A Collection of Contemporary Turkish Literature

AHMET ÜMİT

Born in 1960 in the city of Gaziantep in southern Turkey. He moved to Istanbul in 1978 to attend university. In 1983, he both graduated from the Public Administration Faculty of Marmara University, and wrote his very first story. An active member of the Turkish Communist Party from 1974 until 1989, Ümit took part in the underground movement for democracy while Turkey was under the rule of a military dictatorship between 1980-1990. In 1985-86, he illegally attended the Academy for Social Sciences in Moscow. He has one daughter, Gül. Since 1989, Ümit has published one volume of poetry, three volumes of short stories, a book of fairytales, one novella, and six novels. One of Turkey's most renowned contemporary authors, Ümit is especially well known for his mastery of the mystery genre, as reflected in many of his bestselling novels and short story volumes. Drawing upon the unique political and historical background of his home country, Ümit delves into the psyches of his well-wrought characters as he weaves enthralling tales of murder and political intrigue.

ELKE DIXION

Born in Tacoma, WA in 1969. From 1988 to 1994, she studied Art History and Literature in Washington State and Puerto Rico. After numerous visits to Istanbul between 1990 and 1996, she settled there more permanently, and has since been involved in a variety of projects, from translations to visual arts.

THE DERVISH GATE

Ahmet Ümit

Translated by
Elke Dixon

§

Publication No. 893

Contemporary Turkish Literature 10

The Dervish Gate
Ahmet Ümit

Original Title:
Bab-ı Esrar

Translated by Elke Dixon
Cover Design by Utku Lomlu
Page Layout by Bahar Kuru Yerek

© 2010, Ahmet Ümit
© 2011; Everest Publications. All rights reserved.

First English Edition: February 2011
Second English Edition: October 2012

ISBN: 978 - 975 - 289 - 801 - 1
Certifacate No: 10905

EVEREST PUBLICATIONS
Ticarethane Sokak No: 53 Cağaloğlu/ISTANBUL
Tel: +90 (212) 513 34 20-21 Fax: +90 (212) 512 33 76
e-mail: info@everestyayinlari.com
www.everestyayinlari.com
www.twitter.com/everestkitap
www.twitter.com/baskomsernevzat
www.ahmetumit.com
www.facebook.com/ahmetumitfanclub

Printed by Melisa Matbaacılık
Printery Certifacate No: 12088
Tel: +90 (0212) 674 97 23
Fax: +90 (0212) 674 97 29

Everest is a trademark of the Alfa Publishing Group.

To my dear elders, Zeynep Başaran and Mehmet Ali Başaran,
with my deepest regards...

My infinite thanks to Süheyla Uçum Morrissey and Jasper Edwin Morrissey for helping me learn about London while I was writing *The Dervish Gate*, to Bülent Yıldız and Celaleddin Kara for their unique assistance in introducing Konya, to Elke Dixon for telling me valuable anecdotes about what it's like to live with a Turk, to Uncle M. Sait Çörekçioğlu and Oktay Okukçu for their valuable assistance in helping me understand today's Mevlevi faith, to Oğuz Atabek for providing importanting details about the insurance trade, to Figen Bitirim for not holding back their critical thoughts on this and almost all of my novels, to Anna Maria Arslanoğlu, Kemal Koçak, Erhan Çekiç, Özlem Çekiç, Erdinç Çekiç, Alihan Arda, Gökçen Esra Boduroğlu, Burak Boduroğlu, Hasan Gümen, Ayhan Bozkurt, Hüseyin Özkılıç, Erikli Baba Kültür Derneği Cem Evi, to my wife Vildan Ümit for joining the trips I took both within and outside of Turkey as I was creating this text and to my daughter Gül Ümit Gürak, Gürkan Gürak and Rüzgâr Gürak. If it weren't for their endless support, this book would have never been possible.

The world is a dream within a dream.

An Indian proverb

There was blood on the stone, a full moon in the sky, the
scent of earth in the garden. They were swimming, the trees,
in an unsettling chill. It was the time of burgeoning winter
roses, the season when the narcissus was in full bloom. Seven
men came forth in the garden. Seven wrathful hearts, seven
minds seized by hatred, seven finely-honed knives. Seven
accursed men trod the space, slicing into seven sections the
silence of the garden, toward the wooden door where the
victim was unearthed.

There was blood on the stone. An eerie chill in the garden.
The full moon was alone in beholding the murder. Without
confusion, without dread, without a shudder, it peered
through the dead leaves of the lofty poplars. The youngest
of the seven rapped on the door. The eldest called out to the
person inside. And into that one who was stepping out, the
seven men all at once thrust their blades.

There was blood on the stone, hatred in the hearts of the
men, a deep tranquility in the full moon. An infant cried
somewhere in the distance, an infant wriggling about in
one of the houses. A tender young girl slept somewhere far
afield, a tender girl's body slowly rotting in the earth. As the
youngest of the seven stabbed his knife into the man, the girl
writhed in her grave. A smile spread across her face, which
even death could not drain of its strength. As the youngest of
the seven was thrusting in his knife, a final breath, till now

kept knotted in the young girl's throat, was released with a rush of air, like a sigh of relief.

There was blood on the stone, seven knives slit open seven wounds. From them spouted seven streams of red. Seven tremors shook the body of this man, seven tremors rippled through each of the seven as they plunged in their knives. But the body of the young girl beneath the earth trembled no more. Now, just as the girl's body lay silent, so it was silent above her. It was as though it were the last moment in the world. The living, the dead, all of creation had been silenced, and lay still. The blood on the stone lay still. The moon, doused in the blood of the stone, lay still. Lofty poplars, burgeoning winter roses, narcissus in full bloom, the earth-scented garden... the living, the dead, all of creation had been silenced, all held captive in the blood of that stone...

"...from the steppe a city rose up
in front of me"

※

The plane was only half an hour from starting its descent, but even that wasn't enough to alleviate my anxiety. I knew very well this pessimism wasn't going to suddenly release its grip on me when we landed either. I didn't want to be here, but we could chalk that up to the officiousness of the man who fancied himself the world's best director, Simon. His argument was that I knew how to speak Turkish, that I knew the Turkish people and so on... that the case was so important it couldn't be given to just anyone. It was a three million pound insurance policy we were talking about... Right now, however, I was cursing my familiarity with the Turkish people, regretting that I'd ever been to this city before. I sighed in exasperation, knowing sighing would get me nowhere. At least I was no stranger to this country, I told myself. I hadn't known a thing about Brazil when I went there six months earlier, and yet I'd managed that. I had to stop thinking about it and just jump in and get down to work. I looked down at the numbers on the laptop screen on my knees. The numbers looked back at me, willing me to start. So I did just that. Looking over the numbers in the policy, I tried to figure out what damages might be awarded for the fire in the Hotel Yakut. But after a second calculation, my mind started to wander again. It was useless, my thoughts were all over the place and I couldn't work. I switched off the laptop and returned it to its case. As I bent over to place it under the seat, a thought occurred to me. Doubling over like this, would it hurt the baby? But that was absurd. It wasn't even two months yet and could hardly even be called a baby. And anyhow, I planned to have it taken care of just as soon as I got back to London. Regardless, I sat up quickly, worried about doing it harm. My eyes met those of the middle-aged woman sitting next to me. She'd been dying to talk from the moment we'd boarded the plane. Where was I coming from... where was I going to... who was I? But I was in no mood to chat with her. I couldn't even manage a smile, and just turned to look out the window.

The sky was clear. A scarlet sun was sinking on the horizon. Thousands of metres beneath us, a cluster of thinning clouds stretched over a dark brown expanse of earth. A treeless, streamless, perfectly smooth, colossal expanse of earth. On my first visit here, I'd passed through these lands by bus with my father. Had it been twenty-five years? Maybe longer? In those days there were no flights to Konya, so we'd landed in Ankara. Then there was a four-hour bus journey across this sparse steppe that somehow knew no end. Until suddenly, there in the middle of that eternal brown plain, with no semblance of peak or valley, a miracle appeared. A lake, white as driven snow.

"Daddy, are there any fish in that lake?" I'd asked.

He turned his coal black eyes to look at the pure white lake, and replied, "Afraid not, my girl. There isn't life of any kind. There is something very necessary for life though: salt."

Was I nine years old? Younger? My mother wasn't with us; it was just my father and me. I was dying of boredom after so many hours on that long, flat plain.

"When are we going to be there, Daddy?"

My father had smiled and covered my eyes with his hand.

"Count to twelve silently," he said. I counted, and when he pulled his hand away we were at the end of the road, and from the steppe a city rose up in front of me.

I was stunned. Staring at my father in awe, I asked, "Are you a magician, Daddy?"

He placed a kiss on my forehead.

"Just a man of these lands, my girl."

After my father abandoned us, any thought of him at all just added to my inner turmoil. In those days, however, he held a strange sway over me. I remembered him as a slim man, though not particularly tall. Under his short, sandy-brown hair and narrow forehead with its two compatible stripes for eyebrows, sat wide eyes like big black grapes, a thin arched nose, and a copper-coloured beard, sprinkled with silver. And there in that long, thin face could be seen the chronic melancholy that he took with him everywhere. While melancholy is not an attribute that suits most people, it somehow only added to my father's allure. My mother had been crazy about it. She would kiss him on the lips, claiming she had never met another man whom anguish and melancholy suited so well. It must have embarrassed him, though I couldn't exactly remember. His thin, pale face, and the melancholy in those black eyes, however... that I could never forget, despite wanting to more than anything... because my father, without any explanation, had up and left our lives, and to be with another man no less. So no, I didn't want to remember him. And it was to dispel the memory of him now that I drew my gaze away from the window and turned to face forward again. The woman's prying eyes were still on me. It was so disconcerting that this time, instead of turning mine back towards the window, I simply closed them and concentrated on the sound of the jet's engines. If I could just shake off this anxiety. I tried to clear my mind of all thoughts. Of the child growing inside me with every passing second, of my father and this city of his that I'd come to against my will... I wanted to break away from my past, from this day, from the future. To lose myself for a while in that total darkness, that deepest, most peaceful garden of sleep. To relinquish my body, my mind, and my heart to nothingness...

"Her name is Karen, not Kimya."

✹

It was at that moment I heard the voice. A male voice... soft, warm, and affectionate. I couldn't understand what it said at first, so I tried to tune out all the other sounds around me and only hear the voice. It sounded like grumbling, a friendly scolding or a reproach loaded with affection. I heard it clearly enough to leave no room for doubt.

"Kimya... Kimya..."

Startled, I opened my eyes. I glanced at the woman sitting next to me but she was no longer paying me any attention; her eyes were set on the screen above, perhaps trying to find out when we'd land. I turned round, perplexed. The seats behind me were empty. I faced forward again... to where a young girl and her boyfriend were sitting. There was no one around to call out my name. I must have been dreaming. But when had I ever slept? I must have nodded off when I closed my eyes.

"Kimya!" the voice called out again, but this time the voice came from within my memories. Nobody had called me that in a very long time... not since my father had left us. The only ones to ever call me Kimya were my father and Shah Nesim - my father's friend, soul mate, and the man who eventually tore him away from us. With his sinewy body, sinewy fingers and long face. His golden eyes that peered out with unceasing affection... At least that's how I remembered him. If there were any negative memories to be associated with him, I certainly couldn't recall them. Unless, of course, you counted his ripping my father away from us.

On the other hand, my mother used to refer to him as 'that golden-eyed devil' when she was angry. Though after some time had passed and the pain in her heart had subsided, she started speaking less harshly of him. "Maybe they're luckier than us," she said. "Yes, they are selfish, but luckier too, because they have goals for the sake of which they can even give up those they love." Although not entirely able to wrap my head around what those goals were, I knew it was about religion, some kind of belief. From what I'd heard from my father, from what I'd read from the mystical books he'd given me, stories each more colourful than the next, illustrations, prayers that I'd mostly forgotten... Yes, all of that must have been related to his faith. When I was a teenager, I tried to understand my father, whose face never faded from my memory, and his golden-eyed shah. I wanted a reason, a justification for the father who had loved me like crazy to have one day found it necessary to so abruptly up and leave. But there was none. And though my mother may have forgiven him, that wasn't reason enough for me. That was why I never used the name Kimya which he'd given me. Although it was written on my birth certificate, I'd tried to forget that name, just as I'd tried to forget him. From the start, my mother never took to the name Kimya. Even in those carefree days with my father, while still fascinated with Eastern culture, she never called me Kimya even once. I was always Karen to her. Yet she never minded when my father called me by that name. And she only ever once admonished Shah Nesim for it.

It had been two years before my father left us. Like they often did, my father and Shah Nesim had closed themselves into a room and wouldn't come out for hours. At one point Shah Nesim appeared at the door. "Kimya..." he called out, "With God's blessing, could you bring me a glass of water?"

My mother and I had been in the living room. Irritated not by his request for water but by the hours he spent locked away in a room with her husband, my mother finally exploded, shouting out, "Her name is Karen, not Kimya!"

After which she herself got up and brought a pitcher full to the brim with water to the door of their room. But Shah Nesim, not looking even remotely offended, simply pulled the pitcher through the cracked door as he flatly stated, "God's grace upon you."

My mother went berserk, what with this man not allowing her into her own husband's room under her own roof. But she swallowed her anger, my mother, at least until I had left for school. After that, things reached the point where Shah Nesim wasn't welcome in our house any more. Perhaps that was why my father walked out. I never spoke of it with my mother because it was of little consequence. The truth of the matter was that, for whatever reason, my father had left us to be with this other man. And no one ever addressed me as Kimya again, not even in my dreams. But now, as my eyes were closed for one moment... Or was it possible that I wasn't dreaming? Could my father and Shah Nesim really be on this plane? Knowing full well how ridiculous the idea was, I still couldn't resist putting my chair upright and looking around. The woman next to me, unable to understand my erratic behaviour, started suspiciously eyeing the surrounding seats with me. Of course, neither one of them was anywhere to be seen.

"Are you all right?" asked the woman, unable to hold back any longer. "Nothing wrong I hope."

I forced a smile.

"I'm okay. Just looking for the hostess."

I had to stay calm, I thought to myself as I sat up. I'd just been dreaming. It was not such a short haul from London to Istanbul, and from there I was on to Konya without a break. That would do it. Especially considering my lack of sleep the night before. I'd been racked with anxiety despite having Nigel by my side. This would be a short trip, a few days at most. I would be back in London by the weekend. My thoughts drifted to my mum and Nigel. Thinking of London put a smile on my face and I felt my agitation slipping away. I knew I should get a bit more shut-eye before the plane touched down, but as soon as I closed my eyes, I was startled by a voice ringing in my ears. This time, however, it wasn't my name being called, but rather the hostess announcing to everyone:

Dear passengers, we are approaching our destination. Please return to your seats and fasten your seat belts, return seats and trays to their upright positions, and stow all hand baggage securely under the seat in front of you in preparation for landing.

"...turbaned gravestones"

⚒

I was looking out at the people awaiting passengers in the arrivals hall, trying to catch a pair of eyes searching for mine, a smiling face with a card in hand with my name on it, but it looked like nobody had come to meet me. The woman who'd sat next to me on the plane emotionally embraced two girls who had come to pick her up. Even the couple who'd sat in front of me were greeted by an elderly man. And all the while I just stood there dumbly in the middle of it all with my bags. Now what was I supposed to do? Looking back and forth helplessly was getting me nowhere, so I headed towards the exit, pulling my bag along. As I was pushing through the crowds of people joyously reuniting with their loved ones, I heard a man's feeble voice calling, "Miss Greenwood... Miss Greenwood?"

I turned round to see a chubby man in a grey suit coming towards me. He was out of breath and beads of sweat were shining on his forehead. He must have run to get here on time. Cringing, he asked in broken English, "Sorry. You Miss Greenwood?"

The man's embarrassment, his tense manner and his broken accent, really annoyed me.

"Yes," I said. "Yes, I'm Karen Greenwood."

He should have breathed a sigh of relief, but instead turned red as a beet.

"Very sorry, I come late," he tried to explain in his deteriorating English. "Actually, there is one friend who knows English. He was coming but..."

I really didn't want to listen to this, didn't want this man to stand wringing his hands in front of me. What I wanted was to go straight to my hotel, take a shower, and jump into bed.

"Please don't feel like you have to speak English for my sake," I began, sighing irritably. "I can speak Turkish."

The man's eyes shone with delight, his thin lips broke into a grin as though he had run into a close relative.

"Oh, so you can," he mumbled, his expression now one of gratitude. "Great. I'm Mennan. Mennan Fidan. Owner of the Konya agency."

Sensing my disinterest, he assumed I was angry.

"Again, I am sorry I was late," he tried to explain.

"It's all right, Mr. Fidan," I interrupted. "How do we get out of here?"

He looked around nervously, then waved a hand towards a door on the left. "This way."

I set off, pulling my wheeled bag in the direction he'd shown. Mennan quickly caught up with me and grabbed it.

"Please, let me get that." There was such a pathetic, pleading expression on his face, I surrendered the bag. "Let me take that too," he said, gesturing towards my laptop.

"Thanks, but I've got it," I answered.

We left the airport. The sun, which had accompanied the plane throughout the journey, all at once disappeared as though it had completed its mission, though it still hadn't gone dark out. A strange light had settled everywhere, a silver light cloaking the steppe with soft despair.

Whereas years ago, when I had first come to this city with my father, there had been such a sweet light everywhere... It had been after lunch I guess, maybe late-afternoon, before the sun had set. The streets, the walls of the houses, the glass in the windows, the leaves of the trees, the people's faces, were all bathed in the honey-coloured light - a rust-tinged, golden light which, beyond simply lighting the city, had painted every object it came across with its brilliant dust, transforming everything around into its own colour. For a foreign girl like me, growing up since the time I could speak with the stories of this historic city, its legends and fairy tales, it was an unforgettable moment, like seeing a miracle with my own eyes. We'd gone down to an enormous house, a house made of adobe bricks. It hadn't resembled any of the houses in London, nor did it look like the two-storey houses in the labourers' quarter. There were so many rooms, intricately carved double wooden doors, windows with twisted metal grates, a vast garden covered in trees, and those traditional Ottoman tombstones with their chiseled stone turbans and embossed Arabic lettering. At first I'd thought the tombstones were statues. My father explained what they were, and though I tried not to show it, I was spooked. The graveyard in the garden was just plain creepy. "Is this some kind of church?" I'd wondered out loud.

"You could say that," my father laughingly responded. "It's a kind of convent."

Strangely, I couldn't see any nuns anywhere. Only men. Then finally a woman did come, a large-framed woman with a perpetual smile. She told me her name, which I promptly forgot, then grabbed me and kissed me on both cheeks. She smelled like vanilla. The smell was to die for, maybe I was hungry. I did find it odd, however, her hugging me without any restraint. Because you know, she was neither a relative nor a close friend of ours. But when I noticed the calm expression on my father's face, the joy in his eyes, I kept silent. That must have meant it was normal, this woman's behaviour.

"Here's our car."

It was Mennan who spoke. He was pointing to a black Mercedes. Was I looking in the wrong place? But no, he was going directly towards it. It looked like a recent model, I couldn't help wondering how this man could have afforded it. As far as I knew, we didn't have such a wide client base in Konya. Our biggest client was Ikonion Tourism, the company that owned the hotel that had burned down. While it was true that the amount of the policy was quite high, and they'd always kept up with their payments, it still didn't seem possible that a small-time insurance agent like Mennan could earn enough money to purchase a car like this. Or were the suspicions of our ambitious manager, Simon, founded? Was Ikonion Tourism trying to con us out of three million pounds after buying out our agent, Mr. Fidan? Mennan, oblivious to what was going through my mind, had stopped in front of the car with my luggage and was waiting for me. When I got close, he set down the bag and opened the rear door politely.

"Here you are, Miss Greenwood."

"Thank you," I said, climbing into the back seat. I wasn't falling for his chivalry, however. I'd certainly seen my share of this artificial decorum before. It could especially be witnessed in the exaggerated interest and inflated show of respect of clients trying to pull a scam, trying to distract the insurance expert so that some important detail was overlooked. It would be no big surprise here.

Before getting into the car, he took out his phone and started speaking with someone, glancing at me occasionally as he spoke. I wondered if it was me he was talking about. But there was no sense in being paranoid, the poor man may have only been speaking to his wife. I should just mind my own business.

I turned on my cell phone, too, wondering if my mother had tried to call yet. Despite her love of this country's people, she'd been against my coming here. As I waited for my phone to warm up, Mennan placed my suitcase in the boot, slamming it shut. I turned my attention back to my phone. The inbox was empty. Nobody had messaged while I was on my way here, so I must have been wrong in thinking my mother would be obsessing about me. She must have decided I could cope with things on my own. But Nigel? Love of my life, my boyfriend of three years, father of the child I carried? He hadn't texted either. I was in love with Nigel, and he with me. But it drove me crazy that he was so nonchalant about everything. If only he weren't so charming, too. And those sparkling black eyes, the two rows of white teeth that shined like pearls when they emerged from between his full lips as he smiled, his hot skin... Just thinking about Nigel was enough to warm me up inside. Though apparently he wasn't thinking about me. I mean, he didn't seem the least bit concerned about my coming here. He knew I was on edge. I'd told him I didn't want to come to Konya, especially after finding out I was pregnant. My eyes drifted to my watch. It was coming on six o'clock. Of course, I reasoned, I had reset my watch and it was still early in London, only four o'clock there. Nigel would be in surgery. I relaxed. My mother would also be busy now. She had her meeting for the Aids Support Foundation, just like every Monday at this time.

The car door opened, interrupting my thoughts.

"Sorry to make you wait," said Mennan sheepishly. "They were calling from the office. It was important."

"No problem," I said, trying to look disinterested.

Mennan wheezed as he deposited his corpulent body between the seat and the steering wheel, then pulled the door shut. Pulling a tissue out of the box next to the gear shift to wipe the sweat off him, he stated, "Okay, we're off!" He paused as he was about to turn the ignition key and looked anxiously at me in the rear-view mirror as though he'd overlooked something. "You're comfortable there, aren't you?"

"Yes, thanks. We can go."

Mennan took a deep breath and after muttering "*Bismillah*," turned the key in the ignition.

"What is yours, I have delivered to you."

⚉

We were moving along through the perfectly flat city. Up wide boulevards with trees on either side, past low lying buildings with gardens, through airy open spaces that offered one a feeling of relief... This was not the Konya I remembered. My memory was of mysterious, antiquated houses and age-old mosques, sunlight filtering through narrow lanes which opened onto the unknown, and those turbaned headstones at every step that filled one with dread. Where was that adobe house with the garden that I'd been to with my father? I peered out the car window hoping to find it. A tram passed by, blocking my view with its colourful carriages; it was close enough for me to see the students in their blue school uniforms horsing around inside. The tram passed and a young woman sitting on a bench on the pavement came into view. Her clothes were worn and faded, and she was holding something under a blanket in her lap. I took a closer look and realised it was a baby. She was nursing it, and had covered the baby's face with a corner of the blanket so her breast wouldn't show. I suddenly felt my eyes grow moist; a knot was forming in my throat. My hands unconsciously slid down to my belly but my eyes lingered on the young woman breast-feeding. She lifted her chin and our eyes met. She smiled, but I didn't return the smile, not because I didn't want to, but because I couldn't. Flustered, I abruptly looked away. I wasn't being condescending, perhaps I was just afraid.

15

Not of this young mother but of myself, of this child growing inside me. And my indecision over what I was going to do about it. I couldn't reconcile myself with having cranked my head away so rudely, so I turned back to the young mother to smile at her or nod hello. But she had long since forgotten me and directed her attention back to her breast-feeding baby. My phone chose that moment to ring. I eagerly pulled it from my bag, hoping it was Nigel. It turned out to be Simon, our director. I picked up, trying not to let the disappointment in my voice register.

"Hello?"

"Hi Karen. How was the trip?" Simon asked, in a voice as shrill as a woman's.

"It was fine. We just landed. Mr. Fidan met me at the airport and we're on our way to the hotel."

"So Mennan picked you up. Great. But look, let me just say you would do well not to trust that man too much." He was whispering now, as though he would be heard. "We haven't been working with him so long now and don't know much about him. But that's not why I'm calling. I've got a supplemental contract here, one that assures some pretty big advantages for the client. Five of the seven clauses have to do with fire. The thing's giving me an ulcer. I want you to be meticulous in this job, Karen. Try not to overlook any detail. The owner of Ikonion Tourism is a cunning man, and an educated one. He knows this business as well as we do and he'll try anything to pull the wool over your eyes. He may even have paid off Mennan."

I glanced in the rear-view mirror at the man driving his car with such a sober expression. He looked innocent enough, but who could say. Perhaps he knew English better than he let on. In this business I'd come across tricks the devil himself couldn't have conjured up. It wouldn't surprise me if someone I'd thought was Mother Teresa herself turned out to be the crook of the century. I tried to speak in circles with Simon so Mennan wouldn't understand.

"Don't worry. I'm aware of that, and I'll handle it."

"All right. I've mailed you that additional contract. You might want to look it over before you go to the meeting tomorrow. And as for those two waiters who died in the fire, there's some news about them in the Turkish press. The newspapers are claiming the deaths were not so much an accident as they'd have you believe. And sure, those journalists love to exaggerate, but it still wouldn't hurt for you to give them a read."

"Of course. I'll definitely do that."

"Good. Then we'll talk later. Call me immediately if there are any developments. I'll have my phone on twenty-four seven."

"Okay, I will."

As I hung up and was putting the phone in my bag, I felt the weight of someone's eyes on me. I looked up and caught Mennan's narrowed green eyes in the rearview mirror. I responded with a superficial half-smile, but our authorised agent wasn't going to leave it at that.

"Call from London?" he asked with interest.

I knew all about this Turkish habit of becoming instantly over-friendly with foreigners, and if it hadn't been for Simon's warning, I might have attributed Mennan's question to that. But then I thought of the three million pounds.

"Yes, just a friend," I answered, hoping to close the subject. But Mennan didn't give up.

"I was in London last year," he said, trying to keep the conversation going. "On a tour with a big group of friends from Konya. The Thames River, Big Ben, Hyde Park, and that museum with the wax statues of famous people..."

"Madame Tussauds," I prompted.

"Yeah, that's it. The only thing we never managed to get used to was the traffic driving on the left, though we loved London. It's such a green city, not like here. Not much sun there though..."

Growing weary of the man's idle chatter, I looked out the window and again started searching for the house with the turbaned headstones in its garden. It had to be here in the city centre somewhere. After getting off the bus at the terminal, my father and I had jumped into a taxi, which had driven us through the narrow streets. I remembered a stone mosque with a short, stumpy minaret, and a broad public square where they'd set up a little open market with stalls displaying their colourful fruits. The house had been near that square. We'd entered the garden through a large, imposing door. An elderly man had met us there, and my father reached out and kissed his hand. I thought he must be a relative, my father's uncle maybe? But my father had never talked about any relatives. Strangely, the man then bowed to kiss my father's hand. I knew it was customary for Turks to kiss their elders' hands, but I'd never heard of an old man kissing the hand of a younger one.

"Looking for something, Miss Greenwood?"

I jumped. Mennan's green eyes were on me again.

"Yes, I was looking for a house." I hesitated, thinking it a bad idea to disclose anything personal, but then I considered that this little bit of information didn't really count as my private life and continued. "An old house with a big garden, a garden with those turbaned gravestones in it."

"Did you see it in a magazine? I mean the house... in a travel magazine or something?"

I couldn't bring myself to lie.

"No," I answered. "I've been to Konya before."

Mennan's eyes lit up with curiosity again.

"Really? When was that?"

"A long time ago, when I was a child. They took us to an old house. Well, not a house really, it was more like some sort of religious building."

"A mosque?"

"No. It wasn't a mosque. There were people living there."

"It might be the dervish lodge," he speculated. "Who took you there?"

I was going to say my father, but changed my mind.

"An acquaintance... a neighbour from London."

I saw Mennan's brow furl in the mirror, like he had just encountered a problem.

"To tell the truth, Miss Greenwood, there are a lot of places like that here. I wonder which one it was?" Then his eyes lit up like he'd stumbled on a solution. "Let's drive round some side streets. Konya isn't such a big place. Maybe you'll recognise it."

Before I could object, he cranked the steering wheel and lurched into the first street on the left. As soon as we'd passed the unsightly apartment buildings at the head of the street, which was only just wide enough for one car to pass through, the style of the residences changed. Here was a row of charming two-storey clay houses, and it was as though with the change in the design of the houses time itself had also changed, like we'd gone back a couple hundred years. Could this be the narrow alley I'd come down with my father? These engraved wooden doors, the windows caged in iron-work... But when I looked at this street, which appeared to have been untouched for centuries, my faith in my memory started to falter and I couldn't be sure about what I had or hadn't seen. But it didn't last long. A few hundred metres beyond, that row of darling houses came to an end and our vehicle brought us to a small boulevard in which there were newer buildings.

"So what do you think," Mennan asked, as he pulled out of the street. "Does it look like the same place?"

"I can't be sure," I said, tossing back the hair that had fallen over my eyes. "I was a child then, it must have changed a lot."

We were now passing in front of a park with a small mosque in it. Though it didn't look familiar, I couldn't help staring at the mosque in awe. It looked so old. While I was trying to read the lettering over the door, Mennan suddenly slammed on the brakes.

"Damn it!" The car shook and then came to a halt. He turned to me with a look of distress. "I'm so sorry. I think we've got a flat tyre," he said, pointing towards the front, right-hand side of the car. This was all I needed, I thought to myself as Mennan kept talking without allowing a word in edgewise. "Don't worry, I'll get a taxi to take you to the hotel." I really couldn't be bothered to take my bags back out of the boot and haul them to a taxi. Noticing my hesitancy, he added, "It'll take a while to change the tyre."

"That's all right, I'll wait." I said decisively, but he looked uncertain. "Go on. We'll get to the hotel eventually. It really doesn't make any difference when."

"All right then," said Mennan, taking off his jacket. "I'll try and be quick."

He got out of the car and went towards the boot. While he was opening it, I watched the people in the park, dusk wrapping around them as evening descended. Two uniformed police officers were performing the Muslim ablutions, washing their feet under the spouts of the fountain in front of the mosque. Though I couldn't distinguish their faces so well, the guns strapped to the smalls of their backs were clear as day. I knew they would soon be asking God to pardon their sins, and was struck by the hypocrisy of it. Entering into God's presence with guns hanging off their belts - a God who commands "Thou shall not kill!"

It brought to mind a discussion I remembered my father and Shah Nesim once having, on one of those rare days when they weren't closeted away in their room. They were sitting in the living room drinking tea, and I was drawing a picture, listening carefully to words I could barely grasp. I don't remember how the subject came up, but at one point my father had said, "I don't believe God to be retributive. God is full of compassion and mercy. There is no violence in him."

Shah Nesim planted his golden eyes on my father's face and looked at him long and hard. "You are wrong," he stated, then nodded gently. "God is above compassion, above mercy. And also above violence and punishment, of course. He is all those things, they are all one in him. To be one means to amass the many into one single aspect, without forsaking the diversity of each, without making them uniform or assimilating them. Because everything in existence has a meaning, a purpose. Most of the time it's not a question of what God is, but of what we see in him. Those who love see compassion. Those who are cruel see violence. Intelligent people see reason. Those who are dim, blind faith. Scholars see science. The ignorant, miracles."

Mennan dropped the spare tyre he had taken out of the boot and the clamour of it interrupted my thoughts. I watched as he picked it up and rolled it towards the front of the car. It looked like his spirits were up again, he even made a point of smiling at me as he passed by. He left it there, then went back, took a jack out of the boot, and got down to work. I

felt the jack begin to lift the car. At the same moment, I heard a sound that I hadn't heard in a very long time spread across the darkness of the evening as it fell away. *Ezan*, the call to prayer, was being recited from the mosque. My father used to recite it too, and beautifully. The words were intoned, as though it were a soulful song of passion rather than merely words from a religious text.

As for Shah Nesim, he didn't really pray five times a day as most Pakistani Muslims do, but would occasionally shut himself in his room and lie prostrate for a time. My father's worship wasn't restricted to prayer rituals either. Sometimes he would sit motionless the whole night long, other times he'd chatter quietly to himself in whispers or play his ney. If he came out of the room he'd been cloistered in, his wide black eyes would be moist, a strange, deep calm settled on his face.

I once overheard Shah Nesim tell my father, "One must die before death." The words had a terrifying effect on me. On hearing them, I'd run to my room and cried, thinking my father was going to die. He heard me and came after me.

"Are you going to die, Daddy?" I'd wailed, throwing my arms around him.

My father was thrown by the question.

"Where did you get that idea?"

When I repeated what I'd heard, he broke into laughter.

"I'm not going to die, my girl. And anyhow Uncle Nesim isn't telling me to. Those words have hidden meaning. When you grow up you'll understand. Let me just say this much, it has nothing to do with death."

I'd been ecstatic that my father wasn't going to die. And even before I was grown, I figured out the meaning of the words 'die before death'. They were elucidated by the serenity in my father's eyes. Though they may have meant different things to different people, for me, these words, despite their chronic melancholy, explained the deep tranquillity that never left his face. Whenever I heard them, a silent, still, perfectly calm ocean stretching into infinity seemed to materialise before my eyes. Grand, powerful, extraordinary, but equally calm, vast, and just as tame. I once saw that same look on the face

of a classmate after she'd had a seizure. Janet was an epileptic and the unhappiest girl in the class. Occasionally, her illness caught up with her in the classroom, and she would shake like a leaf caught in a storm, the poor girl. But then when it passed, she would have my father's same look of profound calm in her ash-grey eyes. It was the stillness that comes after serious stress reflected as gentleness in a person's face, the peacefulness which appears in the wake of that horrific storm which breaks out in a person's soul. What I wouldn't give for that state of mind now, I thought. Unfortunately, it was as far from my present state as it possibly could be. Instead it was pessimism that stirred inside me, again that intense uneasiness. For a moment I couldn't breath. I opened the door and tumbled out of the car.

Mennan noticed I'd got out and gave me a puzzled look.

"I'm all right," I said, not letting him ask any questions. "You can keep working."

While he got back to work, I walked round to the other side of the car and looked out over the park, hoping it would put me at ease. The minaret was no longer distinct; the falling darkness had transformed it into a tall, slim silhouette. No other sound but that of the imam reciting the call to prayer could be heard in the square. The people passing in the street, the black dots of birds circling in the sky, the wind tossing about in the branches of the trees, the city in motion as it is every day - it was as if everything and everybody were suddenly wrapped in silence. I couldn't be sure whether it was the voice of the imam which had caught me in the middle of the park, the birds gliding in perpetual circles overhead, or the slow, heavy fall of night, but I suddenly felt totally alone. It felt as though everyone I loved had gone and left me all alone in this unfamiliar city. I felt that suffocating feeling again and was thinking I should have stayed in the car when I heard Mennan's voice.

"Would you like a cigarette? There's a pack in the glove box."

I didn't smoke, I'd never really liked the taste of tobacco. And yet the offer made me so happy, pulling me out of the dark vortex I'd nearly been sucked into.

"No thanks, I don't smoke," I said.

He stretched his head round from where he was kneeling, saying, "I gave up too. The packet is left over from the days when I still did."

Then he bent his head down and carried on struggling with the tyre.

I had to pull myself together. It wasn't like anything bad had happened to me. As night fell I was feeling the loneliness of being a stranger in a strange country, that was all. Some kind of melancholy. But it should end here. I had to shake off this ill-omened pessimism, this nasty feeling that hadn't left me since I'd got on the plane at Heathrow. Maybe if I were to go splash some water on my face at the fountain in front of the mosque? With that intention, I turned round. And there he was, he'd come out of nowhere. A man, covered head to toe in black. Tall, slim, his hair and beard in tangles. He was standing so quietly there in front of me, if I had been taken any more unaware I could have screamed. As it was, all I could manage was a gasp.

"Do not be afraid," he whispered. His voice was calm like water, soft as silk, and as soothing as the coolness lightly falling in the air. "I mean you no harm."

My eyes were drawn to his. There was no threat in them. No cunning nor menace in those two moist, black pools with their impossibly long lashes. It was more like they were appealing for help. I stood frozen in front of him, entranced. I hadn't seen him take a step yet he was closer. Couldn't sense him move even slightly, but he was closer still. He seemed to be gliding, like a silent, nighttime wind. He reached out and took my right hand and placed it into the palm of his left. His hands were warm. Anybody else I would have long since harshly driven away; but with him I couldn't, and didn't, do that. I stood mesmerised, staring into those eyes which appeared naturally- lined in kohl, as the man gently opened my hand and, placing something in my palm, closed it back up finger by finger.

"What is yours, I have delivered to you."

It was like a dream. I turned the hard object over in my palm, then opened my hand and looked. I was unable to make out what it was in the pale light of dusk, so I held it up. It was a ring. A silver ring with a brown stone. I immediately fell in love with it. But why had this man given it to me? Was he trying to sell it? So then this enigmatic man who had stepped out of the night had just been a hawker. I looked up to ask, to try and understand, but he had gone. Where could this man who had just seconds earlier stood in front of me have gone? I look around, but the tall man in black was no longer there. He had disappeared into the night much the same way he had materialised from it.

"Where did he go?" I whispered softly.

"I'm over here," said Mennan, straightening up. "Did you say something?"

I pointed to the empty space where the man had just been standing.

"There was a man..."

Mennan frowned, tightened his grip on the crowbar and came towards me.

"What man? What did he do?"

I shook my head helplessly, knowing I wouldn't be able to explain.

"He wasn't bothering me or anything. It's just... he disappeared so suddenly."

"Disappeared?" he repeated, looking back and forth. But not seeing anyone, he didn't give it much consideration. "He must have run away. Your bag and your purse are still here?"

The thought hadn't even crossed my mind. Of course. The man could have been a pickpocket. Perhaps he had grabbed my bag while keeping me distracted with the ring. I opened the car door and looked inside. My bag, purse, and laptop were still there on the back seat.

"No," I mumbled contentedly. "Nothing was taken. And the man didn't look like a thief. On the contrary, he gave me something. A ring."

I held it up, but he didn't bother to look at it too closely. Pleased I wasn't upset by the incident, he just wanted to close the subject.

"A present," he said softly. "It's lovely."

His explanation did nothing to curb my bewilderment.

"Yes, but I don't know him. He has no reason to give me a ring."

A cheerful, knowing smile spread across his face.

"The people here can seem a bit strange. Presenting tourists with gifts just for the sake of it is not unheard of, just consider it an act of kindness."

"But then why did he run off like that?"

"He was probably embarrassed," he answered, without hesitation. "Our people, they are shy with foreigners."

Mennan's explanation wasn't convincing. I started to look round again. My eyes combed the dark corners of the park, the entrances to streets that were not yet totally veiled by nightfall. The tall man in black with the beautiful eyes was nowhere to be seen. So who was he? The answer seemed to materialise under the lights of the small mosque, in the form of the brass lettering on the sign above the door: *Mosque and Mausoleum of Shams-i Tabrizi.*

"...the ability to touch people's hearts with my hand."

⚒

The hotel was better than I had hoped. It wasn't like the tourist accommodation I was used to, but it was simple, clean, and quiet despite being in the town centre. The lighting in the lobby was soft and not at all harsh on the eyes. Mennan snatched up my passport and headed competently towards the man at the reception desk. I stood back a few steps trying to take in the hotel. Two young men sat in large armchairs in the corner. They'd been watching me with interest since we came in. I'd always hated this hungry, insistent look in men's eyes, whether in London or anywhere else in the world. I turned to look out the window at the street, now totally consumed by the hazy night. There was an historic mosque lit up beyond the pavement in front of the hotel, in front of which was one of those traditional ablutions fountains. Had I seen it before with my father, this historic fountain covered in wood and thin aluminum plating with its numerous taps sticking out all around? If not this one in particular, it must have been a very similar one. We'd stopped to drink water from it one afternoon. I could picture the tin cups hanging down next to each golden tap. The idea of using a cup that everyone's lips had touched was enough to turn my stomach, so I'd struggled to drink from my cupped hands. As for my father, he'd quenched his thirst drinking till satiated from the cup, without so much as a thought to whether it was dirty or not. I was about to ask Mennan about the fountain when I heard the voice.

"Kimya... Kimya Greenwood..."

I was still focused on the fountain illuminated in the pale light. For a moment I had that same strange sensation I'd felt on the plane. I turned towards where the voice had come from and saw the man at reception looking at me and smiling. "Miss Greenwood, could I have a minute?"

How did the man know my middle name? Noticing my stupefied expression, Mennan came to my aid.

"Miss Greenwood..." he interjected. "You have to sign the registration form."

Finally I understood. The receptionist had read the name written in the front of my passport. I went over to the desk.

"Of course. Where do I sign?"

He passed me the form.

"Here please." As he showed me where to sign, he kept talking. "Sorry, but I really am curious. Your name is Karen Kimya Greenwood?"

"Yes, it is," I answered without looking up.

I guess my voice had come out a bit harsh. The receptionist was embarrassed, but his curiosity must have got the best of him because he kept prying.

"I mean, your middle name. Kimya. The English don't really use that name so... I'm guessing you have some Turkish in you?"

Unable to ask why it was any concern of his, I just answered curtly, "No, I'm English."

Mennan sensed my irritation and glowered at the man, who took the signed registration form, grinning stupidly as though nothing were wrong.

"Thank you, Karen," he said, emphasising my name. He handed me the key and instructed, "Room 131. It overlooks Sultan Selim Mosque. You can also see Rumi's Mausoleum from your balcony." Rumi's Mausoleum. Of course, my father had taken me there as well. It was that place with the domes that looked a bit like a church, but with row after row of those strange tombstones covered in Arabic script in the courtyard. Had I asked the receptionist, I'm sure I could have learned more about it, but I didn't want to get on overly familiar terms with this nosey young man. Besides, I was really impatient to get up to my room and into a hot shower. Mennan wasn't going to let me go so easily though.

"What should we do for dinner? We have some really nice restaurants here where you can get traditional local dishes."

He was trying to show me his hospitality, and though I knew it would be impolite for me to refuse, I really didn't want to go to dinner with a man I hardly knew in a city I knew so little about.

"Actually, I was thinking of grabbing a bite here..." I began to say, as the light in Mennan's perfectly round face clouded over. Still, he didn't give up.

"Is it, you know, because there is no alcohol?"

I didn't know what he meant. He noticed my puzzled expression and clarified, "I mean, maybe you've been told there is no alcohol in the restaurants in Konya, but that's not true of all of them. You can easily drink in the restaurant we'll be going to. No one will think it's strange."

I broke into laughter despite myself. Mennan suddenly seemed so sweet.

"No, it's not that. I'm just really tired. Maybe I'll eat in my room. Get a bit of rest. Tomorrow will be a long day and I should gather my strength for it."

"I understand," he said, nodding his large head slowly. "You can be our guest tomorrow evening then."

"That sounds good. All right, I'm off to my room then. Thanks for everything, Mr. Fidan." I stuck out my hand.

As he took it he averted his eyes. He was changing colour, flushing like a little girl.

"Don't mention it, Miss Greenwood. It's my job. Good night now."

"Good night."

Leaving Mennan dutifully planted there, I followed the bellboy to the lift. I was about to step inside when my mobile started ringing. The moment I saw it was Nigel calling, a thrill went through me and I forgot everything else - the open door of the lift, the bellboy waiting with my bags, and Mennan, who was determined not to leave the hotel until I had gone upstairs. My spirits lifted as I took the call.

"Nigel. Hello, my love."

Nigel's voice was cheerful and self-assured as always. "Hey, sweetheart. How is your Turkish adventure going?"

I wanted to blurt out everything I'd been through, to explain what I was thinking and feeling. But I looked up at the bellboy standing a few steps in front of me, then over at Mennan still watching me from in front of the reception desk, and I stopped short.

"Good," I said tersely. "It's going well. Can you hold on a minute?"

I turned back to the bellboy. "You can take my bags up, thanks. I'll take the stairs."

I waved at Mennan and headed towards the stairwell, finally free to speak with my lover.

"Nigel, I can't tell you how happy I am to hear your voice."

The lightheartedness in Nigel's voice disappeared.

"Karen, are you all right?"

My eyes were moist. I was having a hard time not crying and felt so confused. I wanted to ask Nigel why he hadn't stopped me from going on this trip, even though I knew it wasn't his fault. Why should I take it out on him? It wasn't as if anything bad had happened, or I was stood up at the airport and left to my own devices in the big city. No, the uneasiness was all me; my mind was uneasy, as was my heart. What's more, it had started long before I'd come to this Anatolian city. It was stirring even before I'd got on the plane in London. When Nigel didn't get a response, he nervously asked again. "Karen? What's going on?"

"Nothing," I finally managed to say, wiping the tears away. "It's nothing. I'm at the hotel. It's nice."

Nigel wasn't convinced. My voice had cracked, giving me away.

"You sound upset."

"I don't know, Nigel..." I covered the phone with my hand as I sniffled. "I guess I am a bit on edge."

"Why? Is something wrong?"

"No. Things are going well enough."

"Did the trip wear you out?"

"No, it was fine." I couldn't hide it any longer. "I don't know, I just have this bad feeling."

"What kind of bad feeling?"

I felt bad knowing I was upsetting him.

"It's not important. I'm sure it'll pass. You're right, it's probably just the stress of travelling."

"You're not getting ill or anything, are you?"

I knew what he was implying. He assumed it had to do with the pregnancy. We'd spoken about it two days before at the Jazz Club in Soho and decided I wasn't going to go through with it. Or to be honest, Nigel had made the decision. According to him, we couldn't spend the best years of our lives running around after a child. We were both earning good money, our health was good, we were both young and crazy about each other... There were so many places to see in the world and a child would just get in the way. Perhaps he was right, but I was well into my thirties and my biological clock was ticking mercilessly away. I knew it might be my last shot at having a child. Nigel had noticed my hesitancy but chosen to ignore it. He was sure of his decision. "All right then," I'd said, finally acquiescing. "I'll get it taken care of."

"I'll get you an appointment at the hospital tomorrow," he said, wanting it taken care of right away. But it wasn't possible, because I had to be in Turkey the day after that. Although it worried him, he didn't persist. Instead he just smiled, showing off those perfectly white teeth that looked so great against his dark skin. "Don't worry, it won't make any difference so long as you don't leave it longer than a week. We'll deal with it as soon as you get back." Then he refilled our glasses with the Chilean wine he loved so much and made a toast. "Let's drink to life!" he'd said, as he decided to end one. A life where he could be happy, I thought. As he'd sipped his wine, the tension in his face disappeared and he completely relaxed. But right now his voice, a thousand miles away, was swimming in concern.

"Karen, you're not keeping anything from me, are you?"

I can't deny I loved Nigel's worrying over me, but I also couldn't bear his being any more upset.

"No, there's no problem. It's not nice being alone in a foreign country of course, but this is my job after all. Let's change the subject. I'm fine, really. How did your surgery go? You said it was going to be difficult."

The concern in Nigel's voice didn't instantly disappear, but I guess he saw no harm in answering my question.

"It was difficult. It took longer than I expected. The patient was seventy years old and we replaced a valve. Pretty risky, but it went well in the end and we think it was a success. Of course it'll be a while before we know for sure."

I was listening to him admiringly; despite the calibre of the work he did, he managed to express it in extremely simple terms, without any exaggeration.

"Do you know," I said, "sometimes I envy you."

He didn't understand.

"What? What do you mean?"

"I mean your work. It's wonderful. You're always saving people's lives."

That cheered Nigel up. "Just doing my job, like you," he said, assuming an air of humility.

I shook my head as though he were there in front of me.

"No, I... I am working for other people's money. You are working to keep people alive."

Nigel's laughter rang out from the other end of the line.

"Don't get carried away, I'm no saint. In the end I get paid just like everyone else. The only thing that sets me apart is my ability to touch people's hearts with my hand," he said teasing me. "But I prefer touching that gorgeous body of yours to touching the bloody hearts of people I don't know."

I felt my face turn red. I was only ever like this with Nigel. With previous boyfriends, I had played the role of bad girl on numerous occasions, but when it came to this tall, dark man it was a different matter.

"You are already touching me," I finally managed to say.

There was a pause. Neither Nigel nor I could say a word. As I stared at the pastel pink wallpaper with the evenly spaced purple tulips in the stairwell, I thought about how badly I'd rather be looking into the face of the man I loved. I wanted to be by his side, to snuggle into his chest and sleep with the peacefulness of a kitten.

"I wish you were with me right now. I miss you already," Nigel whispered.

A choked, disheartened moan escaped my throat. "Me too."

Just as I was about to start crying again, Nigel lightened things up, saying, "So. Have you seen anything interesting in Turkey yet? Come across any sheiks who desire you for their harem?"

I laughed despite myself and played along.

"Ignorant man, this is not Arabia. There are no harems here, no sheiks..."

But then I saw the image of that man before my eyes, the one with the long beard, dressed head to toe in black. I didn't drive the image away, however. Even better, I drew it into our farcical dialogue.

"Well, there was this man who gave me a beautiful ring as a present..."

"A bribe?"

"No, not anyone from the agency. I don't know who he was. It's a mystery..."

"A mystery? You sound chuffed."

His voice had gone serious like he was jealous. I almost fell for it, but then Nigel started to laugh.

"You wouldn't leave me for this mysterious man, would you?"

"Why not?" I answered ruthlessly. "He might offer me a very interesting life. Full of exoticism, mystery, allure..."

"Allure, huh? Wait, I'll get the next flight there."

Defeated by the longing inside me, I couldn't take the joke any further.

"I wish you would do that."

"I'd love to." His tone of voice changed again. "But I can't. I have another surgery to perform tomorrow."

"You mean you are going to go touching another person's heart?" I glumly protested.

The misery in Nigel's voice echoed mine.

"Yes, but my own heart will always be with you."

"And mine with you," I half-jokingly whispered. "You know it doesn't beat otherwise."

"...the ice blue door in the wall"

※

I was lying on my bed in the darkened hotel room, staring blankly at the wall. I didn't feel like walking about in my room, turning on the TV, or going onto the balcony to look out at the now considerably calmer street. Yet as soon as I'd entered the room, I felt as though I'd left my troubles behind me. Speaking with Nigel had cheered me up, and after jumping into the shower, I'd come out with quite an appetite. As I eagerly looked over the room service menu beside the bed, I was quite surprised to come across a dish I recognised – an okra soup that was peculiar to Konya.

How long was it since I'd tasted this soup? Had it been more than twenty years? My father could by no means be called a good cook, he wasn't really interested in drinking and dining, but all that changed when it came to this okra soup. The little dried okra pods were the only thing my father ever asked his fellow Konyans to bring him when they came to London. It may be that the soup evoked his fondest memories of the city he loved. As for me, I could only vaguely remember how it tasted, but I would never forget the way we would take the string of dried okras into our hands, kneading the pods between our fingers and dropping them into a sieve. I was always eager to help with the process, but because I handled them too roughly, smashing them and ruining their appearance, I was always quickly relieved from that duty and had to make do with the task of washing the tomatoes that would go into the soup.

Once, in the spacious kitchen of the house where my mother still lived in London, I asked my father where he'd learned to make the soup. Stroking his chin, he'd replied. "In the dervish lodge."

"What? You mean that's what they taught you in the dervish lodge, how to make soup?"

He laughed as he responded to my question.

"Well, not just how to make soup; I also learned a lot about life's secrets."

"Daddy, what was the dervish lodge like?"

He thought for a moment before answering. "The kind of place where people mature, bloom, and are purified."

Although I had no idea what my father meant by 'purified', I did understand it had something to do with Sufism. But I'd never taken much of an interest. Not in the hippy movement my mother was drawn into during her youth, nor the Sufism that had affected my father throughout his life. I didn't even pay much attention to the questions Nigel asked with curiosity about Sufism, skipping over the subject saying I didn't want to talk about my father, whom Nigel had never met anyhow. However, here now in this Anatolian city, while alone in this hotel room, I remembered my father and ordered the food that he'd loved.

In the end, I couldn't say whether the okra soup was like the one my father used to make. I enjoyed it though, and apart from the ridiculously spicy green peppers, the salad wasn't half bad either.

After I finished eating, I turned on my computer hoping to get some work done. Simon's email had come, along with the supplemental contract and the news from the Turkish press. I first looked over the newspaper clippings, curious what they had to say. I read through the first article, headed "On the Job Deaths No Accident". It was claiming negligence on the part of the hotel management, saying that their failure to take precautions against fire made them guilty of manslaughter. The other newspapers all held similar views. But the newspapers had no real proof of anything. If they had, they would have reported it. As usual, it would be up to me to head my own investigation. For the time being, however, all I could do was get back to preparing for my meeting with the hotel management. I read through the contract and, sure enough, there was that clause that was going to pay off so well for Ikonion Tourism. In fact, everything seemed flawlessly in place for them, as though the company management had set themselves up for the impending accident. If we couldn't manage to prove that the fire was set on purpose, the insurance company would have to pay out every penny of the damages. No wonder Simon was suspicious, simply being an irreproachable client made them suspect. But Simon could always be wrong. The fire brigade's report wrote that it had been an accident, and the attorney general ruled there was a lack of significant evidence. Maybe it was because the men were beyond reproach that every clause in the contract worked in their favour down to the letter. Of course, our manager hoped the former was the case, that is, a situation would come to light that wouldn't require us to pay any damages at all. As for me, I would to try to do my job to the best of my abilities, but not at the expense of the truth. If the fire really were an accident, Ikonion Tourism had a right to their three million pounds.

Despite all this, there was a nagging voice inside me that kept asking why I was here. It wasn't my usual ambivalence, this was something deeper. I suddenly felt like I was going to throw up and wondered if it was due to the pregnancy. I sat up and tried tuning in to my body. It wasn't violent enough that I needed the toilet, but I did feel I had better lie down. I left the laptop as it was, turned out the lights, and climbed into bed.

Why couldn't I shake this feeling of apprehension? Maybe I'd made a mistake, and I shouldn't have come here in the first place. I could have come up with an excuse and refused Simon's proposal. Perhaps sub-consciously I'd just wanted to see my father's city again, to relive those days I'd spent with him here. Or was there more to it? Was it something else that had dragged me here? I looked down at my belly. There was still no sign that I was pregnant, but if I allowed it - if we allowed it - there soon would be.

All at once, I understood that my accepting this assignment had nothing to do with my father, that my being in Konya was incidental. Simon could have sent me anywhere, Cairo for example, and if he had, that was where I'd be now. What it all came down to was that I'd wanted to get away from Nigel. Deep down that was what I'd needed, whether I realised it or not. To get away from Nigel, to be alone, to keep my thoughts from being influenced.

All this had started when I found out about the baby. I knew at once that I wanted to keep it, and strangely enough, I'd assumed Nigel would too. That was why, without thinking, I'd called him and happily chirped the news over the phone. But Nigel's tone was as cold as ice. "Is that so?" he'd said. "Why don't we meet up later and talk this over?" So we met up later and talked it over. Or more like he talked it over, flatly stating, "No way."

But me, I wanted it: *This child is important for me, it's important for us. A relationship is not only about travelling the world. Not only about sharing beautiful music, or fine Chilean wine and steak with some fancy French sauce. A relationship is not just flowers on Valentine's Day, presents on birthdays, anniversaries in expensive pubs, sex five times a week... A relationship is the desire of two individuals to consciously, willingly, create a whole life together. And that's the kind of relationship we should have. Either I should be moving in with you, or you with me. We should raise this child together. Be a real family.*

It was what I wanted to say but didn't. Though I couldn't for the life of me figure out why. I didn't think it was the fear of losing him, because from what I'd learned through my painful experiences as a young woman, the easiest way to lose a man was to go along with everything he said. If you tried to think, feel, and behave just like the man you were with, you became completely uninteresting to him. Not that this just applied to men, the same went for women, of course. Why would anybody love or value a person who never gave them need for contemplation or concern, nothing to analyse? Wasn't love in one sense about reaching out for something you didn't have in yourself? What good was there in reaching out for someone who wasn't any different from you. So then why hadn't I stood up to Nigel? I supposed it all came down to my mixed feelings. One part of me was urging me to have the child, the other was telling me what a stupid urge that was. I didn't actually know yet what I wanted. And though it was hard to admit it to myself, I knew I was genuinely afraid. Not so much of having the child, more of not being able to love it enough, not being a good mother, failing. If even my father could abandon me without explanation, despite having claimed to love me like crazy, how could I trust myself? And here we were back at my father again.

It was then that I noticed the ice blue door in the wall. I blinked, thinking I was imagining it, but the door stayed in place. I sat up and looked again, trying to keep a lid on my excitement. Then suddenly I caught on to what it was. The light reflected from the computer screen I'd left open on the table had bounced off the mirror with its ornamented wooden frame, creating the illusion of the door. I felt strangely let down by this extraordinary vision, which had turned out to be a mirage. As a young girl I had loved the tales of knights who battled sorcerers, which I read in my illustrated books - and equally so, my father's colourful Eastern legends, which were peppered with miracles and marvel: the thirty courageous birds who searched for their padishah, passing through the seven Valleys of Wisdom to reach the mystical Kaf Mountain; the headless prince who rescued the peasants from the cruel giants and won back his head; the war between the people of The Land of Reason and the sorcerers of The Land of Fantasy... Fantastical heros and extraordinary events we would never encounter in real life, that nevertheless rendered the world we lived in more beautiful, more thrilling and meaningful. I suddenly felt overcome by melancholy. I wished this ice blue door were real and, like one of those heroes from the legends I'd loved so much, that I could step magically through the passage and come to a world where I was free of all my troubles and sorrow. But believing in these supernatural encounters had never come easy for me. I was prone to take after my mother on these things. Like her, I thought heroes and tyrants were just a part of our lives, virtue and evil were simple realities. My father, however, was of a different mind. Once he spoke of a dervish who performed his ritual midday prayers in Konya, Baghdad, and the Ka'aba of Mecca all at the same time. When I objected, saying there was no logic to it, he confidently replied, "You can't grasp miracles with logic." I didn't argue with him more, but with the reasoning of a child, I told myself that if it were truly possible, my father would be living in both Konya and London right at the same time.

I laughed at the state I was in. No matter how hard I tried, I couldn't stop thinking about my father. Nigel must have been right when, after we'd left the Jazz Club, while walking along the canal, he'd told me, "This trip may end up being a good opportunity for you. To face your father, your memories of him." He'd stopped at the edge of the canal, his long shadow stretching into the dark waters. His moist eyes sparkled as they looked into mine and reiterated, "Maybe this will be your chance to come to terms with him." I couldn't help wondering if maybe it was Nigel I should be coming to terms with even before my father.

My pre-occupation with these thoughts was beginning to annoy me. I went over and shut off my computer, still hot from being left on so long. For a while I stared blankly into the room again, until a sudden cool sensation on my cheek brought me back down to earth. A light breeze with a fragrant scent of dried grass and geraniums had broken away from the steppe and drifted over, making its way through the open balcony door. As it intensified, it lifted the tulle curtains into the air, before wrapping itself around my body. I closed my eyes and turned to face it, taking in its pleasant touch. And that's when I heard the whisper.

"Kimya..."

Startled, my eyes popped open. I spun round, my initial reaction being that it was coming from inside. There was no one there, yet I was sure I'd heard that voice again. It was the third time that day someone had called out to me like that. Or was I dreaming again? But standing, with my eyes open? My thoughts went back to the bottle of wine I'd had with Nigel the previous night, before making love. Some might worry the bottle had been tampered with. But that was ridiculous, even in the unlikely event that it had been, the effect would never last this long.

The same whisper resonated throughout the room again. "Kimya..."

I couldn't quite grasp the meaning of it. Was it a summoning perhaps? A cry for help, or some kind of gripe from someone who knew me? The voice had drifted in with the fragrant breeze. I spun back round and, moving with determination towards the open balcony door, lifted the curtains and went outside. The small balcony was empty; there was nothing out here but a wooden stool standing mutely in the corner. I examined the wall that separated my balcony from the others and concluded it couldn't have been a voice from one of the neighboring rooms. I glanced down to the small, deserted square below me, then up to the stone walls of the Sultan Selim Mosque. The old mosque was lit with a pale yellow light, which was responsible for its dejected appearance. Immediately behind it, the glow of Rumi's Mausoleum had the opposite effect – the darkness was powerless against the bright green of this shrine, which carried on shining with hope, like jade.

The wind started up again and my hair began to blow about. I gathered up my unruly hair and held it, as I watched the trees swaying in front of the mosque. I could hear the wind blowing through the branches and I relaxed. The voice must have just been the wind whistling in the trees. But then something in front of the mausoleum caught my eye. Despite the distance between us and the lack of light, I could still make out the kohl-lined black eyes and well-defined, parted red lips. Calling out to me from in front of the fountain was the man, still dressed in black, who had given me the ring.

I felt my blood go cold. My head began to spin and I would have fallen if I hadn't grabbed hold of the railing. With difficulty I pulled myself together, stood up straight, and looked down again. I scanned the area around the mosque and its fountain, but could see no sign of life around the small square. Just like the first time I'd run across him, the mysterious man had vanished. "What is this?" I uttered to myself, completely unnerved. "Who is this man, and why does he keep following me?" My searching eyes came to rest on the mausoleum again, as I suddenly wondered if the ring had also disappeared. Maybe nobody had ever given me a ring to begin with. Was it possible that I'd made the whole thing up? I rushed inside on the brink of panic, then turned on the lights and started rummaging through my bag. But no, the ring was there, just under my passport. I hadn't been hallucinating after all, and I wasn't losing my mind. Relieved, I held the ring up and looked it over. It was gorgeous - silver, with very fine detail. A tulip, a rose, narcissus, ivy... I touched the dark brown stone. It was as warm as blood, its surface misted over. I polished it on my top and the cloudiness disappeared. "What power does this ring possess?" I mumbled to myself. I wasn't expecting an answer, yet I felt the presence of some obscure figure opposite me. Alarmed, I looked up and came eye to eye with my image in the mirror. I looked disheveled, tense, and agitated. The state of my image in the mirror depressed me. "I'm exhausted," I said, looking warily into the strained face of the woman in the mirror. "I'm just really tired, that's all."

"Will you unveil for me the face of Muhammed Jelaleddin Rumi?"

✖

I was woken by the light on my face, but it was not yet the light of day. The room was under the near darkness of dusk, so where was this light coming from? I sat up and tried to find its source. It appeared to be coming from the mirror, but where was the mirror getting it from? Then I noticed the open laptop. I was sure I'd turned it off before I went to sleep, but I must have been mistaken. Confused, I got out of bed to turn it off for good, but was distracted by a spot on the wall. The ice blue door was back in place. That was normal, I reasoned, since I'd left the computer on. I tried to ignore it, but then I noticed that one side of the double door was slightly ajar. I paused, wondering why on earth it had sides to begin with. Wasn't it just a reflection? As I was going over to take a closer look, its shape distorted. It began to stretch upward and outward, then down to where it was right at my feet. I stood there, dazed, as it creaked wide open. I was seized by an emotion I couldn't put my finger on. It wasn't fear exactly, more like a combination of nervousness and curiosity. Finally, I poked my head in, to try and see what was behind it. It was like a secret passage opening onto the unknown, I couldn't make anything out in the pitch black. Unable to take the suspense a moment longer, I felt compelled to slip through the open door.

A biting chill hit my face at the very first step, the dizzying howl of wind ripping through a forest. I took a second step and found myself in a garden. Was this the garden of the house I'd come to with my father? I couldn't place it, as everything was bathed in a dim silver light. I could just barely make out the glazed ceramic pool directly in front of a clay brick building. In the middle of the pool was the full moon. I would have been shocked if it weren't for the smell of geraniums flooding in on all sides, but the fragrance was intoxicating, causing me to confuse appearances with reality. I wanted to be lucid again, to touch this bewildering vision in order to come to my senses, so I bent down and put a finger to the translucent skin of the full moon which had painted the pool silver. The moon shuddered and the water in the pool shuddered. Then the flowers, the poplars, the whole garden with all its insects and night birds shuddered. That same tremor rippled from my fingertips throughout my entire body. I felt connected with it all - the garden, the mute adobe house, the tiled pool and the full moon which stretched the length of it - like I was swimming in its silver, biting cold.

There was a whisper. It sounded like a prayer, like someone casting a wish or unburdening their troubles. I looked around to determine where the voice had come from. It seemed to be coming from the open space to the right. I walked towards it, passing a row of tall poplars, and there saw a man. He was kneeling on a stone slab, his hands raised to the full moon in the sky, mumbling. I couldn't see his face, nor could I hear clearly what he was saying. Though he seemed familiar, I still thought it wise not to make myself known. Shielded by the slim bodies of the poplars, I scanned the area for a vantage point from which to see his face. The moon ducked behind the clouds giving me the opportunity to pass beyond the climbing roses that had formed a thicket just opposite him. Though I still couldn't see the man's face, lost as it was in the dimness of the moonlight, I could now easily hear what he was saying. I recognized the voice, but what really had my attention was what it was saying.

"O he who created the heavens and the earth, O he who makes possible that which is not possible... I beseech you to name for me one of your recondite beloveds."

I glanced round, trying to see who he was talking to, but there was no one there. At the same time a howl descended on the garden. The leaves of the poplars, the tulips and the hyacinths trembled. The rose vines that hid me shook gently. Then a booming voice could be heard, from where I couldn't discern.

"The life you ask about, hidden from the eyes of all, a life with favour and grace upon it, is Muhammed Jelaleddin Rumi, son of Belhli Sultanü'l-Ulema Baha Veled."

I stood transfixed as the kneeling man continued his appeal with a relaxed and natural insistence, as though speaking with an old friend.

"O hope of hopes, O sacred light of our existence. Will you reveal the image of Muhammed Jelaleddin, the blessed face of your beloved?"

Once more a roar shook the garden and again the voice could be heard.

"How will you repay your debt of gratitude?"

Without faltering, the man drew a finger across his throat and exclaimed, "With my head!"

Just then the moon broke away from the clouds and lit up his face like a torch. It was the dervish who'd given me the ring, who later called out to me from in front of the fountain, addressing me as Kimya. What was he doing here? And who was he talking to? As these questions vied for space in my mind, the man turned to look at me. He stared into my face through the climbing roses as if he had known all along that I was there. I ducked down behind the willowy branches and delicate rose petals so as not to be seen, but the moon seemed to deliberately light up the thicket like a nighttime sun. A childish feeling came over me, as though by not looking at him, he wouldn't be able to see me either. I stayed like that for a while, but when he didn't make a sound, I looked back at the stone courtyard where he'd been kneeling. He wasn't there. I stayed alert as I headed out of the thicket, moving forward with small steps and crouching beneath the poplars, quietly making my way back. My fear had proved unnecessary though; I made it to the pool in front of the clay house with ease, where I stopped to regain my composure. The sudden clatter of wood being dragged across stone startled me, and I turned towards the sound. A door to one of the rooms had opened, and the faint reflection of light from inside spilled across the stone foundation of the garden and fell onto the pool. In the open doorway stood the silhouette of a man in a turban. I couldn't see his face but he was clearly looking for someone. I pulled back, alarmed, and was just thinking that if I could reach the trees he wouldn't be able to see me, when a strong hand wrapped firmly around my wrist.

"Kimya..." came the voice.

I turned round to see the bearded man in black. There was such fury in his almond eyes that I cried out.

It must have been my own voice that woke me. I sat bolt upright and looked round the room, now bathed in harsh daylight. Trying to calm my beating heart I told myself, "It was a dream... a dream."

I settled back, propping myself up on my arms.

"It was just a dream," I repeated under my breath. The words should have had a calming effect, but when I recalled the penetrating eyes of that strange man in black, I couldn't keep my skin from crawling.

"God's work is an enigma."

✵

The picture on the wall of the breakfast room was of a dervish whirling, his right hand opened up towards the sky, his left down towards the earth. There was meaning in this movement. I knew because my father had explained it, though what it was I couldn't recall. The sky in the picture, and the earth, were in darkness. Not even the dervish's face was clear, only his white robes were illuminated. As though all the magic were in this white cloth, it was the long and flowing, sleeveless, collarless cloak that transformed the dervish into a divine, magical being and made the painting so affecting.

"Nice picture, eh?"

I turned my head and came face to face with Mennan. His green eyes looked casually into mine as though we'd known each other for years. I didn't know how to answer, couldn't decide if I should smile or say hello. Mennan looked disconcerted when the warmth he'd shown wasn't reciprocated. "I'm sorry. I guess I'm bothering you," he said graciously enough, though his pride was injured.

"Oh no... no you aren't," I answered, regretting my reaction. "Good morning Mr. Fidan, have a seat, please."

I even managed to smile while waving a hand at the chair opposite mine. The tension in the man's plump face disappeared.

"Good morning," he said, taking a seat. "How were you last night? Did you sleep well?"

I wasn't about to tell him what I'd been through, about the dream I'd had.

"I slept fine, thanks."

"This is a nice hotel," he said. He pointed at the picture of the dervish. "I guess you were looking at the painting?"

"Yes. The dervish's robes caught my attention. They look less like clothing and more like an extension of the dancer's body. Like some sacred garment."

A pleasant light spread through his eyes.

"*Tennure,*" he stated.

"*Tennure?*"

"*Tennure,*" he repeated enthusiastically. "That's what it's called."

I turned to look back at the painting and asked, "Does it have a meaning? Or is it just a dance costume?"

"Just a dance costume?" he squealed. "God forbid!"

It was the first time since we'd met that I detected a tone of criticism in his voice.

"*Tennure* symbolises a burial shroud." He paused. Perhaps thinking I didn't know what that was, he explained, "A shroud is a white cloth we wrap our dead in before we bury them. God's subjects should be swathed in nothing more than this when they appear before him. Pure and spotlessly clean in white cloth."

I pointed at the cone shaped hat on the dervish's head. "And this?"

"*Sikke...*" he chirped. "The *sikke* symbolises a tombstone."

"A tombstone? How odd!" I exclaimed. "So much death. Why is that? It is just a dance after all. And the dervishes are living, breathing dancers."

He looked away, stumped as to how to answer. His uncertainty didn't last long however, and he tried to put it into words.

"No... No, don't say such a thing. Just a dance? The *sema* is not a dance. And the *semazen,* or dervish as you call him, is not a dancer."

He struggled to find the right words.

"Now, the *sema* is a kind of worship, like *namaz,* the Muslim prayer rituals," he continued, trying to piece it together. "I mean, you know how you have confession... in the church in the presence of a priest and so on? It's like that."

Unconvinced with his own explanation, he tried again.

"The *sema* doesn't depict death, on the contrary it depicts life. I mean, rebirth. Being cleansed of your sins, passing beyond the physical world to the kingdom of truth. During the *sema*, dervishes wear black cloaks called *hirka* over the *tennure*. And that black cloak is actually the dervish's grave."

Hearing all this did nothing but add to my confusion.

"And that's exactly what I don't understand. The grave, the gravestone, the shroud... What do they have to do with life, or dancing?"

He scratched his broad, smooth-shaven chin.

"To tell the truth, I don't know much about it," he admitted. "But from what I do know, the dervish first removes the black cloak, meaning he emerges from his grave, then he starts the *sema*."

"You mean he whirls?"

He let out a sigh of exasperation.

"It's not whirling. The Mevlevi sufis don't find this word appropriate. They prefer the term *sema*. So, when the dervish casts off his black cloak, he is risen from the grave. And when he starts the *sema*, he is setting off on the true path towards *insan-i kamil*."

"What does *insan-i kamil* mean?"

"A spiritually wise being who has arrived at God. That is, a person who has become one with him. It's the the most difficult task one could ever set out to do. A person must pass through four separate stages, or gates. It's the passage through these gates that is enacted during the dervishes' *sema*. Four distinct musical movements during which four distinct salutations – that's what the parts of the dance are called - are depicted. The first gate is *shari'a*, a strict set of rules that some Muslims still live by, that dictate their behavior. The second is the gate of *tarikat*, that is, the inner, mystical dimension of Mevlevi Sufism. The third is the gate of *marifet*, which is like... like a crowning achievement, as in the moment we grasp the ultimate truth. The fourth gate is *hakikat*, or reality. That's the final phase, where the enlightened dervish shares his wisdom. With his right hand opened upward, a dervish receives the blessings of God, and with his left opened down towards the earth, he bestows them on the people. The dervish completes his cycle of rebirth in this way. A divine birth of course..." With the back of his hand, he wiped the beads of sweat from his forehead. "Like I said, I'm not too deep into these subjects. But if you'd like I can take you to the dervish lodge. The people there know more about these things."

In fact, his explanation had been more than sufficient, though I still wasn't convinced and had no intention of going to any dervish lodge or anything. If my own father hadn't been able to enlighten me by the time I was twelve, how would anyone from the lodge? My father and I must have spoken about these things. I was sure I'd heard the words *hirka*, *sikke*, and *tennure* before. The grave, the gravestone, the shroud... Why was I having such a hard time remembering? Maybe my father hadn't gone into detail, worried he'd frighten me. Perhaps he'd been waiting until I was older, or was holding back because of my mother.

My mother had never been religious. She certainly didn't consider herself Christian and wasn't afraid to say so. "If there is a god," she would say, "it couldn't just be a Christian god. At the same time, it would be Jewish, Muslim, Buddhist, Zoroaster, Shaman... even a god of atheists. And even if there were a god, what I'd never be able to wrap my head around is why that almighty god would be so hard-hearted? Why he wouldn't find a remedy for illness, hunger, and war? Why he would turn a blind eye to all the atrocities and suffering?"

Once, my mother had put that very same question to a Catholic priest she met at a party. Looking into his wide blue eyes, innocent as a child's, she asked, "So tell me. Why is it that God doesn't intervene in evil?"

He was a good man, that priest. Without even the smallest sign of belittlement in his expression, he'd given the woman opposite him all his attention and, with a sincere smile, responded, "God's work is an enigma."

My mother's look had been one of disappointment. "I wish it weren't," she said, shaking her head. "I wish God's work were as unambiguous and easy to decipher as those big blue eyes of yours." The blue-eyed priest didn't know what to say. He bowed his head and went quiet.

"If you'd like we can go tonight." Mennan's words shook me out of my daydream.

"Where?"

"To the dervish lodge. Don't worry, they're good people. They appreciate foreigners who are interested in the Mevlevi teachings and will be happy to answer all your questions."

I was sure that was the case, but I didn't feel like seeing anyone, and was about to say so when my mobile rang again.

"Sorry," I apologised, taking the call. It was my mother. So then she'd finally remembered her daughter.

"Hi Mum. It's about time. Where have you been?"

She sounded tired, her answer was brief.

"At the hospital."

I was momentarily filled with apprehension, wondering if something had happened to Nigel.

"The hospital? Why?"

"He's dead."

"Who?"

There was no answer. She was driving me crazy, this woman. Panicking, I asked again, "Mum, who died?"

"Matt. Last night."

I relaxed. Uncle Matthew had been undergoing treatment for cancer for three years. His situation had been deteriorating the last two months and we were all praying he'd be put out of his misery.

"Thank god. His suffering is over," I said under my breath. My mother was silent. Whether to understand her, console her, or perhaps just to break the silence, I asked, "Did his wife call you?"

"No, the hospital did."

"The hospital?" I asked, surprised.

"He said my name as he was dying," Her voice was shaky. "My name, Karen. Do you understand? Not his wife's, not his daughter's. He just said, 'Susan'."

She began to cry.

"Don't, Mum. Don't be sad. The poor man is finally at peace. He's been in hospital for months. You yourself told me how much he was suffering."

There was a brief silence. From the other end of the line my mother's sniffling could be heard. She must have collected herself though, because she continued speaking.

"You're right, he's finally at peace." She sucked in her breath and carried on. "I'm not crying because he died. I'm crying over the past. Our past, what we let slip away..."

The man I knew as Uncle Matthew had been my mother's first love, from way back in her high school years. In fact, they were distant cousins. I once saw a yearbook photo of Uncle Matthew as a sixteen-year-old private school student. His red hair, which he kept cut short, adorned a wide forehead. He had shy grey eyes set deep in a freckled face, and a long chin under thin, pallid lips. Lips that were born with a silver spoon in them. Uncle Matthew's family were rich, and every bit as conservative. They came from old money, and their roots stretched back who knew how many generations to the royal family. My mother's family had also been well-off, though not nearly to the same extent as Matthew's. Even if they had been, it wouldn't have made any difference. My mother and Uncle Matthew were as polar as fire and ice. When my mother first told me about their romance, I visualised a young Matthew climbing out of his father's Rolls Royce for a stroll in the vast gardens of their Richmond manor, and conversely, my mother in the hippy clothes of her youth at a peace protest in Trafalgar Square. Even back then I understood their being together was out of the question, and it was because my mother felt the same when she was young that she had no qualms about breaking up with him. But now that one of the most important people in her life had passed on, perhaps she'd started to have regrets despite all their differences, and was suffering because she had loved him so much in her own way.

"Maybe I should have stayed with him," she mumbled, her voice injured. "Matt should have been the only one in my life."

Though I knew how impossible it would've been for someone like my mother, who even at this age couldn't sit still, I also realised this line of thinking was doing her good. Despite all her grief, and the very real bereavement she carried in her heart, Matthew's mentioning only her name as he died was one of the most beautiful, meaningful moments she'd had in years. There was no sense in spoiling it for her now with a reality check.

"Yes, maybe you're right, Mum," I said. "But that's not how it happened. Life has its own strange logic. Try not to be too sad. When is the funeral?"

"I don't know," she said gloomily. "What does it matter? Matt's gone for good. I may not even go to the funeral."

I knew she was just avoiding seeing Matthew's wife and daughter in mourning, she wanted to bear the pain of her first love alone and wasn't prepared to share her misery with anyone. But I had my doubts; she may later regret it.

"Seeing as how he played such an important role in your life, don't you want to say your goodbyes?"

"I said my goodbyes last night," she answered. She sounded resolute. "Until the others came and interrupted us... I poured out my heart to him. Told him all those things I'd left unsaid." She started to cry again.

Aware that I couldn't console her anymore, I waited for the woman at the other end of the line who was lost in all the memories of her youth with her first love. I waited to hear her voice, which couldn't quite manage to regain its composure.

"No, Karen," she finally said. "I will not go to that funeral."

If I thought for a minute that she wouldn't live to regret it, I'd have supported her decision. But knowing my mother, I was sure that after Matt was buried, before even a week was up, she would be agonising over not having gone.

"Well, it's up to you, I guess. But won't it be poor etiquette?" I persisted. "What will people say?"

"I don't give a damn about them," she growled. "I don't have to share my heartache with anyone."

It was pointless to keep insisting.

"It's your decision, Mum," I said again, wanting to change the subject. "You are my concern, just try not to get so upset."

"That's easy for you to say."

Here she went again, she was always doing that. If you said "Fine, Mum, you're right," she would reply, "Don't say that, I'm wrong." If you said, "Okay then, you're wrong," then this time she would get offended and say, "You always think I'm wrong anyhow." But now was not the time to quibble.

"Well, that's all I've got," I muttered. "What else can I say from so far away?"

Though I hadn't meant it to, my voice came out reproachful. I supposed she understood.

"You're right," she whispered. "I don't know what I'm saying. There's nothing anyone can do about it anymore, dear." Her voice had softened. "Never mind me. When are you coming back?"

At last she'd calmed down.

"I don't know yet," I said, taking a deep breath. "I have a meeting a little later. I guess it will be clear after that."

"Well, don't stick around there too long," she said, after a pause. "We want you back here."

She was going to say something else - about my father perhaps, or maybe about this city she had been to years before - but in the end she just left it. She probably no more wanted to remember my father than I did, though not wanting to remember and not remembering were two entirely different things. Just like me, she often thought about him against her will. And in the same way Uncle Matthew had always cherished his first love though she'd left him, even calling out to her with his very last breath, my mother still couldn't forget the husband who had left her and gone away. Talking about the death of her first love, which was forcing her to reexamine her own life, had worn her out. She didn't have it in her any more to discuss Konya or my father, and I was happy to oblige.

"Take care of yourself then, Mum."

Again there was a brief silence. Was she going to reopen the subject after all? I figured she had started to think about my father a lot these days. Maybe he hadn't left her mind since I'd told her I was coming to Konya. Right up until Uncle Matthew died. In fact, even while she was pining over Uncle Matthew, I knew it was also my father she was mourning. Yes, she'd been about to mention him but changed her mind. Maybe she couldn't swallow her pride, or perhaps she didn't want to bring him up out of respect for the memory of Matthew.

"You take care too, Karen" is all she said, her voice cheerless. Then she hung up. I felt a profound sadness. Not for my mother or father, but for poor Uncle Matthew and the unrequited, passionate first love that he had held onto till his last breath.

"Bad news?" asked Mennan, his expression one of concern. He was sitting just opposite me but it seemed I had forgotten him. Could this man possibly have understood what we were talking about? But no, there was nothing in his face to that effect.

"Family matters," I said, avoiding the subject.

He gave up. I reached for my cup and took one last sip of my milky tea, not because I wanted it so much as out of habit. Mennan didn't insist, but he kept his inquisitive eyes on me. His heart may have been in the right place, but it was making me uncomfortable. "Shall we go?" I said, suddenly standing up and smiling.

He immediately pulled himself together.

"Sure, whatever you want."

I put my phone back in my bag.

"We have time to see the hotel that burned down, don't we?"

"The hotel?" he uttered, as though the request were outrageous. "What for? It's in ruins."

"I want to check it out," I stated flatly, looking him directly in the eye. "To try and see how the fire started. Determine if it was sabotage. That is my job you know."

"Sabotage? But the fire brigade's report clearly states that it was an accident."

Whose side was this Mennan on, anyway - our insurance company's or Ikonion Tourism's?

"I've read the report," I said, managing to stay firm. "But statistically, at least thirty percent of incidents that fire brigades originally call accidents turn out to be arson. Not only here, but in England, as well. That's why the only report I'll believe is my own. And in order to prepare that report, I have to visit the scene."

He sighed and looked at his watch.

"All right, I'll take you there. But we haven't got time now; we're supposed to meet with Ikonion's managers in half an hour. We can go after that. Maybe they'll want to come along."

"Fine. We'll go after the meeting then, but they aren't coming with us."

"Why not? They're honest people, which you'll see for yourself once you get to know them."

I'd had enough. It was time for me to speak my mind.

"I am not the least bit interested in getting to know anybody. All I want to do is to make sure this investigation is conducted properly."

For a moment he stared indignantly into my face. Could he really be this naive, or was he trying to hamper the investigation? I tried again.

"Look, Mr. Fidan. As you know, this policy is no small amount of money, even for a big company like ours. Ikonion Tourism is considered suspect until this investigation is concluded. Of course, we aren't going to say that to their faces, but we'll stay vigilant until we're certain that our suspicions amount to nothing. That's how the procedure works with us. And you conduct yourself accordingly, please, will you?"

His face turned beet red. He clearly didn't like what I was asking of him, but at least he finally understood who was boss.

"All right," he said, hanging his head. "As you wish."

I took a deep breath. These things were always happening to me. Trying to cool down, I looked at the picture of the dervish on the wall again as I slung my bag over my shoulder. Suddenly, an image of Uncle Matthew appeared before my eyes. Not in his old age, but as the sixteen-year-old I'd seen in the yearbook. For some unexplained reason, I pictured him in those pure white garments. I saw his grey eyes, full of love, looking at my mother from under a brown felt hat. I envisioned him performing the *sema,* imagined him coming back to life - a life where he would be able to accomplish all those things he hadn't been able to in his previous one. My anger seemed to taper off, all the tension up and flew away and with it went my sorrow. I wished I could have explained all this to my mother. Maybe it would offer her some peace, make it easier for her to reconcile the death of her first love. Then again, mentioning the dervish may just reopen the old wound of my father, whom she was already incapable of forgetting. To turn Uncle Mathew into a dervish like my father... I seriously doubt my mother would want that. As I tried to get this thought out of my head, the honey-coloured light of the morning sun filtered in through a crack in the curtains and fell onto the dervish's robes; the glass began to glimmer as it reflected the light, and I was lost in its white radiance.

"What makes it precious is its ineffability."

✳

Mennan's black Mercedes pulled up in front of a large wooden double door, one side of which was wide open. It was an old neighbourhood; a golden-brown clay wall stretched out the length of the street on either side of the wooden door. I couldn't understand why we'd stopped here.

"What's going on, is it the tyre again?"

"No, Miss Greenwood," Mennan replied, pulling the hand brake. "What are the odds of two flat tyres in one day? We're here. This is the Ikonion Tourism head office."

I was surprised. It had never occurred to me that our client's offices could be in a building like this. Through the open door, I could make out a spacious garden, and beyond it a two-storey building of the same clay as the outer wall.

"You're kidding. This traditional old house?"

"Yes." He turned towards me as he explained, "A lot of the old Konyan houses are being restored and turned into apart hotels these days as the locals catch on that there's a whole new breed of tourist out there who actually prefers them to your standard hotels."

He could have been quoting Simon's wife, Margaret, when she was on one of her rants about 'the new conception of tourism'. She, too, was always going on about how she preferred the locals' homes to luxury hotels when abroad, how they helped her to better understand the authentic side of a country. Though if someone were to welcome her into their tin shanty in some Latin American country or other, she would no doubt snatch up her bag and passport and be on her way to the nearest airport in no time. Still, there were plenty of others who shared Margaret's preference for historic boutique hotels, and it looked like Ikonion's management would be among the first to take advantage of that.

"Interesting clients we have," I said under my breath. "Not only shrewd, but tasteful."

He looked puzzled, like he was trying to figure out whether I was genuinely admiring them, or insinuating we should watch our step. "Yes, they are interesting people," he finally said, leaving it at that.

Apparently, he too was avoiding speaking openly now. Even that was an improvement; better to have his stance clear than have him acting all earnest while actually up to something behind my back. I opened the car door and, stepping out, was enveloped by a heat one rarely encounters in London. Although still only spring, the sun was already burning hot. After a long northern winter, this early southern summer was a delight for me. I had a hard time keeping myself from just throwing my arms open wide and stretching like a cat. Mennan caught up with me as I closed the door. With his usual chivalrous demeanor, he fastened a button on his grey jacket and politely put a hand forward.

"Let me get your laptop."

I smiled despite myself.

"Thanks, but it's not so heavy. I'll get it myself."

He knew me well enough now to not insist. We started towards the wooden door, to the right of which was a worn wooden sign with 'Ikonion Tourism' carved into it. The aged wood, the character of the script and style of writing, had all been so skillfully designed that it gave the impression of having been there since the day the wall went up. The path up to the door was paved with small brown and yellow stones. A few steps beyond I spotted a mosaic in the path. I couldn't make out what it was, so I bent down for a closer look. At first I fancied it was an enormous daisy. I squinted. It was a bust. A head of curly hair. But wait, it wasn't hair, it was snakes!

"Medusa!" I cried. "It's the head of Medusa." I turned towards Mennan, who'd been watching me warily, wondering what on earth I was doing. "What has Medusa got to do with Ikonion Tourism?" I asked.

He swallowed uneasily. I was always asking him questions he couldn't answer, poor thing. He looked down at the mosaic, studying it carefully for a moment as though the answer were written there. Then he shrugged and gave up.

"I don't know," he said with a self-conscious smile. "Must be related to Konya's history. Mr. Kuyumcuzade is really interested in these things. We can ask inside."

"Okay. But it's not so important. I was just curious."

We started ahead again. This time, it was the black Arabic calligraphy painted on the wooden doorframe that caught my eye. Though I couldn't read it, I was struck by its beauty. Flowing lines that twisted into circles, arches that met with upward strokes and completed them, elliptical loops, lines that drooped forward and hung just so. Letters, words, and symbols of a culture I didn't know, the script that told the story of that culture... My father also used to write Arabic lettering beautifully, just like this writing on the facade. He had a special ink he used and pens cut from reeds. Once he even wrote my name - *Karen Kimya: fruit of paradise bestowed upon us by God*. I didn't understand what the Arabic words represented, so my father patiently explained the meaning behind each letter. Though I never managed to retain their meanings, I remembered our conversation very well.

"What is the fruit of paradise, Daddy?" I'd asked him.

My father smiled. "A thing of beauty that is beyond description, my girl. Its colour cannot be described, nor its taste, nor smell, nor form. In fact, what makes it precious is its ineffability."

"But look, you can see me," I objected with a spoilt affection.

My father took my head lovingly between his hands and sniffed at my hair like it really was a pleasant smelling fruit.

"And I can smell you, too. But you are more than just this lovely smell, this lovely face and voice, my girl."

He had such a touching look on his face that I couldn't find the courage to ask what more there was. I thought if he said any more he would break into tears.

"Watch your step, Miss Greenwood."

Mennan's warning came too late, as my foot had already caught on the massive slab of rock that was the threshold to the garden. Fortunately, I didn't totally lose my balance; even while stumbling I grabbed the doorframe with my left hand and managed to stay on my feet. I looked gratefully at Mennan, who had latched on to my arm so I wouldn't fall.

"Okay, okay. I'm fine. Thank you." I nodded towards the inscription over the door. "I was distracted by the calligraphy for a second."

A flash of triumph spread across the face of my colleague as he let go of my arm. As if on cue, he read it in a voice heavy with significance.

The East is Allah's, as is the West. Or something to that effect."

What interested me was not what it meant, but that Mennan could read it.

"So you know Arabic."

"A little. They taught it in the *imam hatip* schools - the orthodox high schools of Islamic law. Of course, I've forgotten most of it since I didn't become an imam."

Surprise, surprise. The man had started off as a Muslim prayer leader and ended up a businessman.

"Why didn't you become an imam?"

"Actually, it was my dear departed father's idea that I become one. But he passed away when I was in my final year of high school and I was obliged to join the world of commerce."

While we were on the subject, I wanted to hear more about him.

"So, do you enjoy being an insurance agent?"

"I love it. It's a decent job. Albeit the people of Konya haven't figured out the whole insurance thing yet. They will soon enough though, God willing."

"So you're hopeful?"

"Of course I am. If we get just five more clients like Ikonion Tourism we'll have nothing left to worry about."

I took on the role of responsible manager and half-jokingly cautioned him, "Then you'd better get down to work."

His green eyes glinted craftily.

"We're doing what we can, Miss Greenwood. For our company and ourselves."

Instead of responding, I let it go with a smile and carried on walking. But I'd barely stepped through the door when I froze in shock. The clay brick building with the tulips in front of it; the hyacinths, roses, and towering poplars; the ceramic tiled pool, this fragrance...

"I've seen this." I shuddered. "This place..."

"Is this the house you came to?" Mennan asked nonchalantly. "You know, years ago. You explained it yesterday, remember?"

Without looking at him, I shook my head.

"Not that one. I dreamt about this one last night." I spooked myself with what I was saying. "But that's impossible. I had no idea I was coming here."

Mennan also looked baffled.

"Maybe you've seen it before."

I looked over at the poplars. There was no one there. No strange voice, nor the man from the previous night.

"No," I mumbled. "Where would I possibly have seen it?"

"In a magazine, maybe?"

"I didn't see it in a magazine," I stated. "It's so strange..."

He looked confused.

"How so?"

"I don't know, just strange is all," I repeated, raising my voice. "Some pretty odd things have happened since I arrived in Konya. That man who gave me the ring yesterday evening..." I began excitedly explaining to Mennan, whose green eyes were wide with surprise. "I saw him again last night, in front of the mosque opposite the hotel."

"Your hotel's not so far from where we got the flat tyre. He could easily have been passing by there."

"He wasn't passing by. I know what I saw. He was planted in front of the fountain looking up at my room."

"Come on, Miss Greenwood." He smiled smugly. "It's not possible for anyone to see your room from the fountain."

I ignored him and, like a clock spring unwinding, began recounting the whole episode.

"I was on the balcony. Last night. I don't know exactly what time, but it was quite late. I saw him. Came eye to eye with him actually. His eyes had been riveted on my balcony as if he'd known I was going to go out there. He may even have been following me since where we had the flat. You may think it's absurd, but that's what happened." I was about to explain how someone had called out "Kimya" to me when I noticed the smile on Mennan's face had become one of open ridicule. What was I doing? They were going to think I was mad, and I was under no illusions as to where that would lead. My report would be considered obsolete and, in the end, no matter how much evidence I accrued against Ikonion Tourism, nobody would take it seriously. I immediately came to my senses. Maybe all this was part of their carefully crafted scheme. Maybe they'd slipped something into the okra soup I'd had the night before. It's not like I'd watched them make it; they'd brought it up to my room. It would explain the hallucinations, the nightmares... It all made sense. Mennan had booked the hotel, so if Ikonion Tourism had bought him out, that meant they were all in it together. Even the bearded man. Why not? I suddenly thought of the German specialist they'd kidnapped in Athens just last year. Turkey wasn't so different from Greece. And even in London there was an incredible amount of insurance fraud. I gave him a dubious look. He wiped the mocking smile off his face and settled back into the role of helpful, charming insurance agent yet again.

"Maybe it's a coincidence," he said. "The man was probably a beggar. They like to hang around in front of mosques so the people, fearing Allah, will give them more alms. And when you went out onto the balcony..."

"I don't know," I conceded, thinking it best to go along with him. "Maybe you're right. No, I'm sure you are. After all, this is your turf, you can assess these situations better."

If Mennan were on the straight and narrow, he'd be pleased that I'd started talking sense and would end the discussion as though it had never taken place. But I had no such luck.

"Still, I can't make heads or tails of your dream," he said, dredging it up again. "Did you really see this exact garden?" Apparently, he was hoping to enjoy the fruits of his labour.

"On second thought..." I said, looking hesitantly over the garden again. The clay brick building, the ceramic tiled

pool, the poplars, the flowers, the sweet-smelling fragrance...
everything was exactly as it had been in my dream, but I lied.
"No, this isn't it. There was a building there, but it was stone.
And the flowers and trees were also different from these
ones." I looked back at the pool. "And it was a fountain rather
than a pool, come to think. No, you're right. I guess I just got
wound up over nothing."

He looked me over skeptically, certain I was holding back.
It had been a bad move, going off on a tangent like this.

"Must be foreigner's syndrome," I continued. "The
mistake of thinking every place looks the same in a city you
know nothing about. People can only really distinguish those
differences over time. Like once in Morocco, I got two very
distinct mosques mixed up."

When he kept silent, I persisted. "Really, hasn't that ever
happened to you? Like in the streets of London, didn't you
ever think the houses all looked the same?"

"I got the hotels mixed up," he stated matter-of-factly.

Just as I relaxed, thinking I'd remedied the situation, he
cut in, "But I've never had a dream about a place I would
incidentally visit the following day."

We both went quiet. My forced smile broke down with the
passing of a few strained seconds.

"I haven't either, I just thought I had."

Mennan kept a straight face, but looked me over as though
trying to understand what I was up to.

"In that case, there's no cause for concern." He waved a
hand towards the door the turbaned man had stepped out
of the night before, adding, "Here we are, let's go speak with
our client."

I was hit by another wave of apprehension as it occurred
to me that the bearded man in black who had grabbed me
by the wrist the night before may be the one we were going
to see now. I told myself to be ready for anything. Stepping
through the door of the house, I imagined myself stepping
into an intricately woven web.

“A warrior with the severed head of Medusa in his left hand.”

When I saw the man who greeted us, I felt a wave of relief. It wasn’t the tall, mysterious man with the tangled beard and drab, black garments from my nightmare, but a dynamic one in his early forties, his straight hair shining as though combed back with brilliantine, and a slick, dark suit that made him look taller than he actually was. He smiled at me with exaggerated warmth as though we’d met before, and then extended a hand.

“Welcome, Miss Greenwood. I’m Ziya. Ziya Kuyumcuzade, CEO of Ikonion Tourism.”

He was speaking with an American accent, and his tone of voice was impressive; the look in his eyes, his body language, his posture and poise, all conveyed his unfailing self-confidence. I returned his smile, though with more reserve and, after shaking his outstretched hand, said politely, “If you don’t mind, let’s speak Turkish, Mr. Kuyumcuzade.” I tilted my head towards Mennan. “I’d like our Konyan agent to know what we’re talking about. I’m sure he’ll also have some input.”

I’d caught Mennan off guard, but could see he was pleased by the comment.

“Of course,” he agreed, with a self-confidence he himself wasn’t completely convinced of. “We should speak Turkish.”

Ziya gently slapped his fellow countryman's back and said with levity, "Don't worry, Mennan, Turkish it is. You won't miss a thing."

Their familiarity came as no surprise now. With the coolness of a clairvoyant, I waited for my suspicions to be confirmed, prepared to hold out until everything was out in the open so that the investigation could move soundly forward. Pretending not to think anything of the warm relationship between our agent and client, I began looking around – and was totally caught off guard for the second time since arriving here. It was as if I'd suddenly stepped onto a sci-fi film set, rather than into a historical residence. The adobe walls, aged wood, and twisted iron window grilles outside had all disappeared and been replaced with every manner of objects in dark synthetics, shiny metals, thick black glass, and glossy paints. In the middle of the room was an elliptical, black glass tabletop balanced on a single silver metal leg, around which orbited shiny leather swivel chairs in various colours. The windows were of the same black glass as the table, and steel plated bookshelves stood on the powder blue, ceramic tiled floor. On the wall directly behind Ziya's desk was a Medusa mosaic similar to the one outside, though this one not only depicted the head of Medusa, but also the warrior who had killed her. It was even more impressive - a warrior with the severed head of Medusa in his left hand and an enormous sword in his right.

Noticing my interest in the mosaic, Ziya offered an explanation. "The boy who killed Medusa. Perseus, son of Zeus..." He looked uncertain. "You know the legend, right?"

Of course I knew Medusa, with her hair of snakes and her gaze that turned men to stone. I'd seen statues and pictures of her in various places throughout the world, though I wasn't familiar with the details. Then again, I didn't really care. It wasn't the story of Medusa I wanted to hear, but rather the story behind it's connection to Ikonion Tourism. Why my client had chosen it as a logo. Why they were so interested in mythology.

"I know a little about it," I said, trying to appear engrossed. "But I'd be interested in hearing it from you. Let's see what the Turkish interpretation is."

Ziya let out a brief guffaw.

"Don't worry, Miss Greenwood, the Turkish interpretation is not so different." He gestured towards one of the chairs in front of the table. "But you're still on your feet. Have a seat, what can I get you to drink?"

"Tea, please," I replied, sitting down.

"Of course. With milk." It had come out sounding more like an assertion than a question, but I let it go with a smile of approval.

"I'll just have regular Turkish tea, please." Mennan said quietly, as he loosened the constrictive blue tie around his neck. "But make mine weak. I get heart palpitations when it's too strong."

And sweats when he's too nervous, apparently, I noted to myself. At least I knew I looked cool in comparison, despite being surrounded on all sides by con artists. I leaned back and prepared to listen to the myth, which, after giving our drinks order to the secretary over the intercom, Ziya launched into with gusto.

"As you know, Medusa was not always a hideous monster. On the contrary, she was once a girl of extraordinary beauty. She was so stunning, in fact, that she not only got the attention of the mortals, but that of the gods as well. Unfortunately, Medusa had also fallen in love with her own beauty. She was dizzy with narcissism. So she did something she shouldn't have. She broke a sacred rule. In the acropolis of Athens, she made love to the god of the seas, Poseidon, who had been enamoured of her for a long, long time. Some thought she hadn't done this willingly. That it would be more apt to refer to it as the rape of Medusa by Poseidon. But Athena never forgave the sacrilege that had been committed in her temple. She changed Medusa into a monster, turning each lock of hair into a snake, and that beautiful girl became the horrific creature who turned to stone anyone who looked into her face.

"After that, the monster she'd become would often descend on the town from where she lived in the Taurus Mountains, killing people and laying havoc to the surrounding area. The citizens of the town were just waiting for a hero to come along and kill the monster, but it's not so easy to kill a monster that turns you to stone when you look at it. Eventually, Zeus's gallant son, Perseus, undertook the formidable task. Athena, whose jealousy of the young girl still hadn't passed despite having made her a monster, rushed to the aid of Perseus with great enthusiasm. A difficult struggle ensued, in which Perseus severed the head of Medusa, rescuing the townsmen from this monster. In order to show their gratitude to their hero, the citizens erected iconic statues of him all about the town. And this town, surrounded on all sides by these icons, was given the name Ikonion."

"Ikonion," I repeated under my breath. "You mean Konya..."

Ziya didn't allow me to complete my sentence. He whistled and said, "Very clever, Miss Greenwood. I'm impressed. That's right. The name Konya comes from Ikonion. Or Ikonium, as others knew it."

I pursed my lips, aware that many cities in the world had created these founding myths for themselves.

"I've never heard that anywhere else..."

"And you won't." With great solemnity, as though divulging a trade secret, he explained, "The tourism sector is relentless. Everyone wants a piece of the pie. The Greeks, the Italians, the Egyptians... No matter how many legends, how many stories there are, they all get snapped up. But believe me, that Konya's name was once Ikonion is a fact."

"Thus the company name Ikonion."

He looked at me with the confidence of one who doesn't doubt the integrity of his actions.

"Right again. We then chose the head of Medusa as a logo, to draw attention to the seven-thousand-year history of our city. After all, we're in the tourism business, too."

"I heard a different story," Mennan put in, fiddling with his kerchief. Turning to Ziya, he continued. "Look, please don't get me wrong Ziya, I'm not trying to contradict you. It's just, one of the dervishes from the lodge told me an entirely different story."

Ziya seemed much more interested than I was.

"Really? What was that? Why don't you tell it? Maybe I've also heard it before."

He dabbed at his forehead, then set out to explain.

"All right then. This is the legend: From the province of Khorasan, two dervishes came flying towards Anatolia."

I couldn't understand what he meant.

"You mean they came by plane?"

"What plane, Miss Greenwood?" Mennan laughed. "We're talking about almost a thousand years ago. The arrival of the Turks in Anatolia. These men of God were flying by themselves."

This time I laughed. "You mean like birds."

"I told you it was a legend. I'm just repeating someone else's lie," he said, though not offended by my disbelief.

"Not lies, my friend. Myths," Ziya corrected him. "But go on. They were flying and then..."

"When they were above these very lands, they looked down and saw a place abounding in gardens and vineyards." He turned to me to clarify. "They say that in those days, a thousand or so years ago, Konya was greener than it is today." He smiled. "I mean, there were still plenty of gardens, even if not as many as in London. Anyhow, one of the dervishes, upon seeing the beautiful lands below, asked his traveling companion, 'What do you think, venerable old man, shall I perch here?' The other dervish looked down, and also finding the view to his liking, answered, 'Kon, ya!' meaning 'Yes, perch here!' And that's how they came to perch here, and the city's name became Konya."

Ziya slapped his knee as he recalled the story.

"Yes, of course I have heard that one," he exclaimed.

While a conspiratorial smile passed between our agent and our client, or should I say our two like-minded fellow townsmen, let's not go so far as to say partners in crime, I tried to put into words the question turning about in my mind.

"That legend seems far more suited to Islamic culture, doesn't it? So why choose Medusa for your logo?"

Ziya had his response on hand.

"If we'd wanted to use Islamic culture, there is a bottomless wealth of treasure at our disposal. A treasure that stretches from the Seljuk Palace to the Karatay Madrasah, from the

Mosque and Mausoleum of Shams-i Tebriz to the Mosque and Mausoleum of Sadreddin-i Konevi, and to the priceless jewel that is Mevlana Jelaleddin-i Rumi himself, of course. No doubt it's what we would have preferred. But it wasn't our best option. In Konya, even the shish kebab stalls use Rumi and other various Islamic figures. Not only that, but our target is foreign tourism, not domestic."

"Because it's the foreign tourists who bring in the money," I half-jokingly rebuked.

His dark eyes lit up shrewdly.

"Foreigners better fit our customer profile. That's how I would have put it."

"But there's something you've overlooked," Mennan objected. "Rumi's relevance to tourists is very great indeed."

Ziya squirmed uneasily in his chair.

"I never said we have zero regard for Rumi." His tone was harsh. He gave Mennan a look like he'd overstepped his boundaries, then carried on sternly. "If that were the case, we wouldn't have restored all these old Konyan houses and reopened them as residences." He turned to look at me, and the severe expression on his face vanished. "Moreover, my own father is a Mevlevi dervish, just like Miss Greenwood's."

I didn't catch what Ziya said at first. He'd said my name, and made some remark about fathers... Pointing a finger at the transparent whirling dervish trinket on the black glass table, he reiterated, "Isn't that so, Miss Greenwood? Your father is Poyraz, and he was a dervish in Konya."

How did this man know my father? He must have been snooping around on me. This was too much. All the autosuggestion I'd used in order to keep myself cool-headed just up and flew away. I felt like raining down the insults, putting this slick-haired fop in his place. I was about to ask him just what right he thought he had, when Mennan, clearly agitated, exclaimed, "Miss Greenwood, your hand!"

I looked down at it in dismay. A red stain was spreading out from where it rested in my lap. For one short instant before remembering I was pregnant, I worried that I'd started menstruating. Then I panicked even more, thinking I was having a miscarriage. I lifted my hand and discretely looked down to between my knees, but there was no blood there.

"It's your hand all right. It's bleeding," said Ziya.

I held it up and looked. Sure enough, the blood seemed to be coming from the finger with the ring. The ring? Yes, the silver ring was there on my finger, its brown stone turned scarlet with clotted blood. I had no recollection of having put it on, but this was not the time to think about it. Cupping my bleeding finger in my other hand, I stood up.

"Where are the toilets?"

In one agile movement, Ziya leapt to his feet, ushering me through a metallic grey door in the corner of the room, as he hastily told me, "Here you are. Right here."

"The wife of Shams-i Tebriz was also called Kimya."

※

The water rinsed the blood away and my fingers were now clean. I took off the ring and, leaving it on the edge of the sink, looked my finger over to find the wound. But there was no cut, not even a scratch. I looked down to where, on more careful inspection, I saw that it wasn't my finger bleeding but the ring's stone. Tiny red droplets spread out over the white marble countertop as it was bit-by-bit being silently painted red. The ring must have been cheaper than it looked. It was the dye running off, I supposed, though it's resemblance to real blood was so uncanny that I got goosebumps despite myself. That's exactly how these men must have wanted me - spooked, panicky, off my head. But I wasn't going to let them get to me. I swallowed my fear and touched the dark red liquid with the tip of my index finger, then rubbed it between my finger and thumb. It even felt like real blood, warm and thick. I wondered how they'd pulled it off. I was dubious for a moment, were they really capable of accomplishing all this? Maybe it was just another fit of paranoia I was having, as I did from time to time. But none of this could be explained any other way. It had to be about the three million pounds, the men were doing their best to get hold of that money. I tried to remember putting the ring on. Had I slipped it on the night before? I was sure it hadn't been this morning. All the blood rushed to my head as I imagined them coming into my room as I slept half-naked in my bed to slip the ring on my finger. "Dirty bastards," I exclaimed.

"Miss Greenwood? Are you all right?"

It was Mennan's voice. They hadn't heard what I'd said, but they would hear me now. I wanted to go out, grab them both by their collars, and smack them into oblivion. But when I looked in the mirror and saw the sparks flying from my eyes, I stopped. What difference would it make if I told them off, or spit in their faces even? They would say I was insane, holding them responsible for my dreams. And as it would no longer stand up in a court of law, we could kiss my report goodbye. "Bastards," I uttered, through clenched teeth this time.

"Miss Greenwood?"

It was Mennan again. He sounded genuinely concerned.

"I'm fine," I answered, trying to calm down. "I'm all right. I'll be out in a second."

Simon was right. These men we were up against were not only sly, but bold. I wasn't sure where they would draw the line. I would have to keep one step ahead of them; keep my thoughts and feelings to myself and stay calm at all costs. But how was I going to do that? My hands were shaking as it was, and my face in the mirror was still crimson. I was a slave to my anger. I wadded up some tissue and held it under the tap, then dabbed at my burning temples. The coolness of it helped. "Really, what am I going to say to these men?" I asked my reflection in the mirror, after a lame attempt to clean the stains out of my shirt. "I suppose I should just be straight with them," the frazzled woman answered back. She was right, I would tell it like it was, plain and simple. Some deranged man had given me a cheap ring and the paint had run, spreading onto my hand and clothes. That was the story. There was no need for me to be angry that Ziya had been digging around on my father. On the contrary, what they'd learned might even work to my advantage, helping me to better understand the dimensions of this conspiracy they'd formed. That much decided, I pulled myself together, dried my hands, and looked back at the ring. The dye was no longer running off, but I couldn't trust that, so I wrapped it in a paper towel before stepping out.

When I reentered the room, Mennan was on his feet and Ziya was leaning on his elbows at the head of the black glass table. Both men were waiting in silence, their eyes on the bathroom door. I smiled calmly. "It wasn't my finger," I said, holding up the ring on the paper towel. "The dye on this ring was running off."

Ziya got up and came over, a look of bewilderment on his face as though he weren't in on it. As for Mennan, he'd reacted faster, plucking the ring unceremoniously from the paper and looking it over. "I don't see any dye on it," he glumly observed, before his partner in crime could reach us. Apparently, he wasn't pleased that it had made no impact on me.

"I washed it off," I said, trying not to betray my anger. "But if you want to test it, just hold it in your hand a while and I'm sure you'll be covered in the stuff in no time."

"That's funny. It doesn't look like such a cheap ring," Ziya said, joining his friend.

"Well, I'm not bleeding. So I see no other explanation for it. Unless, of course," I continued sarcastically, "my finger somehow magically bled without there being a cut on it."

"Magically?" Mennan asked, visibly distressed. "Where did that idea come from?"

Ziya shook his head as if to say what a dope Mennan was.

"She's joking," he said, grabbing the ring out of Mennan's hand and taking his turn with it. "It sure is beautiful. Where did you buy it?"

"I didn't buy it. It was a gift."

"Really? How embarrassing. I feel sorry for whoever gave it you. It caused such a mess."

He was really playing his part well. And I played mine, saying, "It wasn't anyone I know. Just some stranger. Some bearded guy all dressed in black."

"I think it was a beggar," Mennan interjected. "One of the beggars from in front of the mosque."

Ziya looked surprised.

"What, did you see the man too?"

"It happened last night as I was taking Miss Greenwood to the hotel." He paused. "I didn't actually see him. I was changing the tyre at that point."

"So how do you know he was a beggar?"

"I figured it out from what Miss Greenwood told me. She said his hair and beard were in tangles. And that the same man came to the mosque in front of her hotel later on."

"No," I said interrupting. "No, I'm not sure it was the same man. I was exhausted. It could have been someone else."

Mennan looked betrayed. I thought he was going to bring up what I'd said in the garden, but luckily he didn't.

"So you've changed your mind and it's not the same guy now?" he asked, sounding bitter.

"No," I answered, trying not to let him get to me. I stared into his eyes without flinching. "I don't think it is."

There was a knock at the door as the secretary brought in our drinks. Ziya smiled and showed us to our places again.

"Have a seat, let's carry on the conversation over our tea."

We settled into our chairs, which were quite plush and comfortable despite the post-modern design. Mennan wasn't looking my direction anymore. He was probably sulking because the person he'd laid a trap for wasn't falling for it the way he intended. I sipped my tea, ignoring him. Ziya had ordered a Turkish coffee for himself, and he also took a sip from his cup. Mennan, however, just sat there sweating in his chair like a chubby, pouty child, his tea steaming away on the table in front of him.

"So, is the tea to your liking?" Ziya asked, finally breaking the silence.

Actually, it wasn't. It was all milk and very little tea. It was hardly the time for me to be considering my palate though.

"It's nice, thanks," I lied.

"Glad you like it. We don't often have English guests. I was worried the boys wouldn't be able to manage a proper milky tea." He turned towards his sulking fellow townsman, whose sullenness he'd also noticed. "So why aren't you touching your tea, Mennan? Miss Greenwood likes it, why don't you?" he flippantly continued.

Mennan sat up in his chair and said sheepishly, "Of course that's not it, Ziya. I'm waiting for it to cool. Look at me. I'm sweating as it is just sitting here."

"Shall I get you a cold soda?"

"No, thanks. I'm fine like this."

It was the perfect time to change the subject and start talking business. But Ziya, taking another sip of his coffee, didn't do that.

"Just out of curiosity, this man with the beard, where did you see him the first time?"

I wasn't surprised by the question. It was only natural that he'd bring the subject back round to the bearded man or the ring. In the future this whole conversation would be used against me if necessary.

"I don't know," I said, setting my cup down. "In front of a park. With a mosque in it."

Mennan was no longer willing to jump in. He might not have opened his mouth if Ziya hadn't asked him a direct question. "Where was that, Mennan?"

"The mausoleum of Shams-i Tabriz."

"Oh, Shams-i Tabriz..." Ziya repeated. He looked straight at me without blinking. "Do you know who Shams-i Tabriz is, Miss Greenwood?"

I thought about it, as I had the day before when I saw the name on the sign at the mosque. I must have heard the name somewhere before. From my father, I guessed.

"I don't know," I said with a shrug. "Must be a dervish."

Nodding his head, he reflected, "Not just any dervish, a very important one. The man who made Rumi Rumi, we could say."

"I get it. He was a great man. Still, why should I know about him?"

He must have thought he'd upset me because he immediately started defending himself.

"You don't have to..." He was about to explain, then changed his mind. He looked torn. "You don't have to know about him of course, but..."

"Yes?" Why was he beating around the bush?

"It must be a fluke."

"What fluke?"

"You know how your middle name is Kimya, right? From what I understand, your name is Karen Kimya Greenwood."

"That's right."

"Well, Shams-i Tabriz's wife was also called Kimya. Kimya was Rumi's adopted daughter."

I felt a chill pass through me. The voice that had called out "Kimya..." rang in my ears again. The nightmares that had plagued me were all going to come flooding back in if I let them, which is probably what they wanted. They both stared at me wide eyed, waiting to see how the words would affect me.

"So? My father loved the name Kimya, that's why he gave it to me."

"I'm not saying there's anything to it. It's just an odd coincidence."

They were playing games with me. I wouldn't give them the satisfaction of a response.

"What on earth were you doing there anyway?" Ziya asked, turning to Mennan when he didn't get the reaction he'd hoped for. "Shams-i Tabriz's tomb wasn't on your route."

"Miss Greenwood was looking for a house. A big house with a garden." He paused. He must have thought I was going to contradict him again because he asked, "I'm not wrong in saying that, am I, Miss Greenwood?"

I gave them a smug smile.

"No, you're right, Mr Fidan. I was looking for a large house with a big garden. I went there the first time I came to Konya."

"Your father's house?"

"I don't know." I was doing well, keeping my cool even at the mention of my father. "Actually, it looked more like a religious centre than a house."

He nodded with that irritating self-conviction again.

"The Mevlevi convent. I can take you there if you'd like."

"I'd like that," I said, genuinely wanting to see it. "How do you know about the place?"

He smiled, displaying broad, slightly yellow teeth.

"Remember how I told you my father is a Mevlevi sufi? Maybe your father mentioned him, his name's İzzet. They call him İzzet Efendi the Silversmith because he worked with silver for years. He's the one who knew your father, Poyraz

Efendi. For years they frequented the same dervish lodge. Would you like to meet him?"

"If we have time," I said. It was time to close the subject of families and get back to work. "Shall we talk a little about the fire now?"

Ziya raised an index finger into the air.

"Let's do that. But first, there's one last thing I'm curious about. Is your father still with you? It was twenty odd years ago when my father last saw him. He said he never heard from him again after he left Konya."

"Why do you ask?"

My voice sounded just as I'd meant it to - cold, distant, and formal. His self-assured expression was shattered.

"I'm sorry," he said. "Please don't take this the wrong way. What I'm actually interested in is my own father. It's to try and understand him that I am asking about yours."

"Is that so?"

"Believe me. My father was once one of the most skilled silversmiths in Konya. Even his apprentices are now among the richest people in the city, but he hasn't changed a bit in forty years."

"Well, from what I can see, you don't appear to be doing too badly yourself," I said knowingly.

He stroked the lapels of his of his perfectly-tailored jacket.

"That's thanks to my Grandfather Osman." He paused. "He was my mother's father. My father's side of the family was dirt poor. If it weren't for my Grandfather Osman, we would be wallowing in abject poverty now, I'm sure. Fortunately, Grandfather Osman was cleverer than that. He was a cheese merchant. And a very shrewd businessman. I like to emulate him."

"Well, we all choose our own paths." I said. "Your father just happened to choose religion."

"That's not it," he immediately objected. "Grandfather Osman also prayed five times a day. We are Muslims too, praise God. No, it's nothing to do with religion, they were just men of different moulds."

"A completely different species," Mennan put in. "Their personalities, thoughts and feelings, insights, mannerisms..."

Ziya gave a teasing nod in Mennan's direction.

"He used to be a Muslim preacher so, you know, he would know more about these things... Anyhow, that's what I'm dying to know. My father still lives in his old house, sits in his old chair, flips the same pages of the same old books... When it comes to love, he reads the same old poems, and he still goes to the same dervish convent as always. And all right, that's no crime. But wouldn't you get bored to tears doing the same things day in and day out? It's because I'm trying to figure him out that I'm asking about your father."

A look of hopelessness crossed his face before he continued. "You think I didn't ask him? Well I did, lots of times. He always answered the same way. 'Don't expect answers from me, son' he says. 'The answers are there at the tip of our noses, but where is the eye that will see them?'"

Mennan couldn't hold back and let out a chuckle, at which Ziya shot him a look, though he held his tongue.

"My father and Poyraz Efendi formed a bond of friendship in the sect. They were brethren on the same path. That's why I was wondering if your father is like mine."

I wasn't sure what he meant by 'sect friends' or 'brethren on the path', but I sensed the question was genuine and therefore saw no reason not to provide him with an honest answer. As honest as I could, that is, considering I really didn't know.

"I suppose he is. But he's not with us anymore. He's living in Pakistan. Probably doing similar things to what your father does every day, and also very content."

He hung his bottom lip and said distractedly, "Strange men, these ones. The last of their kind..." He stayed that way for a moment, as though faced with an insoluble problem, then took one last sip of coffee and came to life again. "Okay, we can talk business now."

This time it was I who stopped him.

"One second, please." I took my laptop out of its case, then turned it on and pulled up the Ikonion files. "Here we are. Serhad Gökgöz, Nezihe Bostancıoğlu, Kadir Gemelek... I need to see these people." Ziya's face clouded over again, but I ignored him and explained, "Those are the witnesses to the fire. I've already read the police statements, but I want their firsthand accounts."

"Certainly," said Ziya, leaning back. "Serhad and Nezihe are hotel staff. Arranging for you to meet with them should be easy enough. Unfortunately, Kadir Gemelek no longer works for us. We had to let him go. He was seriously injured in the fire, and we more than compensated him, of course, but the ordeal left him emotionally scarred and he is, how shall I put it, not exactly in his right mind."

"I'll find him," Mennan blurted out. Surprise, surprise, he'd found his tongue again. "He's a childhood friend. We grew up in the same neighbourhood."

Ziya gave Mennan a piercing look.

"Of course you'll find him. I can find him too, but that's not my point." He turned to me. "Kadir doesn't know what he's saying. He's talking nonsense. If you do visit him, I'd advise you to take whatever he says with a grain of salt." I was about to ask what he meant when Ziya continued with an explanation on his own accord. "He claims aliens burned down the hotel. That a man with antennas on his head came into the laundry room and plugged in all the irons."

"Nice story," Mennan chirped. "Did he happen to mention why the aliens started the fire?"

"He did. Apparently, they were led off course by the lights of the hotel and couldn't find anywhere to land."

"Poor Kadir wasn't himself," Mennan said, backing Ziya up. "He was spewing out some nonsense in the hospital. But the doctors said he would get over it, and we haven't seen him for a few days so..."

"I still say it will be a waste of time, though ultimately it's your decision," Ziya counseled.

So then it was someone I definitely should visit, this Kadir who sees aliens.

"And the other two?" I asked, looking back at my computer screen. "Sehad Gökgöz and..."

"Nezihe Bostancıoğlu," Ziya interrupted, finishing my sentence. "Like I said, they are still in our employment. You can see them whenever you want."

"Thank you." I looked gratefully at Ziya. "You've been very helpful."

"It's my pleasure. We're all in this together."

I looked at him with approval.

"Well, your professionalism sure is a breath of fresh air. A lot of our clients are hesitant around us. But it's like you said, we're all in this together. However, I have one last request. Could you please send those two employees to the scene of the fire?"

He and Mennan were both caught off guard.

"To the hotel? Why?"

"I want them there when they explain what happened. It'll make it easier for me to visually reconstruct the incident, and consequently my report more realistic. And of course, that means less trouble getting the compensation check signed in London."

Ziya's face lit up with gratification.

"That would be great, thanks. The quicker we resolve this, the easier it will be for us to get the hotel back up and running again. We're losing money by the minute, and we'll be all the more grateful to you if we can get this sorted out quickly."

I was certain he was going to offer me a bribe. But then he just smiled and said, "Don't worry, I'll send Serhad and Nezihe to the site."

"With Allah's blessing, a prayer of *El Fatiha* for the souls of the dead."

※

The Yakut Hotel was situated on a wide, newly opened boulevard in the north of the city. This, the best hotel in Konya, along with its gardens, swimming pool and various other annexes, had been built on a total of 3,500 square metres, and now stood in front of us a scorched skeleton. Charred wooden windows, rooms dusty with black soot, metal that had twisted under the heat, melted paint, shards of darkened glass... all nine floors had burned. If the hotel hadn't been undergoing repairs, the number of casualties would have been much higher. It brought to mind a case in Malaysia I'd heard about. Although only the top four floors of the eleven-storey building were destroyed by fire, seventeen people had died, five of those burning to death while the other twelve were asphyxiated by the smoke. Luckily, this hotel had been empty.

Before Serhad and Nezihe arrived, Mennan and I did a small tour of the ruins of the hotel. In the confusion of debris, it was impossible to tell what had taken place. We couldn't take the heavy odour of burnt wood and melted plastic for too long though, and rushed out just as a dark blue Mercedes pulled up in front of the hotel. From it emerged a middle-aged woman and two young men. The driver was burly, with a clean-shaven head and sunglasses, the lenses like mirrors over his eyes. But it was the brown suede gloves he was wearing despite the heat that really got my attention. He kept his distance, waving at us in greeting. Mennan responded with a barely perceptible nod in his direction and I didn't bother to wave back either. The man then took a rag from his back pocket and proceeded to wipe down the car door handles.

"What a nutjob," Mennan spouted from between clenched teeth. "That's Cavit, the clean freak. The gloves are so he won't get his hands dirty."

He needn't have whispered though, because the other man was busy looking over Mennan's Mercedes. He walked around it full circle, then stroking the hood with feigned admiration, asked, "Where did you get the car, Mennan? Sure is flashy. Business is going well, huh?"

The young man's words seemed to make Mennan uneasy and he scowled. Perhaps it was Ziya's reward to our employee for his disloyalty to us.

"That's none of your business," Mennan shot back, before turning back to me. "This is Serhad," he continued by way of introduction. "Serhad Gökgöz. And this is Nezihe Bostancıoğlu," he said, indicating the thin, swarthy older woman. She had a drawn face with sharp cheek bones, which were all framed by the navy blue scarf wrapped round her head. Her chestnut eyes, swimming in years of weariness and tedium, looked out with one small part timidity and even more suspicion. As for Serhad, he was young, somewhere in his mid-twenties. His curly hair was cut short, and his unbuttoned shirt exposed an amulet, some kind of good-luck charm, hanging on a hairless chest. He stood in front of me, hands sunk into the pockets of his trousers, and an expression of disregard bordering insolence in his grey-blue eyes.

"Thanks for coming," I began. "I guess you know why you're here."

"No, we don't," said Serhad. He took his hands out of his pockets. "Ziya told us to come, so we came."

"Uh-huh," Nezihe said, nodding. "Ziya said come and we came, God bless him."

I was prepared to hear them repeat verbatim what Ziya had told them to, but then Mennan surprised me, as he roared, "Forget about Ziya now." He stood bolt upright on his short stumpy legs and placed his hands on his hips. "There's no Ziya here now, and the law is on our side." He pointed towards the ruins behind him. "Look at the state of that hotel. That lovely building, a national asset, reduced to ashes. And on top of that two people are dead. People with homes and families, just like you, like us. Miss Greenwood has come all the way from London for this investigation. This is serious business, so let me warn you. If you lie, or make any false statements..."

I couldn't understand why his reaction was so strong. Maybe he was trying to get even with Serhad for his remark about the car, but Serhad didn't look like the type to give in so easily. "Now why would you say that?" he interrupted. "When have you ever known me to lie? Shame on you, and in front of our foreign lady guest."

Strangely, it was his calling me a foreigner that offended me most. To my surprise, I found myself blurting out, "I am not a foreigner." I looked directly into the young Serhad's lashless eyes. "I'm every bit as much Konyan as the rest of you. My father was walking these streets before you were even born."

"Serhad's not even Konyan," said Mennan. "He claims to be from Antalya. And he's nothing like us."

Serhad was shooting daggers at Mennan. I was afraid he was going to jump him, though fortunately he didn't.

"Sorry, Miss Greenwood," he said, the challenge in his eyes morphing into contrived respect. "I have no qualms with you. Mr. Fidan is out of line, that's all."

Mennan was going to answer back, but I signaled with raised eyebrows for him to stop. I still couldn't understand the reason for this animosity. Okay, the young man may be a bit ill-mannered, but he'd done nothing wrong as of yet. Maybe this too was staged, or Mennan was deliberately creating a rift between me and these hotel employees so that they'd change their minds about talking? But when exactly would Mennan and Ziya have found the time to conspire to this? After we'd left Ikonion Tourism, we'd gone to Mennan's office. It was in a humble flat near Alaeddin Hill, where the old Seljuk Sultanate's palaces once were. For a few hours, I sat poring over the papers that hadn't made it to London, during which time Mennan never left my side. After that, we'd gone to my hotel and I'd changed into some clothes better suited to examining the site of the fire. We were there for about half an hour. They could have spoken on the phone then... but planning it all in such detail wouldn't have been easy. What, were all these men actors? I studied Mennan carefully. Maybe he just had a personal score to settle with Serhad. He seemed on the verge of exploding, but was probably suppressing his anger because he was still shy around me. Either way, I couldn't allow this tension to hinder the investigation.

"Serhad is just trying to help," I intervened, before Mennan had a chance to brawl with him, a boy nearly half his age.

Grimacing, his light eyes blinking irately under thin eyebrows, the young man with the amulet put in, "That's what I was getting at, Miss Greenwood. We're honest people and have nothing to hide. We're ready to tell you everything we know. Why else would we be here?"

Nezihe hung her head again.

"Uh-huh, why would we even be here?"

Serhad was getting really caught up in the argument. "The law is on our side... I mean, really. Why do you find it necessary to use scare tactics like this?"

Maybe he was right. We'd started off on the wrong foot by threatening them and Mennan had come on unnecessarily strong. I decided not to let our agent take any initiative from then on.

"You're right. We were out of line, and I apologise. I guess we got off to a bad start. But as we say in English, all's well that ends well. So now that's sorted, let's get on with it."

When there were no objections, I proceeded to take my video camera out of my bag. Nezihe saw the camera and immediately cringed.

"What's that?"

"It's a video camera. I want to record your statements so I won't forget what was said."

"You're going to have me on film?"

"Yes, you could say that."

She covered her face and moved away from the camera as though it were already pointed on her.

"God no, don't do that."

"There's nothing to worry about. It's not like you're going to be on TV or anything. I'm the only one who will see it."

"No, I'll be too nervous. I can't talk on that thing."

"Don't worry," Mennan said, coming to my aid. "It's just a regular camera. You just concentrate on talking."

"No way," she said, throwing her head back obstinately. "Really, forget it. I won't speak on any camera."

Even Serhad could no longer tolerate this woman's pointless prudery.

"Come on, Nezihe," he said, trying to mollify her. "It's just a camera. What's the problem?"

"You think I don't know what it is? I said no, Serhad. I didn't talk to that TV guy with the beard that came here last year either, remember? You know, the one doing a program on our hotel. He talked to Hasibe from the laundry room instead."

The woman was resolute, she wasn't going to be filmed.

"So let's do this then," I said, trying not to spook her any further. "I won't film you, but I'll record your voice."

She didn't immediately consent, she must have thought I was trying to trick her.

"You mean, I won't be visible, right?"

"You won't be visible, just audible."

She still didn't trust me. She looked at her friend, her eyes appealing for help.

"Don't worry, Nezihe," Serhad said. "They won't film you. Look, Miss Greenwood promised."

"All right then." But she didn't stop fretting. "But look, if you do..."

"We won't. We can't do it without your permission anyhow."

"You haven't got my permission," she repeated. "No filming."

"We're just going to record your voice."

"On tape?"

"On tape."

"Okay, then. Tape is okay."

I put my camera back and took out a voice recorder. Finally, I'd be able to start. I pushed the record button.

"Case of the fire in Konya's Yakut Hotel." I stated as introduction. "With us are two eyewitnesses, Serhad Gökgöz and Nezihe Bostancıoğlu."

Worried that Nezihe would keep kicking up a fuss, I first extended the voice recorder to Serhad.

"Your position at the hotel?"

"I was the security supervisor for the lower floors."

"Were you at the hotel when the fire broke out?"

"Yes. I was drinking tea at the reception."

"Alone?"

"Yes, alone. The hotel was undergoing repairs and the painters were scheduled to come in the following day. There were five of us in the hotel. Me, Kadir, Nezihe... and Mecit and Huseyin, who are dead now."

The woman again nodded her head in agreement.

"Uh-huh, there were five of us."

I shut off the recorder. They looked at me, then at each other, wondering what I was up to. Mennan looked as surprised as they were.

"Shall we go into the building? I'd rather have you explain what happened from where you experienced it," I said, stating my intention simply.

Serhad looked troubled. I carried on with my request, using the one word he wouldn't be able to protest against.

"Ziya. This is what we discussed with Ziya. You're to explain things once inside the hotel."

A smug smile spread across Serhad's pale, thin lips.

"It's no problem for us. But the building is a wreck, it's full of broken glass. I wouldn't want you to get cut or anything."

My command of Turkish was good enough to understand what this kid who fancied himself a mafia thug was implying. I'd once worked as a secretary for a Turkish company in London, where an older woman, Turkan, had taught me the secret meanings behind street language and slang. Turkan had such a mouth on her that they used call her 'Turkan the Bloke'. "You don't really know a language until you learn how to swear in it," she used to say. If I could speak and write Turkish as well as English now, I had Turkan to thank for it even more than my father.

So although I knew exactly what this '*dallama*' Serhad was implying – Turkan had taught me the word for 'jerk' and it was one of my favourites – it was still in my best interest to play the clueless English woman.

"That's so considerate of you," I said, keeping my tone of voice even. "But I am quite used to being in places like this. It comes with the territory. Since it's not a problem for you either, let's carry on this conversation inside."

I didn't even bother to ask Nezihe for fear she would refuse to go in. I was hoping she would just follow along behind us, and she did. But she stopped just before entering where the fire had been centered and looked each of us in the face in turn.

"With Allah's blessing, a prayer of *El Fatiha* for the souls of the dead," she said.

Nezihe and Mennan began whispering in Arabic. Serhad pretended to say the prayer also, but was just moving his lips. I just put out my cupped hands with palms turned gently upward like the others had. It was a very short prayer, and they each said 'Amen' in turn, pulling their hands over their faces, which I didn't do. "May they rest in peace," I sufficed in adding.

We started forward again on our toes, taking great care not to step on any pieces of metal or glass shards. Soon we reached the wide open area that had been the hotel's lobby. Mennan looked around miserably, and despite having already been here, moaned forlornly.

"What a shame. Just look at the state of my beautiful hotel." He pointed towards a heap of twisted metal that I took to be the reception desk. "I can't even count the number of times I've been here... I think the last time was when Simon stayed here, actually. We had dinner, he was crazy about the food." His eyes scanned the charred lobby again.

"A shame," he said again. "A crying shame."

I didn't have the energy to deal with Mennan's moaning. The air was so heavy. Whether it was the heat, the smell and taste of ash, the vile odour burning our sinuses, or all that combined, I couldn't help gasping. I turned the recorder back on and held it up to Serhad again.

"Okay, where were you when the fire broke out?"

Instead of answering, he pointed up.

"We shouldn't stop here. The chandelier might fall."

We looked up to see a huge lamp that had blown out, its glass black as soot. Serhad was right, it could come down at any moment. We moved off to the right.

"We should be okay here," I said, extending the recorder again. "So, where were you?"

Without hesitation, as though there had been no fire and the room was unscathed, he casually indicated the right side of the lobby.

"Sitting right there in that chair."

What he'd referred to as a chair was now a lump of half-melted plastic with metal rods sticking out at all angles.

"Opposite the reception desk," I reiterated for the voice recorder. "How did you notice the fire had started?"

He laughed as though the question amused him.

"How could I not. It exploded like a bomb."

I had already been over the details of the report, but I wanted to hear it from him.

"What exploded?"

"A drum of paint thinner."

"What was the paint thinner doing in the hotel?"

"I told you, there were repairs being done here. The painting was supposed to start the following day, and all the paints and thinners were in the same room. They all caught fire. The explosion was so violent it hurled my chair forward like an earthquake. The tea glass in my hand went flying and smashed to the floor."

I turned to Nezihe.

"And you? Where were you when this explosion happened?"

Caught off guard, the poor woman stuttered, "Me? Where was I...?"

"Yes, you. You were in the hotel..."

Averting her eyes, she answered, "We were in the hotel. In the laundry pressing room. Mecit, Huseyin, and me. Kadir wasn't with us. We were covering the irons and tables with plastic because, you know, they were going to paint the next day so we had to cover everything up."

"And when did you notice the fire?"

She lifted her eyes to look back into mine, finally overcoming the case of nerves speaking had given her.

"Mecit smelled it. 'Something's burning,' he said. Huseyin and I didn't understand at first, then we also smelled it. He was so young and nimble, Mecit, may he sleep in divine light. 'Let's go take a look,' he said. Then he rushed into the next room with Huseyin on his heels. Just as they opened the door, pandemonium broke out. It was like the ground split open and the earth turned upside down. I rolled into a ball and stayed that way. That's when Mecit and Huseyin passed over to the other side. The laundry room door fell on top of me and shielded me. And it's a good thing too, otherwise I wouldn't be with you right now, either."

"All right, so who pulled you out of the fire?"

A look of shame flashed in her eyes. I guess she felt both delight and remorse that she hadn't also died.

"Kadir saved me. As soon as he heard the explosion he ran over, flung me onto his back, and carried me outside."

"Kadir Gemelek? The one who was injured in the fire?"

"Uh-huh. Kadir is in charge of our group. He's the one who got me this job. He's a good man, bless him. If it hadn't been for him, I would already have met my maker by now, just like Mecit and Huseyin."

"Was Kadir injured while he was carrying you out?"

"I don't know, ma'am," she said, her shoulders slumping beneath her wiry neck "I fainted. I didn't see anything."

The woman's deference, her referring to me as ma'am despite being at least twenty years my senior, really pulled on my heartstrings. I was beginning to develop a fondness for her.

"No," said Serhad, interjecting. "After he got Nezihe out, he dived back inside. That's when he got hurt."

"You mean you saw Kadir bringing Miss Bostancıoğlu out?"

"Of course I did. Told him not to go back inside, in fact. But he wouldn't listen. He just said, 'You look after Nezihe, I'll get Mecit and Huseyin out.'"

"Gutsy man, our Kadir," said Mennan, joining in. "I'm not just saying that because he's a childhood friend. Kadir is like a lion."

His voice was shaky, as though he were overcome with emotion. Teardrops welled up in his eyes, ready to spill onto the dust and ash covered floor. I left him to deal with his emotions and turned back to Serhad.

"What were you doing at that point?"

I hadn't meant to accuse him, but he was offended nonetheless.

"What was I supposed to do," he rebuked. "I was helping Nezihe. She'd hurt her head. She had blood on her face and in her eyes."

"Uh-huh," said Nezihe. "Blood all over my face and eyes."

"Did you call the fire brigade right away?"

"Well, at first I was a bit confused, of course. It's not every day you're faced with a situation like this."

Mennan saw his chance and put in, "Go on, tell her you panicked."

"Yeah, I panicked. So what? I wonder what you would have done if you'd been there?"

They were about to have another go at each other, but I was determined not to give them the chance.

"So when did you call them?"

"As soon as I managed to get my wits about me. I mean, it wasn't all that long. Anyways, Nezihe had started coming to."

"But the fire brigade claims they weren't informed until nearly an hour after the fire started."

He scowled, knitting his pencil-thin eyebrows, beads of sweat even bigger than those of Mennan's breaking out on his forehead.

"Because," he said swallowing hard, "because the explosion didn't happen until well after the fire had started."

Although I knew every last detail about what had happened, I gave him an inquisitive look and asked, "Really? I didn't know that."

Mennan, aware that I'd read the reports and was lying, gave me an odd look. I was certain he was going to make some comment giving me away or playing into Serhad's hands, but to my pleasant surprise, he kept his composure and carried on listening.

"Of course," Serhad explained, convinced his contribution was vital. "It broke out in the stock room. That is, the room immediately next to where the thinner was being kept. It started in an electrical socket there. First the carpet caught fire, then the curtains, linens, and so on. Then it leapt to the laundry room where the paints and thinners were. And that's when the thinner blew up. So you see, where the fire started, and where the thinner exploded, were two entirely different places. There was a gap between the two events. The fire brigade calculated when the fire first started and concluded there was a delay in their being informed."

"Didn't you smell anything? I mean, before the explosion?"

"No, how could I? The fire was on the floor below me."

He was getting frustrated. That was a good thing. If he got any angrier, he'd lose control and blurt out anything he happened to be concealing.

"The smell could have come in through the vents," I said, putting pressure on him.

"No, I didn't smell anything," he firmly denied.

"Still, it took the fire brigade quite some time to get here."

His grey eyes were raging.

"Is it my fault if Konya has traffic at that time of day?"

"I'm not accusing you," I said calmly. "I'm just trying to get a grasp on how events unfolded. That's why I'm splitting hairs." His face was swimming in sweat. "What did you do after informing the fire brigade?"

"I called an ambulance. Told them there were some people injured."

"You mean you got Kadir out?" I asked pointedly, knowing he hadn't.

The glare in his eyes clouded over.

"I didn't get Kadir out, the firemen did."

"So you left Kadir inside?"

"I didn't want to leave Nezihe alone." He'd looked away as though he himself didn't believe his own answer.

"Why don't you just say it, you didn't have the guts."

Mennan couldn't resist and had jumped in again despite my warning. He was going to push Serhad over the edge.

Surprisingly though, Serhad kept it together. His guilty conscience was putting him on the defensive.

"I tried to go after him, but the whole place was engulfed in flames."

"The firemen went in," said Mennan, with the audacity having a trump up his sleeve had given him. "They went in when you couldn't and brought our Kadir out safe and sound. Maybe if you'd gone in before them, Kadir would be in better shape now."

Serhad looked like a deer caught in headlights.

"But that's their job. How the hell would I know how to rescue a man from a fire?"

Mennan gave him a condescending look. "You little twerp. And you walk around like some kind of tough guy."

It was the straw that broke the camel's back. Serhad straightened up, bristling in front of Mennan. "Watch your mouth, friend," he growled. "Yeah, I am a tough guy, so what? I've been calling you 'sir' out of respect for your age, but you'd better watch your step."

Mennan didn't back off. With unexpected agility, he ruffled like a gamecock, thrusting out his broad torso towards the erratic youth.

"What are you going to do about it, pal? Come on, let's see what you've got."

They were on the verge of physically laying into each other. I had to intervene quickly.

"What the hell are you doing, you two? Get ahold of yourselves." My voice hadn't come out as strong as I'd hoped, but it had the desired effect. They stopped, not expecting a reaction like this from an English lady in the centre of Konya. Mennan suddenly started hemming and hawing, but I ignored him and turned to the other one. "Look here, Serhad. If you are willing to answer my questions fully and honestly, then do so. If you aren't, then just go. Either way I'll get the rest of the story from Ziya."

At the mention of Ziya's name, he unclenched his fists and his shoulders drooped.

"Sorry," he said, looking away again. "It's just... none of this is my fault and yet everybody keeps accusing me. Even

Ziya is riding me. How could I know a fire was burning in the storage room? As soon as I noticed it, I reported it. What else was I supposed to do? I told Kadir not to go in, but he did anyway. Would it have been better if I'd gone in and got killed too?"

His protest sounded sincere. The demoralizing sight of the lobby, and the suffocating air, had made not just him but all of us tense.

"Stay calm," I said, trying to assuage everyone's temper. "We won't get anywhere by shouting at each other. Let's try to hear each other out."

It was our meek looking Mennan who objected in the end, rather than the young man.

"How can we stay calm, Miss Greenwood?" he asked, staring into my face with bloodshot eyes. "This guy left some of my best friends to die."

Now I was sure he was trying to sabotage the investigation.

"What don't you understand, Mr. Fidan?" I bawled. "There is nothing more you can do for your friends. I am trying to conduct an investigation here. Please hold your tongue. If you can't, then be my guest and wait for us outside."

His face went completely red, but he stayed put. Ziya must have instructed him not to leave me alone, no matter what. I turned back to Serhad.

"Yes, Serhad. Go on, you were saying..."

"No," he said, shaking his head decisively, "I have nothing left to say." He gestured towards Mennan. "If I stay here any longer I'm going to get into trouble. Say what you will to Ziya."

With that he spun round, and I watched him helplessly as he made his way out. With a few steps to go, he stopped and looked back. "Are you coming?" he called to Nezihe, who stood there lost as to what to do.

After a brief glance in my direction, she shot in, "Uh-huh, I'm coming. Wait for me."

She hung her head again and ran to catch up with him.

"You've prepared to pass sweetly
out of this life."

※

Still holding up the recorder, I stood speechless among the ruins of the hotel. It felt like it had got hotter. The smell was burning my nostrils, and the flakes of ash in the air were making it ever more difficult to breath. Mennan stood there in front of me, beads of sweat he'd neglected to wipe away still on his forehead.

"Congratulations," I finally said, huffing angrily. "You've finally succeeded in bringing this investigation to a standstill."

"That wasn't what I meant to do."

"Please, don't add insult to injury by trying to explain." I couldn't bear to listen to him anymore and was afraid if I said any more I would lose control and start screaming my head off, demanding to know what he and Ziya were up to. Instead I spun round and started brusquely for the door.

"Wait, Miss Greenwood," he said catching up with me. "Look, I'm sorry if I screwed up, but you saw that son of a bitch. He's been goading me from the moment he got out of his car."

I shook my head, without even looking at him.

"You're wasting your time. This discussion is over."

"But..."

My phone rang, coming to the rescue. I snatched it out, not waiting to hear what Mennan had to say. It was Nigel. I silently thanked him and answered the phone.

"Nigel?"

I had to get away from the place immediately, so I kept walking while I spoke.

"How are you, sweetheart? How's it going?"

"Well, you know..." I replied. I glanced back at Mennan who was one step behind me. So what if he understood English, I thought, let him. "I try to piece something together, somebody else dismantles it," I complained openly.

"Ooh... someone sounds a wee bit pissed off. I wonder who's been winding up my tigress?"

"Never mind that now. What are you up to?"

"Reading poetry," he breathed cheerfully.

That was a hard thing to picture. My Nigel, flipping through a book of poetry at the clinic on Harley Street.

"You don't even like poetry."

"How do you know I don't like it?"

"Well, you've never read me a poem."

He stayed silent for a moment, trying to remember.

"Are you sure? Haven't I recited for you?"

"It's not like it's something I'd forget," I rebuked. "Just like I never forget the first flowers you sent me, the first present you gave..."

"Hmm, guess I botched that one." He paused. "But just because I haven't read you any poetry doesn't mean I don't like it."

He seemed serious, but with Nigel it was hard to tell.

"Nigel, are you toying with me?"

"Why don't you believe me, eh? I tell you, I'm reading poetry. I had nothing left to do after this morning's operation, so I've put my feet up on my desk and am reading my book."

"Which book?"

"Selected poems."

"Yes, I got that. But written by whom?"

There was a pause.

"Let me read a poem first," he said evasively. "Maybe you'll know who it is."

This was absurd. Only moments before, I'd been in the heat of reprimanding a co-worker. Now I would be listening to my lover's voice reading a poem over the phone from London; expected to identify the poet, no less. I was sure he wouldn't take it personally if I asked him to phone back, but I was worried the mood would be lost and I couldn't do that to him. He'd thought of me while reading a poem, after all.

"All right," I said. "I'm listening. But wait, hold on a second. I'm still in the middle of the hotel wreckage, but I'm on my way out. I want to watch the sky while you read."

"Well, well, well. You want to watch the sky, do you? Who's the poet now?"

"Stop teasing me. This place is horrific; even the loveliest poem in the world would have no effect here. Unless, of course, it were a gothic one."

Nigel burst out laughing.

"You're a funny one, Karen. That's why I love you. Even when things are at their worst, you can joke about it."

"That's the only reason?"

"No. Also because when you get really angry you become ferocious, and nobody anticipates that with you. And because you're such a great kisser. And..."

"All right already, I get it."

I was outside at last. As soon as I got away from the suffocating air, the sickening smell, I took a deep breath.

"I guess you're out?" asked my perceptive lover. "Can you see the sky now?"

Actually, before looking up at the sky, I watched the dark blue Mercedes receding down the boulevard. I turned round and gave Mennan a look as if to say, there you have it, that's your doing.

He hung his head. Distancing myself from him, I cooed, "Yes, I'm looking at it. It's deep blue, with the occasional white cloud. And you may not believe it, but one of those clouds looks like your silhouette."

He let out a guffaw.

"Comparing a snowy white cloud to a black man?"

He loved to refer to himself as black man, Nigel, especially when around white Londoners.

"I didn't say the colour resembled yours, I said the silhouette."

"It all points to the same thing. Apparently, you miss me. You sound better today, though."

"Better?" That was a surprise.

"Yes, better." His conviction was reassuring. "Okay, you're pissed off. But last night you sounded defeated. Like a lonely, orphaned child. Now you are like a big, strong grown-up who knows what her goal is, but is angry because she can't achieve it. Dare I say an ambitious adult?"

He knew me so well. His voice had taken on a criticising tone, as it did from time to time when he accused me of getting too wrapped up in work. "It's not worth it," he'd say. "A pity for your mind and heart." Or, "Stop wearing yourself out so much. We were put on this planet to enjoy it, not to be a slave to it." I agreed, but sometimes I couldn't help myself, as was the case now. I was caught up in a conflict already, when just the day before, I was cursing the very investigation that had brought me to Konya in the first place. Nigel was right, I had to keep things in perspective. On the other hand, I had a job to do. I supposed it was all about knowing where to draw the line.

"What's wrong? Why have you gone all quiet?" Nigel asked. "Have I upset you?"

"Of course not, why should I be upset? You're right. I shut up because I'm waiting for you to read the poem."

"All right. Pay attention then. You have to name the poet afterwards. Here goes."

You've prepared to pass away like a sweet life
Saddled your farewell horse, just to spite
Go, see new lands, roam enchanted realms
But don't forget those lands you dwelled in with me, remember, won't thou?

You've gone, my love, you are now on a journey
The round moon is your pillow, you are fast asleep
May sleep be sweet and colourful dreams be with you
But don't forget those days you slept in my lap, remember, won't thou?

The poem was so beautiful it took my breath away and I couldn't speak. There was no sound from Nigel, either.

Perhaps the poem struck us both so profoundly because it had to do with separation.

"That was beautiful," I finally managed to say. "Exquisite."

"It's probably even better in the original language."

"So then the poet didn't write in English. Careful, you're inadvertently dropping clues."

He laughed. "You, especially, should know who it is."

Now what was he hinting at?

"I don't think so. I've never heard that poem before."

"Impossible. You definitely know it."

Why would he think that?

"Wait, is the poet Turkish perhaps?"

"That's debatable," he said, donning the voice of a game show host. "It is said that his ethnic roots are Turkish. Moreover, he spent all but his childhood years in Turkey, or more accurately Anatolia. But his works of literature were all written in Persian."

"Persian? Is it Omar Khayyam?"

"I said he lived in Anatolia, madam. In the heart of Anatolia." He sounded disappointed.

I turned to look out over the perfect flatness of Konya, extending into the distance beyond. Suddenly the veil over my eyes was lifted.

"Or could it be Rumi?"

"Bravo, you nailed it! Yes, our poet's name is Mevlana Jelaleddin Rumi," he continued. "But I must admit, madam, I had expected you to recognise it from the first line. I am quite certain your father used to talk about him."

He did, several times. What's more, I remembered some of the poems, though only the most popular ones. As for the one I liked best, it was those lines my father and mother had argued over for hours.

How delightful to migrate somewhere new each day
How delightful to perch upon somewhere new each day
How delightful to flow along, neither sullied nor frozen over
My darling - they have passed away with yesterday
Whatever words there were belonging to yesterday
And it is time now for new words to be said

My mother had also loved it, though she didn't agree with the part about flowing along neither sullied nor frozen over. As she put it: "All water that flows over the face of the earth is sullied, collecting dirt, mud, and mildew that compromise its translucence. If it's a hard winter, it freezes. What's important is not that it stays clean and pure, or never freezes, but that it ultimately flows. As long as it flows, there is hope that it will run clear again, or be released from the cold in a thaw. In the same way, no living being is pure or innocent. Everything that lives becomes sullied along the way. What we need to do is make purity and innocence our life's aspiration. It all comes down to living. As long as there is life, there is hope of regaining purity."

But my father was of another opinion: "Water's essence is pure, as is the essence of man. What matters is protecting that essence from evil, cruelty and greed. And that's the hardest job in the world. Our everyday lives spin on a wheel of inhumanity. To distance us from that pure essence, life presents us with a series of relationships, one more dazzling than the next; relationships polished with lies, deceitfulness, and self-interest. Brightly coloured toys that inflate our sensual appetites, enslaving our souls and forcing our minds and bodies into the service of those things. That is what our prophet Rumi was warning us against. And those who aren't sullied, who haven't clouded over or frozen up, are the ones he praises."

The argument ended before it was resolved. I don't remember whose side I took at the time, but from that day on I never forgot the poem. Still, it was only natural that I would love Rumi. What was interesting was that Nigel had taken an interest in him.

"So tell me," I said into the phone. "Where did it come from, this sudden desire to read Rumi?"

"From you. Where else? Last night after we spoke, I looked up Konya online and stumbled onto at least as much information on Rumi himself. It got me curious, so I headed over to that huge shop in Camden Town and picked up a book of his selected poems."

"Well, you've certainly thrown me for a loop. The poem you chose to read was perfect."

"And you say I don't like poetry," he complained, feigning indignation.

"How would I know? You never said you did."

"There's a time for everything."

We both went quiet again. I looked over at Mennan, who was slumped across the hood of his car, waiting for me to get off the phone. He saw me looking and collected himself, attempting a smile. Although I was still angry, I didn't look away. I even tried to smile back. Then I went back to my conversation.

"Thanks Nigel. That really cheered me up. Keep up the wonderful surprises. And even if you don't always read me poems, call me frequently, won't thou?"

"I'll do that," he said, playing along. "But while you are dealing with your insurance policies, remember me. If only from time to time, bear thy black lover in mind, won't thou?"

"I couldn't forget you if I wanted to. I love you, Nigel," I purred.

"I love you too, Karen Kimya Greenwood."

Kimya? That was the first time he'd ever used that name.

"What made you say that?"

He was caught off guard.

"What do you mean? Have I said something wrong again?"

"Why Kimya?"

"Uh... it's your name, isn't it?"

I didn't have it in me to tell Nigel that some strange man here had also been calling me that.

"I just find it a bit odd. You've never used my middle name before. You must be under Rumi's influence."

"It's kind of impossible not to be. But I should let you go. It sounds like I caught you in the middle of an argument. I'll let you get back to it. But listen, don't let it get to you, okay? In fact, maybe it would do you good to read some Rumi yourself."

"If I have time, I'll try," I said, about to hang up. Then I remembered my mother. "Nigel, have you heard that my Uncle Matthew died?"

"Yes, his suffering's over," he said, in that callous manner peculiar to doctors. "He was getting worse by the minute, poor thing."

"That's what I told my mum of course, but it's hard for her to accept. She sounded so heart-broken last night. I'm worried about her. I'm not there and she feels all alone. Could you give her a ring, Nigel? She loves you. She'd love to hear your voice."

Of course, darling. Don't worry, I'll phone her right away. I'll even take her out for dinner tonight if she'll let me."

My mother really did love Nigel. Of all the boyfriends I'd had, she definitely liked him the best. Not just because he wasn't a typical white male, although that also factored into it. My mother had a tendency towards anything people in her day may have perceived as anomalous. Maybe I hadn't married a Turk whose culture was diametrically opposite to that of an Anglo Saxon's like she had, but my being with a man whose ancestors were liberated from slavery wasn't so bad in her book either. However, the real reason she loved Nigel was that this tall, dark man took an interest in her. Nigel really had been the only boyfriend of mine able to bear listening to her rambling on for hours. Oddly enough, he wasn't doing this out of politeness, but rather because he genuinely found her interesting. In fact, they got on so well that I believed they would stay friends even if Nigel and I were ever to break up. Of course, I didn't know what my mother would have to say if she found out about this baby thing. For the last two years her biggest dream had been to hold a grandchild in her lap. "It will be a girl, with jet black eyes and a penetrating gaze, like yours," she said. Yes, she had already even determined the baby's sex. There was no saying how she'd react if she heard I was pregnant and Nigel didn't want the child. I imagined her expression of rage as she shouted, "Never mind what that hedonistic surgeon of yours says - you are having my granddaughter!" Or perhaps she would try and find a middle ground, convincing Nigel she would look after it while he went running off to wherever it pleased him. That way, she would have her grandchild and be helping us at the same time. But right now what I needed was his help, not hers. And Nigel's words put me at ease.

"Thanks, Nigel. I doubt my mother will want to go out for dinner, but you should ask her all the same."

"Don't worry, I'll look after Susan. Go on, get back to work. But keep your temper in check, all right? We'll talk later."

"Okay, bye now."

Hanging up, I realised I'd regained the peace of mind I'd lost while in the ruins of the hotel. Even my anger at Mennan had subsided. What good was it getting angry anyhow? I needed to take another look at things, maybe make a fresh start. But in the way I'd always aspired to, without losing my composure or allowing anxiety and fear to take hold of my mind. Breathing in the hot, dry air of Konya, I headed back into the remains of the colossal hotel, which Mennan stood in front of, filled with apprehension.

"... that strange man was taking on the form of a fiery Medusa."

✳

With each step the smell became stronger. Pressure was building in my ears. It felt like the walls of the burnt building were falling in on us, and the ceiling coming silently down. Perhaps that was why we quickened our pace, passing over the carpet, which the fire had reduced to scraps. We came to a narrow staircase. There was a red light all around, which I supposed was sunlight passing through the blackened windows. Mennan, keeping one step ahead of me, was bathed in the red light. His wavy hair, the chunky nape of his neck spilling over the top of his collar, his bulky hands, one of which held his moist handkerchief, his trousers which seemed one size too big, the patent leather shoes... everything that made Mennan who he was, was painted red.

"This way," he said, turning slightly. The broad forehead, the flattened nose, the cleft chin, the teeth shining in his half-open mouth - his whole face glowed. The sun's rays made the room appear to be in flames again. Mennan's chubby red finger pointed at the descending staircase.

"We'll go down here," he reiterated.

We made our way down the narrow staircase with its red walls, burnt railings, and steps covered in carpet scraps. Traces of the fire were everywhere; in the murky glass of the windows, the mirrors that had lost their glazing, the signs with their melted paint, the plastic flowers warped into odd shapes by the heat... The heat intensified with each step and my eyes were beginning to sting. It felt as if the fire were still burning somewhere on the lower floors. Mennan plowed ahead as though it had no affect on him, though he occasionally turned to look back at me, as I was having difficulty keeping up. Every time he turned round, the gleam in his red eyes looked more sinister.

The stairs brought us to a long corridor. The moment I stepped onto the mauve carpet the red light disappeared. I looked around, dumbfounded. It was like the flames hadn't even put in an appearance here. There was no soot on the olive green walls, nor any burn marks on the carpet, as if I were back in the hotel in its pre-fire state. My eyes searched in vain for the end of the corridor. It seemed to stretch into infinity. I wondered if it were some kind of underground passage running the length of the hotel grounds, but how had it remained unscathed by the fire? As I considered this riddle, I noticed the black, shadowy spots at regular intervals on either side of the corridor. On closer inspection, I saw they were photographs. The second one to the left caught my eye. It looked like Big Ben. That was interesting. What was a photo of our historical clock tower doing in a hotel in Konya? But it wasn't just that one, the one next to it was also taken in London. Wasn't that Trafalgar Square? Yes, and what's more the photograph was a recent one. In the background was a sign for an exhibition that had opened only a month earlier. So it was at the photographer's whim that the photos were black and white. I went on to the next photo. But this was Muswell Hill, my neighbourhood! I stopped in front of the picture. Of course, this apartment on the left was my building, and the man in front of it was none other than my elderly next-door neighbour, Scott. As my mind tried to process it all, my feet carried me to the next photo. My god! It was my flat! Except for the kitchen, the curtains on the windows overlooking the street were all drawn. The photo was so clear. I could see the interior of the kitchen, it looked just as it did now. And there I was, standing at the counter. Cooking, by the looks of it. There was someone behind me, Nigel, I assumed. I took a closer look but couldn't make it out, the face was in shadows. Maybe in the next photo... I was right, the next one was a close-up of the kitchen. I wasn't cooking, but rather stacking the dirty dishes on the counter. We must have just eaten. Beyond me, Nigel stood sipping his drink. I took a closer look. The man behind me wasn't Nigel. It was that man who had given me the ring. I recognised his long, black beard and kohl-lined black eyes.

"Why are you so surprised?" came a voice from behind me.

I thought it was Mennan, but I turned round to see this other man towering over me once again, his eyes peering into mine. His clothes no longer looked black; they were bathed in the red glow, which must have followed us in. His hair, his beard, his long cloak, even his almond eyes were crimson.

"You were searching for the fire, and here you have found it."

He reached out, flames rising from his fingertips. I stepped back, startled. "Do not be afraid," he said again. "You were seeking the truth, and I have brought it to you." He touched his face with his hand, which had now become a torch. His beard caught fire, then his hair. Each lick of the flames then slowly twisted into a snake, as the strange man took on the form of a fiery Medusa. I was terrified. I wanted to run, to break away from this cursed passageway, but I was powerless to even flinch, let alone take a step. I was bewitched by the fiery eyes staring into mine. I stood there helpless, my limbs paralysed as if bound by invisible ropes, as the burning Medusa slowly moved closer. The photos in their wooden frames, the mauve carpets and the olive green walls – everything around me was engulfed by the fire now. The corridor was becoming a living hell. The sweat on my face evaporated, my skin grew taut, and from the whites of my eyes flew ribbons of steam. The pressure in my ears built up until it was unbearable. The corridor, which I thought had been unaffected by the fire, was now completely aglow with that otherworldly red light. And as the fiery Medusa reached towards my face with its blazing fingers, I heard the voice:

"*Allahu ekber, Allahu ekber...*"

I opened my eyes. I was drenched in perspiration. The fire and the red light were gone now, but the voice continued to reverberate throughout my room.

"*Eshedu enla ilahe illallah...*"

I couldn't immediately understand whether I was still in the nightmare or not. I held my breath and listened. No, this was real. The voice was coming from Sultan Selim Mosque, opposite the hotel. They were the same Arabic words I'd heard while Mennan was changing the flat tyre. It was the mosque calling the faithful to evening prayers. So, it must be the same time of day as I'd first seen the man with the beard. After darkness fell, that's right, I had never seen him by day. Was there a reason that he only ever appeared to me at night? Though I should have long ago forgotten them, my father's words came back to me. "There are two kingdoms: the first is the realm of the material, the second that of the spiritual. The material kingdom is similar to the daytime. You see everything that takes place clearly, and it is easy to grasp. As for the spiritual kingdom, it resembles the night. In order to find it, you must switch on the lights of your soul."

The debris from the fire, Medusa, my suspicions of Mennan, even Nigel's call from London, must have all got mixed up in my brain and drawn me into this last nightmare. Maybe it would've been best to confront Mennan. But no, that would only have turned the tide against me more. I had to stay quiet, be patient and strong. I'd done the right thing today, not going back into the hotel after Nigel's call. I was exhausted and needed time alone to think. I mulled over what the man had said. "You were seeking the truth, and I have brought it to you." Was he trying to tell me he had started the fire himself? But that made no sense. My subconscious, left unchecked by sleep, was playing games with me. But the first time I'd seen him, it hadn't been a dream. And he'd used the words 'Do not be afraid' in both the real life encounter and the dream. I had to admit that despite the horrific aura of this recent nightmare, neither the man's voice, nor his eyes, had contained any threat. The experience was terrifying, but it wasn't like I was afraid of him.

The sign over the door of the mosque where I'd first seen him had read: *Mosque and Mausoleum of Shams-i Tabriz.* Maybe it was just some delusional old man who thought he was

Shams-i Tabriz incarnate? Who exactly was Shams-i Tabriz? Rumi's mentor, isn't that what Ziya had said? If it hadn't been for Shams-i Tabriz, Rumi would have remained an ordinary religious scholar. But Shams had been more than just Rumi's mentor. He'd also been Kimya's husband. Kimya - Rumi's adopted daughter. Still, what did any of this have to do with me? Not a thing. And yet this Shams character kept following me around calling me Kimya. Was it all just to scare me? But then what about the voice on the plane? I hadn't even landed in Konya yet at that point. So then the nightmares must have been due to years of suppressed emotion over my father, all at once awoken and assailing my psyche. That had to be it; it was all that made sense. Coming to that conclusion should have put my mind at rest, but I still had so many unanswered questions.

I got up and turned on my computer, thinking to do a bit of my own research on this Shams-i Tabriz. Within minutes, I'd pulled up dozens of sites.

His real name had been Shemseddin Muhammed. He'd been born in Tabriz, in modern day Iran, hundreds of kilometres from Konya. There was nothing certain about his date of birth, though most of the sites had put it around the year 1185. He'd shown signs of mystic leanings, even as a child. In one of the sites, I read how he'd explained his childhood in his own words:

> I had not yet reached puberty. I had dived into a sea of love and would eat nothing for forty days and forty nights, cutting myself off from every manner of desire. I endured hunger and thirst for days and nights on end. My poor father grew concerned upon seeing me like this.
>
> "My son, you are not crazy, though your disposition is so peculiar, I understand nothing of this behavior of yours. Where will it lead?" he chided me.
>
> I responded thus:
>
> "Father, our relationship is epitomised by this story: Beneath one of the hens was placed the egg of a goose, alongside the other eggs. Time passed and all the chicks hatched, and when they had grown a bit they fell into line

behind their mothers and followed them to the lake's edge. While the other chicks scratched about, the chick which was hatched from the goose egg threw itself immediately into the waters. Seeing this happen, the mother hen fluttered about clucking, 'Alas, my chick is going to drown!' Whereas the baby goose swam about in ecstasy. Behold, that is how you and I are. O dear father, I am searching for a sea in which I may swim. That sea is the place I call home, and my disposition is that of a sea bird who cannot suffer the absence of sea. If you are the same as I am, come, let us swim together. But if you are not, go back among the barnyard fowl."

I couldn't believe how sure of himself this man had been, how condescending towards his father. I tried to visualise the bearded man who'd given me the ring. He'd had the same ego, although he seemed to be trying to be more gentle. There was an impassive look in his eye as though he already had all the world's secrets figured out, and nothing, and no one, had the power to surprise him anymore. Actually, I was no stranger to this indifferent, aloof attitude. My father's friend and soul mate, the Pakistani Shah Nesim for whom my father had left us, was just like that. He was never rude to anyone. On the contrary, he always took an interest. Whenever I ran into him, he would smile without fail. If he were next to me, he would caress my hair and ask me about school. But there was something... whether it was his tone of voice, the glossiness in his eyes, or his reserved manner, whatever he did he would let me feel the distance between us. Even if he weren't trying to, he made us all feel like he looked down us, and everything we did. As though he weren't one of us, but rather from a different world. My father wasn't like that. When he smiled at someone, it was genuine. When he hugged you, it was with all his heart. His was a love without restraints. But when it came to Shah Nesim, the world stood still. My father's full attention was focused on him and nothing else, and he wouldn't care a fig about my mother or me. I never could understand their relationship. I guess Shah Nesim was also like, or trying to be like, Shams-i Tabriz.

I looked back at the computer screen. It wrote that Shams had known Arabic and Persian. That he was versed in the literature of both those languages, as well as having an education in alchemy, astronomy, logic, philosophy, and of course, religion. Shams's first guru, a sheikh who went by the name of Ebubekir the Basketweaver, had so thoroughly opened Shams's mind, heart, and eyes to esoteric knowledge, that as he learned he felt compelled to learn more, and he yearned for the things he already knew to be replaced by even newer things. Because he reached spiritual maturity in such a short time, the people referred to him as *Kamil-i Tabrizi*, the Sage of Tabriz, and they all looked up to him. But as Shams learned more and more, Ebubekir's knowledge, and the sheik himself, were no longer enough for him. Shams explained it this way:

> Sheikh Ebubekir Seddebaf's intoxication was from God. But never did he have the sobriety that follows in the wake of that sacred intoxication.

Shams wanted to spend every moment swimming in the mystic sea of love, including not only his 'intoxicated' moments but also his 'sober' ones. I suppose it was a case of insatiability, or an inability to adapt.

"Chronically maladapted" was what my mother used to call my father. "Not just with us, wherever he goes his experiences will never be enough for him. He will never be satisfied. What's worse, he isn't even aware of it." And just like my father left us, Shams had also separated from his sheikh and chosen his own path. Throughout his life, he'd been a wandering dervish, and because of this was also called *Shamseddin-i Perende,* or 'Flying Shams'.

In one article by an Iranian historian, it was written that Shams was on a lifetime quest that continued up till the day he came across Mevlana Jelaleddin Rumi. Rumi, whom he discovered in Konya, had been the climax and finale of the wandering dervish's life. I remembered the name from my dream last night, Muhammed Jelaleddin. The bearded man, his hands opened upward under the full moon as he made his invocation, was answered by that voice, "The life you ask about, hidden from the eyes of all, a life with favour and grace upon it, is Muhammed Jelaleddin Rumi, son of Belhli Sultanü'l-Ulema Baha Veled."

I was confused again. Hadn't Ziya said of Shams that he was the one responsible for making Rumi who he was? Yet it was always Rumi who was the focal point of the articles I found on Shams. Everyone showered Rumi with praise, while Shams always seemed to linger in the background like his sidekick. Maybe it was time to make a visit to Ziya's father. He was meant to be an expert on the subject, I could go to him for my answers. But was this really about Shams? Or was it my father that was the real issue? Maybe the real question I should be asking was whether I was here in this city to investigate a hotel fire, or to find out what had happened to this father of mine who had not sent word, not written so much as a single line in so many years? Perhaps these dreams about the man I suspected was Shams had nothing to do with Ziya and Mennan. And what about the ring? I was at a loss.

I looked back at the computer screen, returning to an article entitled "The Encounter Between Shams and Rumi." Just then the phone in the room started ringing. Damn, I thought, it must be Mennan. When I left him I told him I wasn't feeling well because I'd wanted to get out of dinner. I guess he wasn't convinced. He'd really irked me today, and he knew it. I supposed he wanted to offer me some kind of apology, but I was in no mood to deal with him. On the other hand, if I didn't answer he might get worried and come to the hotel. I had no choice but to reach for the receiver.

"Hello..."

"Hi, Miss Greenwood."

It wasn't Mennan's voice. I knew it, but before I could place it, it divulged, "Ziya. Ikonion Tourism..."

"Mr. Kuyumcuzade. How are you?"

"Very well, thanks. How about yourself?"

"Fine. What can I do for you?"

"Actually, I'm calling on Serhad's behalf. I heard he was a bit rude today, that he walked out in the middle of the interview. I just heard about it and I'm quite angry."

"Never mind. I just couldn't figure out why he was behaving like that."

He gave a knowing laugh.

"It's nothing to do with you. The problem is between him and Mennan."

"Is that so? Anything to do with work?"

"Oh no, not work. Love would be more accurate."

"Love?"

"Last year, Serhad proposed to Mennan's daughter, Hulya. The girl was totally smitten with Serhad, but Mennan wouldn't give her away. He told him he was sending his daughter away to university, and from there on out, they hate each other. So you see, what happened today had nothing to do with you or the fire."

Like always, his explanation sounded doubtful, but I laughed despite.

"Now I understand. I was starting to think Serhad was a bit of a nutter."

"I know he acts like a hooligan," he said, after a brief pause. "He is definitely impulsive. But he's not actually a bad guy. He's very competent, very loyal. That's why I keep him around."

"Please," I said jokingly. "You don't have to defend him. Our company doesn't concern itself with the staff politics of our clients."

He let out a raucous laugh.

"Thanks a lot. You're very understanding."

"Not at all. Just trying to stay within our jurisdiction. I was about to call you actually, to ask when I can meet your father. You said you'd introduce us, remember?"

"Certainly, whenever you want. Tomorrow morning, for instance..."

I'd planned to visit the witness Kadir Gemelek that day, the one who claimed the fire was started by aliens.

"Can we make it afternoon?"

"Sure thing. Three o'clock in my office, then?"

"Perfect. See you then. Have a nice evening."

"Thanks. You too."

Hanging up, I wondered if I'd been mistaken in thinking the scrap between Serhad and Mennan was designed to sabotage the interview. It looked like the conflict had been over Mennan's daughter. Could it be that simple? If not, I'd have to accept that Ziya was working overtime on his plan to foil my report. Maybe it was all in my head. Just an occupational hazard, stress-induced paranoia, this linking everyone and everything to the investigation I was conducting. I was sure that was what our company psychologist Oliver would have said.

Once, while investigating a diamond theft in Manchester a few of years back, I'd blown the whole thing out of proportion, claiming a client had murdered his wife. I believed so strongly in what I was saying that when the woman returned home from her holiday in Majorca a week later, I was gobsmacked. In the end, even that hadn't convinced me. If they'd let me, I'd have gone so far as to contend she wasn't his real wife. Thankfully, Simon wrapped up the case and sent me to talk to Oliver, who had recommended I take a holiday of my own. He did offer me a mild antidepressant as well, but although I got the pills, I never took them. Instead, Nigel and I went on a tour to Tunisia, which straightened me out. I still carried the pills on me, but I didn't think it necessary to take them now either. I had shaken off the pessimism, as Nigel put it, and though I was still a little on edge from the nightmare, I definitely felt better.

Maybe the nightmare was somehow related to my childhood. My mother claimed I'd walked in my sleep until I was nine. Once they had even found me on the edge of the pool in the garden. Another time, in front of a bookrest my father had brought back from Konya. I'd been staring down at the pages of the Qur'an, my lips moving as if I were reading it. Apparently, that signified that I didn't possess nerves of steel. Go figure. Behind this tough exterior of mine lurked some serious vulnerability. I supposed that was it. The affect of the stress I experienced while awake was resurfacing as a nightmare when I closed my eyes. I had to try and relax, to care as little as possible, as Oliver had instructed. At the end of the day, this was just a job. Even if I failed, it wouldn't be the end of the world, I'd already had countless successes for the company. With that resolved, I suddenly realised I was hungry. I felt like calling room service and ordering some food, then immediately changed my mind. I may be experiencing temporary paranoia, but I should still hold on tight to my job. I would eat out tonight.

"Because secrets are concealed in the depths of a sea of patience."

✵

The oven baked kebab was quite tasty, like the okra soup it was a speciality of Konya. I hadn't heard of it before, my father had never been one for heavy, fatty meat dishes and the oven kebab was by no means light. Even worse, it was served with nothing but a raw onion. Luckily, the young waiter, tired of this Turkish-speaking English woman's constant demands, had the courtesy to have an extra plate of sliced tomatoes and cucumbers prepared. I polished off the salad, but left half the kebab on my plate. The Turkish coffee that followed the meal, however, left nothing to be desired. It was steamy and foamy, the consistency perfect, and it was served in a delicate cup with double baked Turkish Delight on the side. Before taking a sip, I breathed in its delicious aroma and thought of my mother, who loved Turkish coffee. My father had never cared about it one way or the other, despite its being his country's traditional drink. His passion was for well-steeped tea, without so much as a drop of milk, of course. But the Turkish coffee wasn't the only thing to get my mother's attention in this city she'd come to thirty-six years before. She loved the adobe houses, the stone and wood madrasahs built by the Seljuks, the ney and the whirling of the dervishes... and most importantly, the reason behind her fondness for all these things - my father - the dervish Poyraz Efendi, as Ziya called him. But in time my mother got bored with the sound of the ney and the whirling of the dervishes, going so far as to say she no longer loved my father either, though that was a lie. She could no more do without him than without her Turkish coffee, her little cups from Istanbul with their turquoise Seljuk motif, the ornamented trays she'd serve it on, the traditional copper stove-top coffee pot... She would cook the coffee slowly over a low flame until the foam, the consistency, and the smell were just right. It had to be perfect or she'd dump it out and brew another. Seeing her drinking her coffee, one leg pulled under her on the purple armchair a beloved aunt had left her, she looked more like an Anatolian woman than an English one. My mother always said that to love someone meant loving them along with their culture, but she herself was proof that that was untrue. However crazy she may still have been about the coffee, she had come to despise the ney and the dervishes' *sema*, when in fact they were the very things that had originally caused her to fall head over heels for my father in the first place. It had been thirty-six years since she'd stopped off at Konya on a friend's advice, on her way back from India and Nepal. She'd been looking for answers, trying to find out if it were possible to start a new life within an ancient belief system, after running away from the washed-up, repetitive culture of a Europe which had exhausted her interest. After the old Buddhist and Hindu temples of Katmandu, she'd carried on to this sunny city in the heart of Anatolia, where the dervish dance rituals at the Mevlevi convent had had such a profound effect on her. It didn't end there however, as my mother's heart had been captivated by the slim, young dervish spinning in the *sema*.

"It wasn't dancing," she'd say. "More like he'd abandoned himself to the delicate voice of the ney and was floating on it. What really affected me though was not so much your father's transcendental dance, but the anguish I saw in his eyes when his eyelids momentarily parted."

Nevertheless, years had passed, and my mother could no longer stand the sound of the ney. Whenever my father would reach for that musical instrument that never left his side, she was out of the house in a heartbeat.

"I also appreciate the soulfulness of the ney, but it's not the only instrument under the sun. Your father played that instrument for all of twelve years, and it was all he ever listened to. But there's more to life than that."

I wondered what my father had had to say about his wife's sudden change of heart towards this instrument she'd once ached to hear. Most probably he'd said nothing, though he never gave up playing it either. He couldn't, because for my father the ney wasn't just an instrument, it was an integral part of his beliefs.

"Our Father created the prophet Adam from soil," he explained, comparing the ney to what he believed was the very first man. "Adam, at first lifeless like a statue, was awakened when our Father blew the breath of life in through his nose. He wasn't just made mortal though; with that breath a godlike soul passed into him. Just like the ney. When a master of the ney breathes into it, this ordinary reed instrument produces a holy sound of magnificent beauty. Like a human who has discovered the soul of God within themselves."

But my mother no more wanted to hear the ney than to share our house with Shah Nesim, the man assumed to have reached that state of discovering God's soul within himself. Despite her love for my father - and in those days she even questioned that - she no longer felt her old connection with his culture. There was only one thing left that she loved from the Konya she had been to thirty years before, and that was Turkish coffee. When my mother occasionally tired of drinking it, I read into it that she'd given up on her love for my father. But she never really did give up, even now, and it looks like she never would. As for me, even though not as addicted to Turkish coffee as she was, I did enjoy drinking it from time to time. Especially after a heavy meal like this oven kebab.

As I took another sip, I noticed an argument taking place in front of the restaurant. The young waiter was standing outside with a dish of food in his hand, shouting, "What's wrong with you? So I put a little meat in your soup. It was just so you'd get your fill, to bring a little colour to your face."

"Did you hear anyone ask you to put meat in my soup?" the man replied.

He was standing at the door, his back to me, in a long black garment like an overcoat on top of traditional, baggy Turkish şalvar. What I first thought were slippers on his feet turned out to be pointy, rawhide çarık. He must have been homeless, perhaps a beggar, though he certainly didn't talk like one.

"Who do you think you are?" he continued, scolding the waiter.

The argument was making the sullen-faced owner at the cashier's desk uneasy; he pushed his bottle-lens glasses back into his eyebrows and stood up. His stout body shuffled on small feet towards the door.

"What have we here?" It wasn't clear whether his raised voice was directed towards the waiter or the old man. "What seems to be the problem?"

The waiter turned towards his boss with a flushed face.

"It's nothing, Rahmi Usta," he attempted to explain. He looked upset that his boss had come all the way to the door. Gesturing towards the man he was quarreling with, he explained, "This old guy comes here every evening with this bowl in his hand and gets soup from us. The cheapest soup, without any meat. This evening I felt sorry for him and put a little meat in it, and now he's raising hell."

The boss turned to the customer, irritated.

"What more do you want, Gramps?" he said. "The kid was doing you a favour. Why are you kicking up a stink in front of my shop?"

"I am not your grandfather," growled the man. "And I don't need any favours. I pay for my soup, and if I'd wanted meat in it, I would have asked. Your job is just to serve the customer. If I say no meat in my soup, then that's how it will be."

I was expecting the boss to give him a piece of his mind, but instead he looked into the man's face and took a step back, as though his irritation had been snuffed out by what he saw there. He turned to the waiter, taking care not to look at the man again.

"Okay, let's not drag this out. Give him what he wants and let him be on his way."

But the man droned on angrily.

"I don't want it. Dump it out. Just give me back the bowl is all."

The waiter shook his head as though trying to summon his patience. His boss wouldn't let him speak.

"Just do it. I don't want any scuffles in front of my shop."

The waiter gave an exasperated huff, and then took the bowl back inside.

"My god, does every nutjob have to come find us?"

He passed between the unimposing wooden tables and headed towards the kitchen. I kept my eye on the man at the door, though still unable to see his face. His back was still to me as he waited silently for his bowl to be emptied, and he stayed that way till the boy returned with the empty dish. When the waiter did finally come back, mumbling to himself irritably and extending the bowl, the old man said, "Look boy, don't think you are the only one who has it all figured out. You must respect the requests of others, no matter how strange they may seem. Other people know a thing or two, whether you understand it or not. Don't just go assuming that someone has fallen on hard times."

He looked calm. His voice had softened like that of an adult offering a bit of wisdom. His words, however, were enough to send the already bristling waiter over the edge.

"Would you look at that. Now you're giving advice? I try to do you a favour and you have a go. Then have the gall to stand in front of me and preach?" He thrust out the dish. "Take it already and get out of here. And don't even think about coming back." Amazingly, the man didn't get angry again. He just shook his head sadly.

"You don't know what you're saying. I've been having my soup in this shop for a hundred years."

I hadn't misunderstood, he'd definitely said a hundred years. The poor man must have a screw loose. Though he certainly seemed cool and collected for a crazy man.

"Without me, this place will no longer be blessed with wealth or abundance." He turned slightly as he took his bowl, though not enough for me to see his face. The waiter was about to answer back when the old man raised his voice shutting him up. "Don't dare to open your mouth. Don't you dare scowl at me. Your insolence will bring down my wrath, and then there will be no place for your profanity, nor for your goodwill. You will cease to be here, as will this shop."

Just as his boss had done, the waiter took a step back, a look of fear on his face. The light in his youthful eyes dulled and a subtle shadow spread through his complexion. He took another couple steps back and, after looking one last time at the man, turned round without uttering another word and came back into the restaurant. This deranged homeless man had managed to frighten two grown men, one of those the restaurant's owner no less. I was dying to know who it was. Just then, he turned his head and I caught those eyes, naturally-lined as though with kohl. The ones I'd been dreaming about only an hour before. He looked straight at me. There was no trace of anger left in them, again his look was of supplication. I felt a jolt as I thought he was going to come over to me. Instead he looked away as though he hadn't recognised me, then started away from the restaurant.

It didn't take me long to act. Up till now it had been him following me, now it was my turn. I left my coffee still steaming away on the table and proceeded to the cashier's. Ignoring the bewildered expressions on the faces of the waiter and owner, I hurriedly paid the bill and rushed out. The man had gone to the right, so I also went that direction. I started off at a brusque pace, trying to catch a glimpse of him through the crowds on the pavement, but I couldn't make out his grizzled hair through the bustling throngs of people. I wondered if he had crossed over the street to the park called Alaeddin Hill on the other side, but the mysterious man wasn't among that crowd either. The pavement connected to a street bearing to the right. I entered the street and there he was, aggravated and pushing through the people. I moved even faster, nearly breaking into a run so as not to lose sight of him, and then saw him stop. As he stood still, I also stopped. He turned round and, despite the distance between us, his eyes locked with mine. I felt myself pulled towards him, as a flash, like a silent explosion, simultaneously burned my eyes. Without warning, everything went dark. The street lamps, the shop lights, the headlights on the cars - whatever light there had been was absorbed by the flash, and the street was left shrouded in impenetrable darkness. But it wasn't just the light that had disappeared, the noise was gone too. The two kids horsing around in front of me, the clatter of a metal shutter being pulled down by a stationer closing his shop, the chubby-cheeked sweetshop assistant who'd been touting for customers next door to him, the din of traffic, the city buzz... none of it was there anymore. There was a profound silence all around. I stood rooted to the spot, unable to figure out where to go, who to call out to. Then I noticed the light. It was tiny, a mere glimmer under the darkness of night like a diamond trapped in coal, a star stubbornly shining in a sky whose sun had vanished. I moved towards it, feeling drawn to it the way the first human was to the first light. With every step the light crystallised and pulled me closer, and with every step my wonder grew. Then suddenly it was there before my eyes. Motionless, silent, perpetually shining as though waiting for me. I reached out, hoping to recognise by touch what my eyes couldn't decipher. But first I felt a hand. Bony, with warm, wrinkled skin. I flinched and pulled mine back. And then there was the voice.

"Do not be afraid," it said again. "What is yours, I have delivered to you."

Gathering my courage, I reached out again. My fingers connected with a hard object, a stone, warm as though it were alive. If I didn't see it, I still felt it. It was that ring - the silver one with the brown stone. The one that bled like a wounded person. Oddly, touching the ring made me feel better, less vulnerable. I took it and put it on the ring finger of my right hand. The darkness began to clear.

"Do not give that which is yours to any other. For others, it is an ill-gotten gain."

I looked up. The mysterious man was standing in the clearing darkness. For the first time, I looked him directly in the eye without recoiling or losing my nerve.

"Do not become separated from this thing which is yours, Kimya," he continued. "It is for you, and you alone."

"I'm not Kimya," I stated bluntly.

His black eyes clouded over, full of sorrow.

"I know." He had lowered his voice and his skin had gone pale as though recalling an unpleasant memory. "You couldn't be even if you wanted to."

I should have felt relieved, but instead I felt insulted.

"At any rate," I said, skipping over the subject and indicating the ring on my finger, "why are you giving this to me?"

He stared at it intensely as he whispered, "That ring will teach you the truth."

"The truth? You mean about who started the fire?"

His eyes betrayed his deep disappointment. His bottom lip sagged, as if to ask why that was all I could come up with.

"Whoever started that fire is of no consequence, and has nothing to do with the truth I speak of."

"What's it to do with then?"

He put his hand to his mouth, as he stated with repugnance, "That... that is all about material gain. It is not truth you seek in that fire of rampaging demons, it's money. But the truth is far more valuable than money."

I was completely stumped now. "So in that case, what is the truth?" I asked openly.

He paused, studying me with the expertise of a teacher trying to help a pupil.

"Are you ready to learn it?"

"Yes, I'm ready."

An enigmatic smile broke out on his lips.

"Nobody is ever fully ready. We can only ever know if we were ready for the truth after having been faced with it."

He had an answer for everything. I was getting weary of it.

"I can't speak for anyone else, but I myself am ready," I said stubbornly. "Go on, I'm listening."

Before he spoke, he gave me a reprimanding look.

"You are impatient." He sighed, then began to explain slowly, as though I were having difficulty understanding him. "In fact, all God's creatures are tied to one another by a thread of patience. The world revolves around patience. Because the sun, and also the moon, require time. Be patient. Secrets lie hidden in the depths of a sea of patience. To unravel grand mysteries, you must learn to swim in it."

"All right. I'll be patient," I conceded. "At least I'll try."

His face lit up and he stroked his beard.

"Good for you. And be adaptable," he said. "The ability to adapt is a beautiful thing. Adaptability is the most important of water's attributes. Water is the very symbol of patience. A home to the oyster. If there were no water, there would be no pearls. Be patient, so that pearls will be formed."

His manner of speaking was peculiar, like old, poetic Turkish. Yet everything about him was so extraordinary, the last thing I could get hung up on was his style of speech.

"Don't worry. I'll be adaptable, too. Yes, go on, I'm listening."

"Are you?" he asked, trying to read me. "And do you suppose you will learn the truth from my words?"

"How else could I possibly learn it?" I asked, in all sincerity.

He looked dubious.

"Words are not truth, they are sounds that come forth from our mouths. Even the world's most eloquent master of words, throughout all time, does not have the ability to explain to us in the necessary way even the simplest instant in life. He cannot show us colours, allow us to perceive smell, help us to hear sound, make us taste - and let's say by some miracle he does - he is nonetheless unable to convey all that goes on in the human soul. He may employ reasoning. He may mount his ideas on logic, taking them for a ride on the endless horizons of his consciousness... but he can never explain in the necessary way, the ever changing state of the human soul."

Noticing my helplessness, he continued. "Do not allow pessimism to take hold of you. What words cannot explain, life will. To learn the truth, one needs not words, but experiences."

I was now at a complete loss. I was wary of asking any questions, because I wanted to avoid that criticising, didactic look he always got in his eyes. But I knew I'd never understand unless I asked.

"Are you saying I have to live through all this firsthand?"

"That's right," he stated, as though handing down a sentence. "You yourself must experience it."

Seeing the quizzical look still in my eyes, he didn't persist. Instead, he smiled, for the first time broadly and at ease like a child, with no burdening significance or insinuation. From between the lips of that enigmatic, fearsome man, the tiny teeth of a child were exposed. Without another word, I returned the smile, as he put out his hand.

"Then considering you are ready, considering it is time... Come! Come, and experience this."

I took hold of the outstretched hand, and all around me there was suddenly light.

"See the image of my dancing friend in the blacks of my eyes ."

※

It wasn't that the lights had come back on, dawn had broken in the city. There was a sweet, honey-coloured light everywhere, just like on that day years ago when I'd first come here with my father. It was as if the sun were more merciful, more compassionate. Not only the sun, but the wind as well; the smell of the rain from the foothills of distant mountains had wafted in on a delicate breeze. From the gardens behind the clay walls, bolstered with wooden struts, came the sound of birds. That's right; all the walls were clay, or stone, and the roads were dirt. There was no asphalt anywhere, and no cement. The street was calm, and there was not a single vehicle in sight. Two horses tied in front of an inn, one brown the other white, continuously swished their tails to shoo away the flies that landed on their rumps. An old shepherd's dog, hairless from age, slept next to them in front of a wooden door, beyond which stood a grey donkey looking crushed under the weight of its fully loaded saddlebags. There were no women. Just men milling about, most in collarless shirts and dark, baggy şalvar, their age or youth indeterminable due to the turbans on their heads.

How did I get here? Panic-stricken, I tried to take in my surroundings and figure out where I was. I looked over at the thick-walled palace, majestically perched on the hill to the right. Eight soldiers, armed with broad swords on the belts of their armour and tall lances in hand, stood guard in front of an ornamented stone door. Was this the imposing Seljuk palace on Alaeddin Hill I'd passed by not minutes before? An answer was provided by the image of the strange, black-clad dervish, reflected in a large, tin tray that leaned against the coppersmith's shop I stood in front of.

"One who says they are ready to learn the truth does not have the right to look so stunned."

He was right. They were my own words being thrown back at me. I resolved to keep my shock and fear in check. However, if I were back in Seljuk times, what would these people from seven centuries ago make of a woman like me? The leather jacket, my jeans...

"Do not be afraid," said the bearded man in the tin-plated copper tray. "Forget about Kimya, or Karen. She is not here. There is only Shams-i Tabriz, who has traversed a path of thousands of parasangs to meet with God's secret beloved."

The peculiar thing was that as he spoke, it was my lips that moved. As though it were I, not he, who was speaking. I looked down at myself, filled with apprehension. I was now dressed in black *keçe*, the traditional goat hair felt, and on my feet were rawhide *çarık*. I held up a hand - it was dark and broad. My body had already become that of Shams, it was my soul he wanted now.

"Forget!" he commanded in a soft voice, like a breeze playing about in my hair. "Forget what you have brought with you from that other, older world. A life unknown to you awaits, a world some seven hundred years younger. What you are to experience in this city of holy men has no equal. You will know the unknown, see the unseen. Let this city, now seven hundred years less spoiled, fill you with a new soul and teach you what took place here. Karen or Shams, what does it matter? Aren't we all from the same mould? Didn't we all enter life with the same breath? Forget about that woman from London now. Like sweet laughter, open the doors of your soul to this poor dervish of Tabriz."

And what he commanded came to be. When I looked back at my image in the copper tray, I no longer regarded the bearded man, with his kohl-lined eyes and black goat's wool garments, as a stranger. Because I was him. Because I was no longer Karen Kimya Greenwood, but Muhammed Shemseddin, the son of Ali, who was the son of Melek Dad. Because I was Shams-i Tabriz, who was also known as Kamil-i Tabriz, the Spiritually Enlightened, and Shams-i Perende, the Flyer. I was a wandering dervish who had devoted a lifetime to finding that great hidden truth. And as I found it I lost it again, and as I lost it, I chased after it with even more ardour than before. I was a wandering dervish who, to find God's hidden truth, had walked day and night following a lead I'd been given as a gift. Through suffocating desert heat, against harsh mountain winds, I'd descended onto the golden plains of Konya to behold the one who was promised me and alleviate my years of longing.

The one who had betrothed him to me had said this:

"The beloved you ask about, hidden from the eyes of all, a life with favour and grace upon him, is Muhammed Jelaleddin Rumi, son of Belhli Sultanü'l-Ulema Baha Veled."

And I had said unto he who had betrothed him to me:

"O he who created heaven and earth, O he who is omnipotent and almighty. Show me that blessed face of your beloved!"

The one who had betrothed him to me had asked:

"How will you repay your debt of gratitude?"

Without faltering, I had stretched out my neck and said:

"With my head!"

The one who had betrothed him to me had said:

"This is spiritualism. This is love. Love has but one price, and that is one's life. Love that is not consecrated by death is not really love. And because of this Muhammed Jelaleddin Rumi, son of Baha Veled, is for you lawful and legitimate. Go now and find him. Go, find him, but do not forget the promise you have made."

When he who had betrothed him to me said this, I came to with a start, and immediately stood up from the worn prayer rug in my humble room. In accordance with the saying 'There is wisdom behind God's every word', I left to travel far and wide. But there were always obstacles. Mountains, seas, cities, madrasahs, dervish lodges, people... Our separation dragged on and on. And to remind the one who had betrothed him to me, I made mention of it, and once again he brought us face to face.

In the city of Damascus, while wandering around in a trance among others who were also in a trance, a hand touched mine. I looked and saw a form in drab attire, but radiating light. I looked and saw Muhammed Jelaleddin Rumi, the son of Baha Veled. He took my hands between his palms and whispered "O great appraiser of this world, fathom me." I stood fixed in front of him as though I'd become a massive boulder. Once again he opened his blessed mouth. "O great appraiser of the spirit world, find me," he whispered. His warm, sweet-smelling breath wiped the filth from my face, removed the slumber from my eyes, and rejuvenated my skin like fresh rose petals after spring rain. His face, and his words, transformed me into a child; my soul was cleansed, and my purity blessed. By the time I woke up from this delightful kingdom of dreams and opened my eyes, that sweet-faced, sweet-tongued friend of God had vanished. But now the time had come to find the one who had gone and disappeared. What was promised me should be brought to fruition, let events fall into place one after the next so that I also could fulfill my promise. Let this world, its enthusiasm long since beaten down, once again flourish with brand new meaning.

I turned my eyes towards Pembe Füruşan Madrasah and waited. I waited because I had been told, "See the image of my dancing friend in the blacks of my eyes." I waited, because the beautiful friend promised me, Muhammed Jelaleddin Rumi, would be completing his lectures at this time and leaving Pembe Füruşan Madrasah to go home by this road. While I waited, a shadow fell across my face.

"May the peace and felicity of Allah be upon you."

I looked and saw the proprietor of the coppersmith shop in front of me. I put my right hand to my heart and gave a slight bow, answering, "The abundance and wealth of Allah upon you."

With a hand blackened from tinning copper, he pointed towards one of two small wooden stools in front of the shop.

"Don't stand there on your feet, stranger, come sit here."

But it wasn't the time to chat with him.

"Thank you for your hospitality," I said amicably. "But I am in no condition to sit. He who I wait for will soon arrive."

He smiled; his mouth, like a deep gash in his round face, opened slightly, exposing a row of yellow bottom teeth with gaps where some were missing.

"Will the one you wait for come more hastily if you are on your feet?"

He obviously thought I was an unworldly pilgrim. Frankly, he deserved to be taught a lesson, but I spoke in a language he could understand nonetheless.

"Of course, he will not," I said smiling. "But if I sit, I will have shared the pleasure of waiting for him with you, whereas that pleasure has been granted me alone."

His lashless, Asian eyes shined with curiosity. Alas, this long-winded man was not going to leave me be.

"I wonder who it is you wait for."

"I know not either," I rebuffed. "We will learn of who he is when he arrives."

He clearly wondered if I were making fun of him.

"What is this? Wouldn't a man know for whom he waits?"

"One who has one's wits about him, perhaps. But how can the person whose mind is imprisoned in his heart possibly know?"

The coppersmith burst out laughing.

"I like you, stranger," he stated. "You are very entertaining."

"And you are even more entertaining, though you are unaware of it."

He couldn't understand whether I was praising him or criticising. Either way, he was vexed.

"Away with you, stranger!" he said, scowling. "You've outstayed your welcome. Do not tarry, be gone with you at once!"

"I cannot go," I said resolutely. "I couldn't if I wanted to. Your shop front, your shop, and you and I, and this sun shining in the sky... everyone and everything are here for his sake."

His almond eyes flashed with anger.

"Lout!" he roared. But just then his eyes were drawn to a point in the distance. He swallowed, and said under his breath, "Lunatic! Don't you bring your trouble upon me..."

I turned to face where he was looking and saw him. He sat astride a mule, on his head a modest turban, on his back a dark flimsy cloak. He was leaning forward, swaying slightly on the leisurely advancing mule. Surrounding him was a crowd of seven young disciples. I couldn't say whether they feared he may come to harm, or simply wanted to be in the presence of his beatific face, but they hovered around their sheikh, keeping pace with the mule. When the incensed coppersmith caught sight of God's secret beloved Rumi, he softened and swallowed his curses. Forgetting all about me, he watched Konya's most blessed holy man pass in front of him. His mouth, like a crater, hung open in awe. I touched his shoulder before parting so he'd know I hadn't forgotten about him.

"Have you seen? Alas, he has come. Tell me, how could I have known who it was before laying my eyes on him?"

Then, before the wretched coppersmith could stop me, I threw myself in front of the mule. The seven disciples gathered together, forming a wall in front their master.

"Who is this black-haired, black-eyed, black-bearded man?" one of them cried out.

"If his heart is also black, then woe be the state of affairs!" said another.

But the Mevlana was like calm, still water; and when he looked into my eyes, I saw a flash of divine light, although it was midday. Yes, Rumi looked into my eyes! And when he did, the buds of spring that were not to bloom till the following days, suddenly broke into a profusion of roses throughout Konya's gardens. When he looked into my eyes, dimples appeared on the cheeks of each child still in its mother's belly. Rumi looked into my eyes, and raising his hands to his disciples, said simply, "Leave him be."

Because as soon as he laid eyes on me he knew me. As soon as he saw me he understood why I had come. Yet he didn't smile, nor did a sweet word escape his lips. He only stated simply to his disciples, "Leave him be." The world had been decreed a trial. He who cannot clear the hurdle of ignorance, cannot bear the weight of knowledge.

The tight knot of the seven young disciples unraveled, in the same way a wall built by adept Armenian craftsmen only comes down stone by stone. I walked through them as though I'd broken through an insurmountable fortress gate. Looking into Rumi's eyes, I drew closer to the most promising friend God had on this earth.

"O leader of Muslims," I said deferentially, taking hold of his mare's reins. "I have a query to put to you. One which I myself could not resolve. I have been all around Khorasan, all around Samarkand, Damascus and Bagdad, but could not find one who could answer it. You were highly commended, and I have travelled day and night from lands far away in the hope that you can solve it."

"Go on, pilgrim," he said stroking his wispy beard. "Inasmuch as you have chosen our city from tens of them, inasmuch as you have come to us after bearing your tribulation such a long distance, let us draw from the well of knowledge in our hearts and drench you with it. What is it then? What is your query?"

As the words poured forth from his lips, there was neither hesitation nor doubt in his face. It was as if he knew before I even opened my mouth, not only the question I would put forward, but also the solution he would offer. I followed his lead, hoping he would answer the question in my mind."

"Now tell me, appraiser of the spirit world," I said in all my innocence. "Which was greater: the scholar and man of God, Bayazid of Bistam, or the prophet Muhammed?"

Rumi furrowed his lovely brow. He hadn't expected this much. Who would be mad enough to compare a mere religious scholar to Muhammed?

"What question is this?" he thundered, an unwavering righteousness commanding his voice. A shiver coursed through me, though I stood beneath the midday sun. My dark skin went pale, the marrow in my skull was on fire, and the heart under my breastbone had become a timid sparrow. I was afraid. I, who was afraid of no one. I doubted myself. I, who never bowed even to the words of Muhiddin Ibn-i Arabi, the greatest of sheikhs.

Rumi took no heed of my condition.

"What question is this?" he asked again. "There is no doubt that the prophet Muhammed, messenger of Allah, is the greatest of his creatures. What mention of Bayazid here?"

While he spoke, I composed my retort in my mind, so that I may immediately come back with it, and my voice would not betray my fear.

"You say this, and yet while the Prophet in all his grandeur says, 'O Allah, we have not properly known Thee,' Bayazid of Bistam dares to say, 'I absolve myself, how glorious is my name. I know all that needs knowing, exactly as it is to be known. I am the Sultan of all Sultans.'" The fury in Rumi's face subsided as he understood. His eyes filled with a divine light, and he could no longer hide his delight. Even so, he didn't withhold his response.

"The heart's capacity is slight for some people, they are fulfilled after one jug of water. For others it is boundless, even oceans cannot quench their thirst. Bayazid quenched his thirst with one sip of water, then pretentiously professed to be saturated. As for the prophet Muhammed, peace be upon him, he suffered from a terrific case of insatiability. He was parched for water while submerged in it. Each day he saw more, understood more, and knew more. But as he saw, the number of things to be seen increased; and as he learned, the number of things he didn't know multiplied; and as he understood, those things he didn't understand grew in size. For that reason he proclaimed, 'We have not properly known thee!'"

I had no chance to wipe away the tears before they fell from my eyes. This was he, the man I'd been seeking all these long years. The one I'd sought throughout all the lands, during all four seasons. This was the one betrothed to me. This was the most sacred of all God's beloveds.

A wail rose in the air. Was it from my throat, my mind, my heart? I couldn't say.

"Where two seas meet."

※

"Karen Kimya... Miss Greenwood... "

In the darkness someone called my name. The voice was distant and muffled, like a cry from the depths of a well. My eyelids parted; a raw white light burned my eyes and I shut them.

"Karen... Miss Greenwood..."

The voice crystallised. It was closer now, as well as familiar.

"She's coming round," said another voice I'd never heard before. "Get back, let her breathe."

My lids parted again. This time the light didn't burn so badly. A man in a white smock stood at the head of the bed, with Mennan's anxious face over his shoulder. Disregarding the doctor's advice, my chubby colleague moved in closer.

"Miss Greenwood, are you okay?"

I looked around the room, which was flooded in stark white light. The smokey-grey walls were bare, not a picture or any sort of decoration on them. A heavy medicinal smell hung in the air. Looking down, I saw that my arm was attached to an IV drip.

"Where am I?"

"The emergency room. You were knocked unconscious." The man in the white smock spoke in English with a heavy accent.

"Emergency room?"

131

As the words left my mouth, I realised that I, too, was speaking English. I must have naturally switched to my mother tongue while coming to.

"We're in the hospital," Mennan explained in Turkish, weaving his stubby fingers together nervously. They found you passed out on the pavement. We don't know how long you were out."

While he spoke, it all came back to me. The argument outside the restaurant, my chasing after the bearded man, the power outage, my transformation into Shams... It wasn't like I'd just felt like him though, I had become Shams-i Tabriz himself. Nothing of myself, or the contemporary world, had remained. Even more surprising was that I could recall every last detail of the experience with spot-on precision. I still felt haunted by the unfathomable beauty of the man's sparkling eyes, as he looked into mine from where he sat on his mare. In the end, I'd cried out. And then fainted. Or Shams fainted. Maybe we both fainted together. And then there was darkness.

"Nobody saw your assailant," said Mennan, startling me. "But of course it was dark out."

"What assailant?" I asked, switching back to Turkish as I tried to sit up. "What are you talking about?"

The man in the smock caught me gently by the shoulders. As he did, I saw his face up close. His pale green eyes, the huge mole on the right side of his nose... I read the ID card hanging from the pocket of his smock. Dr. Bulent Aslan.

"Better you don't make any sudden moves," he warned, also speaking in Turkish now. "Keep it slow."

I lay back down, but I couldn't shake the panic that was building in me.

"What happened to me?"

I had looked at Mennan and asked, but Dr. Aslan beat him to a response.

"Nothing serious. You took a bit of a fall, but there are no cuts or bruises on your head. You may have a bit of stiffness in your neck, but you are otherwise in perfect health."

I guessed that meant the baby was also okay. That was a relief, at least.

"We're not exactly sure why you fainted, though," Dr. Aslan continued. "It may have been the shock of what happened. But we've done some tests and there's nothing you need to worry about. We've hooked you up with an intravenous solution, and you should be feeling better soon."

I couldn't figure it out. Had I really gone back seven hundred years with the man who calls himself Shams? Or should I start worrying again that they'd slipped something into my food at the restaurant. What next? Was I going to accuse all of Konya of conspiring to drug my food and drink? I had to quit with the paranoia. Still, what explanation was there for what I'd been through?

"You said I was attacked?" I said, directing the question at Mennan. "What kind of attack?"

"We think someone may have assaulted you when the power went out."

"So the power really did go out?" I asked excitedly.

He looked at me, trying to make sense of why that was important.

"Of course it did. There was a malfunction in the city's power station and most of Konya was affected. That must be when you tripped and fell, or..."

"Or when someone jumped me," I said, finishing his sentence for him.

"Is that what happened?" he asked, his eyes opening wide as though it hadn't been his suggestion.

What was I supposed to say? I didn't have a clue about what had really taken place. If I told them I'd gone back seven centuries and witnessed Shams-i Tabriz's first encounter with Rumi, possessed by Shams's spirit no less, they'd think I was mad. Our doctor would corroborate, saying it was normal, what with the trauma caused by hitting my head and all.

"No..." I said, shaking my head. A pain shot through the back of my neck and I let out a small cry.

"You okay?" asked Dr. Aslan, looking calmly into my face with professional interest.

When I held still the pain subsided. "Um, yeah. I'm fine."

"The pain is normal. It'll take a few of days to get over it. In the meantime, I've given you some painkillers."

"I've got the pills," Mennan interrupted, though I knew he was more interested in what I'd been through than the state of my health. "Can you remember how you fell, Miss Greenwood?"

"I can't," I said, taking care not to move my head again. "I just remember the lights going out. I couldn't see anything, and I don't remember falling or anyone hitting me. Then when I opened my eyes, I was here."

Mennan scratched his stubbled chin.

"Strange where they found you unconscious," he said. He was obviously stuck on some detail, but looked unsure as how to open the subject. Finally, when he could hold back no longer, he put in, "They call the place Merej el-Bahrain."

"What?"

Passionately, as though reciting sacred words, he repeated, "Merej el-Bahrain. The place where two seas meet. The expression comes from the Qur'an, in fact. 'The Creator brought two seas together, one saltwater, the other fresh,' it is written. Inspired by the Qur'an, they called the first meeting place between Shams-i Tabriz and Rumi Merej el-Bahrain."

I was stunned. If I hadn't experienced that meeting myself, I would have said I was being tricked again and looked for a more logical explanation. But I'd seen it all with my own eyes, heard it and felt it in my bones even. What Mennan said only backed up my crazy experience, so I couldn't object. The doctor in the white smock did it for me.

"What's that got to do with anything?" he asked, giving Mennan an exasperated look. "What possible connection could there be between Miss Greenwood fainting and something that happened hundreds of years ago?"

Mennan, in another fit of obstinacy, tried to convince the man.

"More than you know, Doctor. When she first came to Konya, we got a flat tyre right in front of Shams-i Tabriz's Mausoleum and..."

The doctor pursed his lips patronisingly.

"Please," he interrupted. "We've been out of the Dark Ages for some time now. Could you please try not to confuse my patient with your superstitious fantasies? Let me offer you a simpler explanation. Taking advantage of the power outage, a thief yanked on your bag. You lost your balance and fell."

I looked around anxiously. "My bag... was it stolen?"

Mennan's face went completely red, as though he himself had taken it.

"Yes, but we found it. Someone had tossed it into the Iplikçi Mosque's garden..."

"But..."

"Unfortunately, there was no wallet or passport in it."

Just great. The thing I was always afraid of, every time I went abroad, had finally happened. I lost my passport. I would have to get in touch with the embassy and apply for a new one. Maybe I should call them now, I thought. I wondered where my phone was. The possibilities occurring to me were really unnerving.

"What about my phone? Is that gone too?"

"Don't worry. We found your phone in your jacket pocket," Mennan replied, smiling childishly as though pleased to be the one giving me the good news.

"Well, at least there's that." I gave a sigh of relief, before the dread of losing my passport settled back in again. Forgetting the doctor's warning, I tried to get up again. "Shouldn't we be looking for my passport?"

"The police are on it," Mennan said, trying to calm me. "Combing the city as we speak. They are the ones that informed me, after all. After finding my card in your bag."

The situation must have been pretty bad if the police were involved. It could take them days to find my things. I wanted to get back to the hotel, contact the English Consulate, and perhaps let Simon know what happened. He would know better what to do next. I glanced down at the IV in my arm, then at my hand. My fingers were bare. The ring was also gone. Maybe they'd taken it off when they hooked up the IV. I turned hopefully to the doctor.

"And my ring? There should have been a silver ring on my right hand."

Dr. Aslan didn't appear to know what I was talking about, though Mennan was all ears.

"The ring is gone, too? The one that bleeds?"

He seemed really caught up in the course of events. If it weren't for what I'd just been through, I would have maintained that the ring wasn't bleeding, that it was just the dye running off. As it was, I couldn't say anything but, "Yes."

A ring that bleeds, the meeting of two seas, Shams-i Tabriz... Our doctor looked at us warily in turn.

"Are you sure you're all right?" he asked glumly. He was polite enough not to point out how crazy we sounded. "You sure you're not dizzy or anything?"

"No, I'm fine. But the ring... it was really important to me and they've stolen it too."

"Yes, well, sorry about that," said the doctor, not trying so hard to hide the tedium in his voice anymore. "Look, if you two don't need me anymore, I'll be off to my office."

"Of course," I said, thanking him and giving him a grateful smile. "But when can I leave?"

He gave me a quick once over, as though he could judge my condition by just looking.

"If you feel all right, you can leave when the drip is finished. Just so you know, there's a police officer outside waiting to take your statement. After that, you should get straight back to your hotel and take it easy." He took a card from his pocket and held it out. "Call me immediately if you feel nauseated, or funny in any way."

Before I could respond, Mennan plucked the card out of his hand and answered, "Don't worry, we'll be fine. At least I hope so. But if anything does go wrong, we'll call you right away."

He waited till the two of us were alone in the room before continuing. "Anyhow, you're in good shape, Miss Greenwood." All his tension had left the room along with the doctor, like he was experiencing the deep comfort you get when alone with your loved ones after guests have gone home. He must have assumed I felt the same, and was expecting me to let him in on a secret, because he asked in a conspiratorial whisper, "So really, what happened to you?"

"I can't remember. Is it really so important that I do?"

"No... but I mean... I thought maybe you saw your attacker. Maybe it's someone you know."

Now what was he implying?

"Someone I know? Do you know something that I don't?"

"Of course not, why would I?"

But I was sure he did, or at least there was some idea he was toying with. It didn't take long for him to confirm my doubts.

"Actually, I do have my suspicions. I was thinking about that talk we had this afternoon."

"What talk?"

"You know. This afternoon. At the Yakut Hotel."

"And?"

"That good for nothing Serhad, he really got our goat, eh?"

"Are you suggesting he's the one who attacked me?"

"Ziya is an honest man, I have nothing to say about him. Serhad, on the other hand, is a total scumbag. As is that cue ball, Cavit." Thinking I may not remember, he clarified, "You know, that clean freak who was wiping down the door handles on his Mercedes. Neither one of them can be trusted. Nothing is beneath them. So I'm just saying, they were pretty angry today and..."

Was he using me as an excuse to get back at Serhad, or did he really believe what he was saying? Not that the idea was so far-fetched. Though Mennan was always trying to protect Ziya, the attack on me – assuming I really was attacked – could well have been all three of their doing. In that case, I would have to accept that Mennan wasn't one of Ziya's henchmen after all. That my suspicions about my colleague had been ungrounded from the start. It was hard to tell.

"I don't think so," I finally said. "Even if that were the case, I didn't see anyone. Not Serhad, and not his sidekick, Cavit. I don't know what happened. But right now I'm exhausted and don't want to think about it anymore."

I checked the IV again. The last drops were just emptying out.

"If this damn thing would just finish so we could get going," I grumbled, noting his unhappiness at the change of subject. I was sure he would have been happier if I'd blamed Serhad, but I was in no mood to go flinging mud just to please him. "So, where do we pay?" I asked.

With the mischievous expression of a naughty child, he gently raised his hand and, proud of his competence, responded, "Don't worry, it's taken care of."

That was one of those Turkish characteristics I'd never understand. The habit of being overly self-sacrificing for others, insisting on treating, or footing the bill as was the case here. Was it a sincere impulse to be selfless? Or an artificial show of generosity, a martyr complex? The innocent look in Mennan's eye was saying that the former was the case, but either way I wasn't going to let him pay for my treatment.

"I can't accept that. And anyhow, the expenses will all be covered by the company. We do work for an insurance company, remember?"

The situation was getting on my nerves, and I couldn't help pointlessly chiding him.

Wiping the sweat from his forehead with his handkerchief, he answered, "But you are my guest..."

"No. I'm no one's guest." I frowned. "I'm here on business. And you've been very helpful, thank you, but you are also just doing a job."

He looked away, giving in without a fight.

"All right then, I'll give you the bill later."

His plump cheeks turned crimson again and sagged forlornly. I was sorry I had snapped at him.

"Thanks, Mr. Fidan. I really appreciate it. I couldn't have paid now even if I'd wanted to. You know, seeing as how my wallet's been stolen. We'll settle it later." Smiling, I patted his shoulder. "And you also owe me a dinner. Don't think I've forgotten."

He immediately shrugged off his hurt feelings and his face shone.

"Whenever you want." The light in his eyes intensified and he became downright giddy. "In fact, if you're peckish right now..."

"No, no thanks. I'm not hungry. Later."

He pulled himself together with his usual impulsiveness.

"Let me have a word with the police outside. We'll take care of this statement business without wearing you out any further, then head back to the hotel."

"Mankind's greatest mystery is the brain."

✖

It was midnight before we finally drove back through Konya, its streets now liberated from cars and people wrapped in darkness, and arrived at the hotel. I'd called Simon on my mobile from the car and explained the situation. He sounded concerned; I even detected a bit of guilt in his voice.

"Don't worry," he'd said. "I'll call the consulate first thing tomorrow and start the procedures for applying for a new passport for you. You are all right, aren't you?"

"Not too bad," I'd said. "I feel better thanks to the IV drip."

I was expecting him to tell me to quit the assignment and come back if I weren't feeling well, but he didn't. He would never say that. Work was work, and you did what you had to do. Then again, if he had said the job was getting too dangerous and I should abandon ship, I don't know that I would anyway. Yes, unexplainable things were happening around me. And yes, I was afraid. Yet in some strange way I found the situation compelling and couldn't help wondering where it would all lead. Besides, I felt like all this was somehow related to my father, even if I hadn't yet figured out how.

When we arrived at the hotel entrance, Mennan had asked if I wanted him to get a room too. He thought it might make me feel better to have him nearby in case I needed anything. But after thanking him and telling him there was no need, I sent him home. Now I was heading past the reception desk, where the meddlesome receptionist was on duty once again.

139

"Welcome back, Miss Greenwood," he said, staring at me with interest. "Did you have a nice day?"

"It was good, thanks," I replied, smiling coldly and moving quickly towards the lift.

I reached my floor, and while putting my key into the lock under the dim light of the corridor, a shiver of dread passed through me. What if I were to hear the voice of that dervish in black again, or have another nightmare? I wished I hadn't sent Mennan away. And then what, I laughed to myself. Was I going to curl up in bed with the man and go to sleep? Trying to dispel the negative thoughts, I turned the key. The door opened silently. The room wasn't dark; a yellow light reflecting from Sultan Selim Mosque was indistinctly lighting up the interior. The bed I'd left unmade when I went out to eat, the mirror which looked like a pitch black hole in the wall, and the little table with my computer on it, were all just as I'd left them. Nevertheless, I switched on the lights before shutting the door. The room popped up in all its gloominess and desolation. No matter how swanky, how nicely furnished, this desolation and penetrating gloom seemed the common fate of all the areas in the hotel. But right now I didn't care one wit about the gloomy atmosphere. The fear inside me was so intense that even turning on the lights was no comfort. I went into the bathroom and quickly hit those lights too. The emptiness of the bathroom, and its white tiled walls, made it feel icy cold. From here, all that could be heard was the muffled gurgle of water flowing through pipes as a hotel guest showered in one of the neighbouring rooms. I left the bathroom lights on and went back into the bedroom. A pain shot through my body every time I moved my neck, and my head was starting to spin a bit. I lay down in bed straight away, which made me feel better at first, but before long I was thinking about Shams again, what I'd been through with him. Or more accurately, what he'd put me through. It had all started with the power going out. I'd passed out, and brought Shams and Rumi together in my dream world. I couldn't figure out how I'd managed it, when I hadn't known anything about how and where they first met, or what they'd said to each other. Or had I? Couldn't my father have told me the story? Maybe I'd kept it buried deep in my brain somewhere, and it was only resurfacing now that I was back in Konya. I was starting to think like my mother. She always used to talk about how the mystery of the human brain had never been completely solved.

"Mankind's greatest mystery is the brain. The way it works and to what capacity is not altogether known. How aware are we of the billions of things programmed into our genes. Or those perceived by our senses, or learnt through our experiences? Where is it all kept, that information we've gleaned from what we hear, see, feel, taste and touch, but rarely use? How much of it does our psyche erase, how much does it store? It's all a giant riddle."

Maybe it wasn't Shams-i Tabriz coming from the past, or Ziya and his men chasing after the load of cash to be paid for damages, or Mennan, who was drenched in sweat whenever he got nervous or lost his temper, but rather me - I was the only one responsible for all this, this mixed up brain of mine. To what degree were our brains at the mercy of our sub-consciousness? This was the finer point of the riddle my mother spoke of. All at once I felt better. I had my explanation. But then... in that case was Ziya innocent? Of course not, that was another matter. One that I'd need to keep probing into. Even our Mennan may still be guilty. And that was why it was so important that I kept my appointment with this ex-employee Kadir, who claimed aliens had started the fire. Even if he had lost his mind, he was no longer one of Ziya's men. If Nezihe and Serhad were keeping something from me, I would hear about it from him.

I glanced down at my jeans, covered in dried mud, and my jacket which was no better. Sitting up slowly, I got undressed. I went into the bathroom again intending to take a shower, but worried I may pass out and fall again, I hesitated, then changed my mind. I would have to settle for just washing my hands and face, and worry about showering in the morning. Though I wasn't sleepy, I went back into the room and put on my pyjamas. Remembering the painkillers the doctor had given me, I reached for my bag. I found the prescription bottle, twisted it open, and poured some pills into my hand.

Then I remembered the baby and, without a second thought, put the pills back in and popped the lid back on. What in the world was I doing? Was I really going to have this child? Even the word 'baby' felt foreign to me. On the other hand, the idea of having it aborted was horrifying. The first time had been bad enough. It had felt like a huge hole had been opened not only in my womb, but in my heart and skull as well. I was pretty young then, very inexperienced, albeit very strong. These days I felt more vulnerable, more prone to injury. Perhaps that's why I was so frightened. But sooner or later I would have to make a decision. A decision that I would have to defend to Nigel when I got back to London. One that may deeply affect our relationship. My phone rang. Assuming it was Mennan, I picked up without looking. But it was my mother's cheerful voice that rang in my ears.

"Hello, Karen?"

"Hi Mum. Everything all right?"

"Yes, fine. I haven't woken you, have I?" She kept talking without giving me a chance to respond. "This Nigel of yours is such a dear. I'm telling you, if you let him get away I'll never forgive you."

"Don't worry, Mum, I have no intention of doing that. Of course, if he doesn't want me..."

"Don't be silly, he's crazy in love with you. He rang me this evening. And guess what he said?"

Good for Nigel, he'd wasted no time in inviting her to dinner. Though of course I pretended not to know about it.

"Go on. Tell me."

"He asked me out to dinner. To that jazz club in Chelsea I liked so much. The one you took me to."

"Club 606?"

"That's the one. They still have that French chef there, don't they? In charge of the kitchen?"

"Well, I haven't been there in quite some time, but I suppose so."

She giggled.

"We'll be able to gossip about you a bit in your absence."

I wondered where this sudden change in mood had come from. Then it dawned on me.

"Mum, have you been drinking?"

She tittered like a naughty child.

"Who, me? Stop slandering your elderly mother."

"You aren't supposed to be drinking. Doctor's orders."

"Well, the doctors can go to hell," she grumbled. "They restricted plenty of things for Matt, too. And look what happened. He only lived three more months. If you can call it living. Creeping about in the corners of a hospital. He didn't even get to smoke one of his beloved Cuban cigars one last time before he died. So don't talk to me about doctors, Karen. They don't know a damn thing. Besides, I haven't had so much... just two little glasses."

It didn't seem like 'just two little glasses' inebriation to me. My mother was diabetic, and what's more she had hypertension. The doctors had most recently diagnosed her with an enlarged heart.

"Mum, this is like suicide. You are going to slowly kill yourself. Why are you doing this?"

Resentful and hurt she mumbled, "Maybe because I can't do it outright."

I was already in a state, and now I had to deal with her as well.

"Please don't talk like that," I scolded. "Why would you kill yourself? What exactly is so wrong with your life?"

"What's wrong?" Her voice was full of rebellion. "Don't you see all the people I love are leaving me and going away? First your father, now Matt. I'm all alone in this big wide world."

"All alone? I'm here, aren't I?"

"You... You are a lovely daughter. But you've got your own life to live. I can't believe you still manage to meddle in mine even from so far away."

She sounded really emotional, like she was on the brink of tears. What was it with this woman?

"What do you mean, Mum?"

"Don't you dare deny it was you who told Nigel to invite me to dinner. I'm not so old yet that I can't figure that out."

"Of course I didn't tell him to..."

"Karen, stop it! You can't pull it off, lying. You never could. You got that from your father. You told Nigel to call me. And it was a good thing you did. I'm sure he would have done it himself if he'd thought of it. But you know men, they are a bit thick. Sometimes you have to remind them - and you reminded. Now don't deny it. Besides, I was thrilled with the offer. You know I adore that dark, handsome man of yours. But all joking aside, he's a good man, Nigel. The kind of man that's hard to find nowadays."

"Mum, please don't drink," I entreated. "If not for yourself then for me. Look, I feel really bad."

"There's nothing to feel bad about, sweetheart," she said, trying to keep her voice firm. "I'm fine. I haven't drunk that much. Really, two drinks is all. All right, let's say four then. But not more. And I won't drink any more. I'll put my head down and sleep just as soon as I've hung up. So, what are you doing? How is the Konya adventure going? Has that mystical city changed much?"

Her voice was fraught with nostalgia. She must have been remembering the old days.

"I suppose it has. There are some wide boulevards I don't remember seeing before. And taller buildings..."

"They're ruining the place," she mumbled despondently. "Destroying all the old beauty of it. Not just there, all over the world. Wreaking havoc, remorselessly, barbarically. Sometimes I think someone needs to come along and rescue the world from people. Somebody needs to take this lovely world out of our hands."

"It's not all that bad," I said, trying to mollify her. "A lot of the old houses and mosques are under protection. The streets are wide and sunny. They've reclaimed Rumi's Mausoleum and are looking after it better than before."

"Is the dervish lodge still there?"

I was sure she meant the house with the turbaned headstones I'd been to with my father, but I wanted to hear what she had to say about it, so I pretended not to know what she was talking about.

"What dervish lodge?"

"You know. Where your father lived. It's where I first saw him. He used to dance there."

I recalled Mennan's words, that the Mevlevis don't like the *sema* to be called a dance.

"You mean, the *sema?*"

"Yes, I mean the *sema*," she mimicked teasingly, her voice suddenly mirthful again. "You are your father's daughter. Poyraz also used to hate the *sema* being called a dance."

"Have I been there too, Mum? I'm serious, I don't remember."

"You must have. I mean, I don't know for sure, sweetheart. The two of us have never been to Konya together. But your father must have taken you there. That was his home."

"His home?"

"Yes, his real home. Don't tell me you don't remember that either."

When I kept silent, she let out a small, mock scream.

"Oh Karen, you're going to be senile before I am, my dear. You know, they left your father at the door of that lodge when he was a baby... remember?"

No, I really didn't remember. I supposed that must have been buried somewhere deep in my subconscious, too.

"Maybe if you explain a bit, it'll come back to me."

"Funny," she murmured, "How could you not remember? We talked about it so many times. That's where your father's name comes from."

"From where?"

"You really don't remember. Amazing."

Knowing it was amazing wasn't really helping.

"Yes, amazing. But I've forgotten, so there you are," I grumbled. "Now where did his name come from? Tell me, so at least now I'll know."

"Okay, okay. I'll explain." She seemed to have sobered up. Maybe she was telling the truth about not drinking too much.

"Now. When your father was still a baby, his family, for whatever reason, put him in a basket and dropped him outside that dervish lodge. Very biblical, isn't it? It was the end of December. And incredibly cold. If the poor thing had stayed out there much longer, he would have frozen to death. But then the northeasterly wind came up out of nowhere -

the one they call Poyraz in Turkish. And it started pounding on the door of the lodge. Firmly and urgently, like someone in need of immediate help. One of the dervishes inside heard the knocking and really did think there was someone there. He opened the door, and there was the tiny baby in the basket. Your father, that is. The dervish grabbed the baby and took it inside. When the residents of the lodge heard the story, they declared it a good omen. Then a sheikh by the name of Hikmet took him under his wing, raising him as his own son. And in honour of the wind that had rescued him, they called your father Poyraz."

Yes, I vaguely remembered some things. Not memories exactly, more like fragmentary images from my imagination passing before my eyes. Very fine snow that lashed like a whip in the violent wind. The baby's father, who, ashamed of what he'd done, not only hid his face from the people but from the snow and the wind as well. That same father preparing to abandon the baby to this unforgiving world, as it slept inside the basket unaware of its own helplessness. The crazy wind pounding away on the door with all its strength, whether out of a desire to save the baby, or fury over what evil man is capable of. The wind that rescued little Poyraz, and thus somehow bestowed me with life. The dervish with his glowing face, opening the door and finding a baby in a basket at his feet...

"He must have felt terrible when he grew up and found out about these things," I observed.

"Possibly," my mother acknowledged. "But I never saw him obsess on the subject. In fact, even though he said it jokingly, I think he was a bit proud of it. 'Like the prophet Moses, I came into the world as an explorer in a basket, not in a mother's arms like all of you,' he used to say. Maybe that was his way of coping with the pain. Being abandoned is a terrible thing, of course."

"Well, he also abandoned us in the end."

I shouldn't have said it, especially not while my mother was drunk, but it had slipped out. There was a brief silence. A deep, bleak silence.

"He certainly did, damn him."

I kept quiet, not because I wanted to, but because I didn't know what to say.

"But try not to brood on it," she continued, sniffling. There you go, I'd finally managed to make the woman cry. "And don't talk negatively about him, I'm sure he had his reasons."

"I'm sure he did," I replied, trying to stifle the anger rearing its head inside me. "I'm sure whoever left him at the door of the dervish lodge when he was a baby had his own reasons, too."

"He who knows himself knows God."

※

After my mother's phone call I was wide awake. I opened my laptop and jotted down some notes on the day's interviews. Then I turned on the voice recorder and listened to Serhad and Nezihe's statements. Although there were no major discrepancies, I did find two points interesting. First, that it was Kadir Gemelek who had pulled Nezihe out of the fire, and second, that it was the fire brigade, rather than Serhad, who had come to his rescue after he'd gone back inside. These two incidents weren't in their written statements. I would ask Kadir Gemelek about it during the next day's interview. That is, if he could understand and give logical responses. Though they didn't seem like much on their own, it was when small, seemingly insignificant details like these were brought together that puzzles were solved. I turned off the recorder and closed up the laptop; another difficult day lay ahead and I needed some rest. I turned the lights out and settled into bed.

I thought back to the encounter between Shams and Rumi. Actually, it felt more like an arranged meeting than a chance encounter, as though it were God himself who had ordained it. Shams had just set things in motion, beseeching God to reveal the face of one of his 'recondite beloveds' and offering his head in payment. But Rumi had hardly seemed oblivious. Hadn't he faced Shams years earlier in Damascus, appealing, 'O appraiser of the spiritual world, find me'? It seemed their coming together was destiny. A destiny that was merely playing itself out, unable to change or be changed. They were just acquiescing to it. But every chapter had already been written, every conclusion foretold. When Shams set his eyes on Rumi, his heart was filled with such great love, such immense happiness, such unrestrained fervour. Even I, when looking at Nigel, couldn't compete with this rapture. And what about Rumi? I remembered the shining eyes of the man on the mare. He seemed in a worse state than Shams, overcome with some kind of ecstasy, as though he were intoxicated. What kind of love was this? What was this bond they shared? The light that shone in Rumi's eyes was just like that in my father's when he looked at Shah Nesim. They never shone with such passion when looking at my mother or me. And nobody else could provide him with that thrill he got from speaking with Shah Nesim. Neither my mother nor I had any role in this story. That was how he could leave us without the slightest remorse. Who knows what or whom Shams and Rumi had sacrificed in the name of their love. Take this Kimya, for instance. Why would Rumi marry off his adopted daughter to Shams? More importantly, how is it that a Sufi like Shams, who had devoted his whole life to uncovering God's mysteries, could marry such an innocent young girl?

Questions and more questions. Questions which, growing ancient in their open-endedness, became anathema. Questions which paved the way for the mistrust I harboured of everything I knew. Questions vying for space in my mind, allowing no relief. There would be no sleep for me tonight. I sat up. From somewhere came the hum of a television left on, and I couldn't help thinking what a great idea it was.

I reached for the remote on the dresser. At first only jumbled colours appeared on the screen. I had to wait a full minute before they formed a normal image. I wasn't familiar with any of the faces on the screen, but I guessed they were Turkey's singers, actors and actresses, its celebrities, so to speak. They were trying to pull a single glass out from under a pyramid of glasses without toppling the whole stack, while tension-building music played in the background. I quickly changed channels and came across a very rough copy of *Citizen Kane*, which I'd already seen a dozen times, so I skipped that, too. This time I got what looked like a cop show, but the camera was so shaky that I knew I'd get dizzy again if I kept watching. I pushed the button on the remote once more. First the sound of a ney filled the room, then the image crystallized - an image of what was at most only two hundred metres beyond the bed I was lying in - Rumi's Mausoleum. As the camera passed through the mausoleum's entrance to the garden inside, the presenter, speaking in a hymnal tone to suit the atmosphere, began to drone verses of poetry.

O he who probes mysteries
There is a soul within a soul, seek it in your heart
Seek out your own essence within yourself
O he who probes mysteries, seek it everywhere
Yet it is not that which is around you, seek it within yourself

The camera went in, accompanied by the poem. In the golden ochre light of the mausoleum, row upon row of tombstones with gorgeous Arabic calligraphy stretched into the distance.

That mystery was unknown to anyone but the two of them. They both burned with the fire of being apart. They'd been seeking each other for years - perhaps to share their many secrets, perhaps to unite the two parts of one single secret in order to learn the truth behind it.

Now the camera left the mausoleum and was moving step by step up Konya's darkened streets. At some point it stopped and stayed fixed. Morning was breaking. I knew the place; it was what Mennan called Merej el-Bahrain, the place where two seas meet.

This is where Shams fell to the ground in a heap uttering the name of Allah. When he awoke, the prophet Rumi was at his side, and he opened his eyes in the embrace of one of Allah's beloveds. The two great dervishes, the two men of God, were together at last. They took refuge from the world's filth, noise, and oppression in a desolate room without light.

150

For days, weeks, and months, they experienced the solitude of two people in one room. When the door finally opened and they both greeted the world, neither was Shams the same Shams, nor was Rumi the same Rumi. Mevlana had given up the Muslim prayer rituals, the sermons, and the teaching in the madrasah. He was intoxicated, though not from drink, and began to tell of this dizzying love to everyone and everything he came across. To the rain in the sky, to the dry grass that awaited the rain and the fig tree that was watered by it, to the caterpillar that climbed the fig, to the sparrow that pursued the caterpillar, to the stone houses where the sparrow built its nest, to the roses that decorated the stone houses, to the nightingale preoccupied with the rose, to the hawk that chased after the nightingale, to the gentlemen who tamed the hawk, to the palace that housed the gentlemen. Words of love poured forth from his tongue with the enthusiasm of a child who has just learned to walk and yearns to show off its newly acquired talent. And with that same enthusiasm, he wandered the streets of this ancient city with renewed excitement, walking proudly and staggering in turns.

The camera moved forward again, now meandering through a park. Not a big park, but spacious and airy. I'd seen it before, I thought, as the camera panned to a small mosque inside the park. Of course, it was the Shams-i Tabriz Mosque and Mausoleum, where everything had started. As the camera approached the mosque, the presenter spoke in a voice overcome with emotion.

Shams did not part from Rumi's side. The city of saints acquired yet another great dervish.

The image on the TV appeared to be breaking up. When it cleared, it revealed a man in black robes at the door of the mosque. The presenter continued.

The people were overjoyed. The whole city was ecstatic.

Then the presenter's voice cut out.

"That is a lie!" shouted the black-clad man, as he thrust his right fist into the air. It was Shams, the protagonist of my Konya nightmares.

"They are lying," he growled again. "Don't believe them. That's not how it happened." Our eyes locked. How he managed it, I'll never know, but he was using a television broadcast that hundreds of people may be watching to address me directly. I immediately forgot all about the conclusions I'd just drawn on the mysteries of the brain, and the reasons I'd established for why I saw these apparitions. My mind was effectively pulled aside by my heart, leaving the emptied space under the command of my subconscious. Instinct was now giving way to sentiment, and it was curiosity, rather than fear, that I was overcome by. That is why I listened so closely to the words of Shams.

"No one was overjoyed," he carried on, grimacing. "Not the sultan, not the soldiers, not the Muslim theologians, and certainly not the people. They disliked me from the moment they saw me. They all hated me and wanted me out of Konya. They'd have killed me without a second thought if they could have got away with it. All except Khüdavendigar, and his eldest son, Bahaeddin."

Surprised by my own boldness, I asked, "Who is Khüdavendigar?"

"Khüdavendigar means 'the lord'. Who else could it be but Rumi?"

"You called him Khüdavendigar?"

"Not I. His father, Belhli Muhammed Bahaeddin Veled, who was himself known as Sultanü'l-Ulema, or 'the Sultan of Muslim Scholars'. I counseled Khüdavendigar to forget all that his father had said, yet I did not refrain from calling him by that name which his father had called him by, because I also loved the name." He suddenly appeared to be lost in thought, remembering the past. He stood silently in front of the mosque like that for a while.

"Why?" I asked, my voice sympathetic. "Why didn't they accept you?"

His dark face clouded over with renewed melancholy as though the events had just occurred that morning.

"They didn't understand. What they didn't understand, they deemed wicked. The ulema thought I was going take him away from them, when in fact I had come to make Rumi the sultan of the world. Not just of his own lifetime, as his father had been, but throughout all time. But they didn't understand, because what they knew as religion was blasphemy. What they knew as worship was idolatry. They were committing crimes against humanity, and doing it in the name of Allah nonetheless. They believed that faith simply meant observing the writings in a book, as if the Creator needs voluntary slaves. What they thought was morality was intolerance, as though the Creator takes pleasure from hatred. They believed zealotry would buy their salvation in both realms. Shame on them! As though the Creator were a merchant."

"And Rumi? What did he say to them?"

"Khüdavendigar? His was a different nature. The earth he was moulded from was more supple, his blood from the sweetest lake, his breath from the gentlest breeze. He possessed hope but no distrust, tolerance but no anger, love but no animosity. When he saw the image of himself in my soul, he was beside himself. Like a flag of mutiny kept in a chest for years, the moment he saw the wind, he unfurled and flapped about with fervour. He cared nothing about the palace, the ulema, or the people. He packed up his wisdom and his reasoning, flinging them into the abyss. He became a man consisting strictly of heart. This is why his every word was a poem, his every movement one of beauty, his every touch a miracle."

"And your nature?"

Before answering he stroked his beard thoughtfully.

"Khüdavendigar's contained nothing but beauty, whereas mine had both beauty and ugliness. But he saw only my beauty, ignoring the ugliness. I was never duplicitous with him. I presented him with both good side and bad so that he may know me. They call the place we met Merej el-Bahrain. It is an Arabic term. In the Qur'anic sura of Furkan it is explained like this: 'Two seas were brought together, one salty and bitter, the other sweet so that it quenches thirst. Between them was placed an invisible curtain so that the two would not mix.' And this is how Rumi and I came together while maintaining our own respective essences. If you wish to understand the difference in nature between Rumi and me, you must look at our fathers, or rather our relationships with them. Rumi held his father in the highest esteem. He believed every word his father uttered to be true, every word he wrote law. Baha Veled was his exemplar. Whereas I was aware even before puberty that my father was inadequate. If I had felt like him, behaved like him, I would have been an ordinary Tabrizi Muslim. Yes, my father was an ordinary man, an ordinary Muslim like the millions of grains of sand in the desert. He didn't understand me, and even began to judge me because I was different from him."

Sham's arrogance was starting to get to me. Intending to bring him down a notch, I said critically, "And so you belittled him."

His eyes narrowed slyly.

"It's like the story of the goose hatched from the chicken egg. I wasn't belittling him, just trying to explain myself. To demonstrate how I was not like him."

He became serious again, continuing to speak calmly. Not like a teacher but like someone who was misunderstood; in effect, like someone who realised he would never be fully understood but had grown to accept it.

"Everyone assumes we are simple and easygoing, but my nature is complex. The earth I was moulded from was barren, not every plant can grow in me. My blood is unsavoury like sour wine; my breath erratic, like wind breaking on a craggy stone precipice. There is more suspicion than hope in my heart, more anger than tolerance. And although I don't harbour unwarranted animosity, neither do I foster strong affection without good reason. I am on the side of truth and reality. That's why I believe only those who have earned the privilege are deserving of love. Love is too precious to bestow on those who haven't earned it."

"Did Rumi earn that privilege?"

"What does 'earn' mean here?" he answered without hesitation. "My love has been with him from the beginning. It came naturally - as naturally as an ear of grain yielding wheat, a baby gravitating towards its mother's milk, one life being fed by another. But Khüdavendigar wasn't immediately aware of it. He couldn't comprehend."

"And you? Did you know from the beginning?"

154

He smiled; his coal black eyes gleamed.

"I did not fully know either until I came upon him. When I saw him I knew. Ere that, there were only visions, vague images. Colours within colours, scents within scents, voices within voices... But I knew not where they lay hidden, nor in what manner. When I saw him, I understood. According to the words of Muhammed, peace be upon him, 'He who knows himself, knows God'. In the same way, I knew upon seeing Rumi that what I had been seeking all those years was actually myself."

"You saw yourself in him?"

"You do not understand, do you?" he said despairingly. "It is not easy, because everything we know is mercurial. You know they say God doesn't change, but that is entirely wrong. He changes. His divine wisdom cannot be questioned, but it is because he changes so much that we have difficulty in understanding. That which is known becomes unknown, what is false becomes true, good deeds become sins, what's permissible becomes forbidden, and lies become truth. In this way the Supreme Being is beyond reach, and his great secret remains protected."

"What is that great secret?"

His eyes narrowed again and became two glistening pools of light in his long, dark face. Then those pools of light were all that could be seen on the screen. I couldn't see his lips moving anymore, but his voice said, "If you want to know, you must come."

"Where?"

The screen opened out and he stood in front of me, a benign smile on his gaunt face.

"With me. Or have you forgotten what I said when we met earlier? To know, you must live it firsthand. And for that, you need courage."

He was once again inviting me to be him, to live out his experiences. I couldn't say no. Enthralled by his words, I again reached out to take his sinewy hand, darkened by who knows how many years of sunlight.

"... he who succumbs to his urges succumbs to demons."

✳

I was back in that garden where I'd lost myself, inside a man's body that wasn't my own. From the flowerbed just in front of the clay brick building, the varied fragrances of tulips, hyacinths, and roses wafted past, as though to reassert the world was a beautiful place. In the middle of the garden was the pool framed in white stones, its interior covered in blue ceramic tiles. In the pool, a sweetly shining noontime sun. At the foot of the garden wall, soaring poplars leisurely swayed. Behind it was a giant walnut tree. Who was I now? Karen of London or Shams of Tabriz? The image reflected in the water of the tiled pool provided an answer.

"This sun is seven centuries younger than yours. This body is seven hundred years older."

I looked into the pool, once again seeing my bearded, black-clad reflection. Before I forgot all about Karen, I asked my image in the water, "Is this Rumi's home?"

"No, it is God's," replied my image in the gently rippling water. "Like the bee's hive, the eagle's rock, the ant's burrow, the bear's den, and the sultan's palace - this place also belongs to the Creator. It was a gift presented by Sultan Keykubat with the hand of Allah to Khüdavendigar's family for them to use so long as they should live, not only as a home to stay in, but also as a madrasah to teach in."

I turned to look at the house. I hadn't noticed how big it was before, how broad. I wondered how many rooms there were. Khüdavendigar's room was on the upper floor. He shared the room with a beautiful lady of Greek descent by the name of Kira, who before marrying him had converted to Islam. The other rooms belonged to the children and the servants. The smell of food wafting out from the kitchen on the lower floor gave me hunger pangs. I stood back, in order to curb my appetite. While backing away from the kitchen, I nearly collided with someone.

"Make way," I said, sidestepping him. I looked and saw Khüdavendigar's middle son Alaeddin, and behind him, Kimya, who blossomed and became more beautiful day by day. Kimya, who although not Khüdavendigar's flesh and blood daughter, walked about the house head held high as though she were. Kimya, who looked a person in the eye unabashedly, without reserve or trepidation. What was she up to with this boy?

"Slow down," I scolded Alaeddin. "You almost had me bathing in the middle of the courtyard."

Before speaking, Alaeddin shot me a look like a wild animal. If Kimya hadn't been with him he would have no doubt ignored me, but he was obviously not happy about being reprimanded in front of the girl.

"I didn't see you," he shot back, with a total lack of humility. "I, too, was almost knocked to the ground."

Alaeddin was a child who bowed to no one, who was always overstepping his boundaries and would not conform to the mould he was made in. I, who was even unafraid to look into Satan's fiery red eyes, was nonetheless alarmed by the cutting look in the eyes of this adolescent. To conquer my fear a bit, I shouted out as though in anger, "What is this rushing round the house like a Mongolian soldier hastening to deliver news to his commanding officer? I expect an apology."

"Pardon me," he said grudgingly. "I have a lesson in the Karatay Madrasah that I have to get to."

With that he was off, deliberately running as though I hadn't warned him, with Kimya on his heels. That child didn't like me in the least. The spark of hostility in his eyes hadn't waned since the day I first arrived. He needed to be taught a lesson, but for now I kept my cool, muttering, "Lord, give me patience," and walking away. Before I'd gone a few steps further, Khüdavendigar's eldest son Bahaeddin caught up with me. If Alaeddin was fire, Bahaeddin was water. If Alaeddin was a storm, Bahaeddin was stillness. If Alaedddin was fury and rebellion, Bahaeddin was peace and submission.

"Forgive him, my sheikh," he said, grasping my hand and kissing it. "My brother is wild, he doesn't know a person's worth. Whatever my father did, the child was somehow never tamed. Forgive him if he wronged you. Don't take it to heart. It's not you, his nature is flawed."

His face, with its wispy peach fuzz, blushed faintly like an apple beginning to ripen. I gently touched the cheek of this boy with the lovely words, lovely body, lovely soul.

"I was looking for your father," I said. "Would you know where he is?"

"He's in his chamber, my sheikh. At midnight last night, I went to him. You weren't there and he asked about you. I attended morning prayers, but you weren't there either and he asked about you. Just now I brought him his bread and water, and again he asked. So I suppose he also is wondering about you."

I turned and walked towards his room; the smallest, darkest, and humblest, but also holiest room in this huge house. Bahaeddin followed along behind me. I stopped, and he also stopped.

"You wait outside. I need a word with your father."

He bowed his head and clasped his hands together.

"As you wish, my sheikh."

I left him outside and entered through the arched wooden door. Rumi sat cross-legged on the floor in front of a bookrest, reading.

"Peace of Allah upon you."

As soon as he saw me, he sat up straight.

"And Allah's love upon you."

He reached out and tried to kiss my hand but I kissed his first, beating him to it. He didn't leave it at that, however. He also touched his lips to my hand.

"Thanks be to God that you've come, master," he said excitedly. "Thanks be to God you are here again today."

I glanced at the book on the bookrest. It was the *Maarif*, the book penned by his father Baha Veled. I had told him before, "Do not read from what your father has written." So this meant he was still reading it. I knew this habit was the worst form of addiction. It was the hardest thing to give up. But how could a dervish who could not overcome his addictions triumph over his desire. In the Alak verse of the Qur'an it was written, 'In the name of God the Creator, I command you: Read!' I looked Rumi in the eye and bellowed the opposite thrice over.

"Do not read! Do not read! Do not read!"

Like a child, his face went white. Silence fell like dankness over his chamber of trial and suffering. Remorse collapsed like a mountain on Rumi's shoulders. He closed the cover of the *Maarif* with trembling hands. Then he placed the book on the shelf next to him. I looked over to see more books there: Feriduddin Attar's *Esrarname,* Muhyiddin ibnu'l-Arabi's *Fususu'l-Hikem'i,* Ebu'l-Ferec el-Isfahani's *Kitabu'l-Agani,* Kuseyri's *Risale,* Gazali's Ihya-i Ulumi'd-Din's *Kelile* and *Dimne,* and *Binbir Gece Masalları - A Thousand and One Nights.* Even if I could have been okay with those, when I saw the *Divan* by that poet Mutenebbi, who considered himself a prophet and was nicknamed Kufeli, as though he wrote in Kufic like in the Qur'an, I was incredulous. Could I have been mistaken? Had I misidentified the one who was promised to me? Was it not Muhammed Jelaleddin Rumi, son of Belhi Baha Veled, who was Allah's recondite beloved? Was I being dragged along by an illusion, not unlike a dry leaf tossed about in the wind?

Rumi saw my face grow dark as I scowled at Mutenebbi's *Divan.* He recognized the shift in my soul and his chin quivered like a child's. He looked so defenseless that my heart almost shook too. But I didn't allow it; neither my heart to be softened, nor his pride to be roused.

"For how long will you continue to read other people's books, Muhammed Jelaleddin?" I snapped. "How long will you continue to seek out the mystery of yourself in the words of others? Even if those of a theologian like your father, even if those of a poet whose words are crafted like a master jeweler's, even if those of a scholar who erects buildings from words on the thin sheet of ice in your soul, let go of those worn-out words, leave them in the past. For it is only with your own words that you will ever uncover the mystery of yourself."

"But..." he appealed, his blessed lips parting slightly.

I cut him off like the sharp winter wind of Tabriz.

"There can be no 'buts' Jelaleddin. There can be no wavering, no dragging of feet. There is no time for that. Nighttime has parted and the day has dawned. A path has appeared, which will be traversed now or not ever."

His eyes watered, crazed from lack of sleep. A look of anguish subtly spread throughout his pale face. In that moment he seemed to me so beautiful, so innocent, so holy. But I stamped out the adoration roused inside me and, remembering what I had to do, girded myself with my austerity. It was said that life is like a bridge - those who grasp the truth will pass over it in this world; those who don't, in the afterlife. Rumi might not have known it, but he had a trial ahead of him.

"Rise," I commanded. "If you would just budge already, it is not the time for apathy now. I have three wishes I'd like you to fulfill. Seeing as I am your guest, you must grant me these wishes."

He shuddered, then immediately stood up from the cushion he sat on. He bowed his head and clasped his hands in submission, like his son, Bahaeddin, had in the courtyard. He looked into my face with eyes resembling two candle flames flickering with joy.

"You are not my guest," he said, his voice shaky. "This house and this madrasah are your kingdom. If there is a guest, that would be me. Go ahead, appraiser of this world, your wish is my command."

I sat down on the cushion he'd stood up from. Stroking my beard with the cunning of a hunter who has set a pheasant trap, I said, "You know, many days have passed since I arrived in Konya. In short, I need a woman, Rumi. And not just any woman, a beautiful one. Can you find me such a woman?"

I watched him as I spoke. Let's see if the light in his eyes would go out, if a shadow would spread throughout his face.

160

Let's see if he would trust me. But the light in his face did not wane. He never paused, never stopped to consider it, not even for a second.

"Your wish is my command."

Without giving me a chance to respond, he left his humble chamber. I watched him go, delighted. But my first sheikh, Ebu Bekir-i Tabriz Sellebaf, may he rest in peace, had said, "Do not make hasty choices. When choosing both guru and disciple, be patient. Because the sun's time is one thing, the moon's time is another, and the earth's is yet another. Be patient until it is the time to decide." I buried my joy in a deep grave of doubt and waited.

It wasn't long before the arched wooden door of the chamber was opened by Rumi's hand. I saw as he came in that his free hand held that of another. Next to him stood the most beautiful woman in Konya - Kira, Rumi's wife. This was loyalty, this was faith, this was submission. I could barely resist throwing my arms around Rumi's neck. But the sun's time is one thing, the moon's time is another, and the earth's is yet another. I had to wait until the darkness of doubt was erased from my heart. I frowned.

"This will not do. Kira is my soul sister," I said. I bowed respectfully to his wife. "You may leave, Miss Kira."

The poor woman didn't understand what was going on, and though looking briefly into my eyes with consternation, she then honoured my request and walked out. I turned back to Rumi.

"Let us come to my second wish," I said in all seriousness. "Bring me a beautiful boy child to serve me. One that will not disappoint me or make me say things twice. He should understand my demands and fulfill them immediately."

Again, his face did not cloud over. He never paused, never for one moment gave it any thought. He sufficed in repeating the same sentence.

"Your wish is my command."

Then lurching forward, he left the room again. Even though my heart called out, with no reason for doubt anymore, my mind held back the urge. Before the opened door had closed again, Rumi had reentered. With him was his eldest son Sultan Veled, whose beauty was only comparable to that of the prophet Joseph's. Before I could open my mouth, "I hope," he said, bowing respectfully, "this child will be a slave worthy of being in your service."

I had difficulty keeping myself from crying out and kissing Rumi's hand. But because the sun's time is one thing, the moon's time is another, and the earth's is yet another, I had to wait in hope until the shadow of doubt was lifted. My face fell.

"Sultan Veled is like a son to me," I said. "He cannot serve me. Send the young lad away, let him go."

Bahaeddin Veled, unaware of what was happening, stood looking into my eyes in shock as his father's wife had. When Rumi gave a nod, indicating his son should leave, he remained facing us as he backed out of the room. Then, without lowering my eyes, I made my third and final request. "I am thirsty, and the water of Konya is not enough to quench that thirst. My thirst is insatiable and I need wine, I cannot do without it. Go to the Jewish quarter and bring me back wine."

Rumi did not say, "Enough!" He did not say, "Me? This city's most well-known theologian? What do you mean telling me to go to the Jewish quarter and bring back wine?" He did not ask, "Why are you playing with my pride?" Or, "Why are you making me enemies?" What he did was laugh, as though I were a baby thirsty for milk, and he my indulgent mother.

"Right away, my sheikh," he said. "Your wish is my command."

I was very nearly unable to swallow my urge to shriek out, "Stop, man of God! Stop, assessor of both realms! In fact, it is you who are my sheikh, you who are my master!' But he who succumbs to his urges succumbs to demons. I held back. I waited.

This time the wait was longer, daylight gave way to a darkness on the horizon. Perhaps Rumi had been overcome with shame? Had he taken his reputation into consideration and decided not to buy the wine, like Sheikh Evhededdin-i Kirmani, whom I'd met years ago in Bagdad?

"With all my desire, I wish to be your slave," Sheikh Kirmani had said.

To which I had responded, "You are not even capable of enduring my friendship."

"Please. Accept my offer of servitude," he'd implored, clinging insistently to the collar of my black felt garments.

And I'd said to him, "Granted. On the condition that here, in the middle of Bagdad, in front of everyone, you drink date wine with me."

And he became yellow like a date.

"I cannot do that."

In accordance with the saying 'show them the ease with which to do it, for it is ease that lights our path', I said, "In that case, can you find and bring back date wine for me?"

"No, I cannot do that either."

And I said, "Will you keep me company while I drink?"

"No, I cannot," he had answered.

And I'd said, "Then do not try to keep company with God's soldiers. You are not the man to do so, for God has denied you this strength. Being God's soldier, you must not be concerned with the opinions of those who follow you, your pride, or your honour. You must be willing to deny them, even for one glass of wine. You are not a pilgrim on this path. Steer well clear of the company of God's soldiers."

Remembering this so-called man of God, Sheikh Kirmani, I lost hope. Perhaps my suspicions were founded? Perhaps what had happened in Bagdad would be repeated here in Konya? Like Kirmani, did Rumi also put his ego before love? As these negative thoughts cropped up, the chamber door opened once again. Rumi's shining face appeared, full of conviction, with a pitcher full to the brim with wine in his grasp.

"I am late. I apologise," he said with the sweetest smile. "I tried to find the best wine, the most delectable. The one that was most worthy to touch my sheikh's lips, teeth, and tongue..."

I could hold back no longer. The sun's time had come, the moon's time had come, the earth's time had also come.

"You are the true sheikh," I said, falling at his feet. "You are the true friend of God. I beg you to accept me as your disciple."

He immediately fell to the ground, took my hands in his, and kissed them. Tears streamed down my cheeks. He kissed those tears then pulled me to my feet, saying, "A sheikh is not one who believes, it is one who causes others to believe. Not one who explains but one who demonstrates. Not one who teaches, but one who lifts a curtain. You have lifted the curtain before my eyes. You have shown me the true essence of who I am. You are the sheikh, the master, the true friend, the truth..."

"The hands of thieves are cut off at the wrist."

✼

When I opened my eyes, Turkish raiders wielding swords, flags with three crescent moons waving above their heads, chased a Byzantine cavalcade under a flag with the Christian cross. Though it took me a minute to gather my wits about me, I finally grasped the situation. I'd fallen asleep with the TV on. I pulled myself together as the Turkish raiders bellowed the Muslim war cry, "Allah Allah Allah Allah..." The horses ran foaming at the mouth, the sound of their hooves echoing throughout the room. I was surprised how loud I'd left the volume up. I shut it off, pushing the power button on the remote still in my lap, but the noise didn't stop. It wasn't the sound of horses' hooves resounding in the room; something was pounding outside. I must have turned the volume up so loud that the other hotel guests had come to my door in the end. I got up quickly and turned on the light, spruced myself up a bit in the mirror, and went over. On the other side of the door were two men's voices. I recognised the first right away as that of the nosey receptionist.

"She's in there, I'm sure about it. She came back to the hotel close to midnight. Hold on... the volume's gone down. She must have heard us."

"She'd better have," the other voice bellowed. "I don't give a damn about customer privacy. I'll get myself a spare key and march straight in if I have to."

I cracked the door open before the receptionist's reply became necessary. In front of it stood three people. Apart from the receptionist, there was a burly man with a sputtering wireless in hand and an attractive young woman, her hair pulled back in a bun. "Police. Open up. We need to have a talk," the man snarled through the cracked door.

This I wasn't expecting. What business could the police possibly have with me? Trying to appear calm, I swung the door open wide.

"Yes, what can I do for you?"

The burly police officer kept growling.

"We've been trying to reach you for a while now, Madam."

It sounded like he was scolding me.

"Karen," I said, standing up to him. "My name is Karen Greenwood."

I kept my voice cold, distant, and confident, as if to let him know he was up against someone with whom he couldn't just behave as he pleased.

He pulled a card from his pocket and looked at it.

"Isn't there also a 'Kimya'?"

"Excuse me?"

"I said 'Kimya'. This card says Karen Kimya Greenwood. Wouldn't want to be speaking to the wrong person," he said facetiously.

"All right then. Karen Kimya Greenwood."

His weary face feigned deference.

"And I am Detective Ragip. May we please come in?" There was still sarcasm in his voice. "This is not really working, with us in front of the door like this. And we've already disturbed the other hotel guests enough as it is."

"First I'd like to know what this is about," I baulked.

"The mugging. And the things that were taken from your bag. That's what this is about," he went on, looking put out at having been asked for an explanation.

"Couldn't this have waited till morning?"

He stared at me blankly, showing no intention of answering this time. Maybe something else had happened that I didn't know about. I could have told him to wait for me downstairs, but then, what did I have to hide? "All right," I said resentfully. "But give me a minute to straighten up my room."

"You're not going to run away, are you?"

I guess he thought he was being funny. In lieu of a response, I shot him a cutting look and shut the door. My room wasn't really so messy, but I needed time to think. What could have happened that they were planted in front of my door at this ungodly hour? Maybe this was how the police did things in this country. I couldn't get my head around it, but it's all I could come up with. I straightened up my bed a bit, then picked up the trousers and jacket I'd thrown down the night before and hung them on the coat rack. Before returning to the door, I checked my face and hair in the mirror again. I looked tired. There were dark circles under my eyes, and a look of stupor on my face that I somehow couldn't manage to wipe off.

"Here you are. Come on in."

"Sorry for bothering you at this time of night," the young woman mumbled, embarrassed by Detective Ragip's having barged in like a bull at a gate.

"That's all right," I answered, feeling obliged to be polite too. "You're just doing your job."

Ragip looked over at us with interest, as if to ask what was going on.

"I forgot to introduce you," he said, still smirking. "This is Zeynep. Inspector Zeynep." He looked condescendingly at his colleague. "She's more civilised than I am. She's from Istanbul."

"Is there some new development in the case?" I asked, ignoring him.

The question was directed at Zeynep, but Ragip, not allowing her to answer, interrupted with all his vulgarity intact. With a subject that had nothing to do with my question, no less.

"Your Turkish is pretty good, Miss Greenwood. Now where did you learn to speak our language so well?"

As he said this, his eyes looked into mine for one second, then started scanning the room. I wished I hadn't let them in, but it was too late to change that now. "In London," I answered.

His face contorted with exaggerated enthusiasm.

"In London? They speak Turkish in London?"

Look at that. This boor was trying to be charming. Without letting it get to me, I explained, "My father spoke Turkish at home."

"Why? Is your father a Turkish teacher?"

"No, my father is a Turk."

"A Turk!" He chirped admiringly. Then he turned towards Zeynep, who was also looking the room over. "Did you hear that, Zeynep? Miss Greenwood is a Turk."

Zeynep didn't take too much notice of her Detective, she just kept looking around. When Ragip didn't get the reaction he'd hoped for from his colleague, he carried on speaking to me.

"How nice that you've learned our language!"

"Thank you," I grudgingly responded.

"You obviously have a knack." He was no longer looking at me, but trying to lift the lid of my unzipped suitcase with the wireless in his hand. I was about to intervene, in case he started going through my clothes, when he dropped it and spun round. "And let's give your father his due, he taught you well. I swear, you speak Turkish as good as any Turk." His expression changed as he took a step towards me. "But it was quite hard to wake you up. You sleep like a rock, Kimya!" His cigarette breath licked my face; his pale, thin lips broke into that smarmy grin again. "You don't mind me calling you Kimya, do you? For someone who speaks such good Turkish, I'm sure you would feel honoured to be called by your Turkish name."

"I suppose not. Except Kimya isn't Turkish, it's Arabic."

Zeynep giggled. Ragip threw the young woman a look, but then swallowed his irritation and turned back to me.

"Yeah, I guess you're right. So you know it's a Muslim name then, right?"

Just great. Now he was going to ask me my religion.

"It's no problem, you can call me Kimya," I relented, to cut him short. "It's what my father called me."

I wasn't sure if the approval in his eyes was genuine or not.

"Your father sounds like a good man. If all Turks living abroad were more like him, the world would be in better shape today."

Zeynep, who'd been examining the clothes on the coat rack, interrupted him with a question.

"There's mud on the sleeve of this jacket, Miss Greenwood. Were you wrestling with someone?"

"It must be from when I was mugged," I speculated. "I guess I fell when he yanked on my bag."

The explanation was good enough for Zeynep, but Ragip lunged in as though he'd caught me out on something.

"What do you mean 'I guess'? Didn't you know you fell?"

"I passed out about the same time as the power outage," I said, surprised by my own patience. "I don't remember the rest, and by the time I woke up it was all over."

"You mean you didn't see your assailant personally?"

"No, I didn't see anyone."

"Well, that's an odd state of affairs. Some man is yanking on your arm, and you don't even notice." Without giving me a chance to reply, he turned to his colleague. "What do you have to say about this, Zeynep?"

The young girl looked vacantly at her superior officer. Apparently she didn't give a damn about him.

Taking advantage of the pause, I continued my strained explanation. "Everything happened quite suddenly. I told you I passed out. Why are you even asking me these questions?"

"Stay calm. There's no need to get upset. In fact, if anyone should be getting upset, it's us. We were at your door for ages."

"Since when is exhaustion a crime?"

He looked me up and down.

"Frankly, we didn't consider your exhaustion while we were waiting at your door. You did rouse our suspicions, however. Isn't that right, Zeynep?"

Zeynep didn't reply. She'd gone into the bathroom, perhaps to escape this bore's incessant yapping.

"Really, why didn't you open the door? If we did consider you a suspect, we would assume you were trying to hide evidence."

I'd had enough. The man was all but accusing me of something.

"What suspect? What evidence?" I blurted out. "What the hell are you talking about?"

Amused by my indignation, a look of pure pleasure spread on his washed-out face.

"I'll come to the point, sweetheart. Don't get all bent out of shape."

But I had no intention of backing down.

"To begin with, I am not your sweetheart. Watch how you speak to me, please. And secondly, I'm not the criminal, remember? I'm the victim. I'm the one who was attacked, whose things were stolen..."

He wasn't listening to me. He'd just backed away a bit while I was speaking. Not because he was shying away from me, I soon realised, but because the boots at the foot of the bed had drawn his attention.

"We know," he said absently, as he examined my boots. "You were mugged. Your bag, your money, and your ring... were stolen."

"And my passport."

He stood up straight as he considered this, then turned to look at Zeynep as she came out of the bathroom.

"Was there a passport in the recovered items?"

All my tension and indignation melted away.

"What? Have you found my things?"

"We found them, all right," he said, with another artificial smile. "Three hundred seventy pounds sterling, eight hundred twenty Turkish lira, and a silver ring with a brown stone. But no passport."

There was something else he wasn't telling me.

"Maybe," said Zeynep optimistically, "...it's somewhere near the scene. The CSI Unit is still scouring the area. I'm sure they'll find it soon enough."

"Maybe..." said Detective Ragip planting himself in front of me. There was no longer any sarcasm or smugness in his expression. His look was one of outright accusation. "Or maybe you've got it."

"What? You think my passport wasn't stolen in the first place?"

"Oh, it was stolen all right. But whoever killed your assailant could have returned it to you."

"Whoever killed my assailant? What do you mean? The man who mugged me is dead?"

"Not just dead, Miss Greenwood. Murdered."

"Where did that happen?"

He gave me a strange look, as though the question were incongruous with the situation, before conversely stating, "Good question. Yes, it was unusual, where they found your assailant's body. Same exact spot where you were attacked, if you must know."

"Merej el Bahrain," I muttered impulsively. Ragip didn't take any notice, but I'd got Zeynep's attention.

"Excuse me? What did you say?"

It was my good fortune that she hadn't understood.

"I said it's interesting. That the man always bag snatches in the same spot."

Zeynep realised I was holding something back. She may have been about to jump on it, but before she could, Ragip unwittingly came to my rescue. "What bag snatching, Miss Greenwood?" he grumbled. "At three in the morning the place is completely deserted."

"You mean he was killed elsewhere then dumped there?"

Zeynep, still eyeing me narrowly, nodded slowly.

"That's what we think."

I was getting confused.

"What has any of this got to do with me?"

"We don't know." Zeynep had adopted that cold, callous expression typical of police. "We were hoping you would tell us."

"Tell you what?"

"Whatever you know."

"I gave a written statement to the police at the hospital last night."

She gave me a look as if to ask why I failed to understand.

"That was before your assailant was brutally murdered."

I felt my nervousness turning into fear.

"What do you mean by 'brutally'?"

"You don't know, do you?" said Ragip, straightening up again. "I mean, you have no clue about what went down?"

"How could I? I was asleep in my room."

He huffed in exasperation; his breath smelled terrible. He turned back to the young woman.

"Zeynep, could you please fill the lady in?"

"Of course, Chief," she said, collecting her thoughts. "It's a bit odd, Miss Greenwood. His left hand was cut off at the wrist."

"Why the left hand, do you know?" Ragip cut in, unable to hold back.

"No. I don't," I said, my eyes wide as saucers.

"Because the man was left-handed. He was one of Konya's most notorious street thieves - Lefty Kamil. Kamil Tenekeci is his real name. He was pretty good with that left hand of his."

"I don't get it," I said, not quite able to grasp the relationship between the two.

"To punish him," he said, without pausing. He was watching my face intently, so as not to miss even the smallest twitch. "It used to be that thieves' hands were chopped off at the wrist."

"It's shari'a law," Inspector Zeynep took over. But then afraid I would misunderstand, she added, "Of course, there's nothing like that here anymore."

Neither Islamic law nor this county's laws interested me in the least. I was too preoccupied with the murder.

"He bled to death?"

They looked at each other with surprise, not having expected a question like this from me. It was Zeynep who finally answered, "No, he suffocated."

"Was he strangled?"

"No. Actually, it was even more violent than that. Someone shoved his severed hand down his throat."

I pictured a face with bulging eyes and a hand in its mouth with the wrist sticking out. The image was horrific, but it didn't cloud the question in my mind.

"Wouldn't that be a bit difficult? How exactly would a human hand fit into a mouth?"

"We don't know that yet," Ragip said, shaking his large head. "The body is at forensics. We won't have those answers till tomorrow."

"So then they must have definitely killed the man somewhere else."

"Like I said, that's what we suspect," Zeynep reiterated. "The only blood was on the victim. Not one drop in the surrounding area."

"That must have required some serious expertise on the part of the perpetrator."

Ragip's beady, chestnut-coloured eyes looked into mine with exaggerated admiration. "You never cease to amaze me, Miss Greenwood."

"Why? What have I done?"

"You've started to talk our talk. Isn't that right, Zeynep?" he called out to his colleague again.

"That it is, Chief." Her full lips broke into a sardonic smile. "Miss Greenwood is thinking analytically."

Ragip gave Zeynep a funny look. I don't think he fully understood what was meant by 'thinking analytically', but I took it as a compliment.

"In a way, my job is not so different from yours." I said. "I'm an insurance expert. Like you, I also sometimes have to come up with a solution to some unexplained event. Like it or not, I start thinking like police. Thus the 'expertly perpetrated' comment. This murder obviously took some planning."

"Hmm," said Ragip, leaning against the wall. "In what way did it take some planning?"

"Because, well, you have to catch the man, cut off his hand and shove it into his mouth, then move the body to another location. Sounds like the work of more than one person to me."

With his back against the wall and his eyes still on me, he picked up where I left off.

"Couldn't it be revenge? A few years back in Ankara, some unfortunate mugger physically assaulted an on-duty, female, plainclothes police officer. She went mental and emptied all her bullets into the guy."

Both Zeynep and I had the same wry smile now, as we listened to her superior officer. But Ragip had got carried away and continued to expound on his theory.

"In situations like these, people can easily lose control. I mean, even you..."

This was too much.

"Now what are you saying?" I barked. "Are you implying that I went crazy and killed a man for stealing my bag? And on top of that, cut off his left hand in accordance with shari'a law and shoved it down his throat?"

He gently batted his tired eyelids.

"All right, let's say you're right. It would be ridiculous, as well as impossible, for you to pull that off. But what if someone you know killed him?"

"I don't know anyone in Konya."

"Mennan... You know, the man who was with you at the hospital..."

"Huh? You've got to be kidding. I just met him yesterday. You think our Konya branch agent is going to kill a mugger for me? And working meticulously like a serial killer?"

Zeynep could contain herself no longer and started to chuckle quietly, but Ragip didn't take it to heart.

"What about your father?" he mumbled. "Your father is Konyan. Where is he now?"

"I have no idea. I haven't seen him since he left us about twenty years ago."

"What?" He looked sincerely disillusioned. "Your father? You mean the one who raised you according to Turkish tradition?"

"I didn't say that. I just said he taught me Turkish."

"Okay, whatever. But you mean that man left you when you were just a little girl? Really?"

I wanted to ask him what concern it was of his, but then choosing not to drag it out, just bluntly replied, "Yes, really. That's life."

"So tell me, where is he now?"

He spit out the question as though he were asking about a cold hard killer.

"I don't know. And I don't care. More importantly, he also doesn't know I am in Konya. And even if he did, he's not the kind to go around killing people. He's more of a turn the other cheek sort of person."

My speech had no effect on him.

"Abandoning his daughter, when she's just little..." He caught me frowning at him and felt he should explain. "I know this is a family matter, but I also have daughters, don't I, Zeynep? I mean, what kind of man..."

Zeynep sensed the subject was making me uncomfortable, but instead of speaking up, she just shrugged her shoulders and raised her eyebrows as if to say there was nothing to be done about it. Ragip didn't seem appeased, however.

"I fuss over my daughters all the time, I don't want one hair on their heads harmed. I swear, even on nights like this when I'm on duty, my mind stays at home. I mean, a girl's father..."

He was really quite upset, Ragip. Frankly, I wouldn't have expected this strong a reaction from such a hardened police officer.

"Never mind," I said, trying to calm him down. "That was a long time ago."

"Still, I'm sorry to hear it." His tired face was consumed with sadness. "But you're right; never mind him. A father like that is not worth getting upset about. He blinked, then went back to his old self. "Let's get back to work. What did you do after leaving the hospital? Tell me and we'll wrap this up. We've already read about what happened up till then in your statement."

"I didn't do anything. After checking out, Mennan gave me a lift back here. I came up and got into bed. I wanted to watch a bit of TV, but I fell asleep. And then, well, you came."

"Didn't you talk to anyone?"

"My mother called me from London. I didn't tell her about my encounter with the mugger for fear she may fly over here and shove his hand down his throat."

It was my turn to make fun, but he wasn't enjoying himself anymore.

"I understand," he said bleakly, putting an end to the conversation. "Come by the station later today and pick up your things. And you'll have to put what you've told us in writing."

He walked towards the door, signaling to Zeynep with his wireless that she should follow. When he got to the door, he turned round. He still had that weary look on his face.

"Sorry to have bothered you. But if you really do think like us, you'll understand that it's our duty."

"It's not a problem," I said, surprised at how tolerant I was now being. "If you want to do me a favour, just find my passport, that's all."

"... I think I know who committed the murder."

※

Getting caught up in a murder investigation on top of everything else was all I needed, but there you go. This was some coincidence, given that the man who had stolen my bag was murdered and the body found in the very place he'd jumped me. There was more than enough there to warrant Chief Ragip's suspicion. I wondered about Mennan. They'd most certainly knocked on his door as well, maybe even taken the poor guy down to the station. Though there were witnesses to my whereabouts, Mennan had only his family to vouch for him, and I wasn't sure they'd be considered viable witnesses. I thought about ringing the station to see if he was there, but knew it would only add to Chief Ragip's suspicions.

I opened the curtains a bit and looked outside. It was starting to grow light, a red glow was slowly taking hold of the sky beyond Mevlana's Mausoleum. Just then the morning call to prayer began. The muezzin was reciting it beautifully, his voice was truly moving. I stepped out onto the balcony to listen for a bit. Though I didn't know what the words meant, I felt saddened nonetheless. There was something about it that swept one up in its melancholy. My attention shifted to the flow of people heading towards Sultan Selim Mosque for morning prayers. There was not one woman among them, only men. I watched as a few of them performed the Muslim ablutions at the fountain in front of the mosque. One of them wore black. Chills ran up my spine as I thought perhaps it was Shams and he'd been watching me. His head was turned so that I only had a side view of his face, but I couldn't really see clearly anyhow because it wasn't yet completely light out. I focused all my attention on him as he got up and put on the jacket he'd kept slung over his shoulders while washing his hands. As he turned to look back over his shoulder, I braced myself. But no, it wasn't Shams after all. The man had no beard and was every bit as chubby as Mennan. I guess I'd just let panic take hold of me again. Our psychologist, Oliver, would call this a symptom of my neurosis if he were to hear about it.

I watched as the red glow beyond Mevlana's tomb got even brighter. The sun was rising fast; it wasn't long before its golden rays started playing off the green curves of the tomb. As it shone from behind the clouds, I suddenly thought of my imaginary childhood friend, Sunny. With his curly blond hair and wide blue eyes, he was the invisible playmate I'd created for all my games. I'd considered him a weak child, a boy forever in need of my help. I would feed him, put him to sleep, and look after him when he was ill. Apart from my mum and dad, he was practically the only one I ever spoke to. My father never could understand my devotion to this imaginary friend. He found the whole thing abnormal. So much so, in fact, that he began to worry it pointed to a deeper problem, one that would require therapy. In fact, years later, my mother admitted it had been the source of arguments.

"Your father was concerned. Even while sitting with us, you would be chatting away with this imaginary boy you called Sunny. You went so far as to quarrel with him in your room and sing him lullabies to put him to sleep. But plenty of people would have said that was perfectly normal, acceptable behavior. There were even pedagogues at the time who claimed it was healthy, and that it signified a strong imagination. Your father, however, had a hard time understanding that and was convinced there was more to it. He kept saying we should take you to a doctor, despite my maintaining it wasn't necessary. You were just trying to establish a relationship with the world, trying to give meaning to your existence, and I told him so. He asked how it would give meaning to your existence, talking day and night to a child who wasn't real.

Then one day I got tired of it, and decided to have a bit of fun with him, so I asked, 'How do you know he's not real?'

"'Real?' he said. 'What, have you seen him now, too?'

"I suggested that it might be God appearing to you as a child. Reminded him that he was the one who always said God can only be seen by the most pure and innocent. When he gave me a skeptical look, I asked him, 'Why not? Isn't that what you're doing? Trying to curb the desires of your mind and body in order to regain that state of innocence and find God? And in doing so, aren't you also in some way struggling to become a child? Well, your daughter is a child right now, so you should accept the possibility that God is communicating with her.'

She took a deep breath before continuing.

"But then he started getting defensive. He asked me what possible motivation God would have to communicate with you. So I again used his own words, that God approaches those who are really in need of him, and that, well, maybe you really needed him. But what I said was beyond him. He still didn't agree, and repeated that we ought to get you some help. I was losing my patience. I asked him why, when day and night he talked to, pleaded with even, some celestial being who had never put in a physical appearance or uttered so much as a single audible word, why that didn't signify a psychological problem for him, but it did for you. He gave me one of his looks, like I was oblivious, and asked, 'What are you implying, Susan? That Kimya's inventing an invisible friend is on par with my praying to God?'

"I wasn't going to back down. I looked him straight in the eye and with that cool, collected manner of mine that drove him crazy, answered, 'I don't know. But neither do you.' Of course he said it wasn't that simple. That I cannot compare God to a child's imaginary friend, and so on. So with the most self-assured smile I could muster, I told him something to the effect of 'I can and I will.' Then I went on to tell him that in my opinion the two were very similar. There was absolutely no difference between his conversations with God and yours with Sunny. They were both harmless, both naive. Both just a search for meaning, or for a solution to your loneliness, perhaps.

"Your father couldn't take it anymore. 'You cannot judge people's beliefs like this,' he said. 'Faith is not something that can be explained away.' He looked at me as though he pitied me for thinking it could. He told me, 'Think what you like on the subject of belief, but if Karen has problems later in life, don't forget I warned you.' Then he marched off to his room and started blowing on that ney of his. But after that day he never brought up the subject again. And you forgot all about Sunny when you started school."

It wasn't that I'd immediately forgotten about him, though. In school, I'd shared a desk with a boy named Tony. He also had blond hair, though his wasn't curly, nor were his eyes blue. His hair was straight and fine, his green eyes barely visible under languid lids. I must have replaced my imaginary friend with him, after he irritably warned me a few times, "Stop calling me Sunny, Karen. My name is Tony."

Tony had also been my first kiss, I recalled now. We'd put our lips together timidly, not knowing what we were doing. Much later, Tony went on to study at the Vatican and became a priest. Then two years ago we heard he'd died. He'd been bitten by a monitor lizard in the Galapagos Islands while searching for evidence that would help him to put a hole in Darwin's theory of evolution. Although the lizard wasn't poisonous, the open wound from the bite got infected and poor Tony died of gangrene, after which his body was laid to rest near the Vatican. The news had made me quite sad, though my mother dismissed it as 'the curse of Darwin'. And she wasn't joking, she meant it.

I never remembered Sunny, though, not even then. What disloyalty! Whereas when I had no other friends, it was he who helped me overcome my loneliness. I'd shared all my childhood secrets with him. Frankly, I couldn't remember any of my conversations with Sunny, they eluded me; but I knew he'd made me feel happy, safe, and free. How easy life would be if I still had a friend like that now, I thought. But in real life, no actual person would ever show such servile devotion.

Then again, what about Rumi? Hadn't he tried to fulfill all of Shams's wishes with no objections, no complaints, and no

180

regard for his honour? Why had he been so accepting? And what kind of love was this, anyway - that the person you are with feels the need to constantly test you? It went beyond just testing, Shams had expected Rumi to give up the people he loved most. But had he really? If Shams's intentions had been that bad, would Rumi's wife and son have stayed with them after everything he did?

The similarities between my father and Shah Nesim's relationship, and that of Rumi and Shams, was uncanny. Perhaps my father's relationship had been influenced by theirs. Influenced by? Or would it be more apt to say modeled on? Perhaps it was some kind of religious tradition. I'd have to remember to ask Ziya's father about it when we met. İzzet had been my father's friend, and they were raised in the same lodge, so nobody would know better than him.

My phone rang, interrupting my thoughts. Wondering whether it was the police again, I quickly picked up.

"Hello?"

"Hello, Miss Greenwood... Is that you?"

Though the voice was muffled, I recognised it as Mennan's.

"Hi, Mr. Fidan. Yes, it's me. Go on..."

"Have the police left yet?"

He was whispering as though afraid someone were listening in.

"Yes, they're gone. How did you know they were here?"

"Because they came to us first. That officer, Ragip, was treating me like a criminal. He said he was going to pay you a visit next. But no matter how much I insisted they save the conversation with you till morning, he wouldn't listen."

Mennan was excited. He was blurting out everything in one breath.

"Never mind," I said, trying to calm him down. "I've answered all their questions and it's settled now. Though I do find it odd that the guy who stole my bag was murdered."

"It's strange all right, Miss Greenwood."

His voice had become thinner and shriller.

"Not only that, but the body was found right where my bag was stolen."

"Merej el-Bahrain," he breathed, his voice shaking as though the words held some magic. "The place where two seas meet."

Was it his pointless fear overtaking him again, or did he know something?

"Yes. What a coincidence, huh?" I repeated, hoping he'd share whatever was going through his mind.

"Coincidence? The man who steals your things is murdered and his body is dumped in the exact place you were attacked? What kind of coincidence is that?"

His words were beginning to make me come unhinged. To cover up my stress, I joked, "You sound like Chief Ragip, Mr. Fidan. If this keeps up, you'll also be you accusing me of murder soon."

"Nonsense. Don't say such a thing. I would never accuse you of anything."

"I know, I know," I said. "Seriously though, why are you calling?"

"For um... well, I was going to tell you..." His voice was so quiet I was having difficulty hearing him.

"Could you speak up a bit? I can't understand what you're saying."

"Of course." He was so nervous that his incessant swallowing was audible. "Miss Greenwood, I think I know who murdered that man."

I couldn't quite grasp what he'd said.

"You know?" I repeated, without thinking.

"Yes."

"Are you aware of what you are saying, Mr. Fidan?"

"Quite aware. We have to talk right away."

I got chills. He seemed so sure of himself. Maybe it'd been Ziya who was behind all this after all. Mennan was regretting his part in it and wanted to come clean.

"So then, who killed him?" I pressed.

"Not so loud, please..." he said lowering his voice again. He paused. "I can't tell you over the phone."

"Where are you now?"

"Near the hotel."

"Okay, I'll meet you in the lobby in five minutes," I answered without thinking.

"In the Mevlevi faith, people don't die, they just go silent."

※

Mennan was waiting for me perched on the edge of one of the big armchairs in the most secluded corner of the lobby, looking white as a sheet. I watched as he gave a nervous, sidelong glance to the door as though he were being followed. What was it with this poor guy? As I started over to meet my colleague, the receptionist gave a nod in greeting. He rubbed his sleepy eyes, no doubt preparing himself to eavesdrop on our conversation. I changed route, walking straight for him instead. When he realised I was advancing on him, he tried to pull himself together. He must have thought I was going to blame him for what had happened that night, because he got all flustered, upsetting a penholder on the desk and sending all the pens rolling to the floor. I bent down to pick up a black ballpoint that had rolled to a halt at my feet, and by the time I'd straightened up again he was at my side.

"Shouldn't have troubled yourself, Miss Greenwood. I would have got it."

"It's not a problem," I said, holding out the pen. "Could we get some tea, please?"

"Tea?" I could see him wondering where in the world this idea for tea had come from at this ungodly hour. Ignoring his long face, I continued, "And it would be nice if we could have some biscuits or something to go with it."

"Tea and biscuits..." he repeated glumly, as though it were the end of the world.

"And could you check that they aren't stale? If there are no fresh ones, then packaged ones will do."

"Sure," he reluctantly droned. "But the kitchen staff are all sleeping. I mean, I'll have to do it myself."

His eyes were imploring, as though hoping I'd say, "Oh really? Never mind then." But of course I didn't indulge him. I just smiled and said, "Thank you, I'd be grateful. Oh and, speaking of which, please don't forget I take my tea with milk."

"Certainly..." His face now wore a deep frown. "I won't forget."

I left him to pick up the scattered pens and headed towards Mennan again. He was standing now; he must have got up from his chair as soon as he'd seen me. In his hand, he held a thick, leather-bound book. What on earth, I wondered? Has he brought a Qur'an with him? Maybe he didn't know anything after all. If what he had to say came down to this book, I really had got all worked up over nothing.

His expression was apologetic. And was it my imagination or was the man trembling? I wanted to help him compose himself, so I smiled at him and put out my hand.

"Hello again, Mr. Fidan." He didn't make a peep, just gripped my hand weakly. "Let's sit down. I've ordered tea, and something to nibble on..." He seemed surprised by my poise. He couldn't make sense of what I was saying, but he sat down regardless.

"What? Oh, thank you..." he said, as he suddenly understood. His eyes were twitching impatiently like he wanted to get straight to the point. Actually, I too was quite impatient to hear what he had to say. I glanced down at the book in his lap, which he clutched as though it were some kind of priceless gem.

"Is that the Qur'an?" I asked, trying to read what was written on its cover.

He looked down.

"No. It's *Ariflerin Menkibeleri - The Feats of the Knowers of God*." Seeing the puzzled look in my eyes, he explained, "It tells of the life and times of Rumi. And the people around him, too, of course."

The people around Rumi. So the book would have plenty to say about Shams. We'd come back round to him again; I knew Mennan couldn't have brought this book down here for nothing.

"Who's the author?"

"A Sufi mystic by the name of Ahmed Eflaki."

I didn't recognise the name. If he were that important, my father would most certainly have read his books, and probably would have talked about them. I guess, like everything else he'd told me, it must have wilted away in the poorly lit gardens of my mind.

"Was Eflaki one of those people around him?"

"No. The book was written much later, based on what was recounted by Rumi's grandson, Ulu Arif Çelebi."

"Rumi's genuine grandson?"

"Of course. Bahaeddin Veled's son. Actually, it is said that Eflaki met Sultan Veled in the flesh, too."

Sultan Veled must have been that deferential boy who had referred to Shams as 'my sheikh'. So then what about the angry, rebellious one I'd seen with Kimya? "Rumi had another son too, didn't he? A bit younger than Sultan Veled?"

His expression grew dark.

"You're probably talking about his middle son, Alaeddin. He didn't have such a good reputation as the rest of his family."

Funny. Shams hadn't been too thrilled with him either, I remembered.

"Why was that?"

"No one knows for sure. They say he had a terrible temper. There were problems between him and Shams. Rumours that he'd behaved inappropriately with Shams's wife, Kimya..."

In the dream I'd had, Alaeddin and Kimya had seemed quite warm with each other. It was the dervish in black who was cold and aloof. Sure, Alaeddin had managed to rile him, but it wasn't as if Shams had seemed the least bit interested in Kimya. It was time to get to the point. "So, what does this book have to do with the murder?"

He looked down again and swallowed hard.

"On it's own, not a thing," he said, lifting his shaking hand from the bound cover. "But the contents of this book, together with what we've been through..."

Just as I'd predicted, Mennan didn't know the first thing about any murderer. He was just going to reel off a few more of his stories. I leaned back, disappointed. "Don't tell me. You put two and two together, and suddenly came up with the murderer."

He was so worked up, he didn't even notice I was being facetious.

"Yes," he said passionately. "I figured it out with the help of this book."

I knew it was ridiculous, but I took the bait.

"So? Who is it?" I asked impatiently.

He didn't immediately answer, but instead whispered, *"Euzubillahi minesseytanirraim,"* before looking back and forth as though being watched by some invisible presence. I only managed to pick one word out of the string – Satan. It must have been a protective prayer. Though his behavior was irrational, comical even, he was going about it all so seriously that a part of me felt apprehensive despite myself. Convinced the djinn and demons had been exorcised, he leaned in close.

"The murderer is Shams," he said, his voice a mix of fear and respect.

I felt my heartbeat quicken. His fear was contagious. What was wrong with me? Was I really falling for this absurd talk? Who was I now - my mother's daughter, Karen, forever trying to weigh events in a logical manner? Or my father's daughter, Kimya, seeking out meaning in the light of those mystical events? The former seemed more appealing right now, which was why, to buy myself time to think, I asked, "Shams? You mean Rumi's soulmate, Shams?"

"None other," he said, the expression in his eyes bordering terror. "The holy Shams-i Tabriz, may he rest in peace."

My expression was one of disbelief, slight condescension even.

"Please be rational, Mr. Fidan," I implored, though I was cautioning myself more than anything. The words had no effect on Mennan, who looked at me as though I were the naive one. I ignored him and finished what I was saying.

"Try to be sensible. What you are talking about only happens in fairy tales and horror films. Dreaming up a fantasy villain based on someone who's been dead for seven hundred years is not going to help solve this murder case."

"There are things you don't know, Miss Greenwood," he said, as though he pitied me. "In the Mevlevi faith, people don't die, they just go silent. The dead are just people who hold their tongues as they continue to live among us. When it comes to men of God who have unraveled great mysteries, like Shams, by the time the harbinger of Armageddon, the Archangel Israfil, has blown his trumpet, who knows how many times they will have appeared among us. They break their silence, speaking to those they favour." He stared at me, wide-eyed, then raised his voice. "Do you understand what I'm saying, Miss Greenwood? The holy Shams is trying to help you."

He was putting into words something that had been in the back of my mind for a while now. Ever since it had occurred to me that it was Shams who had given me the ring.

"That's absurd," I objected. Though my mind kept resisting, a shiver passed through my body. "But for argument's sake, let's say that by some miracle your Shams has come back from the dead, or 'broken his silence' as you put it, to intervene in worldly affairs. Can you tell me, exactly how would killing that bag snatcher be of any help to me? More importantly, why would a dervish of such high spiritual standing take any life at all, even that of a thief?"

"In the beginning, I felt the same," he said, patting the book. He lowered his voice again. "For instance, His Holiness Mevlana wouldn't hurt a fly. He would never say a bad word against anyone, not the vilest person you can imagine, let alone raise a hand against them. He preferred to just avoid those types. As for Shams though, that's another story."

I remembered what Shams had said. "I was never duplicitous with him. I presented him with both good side and bad so that he may know me." Then I immediately chased his voice from my head. Mennan was still wholly absorbed in what he was saying, unaware of all that was going through my mind. He believed in it so much that his eyes were almost teary. Maybe he was regressing to his days as a superstitious, young student at the *imam hatip* high school.

"It's all in this book. One of the titles Shams was known by was *Seyfullah*, meaning 'Allah's Sword', because he never forgave anyone who slighted himself or his loved ones."

He cracked open the book with his stubby fingers.

"Look, it says here, 'some of the wise elders would call him *Seyfullah*, because whosoever should cause him injury, he would either kill them, or open a wound in their soul.'"

"That hardly proves he's our bag snatcher's murderer."

He shook his head as if wondering why I failed to understand.

"Shams-i Tabriz was anything but your average dervish. Let me share a few of the stories from this book with you: One day, Shams came to Aksaray from Kayseri, where he put up in a small mosque. After calling the faithful to evening prayers from the minaret, the muezzin brazenly attempted to toss Shams out. 'Be gone from here. Seek your lodging elsewhere,' he'd said.

"Shams tried to persuade the man. 'I beg your indulgence. I am a stranger to these parts, I know no one. Allow me to take my rest in peace here,' he implored. But the muezzin pushed the matter to the point of impertinence, hurling down insults on Shams. The holy Shams got up and left the mosque. But as he did, he turned to the muezzin, uttering, 'May your tongue swell up.'

"All at once the muezzin's tongue began to swell. His Holiness Shams headed back for Konya without a second thought. Meanwhile, the imam had come to the mosque and found the muezzin rolling on the floor in agony. 'What is this? What's come over you?' the imam asked.

"To which the muezzin choked, 'It's that wandering dervish who has put me in this state. Quick! Go and find him, or I will surely die.' The imam set off at once and caught up with Shams near Kulkul Suyu. He went down on his knees before the mighty dervish and groveled. 'Have mercy. That wretch could not know how great a man you are. I beg you to pardon him.'

"He pleaded and begged forgiveness, but Shams shook his head. 'The die is cast and judgment has been handed down. I can do nothing now but offer a prayer that he dies a believer and is not tormented in the afterlife.'

The imam understood at once that Shams was a tenacious enough sort to not back down on his word. He believed him, and immediately became his disciple. Returning to the mosque, he found that the poor muezzin had long since suffocated and gone to meet his Maker."

I couldn't understand what Mennan was trying to prove with this debatably unauthentic account.

"Do you actually believe these stories?" I asked.

With the unshakable conviction of one who truly believe in miracles, he explained, "It's not a story. These things really happened. Ahmed Eflaki Dede just wrote it down, drawing from sources among which were Mevlana's own writings, as well as Sultan Veled's accounts and the testimonies of other people who lived during that era. Okay, maybe he embellished a bit, but that is just one of innumerable stories of Shams's greatness. For example," he said, flipping pages, "there was an incident that took place in Bagdad..."

Without asking whether or not I wanted to hear it, he gushed, "One day Shams was passing by the palace gates in Bagdad. He heard music and went inside to listen. When the lord of the palace saw him, he commanded his slave, 'Strike this dervish and be gone with him.' Drawing his sword, the slave made to attack Shams, but he couldn't bring down the hand he'd raised because his arm was paralysed. The lord commanded another slave to strike him. But the arm he raised against Shams also froze. Shams then left the palace. The lord sent his soldiers after him, but nobody could catch him. Within two days, the lord of the palace was dead and gone."

Mennan's face shone with agitation. The beads of sweat on his forehead, the light in his eyes, the fever in his cheeks, the parting of his lips, all of them indicated that Mennan believed heart and soul in everything he was saying. Fortunately, I'd conquered my fears as he was telling the story and my mind was back in control of my body.

"Sorry, Mr. Fidan, but nothing you've said supports your claim that Shams has come forward seven centuries to commit murder."

After looking around as though about to divulge another valuable secret, he whispered, "It wasn't about murder. Shams came back to protect you."

Another wave of consternation swept over me. Mennan went quiet, waiting for me to grasp what he'd said.

"You have to appreciate what that means," he began again, his voice a bit louder. "Thousands of people here in Konya would give their right arm for an opportunity like this. But he came right up to you. Don't back away. Let Shams help you."

He wasn't being offensive, and he certainly meant no disrespect, but I was annoyed nonetheless.

"I don't really need any help," I said, trying to sound complacent. "Unless he can tell us whether the fire in the hotel was an accident or arson."

I heard Shams's voice in my head again. "It is not truth you seek in that fire of rampaging demons, it's money. But the truth is far more valuable than money."

As though Mennan had also heard it, he proclaimed, "Shams's truth is far greater than the fact of who started any fire. I don't know what it is he wants to help you with, but getting a flat tyre right in front of Shams's Mausoleum was no coincidence. Nor was his giving you the ring." His eyes flickered. The sweat on his forehead was about to trickle down between his eyebrows onto his face, but he ignored it and carried on. "And no, Miss Greenwood, it wasn't dye running off that ring. I'm quite certain it was blood. It was not mere coincidence that they cut off that guy's left hand and shoved it down his throat, either. The thief also stole the ring Shams gave you. Not only that, he did it in the same exact place Shams and Rumi first met. Can you imagine any greater sacrilege? You think His Holiness Shams would turn a blind eye? As it says in the Maide verse of the Qur'an, 'As to a thief - man or woman - such restrictions should be imposed on them which render them incapable of committing such crime.' Punishment is every bit as much his right as reward."

It was a persuasive argument. But although he'd strung the events together quite cleverly, the basis of his theory was illusory. It had no foot in reality, so I felt I had to debate with him.

"Let's assume all that is true. Let's say a seven hundred-year-old dervish is trying to help me. You still haven't explained what possible motivation he could have. What am I to him? I only just came here two days ago. And I'm not even Muslim."

"Your father is Poyraz Efendi. He is Mevlevi. A man on the path to God. Then again, he left the dervish lodge and went away to London and we don't know what happened after that but..."

Unbelievable. On top of everything else, he was now making insinuations?

"My father has nothing to do with this."

The words spilled out of my mouth, sharp and angry. Mennan couldn't possibly not have noticed, though he was so caught up in things, he had the audacity to keep trying to convince me.

"But in order to understand what happened..."

"That's enough," I ordered. "Leave my father out of this."

There was a long pause.

"I'm sorry. I didn't mean to offend you," he said softly, trying to figure out where he'd gone wrong.

"How could I not be?" I rebuked. "I've spent the better part of my morning listening to your ridiculous ghost stories without so much as a peep, but it ends here. You have no right to drag my family into this. He's my father. Where do you get off talking about someone you don't even know?"

He was speechless. He swallowed hard, before finding his voice. "I'm sorry, it wasn't my intention to defame your father, or to upset you."

"But you have," I said irreconcilably. His bringing up my father really had rubbed me the wrong way. But what made me even crazier was his dragging my nightmares into daytime in order to advance his theories. His prophesying that my fears would turn out to have a basis in reality.

"You," I accused him, "are presenting things you wish were true as facts. Look here, Mr. Fidan. I respect people's beliefs, so long as they are not rammed down other people's throats. But what happened has nothing to do with Shams, it couldn't possibly. And don't you dare talk like this around the police. They'll think you're mad."

He was about to protest again but at that moment the receptionist reappeared with a tea tray in his hands and a sullen expression on his face. As soon as Mennan saw him, he clammed up. There was nothing left for him to say, anyway. He knew he could no longer convince me. Lowering his head, he respectfully closed the seven hundred-year-old book in his lap.

"Make no mistake, the verdict is his..."

※

When I got back to my room, it was still dark out. The sun had not yet emerged from behind the wispy clouds. Mennan, after proposing stopping by police headquarters at ten, had finally gone. If I'd left it up to him, we would have spent the next four hours debating on the subject of Shams. He hated missing out on this opportunity. The miracle he'd read and heard about from various sources over the years, though never managing to witness personally, had suddenly materialised along with his guest from London. He must have believed this heart and soul, otherwise why would he go searching all night long for a very real murderer among the pages of a seven-century-old book, like some kind of psychic detective. He must have started reading *Ariflerin Menkibeleri* just as soon as he got home. He would have been interrupted by Detective Ragip's visit, then unable to get his emotions in check, had called me the second they'd left. There was no saying how unhappy he must be now. "Go home and sleep," I'd said, but my words had most likely fallen on deaf ears. He probably went straight back to his office to start poking around for new evidence in the pages of the book, perhaps even consulting other sources to back up his theory. I couldn't get over that crazy look in his bloodshot eyes. At the very least the poor man should be trying to hang on to his sanity...

Then again, look who was talking. At least he was reading history in the pages of a book. I, on the other hand, was experiencing it firsthand in my dreams. I had to get a grip, and accept that all this had been nothing more than a string of coincidences. And if Mennan weren't so obsessed with his religious stories, he might have at least recognised the possibility that Ikonion Tourism had been behind the previous night's incident. Now that was a solid theory. A foreign insurance expert is attacked in a city she's unfamiliar with, the aim being to frighten her. To keep her from digging deeper into the prospect of a fire being arson, ensuring that she made her own safety a priority over her company's potential losses and returned to her country without delay. Though I still didn't know the story behind the new Mercedes, I was fairly convinced now that Mennan himself didn't have a hand in any such plan.

I thought about what he'd said about Shams. Even Ahmed Eflaki, himself a Mevlevi, had had some pretty surprising things to say about him. Could Shams really have been that cruel? I guess we'd never really know. The author's accounts had been based not on his own experiences, but on second, or even thirdhand accounts. And naturally his writings would also have been prejudiced by his own feelings on the subject. It would be impossible to separate fact from fiction.

Shams had played such an important role in Mevlana's life, I couldn't help but find it significant that he wasn't buried in the same mausoleum. It looked as if this dervish, though closer to Rumi than his own family, had been driven away by someone hoping to pretend he never existed. What's more, the green dome of Rumi's mausoleum was so obviously revered as a work of art, beside which, the humble mosque and mausoleum where Shams lay buried crouched as though forgotten among the neighborhood's taller, banal buildings. Why had they done that to him? Had he been guilty of some reprehensible act in the final days of his life? Had he hurt someone in Rumi's family? I had so many unanswered questions about the man, not least of which was how he had died in the first place. By what means, exactly, had the life of this fascinating person come to an end? I was annoyed as I remembered this was the second time I'd asked myself that question, when getting an answer would be as easy as turning on my computer and allowing the virtual genie that is Google to provide its instantaneous answer. But right now, I couldn't muster the energy. I looked over at the clock. It was just twenty-three past six. I glanced over at my hastily made bed, but although I knew I needed the sleep, I didn't feel like lying down in it. My head was throbbing, my neck ached, and my eyes burned. Thinking a warm bath would do me good, I went into the bathroom. The tub was nothing to write home about, but it would do. I turned on the hot and cold taps, then after adjusting the temperature to my liking, left them to fill the tub. As I was removing my trousers, I noticed a bruise on my left thigh near my hip bone. I poked it and a deep pain shot through my body. Trying to be gentle, I turned to look at my back in the mirror. There were a few of scratches, but nothing serious. I'd got off easy. If I'd fallen any harder, I could have hit my head and got a concussion. I turned round and looked down at my belly. And of course I could have lost the baby, I thought. But there had been no bleeding or pain. I placed my hands on my belly. There was no movement, nor any sensation indicating the existence of life there, either, but I knew the baby was there. For the first time, I wondered what it would be like. I knew the child would be a good person. We would raise it to be one of the few good people on this god-forsaken earth. But how could I be so sure? It could just as easily turn out to be one of those egomaniacs my mother so despised. A snob, or someone with no tolerance for the opinions of others, thinking they were the centre of the universe. One of those primitive types with stunted empathy that appeared in human form. What was I thinking? Most expectant mothers wouldn't be wondering beyond whether the child was a boy or a girl at this point... Whatever it was that made this brain of mine tick, I was definitely my mother's daughter.

So then, was it a boy or a girl? Would it look like me, or Nigel? A baby with a dark complexion - my mother would be over the moon. Or it may be white like me; who could say? To get these answers, I would first have to decide to give birth. But it wasn't my decision alone to make, I'd have to let Nigel have his say. On second thought, he already had. He'd said he didn't want it, and I'd gone along like a sheep. Or kept my opinion to myself, at least. That, I rationalised, was because I hadn't yet formed an opinion. And it would have to stay on the back burner for the time being, because what I should really be concentrating on was writing my report so I could get out of here.

The tub was more than half full. I touched the water. It was just how I wanted it, not too hot, not too cold. I jumped in and stretched out the length of the tub. The warm water felt great. A deep feeling of relief swept over me from the tips of my fingers and toes to my scalp. I remembered how I used to climb into the tub with my mother when I was little. Our tub, which was big enough for three people, had been specially built by my grandfather, Ken, long before home jacuzzis were even heard of. My mother would throw in everything – lavender, lime blossom, daphne... even grasses, leaves, and roots collected from the outdoors – and after lighting candles and incense, she would turn out all the lights, transforming our bathroom into a room of ancient tribal ritual. Sometimes, she herself would laugh at her efforts. Other times, she would set out to explain. "Water relaxes us, because it is from water that all life springs. With it, we return to our origins, to our mothers' embrace. This is a rite of celebration for that return." I would watch my mother's long, strawberry blonde hair spreading out in the water, with wonder and great respect, as though watching a goddess. No matter how many thousands of kilometres away my mother was at this moment, just thinking about her made me feel safe, and as peaceful and contented as a child in its mother's lap. The warm water was absorbing all my aches and pains; my mind was sliding gently into sweet numbness. A song played round my mind, a piece by a Native American jazz composer called "The Young Mountain Wind's First Jaunt in the Garden". Through the eyes of the wind, it explained seeing a garden for the first time, it's trees, flowers, and grasses. I closed my eyes and imagined myself as that wind. It was like mounting the wind's pellucid wings as a flower spore, drifting in among the trees. I was passing among the varied tones of the green leaves of poplars, oaks, and chestnuts. A moist, warm mist licked my face. As I neared the ground, a delightful surprise awaited me. Before my eyes were yellow, pink, purple, red, and white chrysanthemums, hydrangeas, and violets, all so delicate their beauty made my head spin. Then I noticed the turtle slowly making its way through the fresh grass. As I drew closer to it, I recognised the picture of a daisy on the right side of its shell, and the peace symbol on its left. It was Cornelius, the turtle my grandfather had given my mother when she was eight years old to keep her company. My mother had painted the peace symbol after she'd returned from her trip to the Orient where she'd met my father. And I had drawn the daisy on its right side sometime before my father left us. But hadn't Cornelius died? Didn't my mother bury him under the massive plane tree in our garden? I leaned down to pet the hard shell of this aged turtle, one of the oldest members of our family. As though he could feel my hand, he stuck out his funny head to say hello. At the same time, a familiar voice rang in my ears, chanting a nursery rhyme I recognised from long ago.

Hu hu hu dervish
The dervish opened a dervish lodge
His skirts they scattered secrets
Although no one knew about it

Hu hu hu dervish
His head it reached the sky above
His beard it brushed upon the ground
His lips they scattered secrets
Although no one could hear them...

It was the nursery rhyme my father used to say to put me to sleep as a baby, like a lullaby. My mother said I never forgot it. That right up till primary school I had murmured it to my dolls to put them to sleep. But who was this now? I turned to look in the direction of the voice. Two eyes, blue as a cloudless sky, met mine. Curly blonde hair shone in the morning sun.

"Sunny," I whispered. "Is it really you?"

"It's me," he said, without batting an eye. "Did you think I'd forgotten you?"

It would have been impossible not to notice the slight reproach in his voice. Those blue eyes gave me a look as if to say, though I may have forgotten him, I had never left his mind. I felt a knot form in my throat and my eyes fill with tears. I threw my arms around him and hugged him.

"Sunny! I missed you so much."

"Me too," he answered, as he also held me tight.

My imaginary friend was no longer a phantom; he was a real person with a real voice, a real body.

"You haven't changed a bit," I said, as we let go of each other. "You're still a beautiful child."

"You have." He looked me up and down, his expression bitter. "You look like your mother. I liked you better before."

It looked like I had grown up, while Sunny, my very first friend and confidante, had stayed exactly the same.

"What are you doing here?'

"I was waiting for you."

"For me? Why?"

"Because you told me to. Don't you remember? You know, we were playing over there, near the pool..."

I looked to where he was pointing. It was our garden! There was the pool with the stones around its edge, where white and yellow lilies grew, and little orange fish swam through the green seaweed. Our secret place of games, where every evening a chorus of frogs began chirping their happy little songs as soon as it started going dark out.

"Your father called you," Sunny resumed. "You had to go. But as you left, you said, 'Don't you dare move a muscle. I'm coming right back.' I have been waiting for you since that day."

I felt so ashamed, I reached out and took my little friend's hands.

"I am so sorry, Sunny," I said, my voice heavy with regret. "I forgot about you."

His smile was forgiving.

"It's not your fault, it happens to all grown-ups. When people grow up, they begin to lose faith in their perception and emotions. They stop believing in anything they can't see, touch, hear, smell or taste. They lose their power of imagination. They think miracles can't happen. And you are no different."

It was so eloquently put.

"Where did you hear that?"

I was expecting him to say he'd read it in the books I had given him, but a secretive smile spread on his face as he instead said, "From a friend of mine. A grown-up, like you, who shared my loneliness while I waited for you."

"A grown-up! You mean it was an adult?"

"Yes, he was all grown-up, but he never lost his ability to imagine."

Inside me, something akin to jealousy reared its head.

"Who is this friend?"

"You already know him," he said assuredly. "If you'd like I can take you to him."

Before getting a reply, he grabbed my hand and dragged me towards the house. Who was he taking me to? My mother or father? If that were the case, wouldn't he have just said so?

"The meaning of the name of this person is related to the sun, just like mine," he whispered. Sunny was playing a game we used to play once upon a time, where one of us would think of the name of someone we knew and the other would try to guess it. Just as Sunny had done now, the person who thought of the name would occasionally give a clue. Who else did we know with a name related to the sun? One of the people who worked here when I was a child? Let's see... there was Emily, and Kate... Maybe the gardener, Old Alec?

"I need another clue," I said, caught up in the game. "Is it someone who actually lives here in our house?"

His lips twisted into a little smile, as his blue eyes grew glossy with the secret he kept.

"He's here right now."

"Where was he before?"

"He didn't say, but he knows both you and me very well."

An adult who knew us both. Now that was interesting. That they knew me was to be expected, but how would they know my imaginary friend? It didn't make any sense.

"Someone from my family?"

"No, but he knows your family very well."

He raised his finger slowly into the air.

"I must warn you, you only have one question left."

"What?"

"Did you forget?" he asked, disappointed. "You only get five questions in this game."

He was right. I'd even been the one to make up the rule.

"Of course I didn't," I lied, so as not to disappoint him. "Okay, last question. You said he knows us, but did he used to play with us?"

He looked down so he wouldn't give it away.

"Yes, but one at a time."

"What do you mean, one at a time?"

"He never played with both of us at the same time. But he played with you, and he played with me."

"You mean the three of us never played together?"

He nodded his curly-haired head.

None of the questions I'd asked had helped. I couldn't visualise a face, nor did a name spring to mind. As we passed through the narrow corridors of the house, I realised I'd lost the game.

"Okay, I give up," I said, shrugging. "Tell me who it is."

His face shone with mischief.

"I won't tell you. You have to see with your own eyes."

It was useless to insist. Another rule was that the person didn't have to say. They could tell you or show you whenever they pleased, or never.

We carried on, to where two doors faced each other on either side of a corridor. The one on the right was my bedroom. The one on the left was the den where my father and Shah Nesim used to hole up together. I thought we'd go into my room, but he surprised me by opening the door to my father's room instead. After the dim light of the corridor, the sunlight that flooded through the open door blinded me, though Sunny looked unaffected. Someone sat cross-legged on the cushions in front of the bookshelves in Shah Nesim's usual place, but I couldn't make out if it was him as my eyes had not yet adjusted to the light. Sunny pulled me by the hand, taking me to face the person.

"I have brought you Karen," he said, addressing the seated man. The words were extremely simple, but his inflection held a quiver of emotion that I'd never heard before. "Now we can all three play together."

By the time Sunny completed his sentence, my eyes had adjusted. The wavy black hair, kohl-lined black eyes, black beard and clothes of the seated man were all crystal clear now. Sitting there on Shah Nesim's cushion was Shams-i Tabriz.

"Hello, Kimya," he said, a mischievous look in his black eyes. "So you couldn't guess who I was?"

"You... what are you doing here?" I uttered in dismay.

He smiled and stroked his beard.

"Have you forgotten? It was you who summoned me."

I lost my patience, "No," I snapped at him. "I never summoned you."

As he turned and addressed Sunny, his face betrayed neither anger nor insult.

"What is Kimya saying, Sunny? Didn't she summon us?"

I didn't let Sunny reply.

"Don't you drag him into this. He's nothing like you."

He pulled his right hand away from his beard and his bushy eyebrows furrowed.

"So tell me, what exactly am I like?" he asked, starting to get angry.

"You know that," I answered, holding my own. "What did that thief do to deserve death?"

The acrimony in his eyes seemed to subside, and was replaced by sadness.

"As usual, you understand nothing. There is a curtain before your eyes."

I was fed up with his banter. Whenever I asked a question he couldn't answer, I was either unready to learn the truth, or some ignorant soul who couldn't grasp what I was seeing.

"No. I assure you I understand. You murdered that man, plain and simple."

He looked into empty space as though talking not to me but to some invisible being. "It is God who calls into existence, and God who spirits away. He loves justice. Make no mistake, the verdict was his."

"No. It was you who passed the sentence, and you who executed it. God had nothing to do with it."

He didn't get offended, didn't look guilty or ashamed.

"God is within us," he pronounced, withdrawing into himself like he was praying. "It is he who is primordial, designs the here and now, and knows what is to come. If there were nothing good in the thief's death, it wouldn't have been allowed."

"The God I know takes pleasure from love, not punishment. We were taught he was beneficent."

His helpless black eyes again stared into mine.

"That is the god of Jesus. But in order to know him, one must also know the god of Moses and Muhammad. God condemns, every bit as much as he shows compassion. No one can be more cruel than him when it is called for."

"Are you trying to frighten me?"

"I would never frighten someone in need of my..."

"For the hundredth time, I do not need your help," I interrupted. "Stop saying that."

"If that were true, you wouldn't have summoned us."

"What 'us'? There is no 'us'."

A childish smile broke out on his face.

"You are wrong. It is not only I. There is Sunny." He turned back to my imaginary friend. "Isn't that right?"

I also looked back at Sunny, and froze. Sunny's skin had become dark. His curly blonde locks had turned raven black, and his blue eyes were now the colour of black grapes.

"Yes," said Sunny, with Shams's same look of malevolence. "You called out to us."

"But I didn't," I repeated, though the words came out muffled. I felt sick, and I was struggling to speak. "I don't know what happened, but I didn't..."

Choking, I tried to sit up. My body was submerged in water. I tried to keep my head up, but then slipped and sank all the way under again. Finally, I managed to grab hold of the sides of the tub and pull myself up. As I coughed, I gagged, and as I gagged I coughed more, before finally spitting out the water. I thrust myself from the tub and sat retching for a few minutes until I recovered. Seeing my pale white face in the mirror, I could barely keep myself from laughing at my own stupidity. I had nearly earned a place among the idiotic victims of the world's strangest accidents, by displaying my ingenuity for drowning in a bathtub.

"Hell shall be their cradle..."

※

After we'd given our written statements, Detective Ragip pointed at the yellow envelope on the table and reminded Zeynep, "There's three hundred seventy sterling in it, and eight hundred twenty Turkish lira. Have Miss Greenwood count it and then sign the pay slip."

"Of course, sir..." Zeynep responded formally, pulling the envelope over. "Are you leaving?"

He looked at his subordinate as though asking for her sympathy. "I should go get some shut-eye, Zeynep. I'm at the end of my tether, I swear." He turned to me, smiling. "I used to be able to do three day stint and think nothing of it. Didn't even feel tired. Now I can't even take twenty-four hours. Must be getting old." He pulled himself together. "Anyhow, Inspector Zeynep will look after you. And I'll be back here this evening. See you all later."

As Detective Ragip lugged his hefty body out the door, Zeynep opened the envelope, checked its contents, and handed it to me.

"Here you are, Miss Greenwood. Count it please." She looked even prettier than the night before. She must have gone home and showered and changed, before coming back to the station. She wore a lilac blouse under her black leather jacket, casual jeans, and flat-heeled shoes on her feet. There was not even the smallest sign of fatigue on her face. Her wide brown eyes looked wisely out from under thin eyebrows, and her unpretentious movements exhibited her self-confidence. As I took the envelope, she continued admiringly, "I noticed there's a ring in there too. It's beautiful. Did you get it here or in London?"

When the subject of the ring came up, Mennan's eyes met mine. Just great, I thought, he was going to launch into one of his mystical connection stories again. But reading my thoughts, he averted his eyes. Zeynep appeared to sense something was up, but before she had a chance to fully understand, I answered, "Here in Konya. From one of those souvenir shops near Rumi's Mausoleum."

She wasn't convinced.

"Really? It looks more special than that. Like whoever made it put some effort into it."

I looked inside the envelope. The silver ring rested innocently among the worn Turkish and English banknotes. I was worried it would bleed or the paint would run off again in front of Zeynep, so I hastily folded the envelope up and stuck it in my bag.

"You didn't count it," she politely noted.

"I'm sure it's all there. I trust the police."

A sweet smile spread across her slim face.

"Thank you. I can't say the same for our citizens, so..."

Mennan appeared to be trying to shake off his exhaustion from the night before. He fidgeted in his seat and said, "Oh, come on, Inspector Zeynep. That's not true. This police force is the apple of our eye."

Zeynep wasn't buying that either, but she didn't push the subject.

"I hope you will always feel that way."

Even if Mennan's groggy eyes weren't so convincing, he tried to look confident.

"Of course we will," he insisted, raising his voice. Apparently he thought being louder made him more convincing. "The police will always be by our side, God willing."

Zeynep thanked him, then turned to me. "Could you sign this please? We have to document that your things were returned."

I signed, and asked, "What about my passport? Is there still a possibility it'll turn up? Or should I start looking into getting a new one."

"Unfortunately, we haven't found it yet, Miss Greenwood," she said, throwing back her dark hair. "Not in the victim's house anyway. I conducted that search myself, and it wasn't there. Maybe the murderers have it."

"Why would they keep it?" Mennan broke in. He appeared to have recovered from the stupor brought on by lack of sleep. "Wouldn't it be more prudent to toss it? Get rid of the evidence?"

The question was logical enough. This agent of ours occasionally came up with something that proved he wasn't as dense as he sometimes seemed.

"You're right," Zeynep agreed, fixing her pretty eyes on my colleague. "Taking the passport would be a risk of course. But we don't know exactly who the murderers are, so it's hard to know what motivated their actions."

She'd used the word 'murderers' again. Did this policewoman know more than she was letting on?

"Inspector Zeynep, I noticed that twice while mentioning the criminals you referred to them as murderers. So you must have something on them, if I'm not wrong."

She gave me a conspiratorial look.

"We have reason to believe Lefty Kamil's murder is the latest in a string of crimes."

What, so then Shams-i Tabriz wasn't the killer after all? He hadn't come forward seven centuries to help me? I didn't want to miss the pleasure of this moment, and turned to look at our agent. But I was mistaken. Rather than forlornly hanging his head, Mennan kept at the subject.

"So you have suspects." His green eyes flickered as they had that morning when he'd revealed Shams was the killer. "And you're tracking them."

Inspector Zeynep gently raised her right hand.

"I am not at liberty to say," she said, politely reminding us not to cross any lines. "However, some interesting things have taken place in this city over the last six months. Two kilometres from the Konya-Afyon motorway a hustler-hooker husband and wife team were found dead in a quarry. Both of them had been stoned to death. The killers had left the victims there with the stones they'd thrown, blood and pieces of flesh still on them, as if to lend clarity to what they'd done."

His face lit up. He was probably jumping to all kinds of conclusions about Shams, maybe imagining he'd created a gang to perpetrate his serial murders.

"*Recm*," Mennan stated knowingly. "It was *recm*, the punishment of stoning to death. Someone is administering Qur'anic justice."

"There is no such statute in the Qur'an as to the administering of *recm* against women who engage in prostitution," Zeynep said, bringing Mennan down a notch. "The subject of stoning is touched upon in the Qur'anic chapter of Meryem, but prostitution is not the issue. And *Recm* can be found in the Bible, as well as the Qur'an, in the verses pertaining to a prostitute about to be stoned. When the Prophet Jesus is urged to go first, he challenges them, saying, 'Let he who is without sin cast the first stone.' Of course no one could throw one, because no one is without sin. Death by stoning existed in Judaism, too. It dates back to pagan times even. And although it's virtually unheard of anymore, I suppose there will always be the odd fanatical sect who will claim it's their right to use that horrific form of punishment."

"How do you know all this? Did you also study theology?" Mennan asked admiringly.

"No," the young woman answered. "I had to look through some of the sacred texts while working on this case is all."

"Well, you've done a great job of researching, I swear. Not everyone knows these things."

"Were there any other murders?" I had to interject before he took the subject too far off track. "I mean, with religious overtones?"

"Well, they did set fire to a tavern. Three people were injured, one seriously. The following night they wrote on the wall opposite the tavern in Arabic, "Hell shall be their cradle, and layers of fire shall cover them."

"The Araf chapter of the Qur'an," Mennan uttered, going white as a sheet.

I was thinking to myself that I wished I hadn't brought him with me when Zeynep confirmed, "The 41st verse of the Araf chapter. There are a few other incidents like that. The murder of Lefty Kamil may also have been the work of this fanatical group."

I couldn't see the logic in Muslim radicals going after a purse-snatcher.

"Why would they do that? What harm was Lefty to them?"

"They see themselves as executors of shari'a law. At least that's to be gathered from the actions they've carried out so far. They appear to be passing judgement and punishing those who have strayed from the path, according to their religious principles."

"To warn others," Mennan added. He had started making his own observations, unable to keep quiet on a subject that so interested him. "And also to protect the innocent."

"They're targeting society's best-known criminals," Zeynep carried on, "so that everyone hears about it and they leave an impression. That's probably why they chose Lefty Kamil."

"Was Lefty Kamil really that notorious?" I asked, finding it an odd choice.

"Not as a bag-snatcher." She leaned forward on her elbows. Her hair fell back into her face but she ignored it this time. "It's true Lefty was a very talented pickpocket. Not only because he was left-handed but also because his left hand was unusually small. That's how the murderers managed to stuff it into his mouth after cutting it off. But Kamil's notoriety wasn't about picking pockets. Konya knows Kamil as a brutal murderer who butchered his mother and two brothers."

"Yes... That's right," Mennan said, backing her up. "I remember now. It was in the newspaper for days. That monster, was that Lefty Kamil? He carved up his own mother and brothers with a cleaver."

"And then he lit a fire," said Zeynep, stating a crucial point. "To cover up the murders. I've read the archived newspaper articles. He cried his eyes out at the funeral, tore himself up. They had a hard time calming him down. Turns out, he was just pretending to be grief-stricken, to take attention off himself."

Shams's words rang in my ears again. "Have you any idea what kind of person that bag-snatcher was?" Still, nobody deserved to die before standing trial, I silently answered the Shams from my dream.

"But it sounds like he was caught."

"Of course he was. Not even a week after the murders, it came to light that Kamil was the killer. He was arrested and brought in by our fellow officers, found guilty in a court of law and sentenced to life in prison."

I was bewildered. I looked at Zeynep and Mennan in turn.

"So how did he get out?"

"He was released. He got out on a general pardon," she said, sounding discouraged.

Mennan had began to sweat again. He took his handkerchief from his pocket. "Most of these prisoners who were pardoned went on to commit more crimes and wound up back in prison."

"But this time it was different," Zeynep pronounced. "Kamil didn't commit any more crimes until now. At least none we know about."

Mennan dried his forehead.

"Don't take this the wrong way, Miss Greenwood, but that's some luck you've got. Years later the man decides to start up again and it's you who pops up in front of him."

"Maybe it wasn't luck. What if Lefty Kamil targeted me especially?" They both looked at me, trying to follow my train of thought. "Did Kamil have a steady job? I mean, who did he work for?"

"There was... Hold on, let's take a look at his file."

She got up and reached for one of the red and blue files on the shelf behind her, then sat down at her desk again and, opening the cover, began shuffling through the papers.

"He was a driver," she said, without looking up. "But he didn't come straight back to Konya after he was released. He's only been working here for the last year. Before that he was in Ankara for two years, and it's not known what he did there. He had an alias; he was going by the name of Suleyman. And he grew a beard and moustache and dyed his hair."

"Of course he did. His eyebrows too, I'll bet. Think he'd get a job if anyone recognised him?"

"Actually, he managed to get straightened out. He had a minibus which, ironically, he bought with money he got from selling some land his mother left him. He drove a route in Konya."

"What?" Mennan bellowed. "You mean he was carrying school kids?"

"No. Tourists. Taking them on tours in and around Konya."

"Really?" I asked excitedly. "Do we know which company he worked for?"

Zeynep noticed the change in my voice and, looking up from the file, gave me a look as if to ask why that was of any significance.

"The reason I came to Konya in the first place is because I'm investigating a hotel fire."

"The Yakut Hotel fire," Mennan clarified. "Two people died in it."

"So I heard." Zeynep gathered her hair behind her head and leaned back in her chair. "I was in Istanbul when it happened, but it was on the news. They said it was an accident."

When she noticed my doubtful expression, she asked with curiosity, "Wasn't it? Or do you think it was arson?"

"We're not sure," I said, though it sounded like I believed otherwise. "The thing is, if it doesn't turn out to be arson, the hotel owners will be awarded no less than three million pounds by our company in London."

"Three million pounds," Zeynep said, whistling. "That's big money." Her eyes twitched silently as she did the math. "With even a tenth of that we could open a state of the art crime lab here in Konya."

"Well, Ikonion Tourism, the company that owns the Yakut, want to open apart hotels. Their plan is to renovate some of the old Konyan houses to accommodate foreign tourists."

Zeynep, still leaning back in her chair, studied us with a blank expression.

"Sounds like a favourable enough enterprise to me," she said, though there was no sign of approval in her voice. "At least something good would come out of it."

210

"Yes, but do they deserve it?" I openly asked. "And if the fire was sabotage, the subject will be of interest to you, too, thanks to the two fatalities."

"What does the fire brigade's report say?" she asked circumspectly.

"Accidental."

"Hmm... and the attorney general?"

"They agree. Thus the inconclusive evidence ruling."

She shrugged.

"I'm sorry, in that case there is no reason for us to think it was anything but. So the matter doesn't fall under our jurisdiction."

"What if I were to find evidence?" I optimistically insisted. "A witness, or a clue?"

She laughed benignly.

"Then we'll talk again. For the time being, however, it would be wrong to say the hotel owners set Lefty Kamil on you just because you are conducting an investigation on them."

She paused as though stuck on some detail, then reached out and grabbed a pen.

"Tell me the name of the company again anyhow and I'll look into it."

"Ikonion Tourism," I said, pronouncing each syllable clearly. "The owner's name is Ziya Kuyumcuzade."

As she jotted it down, Mennan couldn't resist blurting out, "I don't know if that Mr. Kuyumcuzade is guilty of anything, but there is another guy there by the name of Serhad. Serhad Gökgöz. That guy is a shady character if ever there was one."

Zeynep looked over at my colleague.

"Fine," she said smiling. "I'll check out Serhad Gökgöz then, as well."

"...it's not our job to solve this murder..."

⚔

It was noon by the time we'd come out of police headquarters. The sun was burning stronger now than it had been the day before. I couldn't even imagine the summer months; it was sweltering already as it was. As I took off my jacket and held it, I hungered for London's rain, its pale skies even. It suddenly occurred to me to call Simon. I'd never get out of this country if I didn't get my passport sorted out.

"Kadir's house is on the next parallel street," Mennan announced, as I took my phone from my bag. "We can walk it if you'd like."

"Okay, let's do that," I said. A little movement would do us good.

As we walked, I scrolled for Simon's number, then pushed the call button. "What do you make of what Inspector Zeynep told us?" asked Mennan impatiently. "This business about the fanatics?"

He must be quite curious if he wasn't even going to allow me to talk on the phone. But I didn't give up. I put the phone to my ear. It hadn't started ringing yet.

"It's possible," I said, turning to Mennan. "If there really is a group of fanatics like that, why shouldn't they also punish Lefty?"

"But Lefty wasn't committing crime anymore." He skipped to one side to avoid a pothole. "He'd become a responsible working man."

Simon's phone was ringing.

"Didn't you hear what Zeynep said?" I hurriedly responded. "He's a known criminal in Konya. Even you had heard of him."

"How could I not. The guy sliced up his own mother. But I still find it strange that this group of fanatics picked up his trail."

"Well, it's not our job to solve this murder. Let's keep to our own investigation."

Before I finished my sentence, Simon had answered the phone.

"Hi Karen... Sorry, what did you say?"

I signaled to Mennan to give me a minute before answering my boss.

"Hi Simon. No, I wasn't talking to you. How are you?"

"I'm all right, the real question is how are you? Feeling better?"

"Yes. Still a bit drowsy, but not too bad. The police actually recovered my purse, but unfortunately my passport's still missing."

"Don't worry. I've contacted the embassy and they said they'll issue a new one with no hitches."

"Thanks, that's great. But it may have to be expedited. I need it to get back."

"Back?" he asked bleakly. "You mean you're finished there?"

"Well, not yet, but I assume you don't want me to spend the rest of my life here."

He relaxed and gave a loud laugh.

"Of course not. Would I leave a clever, hard-working, devoted staffer like you over there? I thought you meant you wanted to come back right away."

"Shame on you, Simon. When have you ever known me to come home with a job half-finished?"

"That's not what I meant. You were talking about coming home, and I was surprised is all. Anyhow, how is the investigation going? Any breakthroughs?"

Taking care to stay on the shady edge of the road, I began to explain.

"Yesterday I spoke with Ikonion Tourism's owner, the young, ambitious Mr. Kuyumcuzade. Then I interrogated two witnesses, Serhad and Nezihe, who both still work for Mr. Kuyumcuzade and I think are trying to protect him. It sounded like they were hiding something, though I can't be sure. And now I'm off to see a man by the name of Kadir Gemelek who was also at the hotel during the fire, though more importantly, he wasn't on good terms with his boss. He also just so happens to be Mennan's childhood friend. We're hoping to get something useful out of him. I'll let you know later if that happens."

When I'd finished, Simon thanked me and hung up.

I felt Mennan's inquisitive eyes on me as I put my phone back in my bag.

"Was that Simon?"

"Yes. It was Simon."

My answer had been curt. I had no intention of talking over the details of the call and wanted him to understand that. It must have worked, because he didn't mention Simon again. We continued in silence for a while before he began reflecting on another of his concerns. "I wonder if we should have mentioned Shams to Inspector Zeynep?"

Just as I'd suspected, his thoughts were still on the black-clad dervish.

"What would we have said? 'Actually, it's Shams-i Tabriz committing all these murders. But you can't possibly catch him because he's been dead for seven centuries. Might as well just drop the investigation...' Is that what we want?"

"But he really..."

"No, he didn't really anything, Mr. Fidan. These are all just fables. What's real is what we've been through. The Yakut Hotel really burned down. Lefty Kamil really was murdered. Forget about Shams-i Tabriz and try to get a grip, please."

He didn't object; he just took up walking silently beside me again.

"Does this Kadir live alone?" I asked, changing the subject. "Is there anyone looking after him or anything?"

"Of course," he said, coming back to life. "His wife Nimet. She's a good woman. They've also got a son who's getting married soon, Zaim. Same age as our Hulya."

By 'our Hulya' he must have meant his daughter. I had to ask while I had the chance.

"What's the deal between Serhad and you?" I must have been on the right track, because he recoiled like I'd hit a nerve. "It seems you can't stand him."

The mention of Serhad so soon after his daughter had raised his suspicions. He gave me a sideways glance, wondering whether I knew something, but I feigned ignorance.

"You would've hit him yesterday if I'd let you."

His face went red.

"I certainly would have," he vehemently pronounced. "Pardon my French, Miss Greenwood, but that guy is a son of a bitch. A real dog. I don't understand why a man like Ziya would employ him."

"Even dogs have their uses," I said. "If you're trying to scare someone, a beast with sharp teeth can come in handy."

"I know you're still wary of Ziya," he said, apparently not sharing my views. "But I'm telling you, that father of his is a saint. You'll see for yourself when you meet him. And any son of his can't be all bad."

"We'll see," I said, stepping onto the narrow pavement of the shop-filled street. "But go on, explain this situation with Serhad to me. Why does he get you so worked up?"

"That guy..." He heaved a sigh of exasperation. "That guy was trying his best to seduce our Hulya. She was only in her first year of high school. So young and impressionable. And this Serhad was always strutting about all over the place."

"So how did they meet?"

He shook his head as though cursing himself.

"It was my fault. Hulya works with me during the summer and I'd sent her to Ziya to have some papers signed. That's where she saw Serhad. He went after her at once. And with the fanciest car Ikonion Tourism had, so naturally the girl was impressed. We were always so lax with Hulya. We'd already lost two children to cot death, so I guess we spoiled her a bit. She was used to getting her own way. But this time I put my foot down. I explained to her what a creep Serhad was, though of course she didn't believe me. And because she wasn't going to, I arranged for her to see with her own eyes what a scoundrel he was."

He looked riled again, as though he were re-living those days in his head. Seeing him for the first time as a possessive father, the chubby man started to grow on me even more.

"How did you manage that? Did you follow him?"

His eyes shone with mischief.

"Even better. I had my daughter talk to Serhad's friend."

"His friend? You mean the bald one who brought Serhad and Nezihe to the hotel? The one with the gloves?"

He stopped in his tracks.

"No, Miss Greenwood." Following his lead, I also stopped, but he couldn't quite manage to explain. "Now, when I say friend..." His face went bright red. "I mean, well... you know those ladies..."

"Hookers?"

The red in his face spread all the way down to his wide white collar with the navy blue tie choking his neck. I was fairly certain every square inch of his body had gone red.

"Yes," he said, swallowing hard. "One of those women like you said."

I burst out laughing despite myself. Then, so he wouldn't think I was laughing at him, I quickly put in, "So then, Serhad also has a penchant for those kinds of things, huh?"

"Does he ever." We started walking again. "Drinking, gambling, hobnobbing with women of ill-repute..." he continued, denigrating the man. "But though his friend Miss Dilber may be a woman of low moral standards, she's actually got a heart of gold. When I explained my predicament, she felt bad for me and you know what she said? 'That's terrible. He's going to bring your whole family down, not just your daughter, the creep. Bring her to me, I'll tell her a thing or two about that man.'"

"What?" I asked, to make sure I hadn't misunderstood. "You took your daughter to speak to a prostitute?"

He got flustered, thinking I was accusing him.

"I had no other choice."

I didn't blame him though. On the contrary, I was tickled by his behavior, and was about to tell him so when he continued.

"Anyway, it wasn't to her house. I would never take my daughter to a place like that. We met in a pastry shop, where Miss Dilber proceeded to recount Serhad's stunts one by one. How he'd eaten up all her money. How he smoked cannabis. How he'd get drunk and cause scandals in their neighbourhood, which led to their moving house four times in just one year... When my poor daughter learned the truth, she fell to pieces. She couldn't take it too long and ran out of the pastry shop. For days she wouldn't come out of her room, though eventually she got over it, thank god. And that's how we got rid of that dog. Semra, my wife that is, has got quite the head on her shoulders. She said to me, 'We've really spoiled this girl. Her expectations are through the roof, and now she's got a thing for fancy cars. So rather than have her ravenously eying any old body's car, why don't we just get a nice, new one ourselves?' She was right. Though cars are normally a boy's hobby, it must have been God's will that our daughter was also so interested. When she was just five years old, she climbed up behind the wheel of the very first car I ever bought. Which would have been fine, but she had her heart set on a flashier model. Where were we going to get that kind of money?"

"In the end you did get a Mercedes though," I said, finally putting into words something that had been hounding me for ages. "That must have been fairly pricey."

"Very pricey, Miss Greenwood," he griped. "With what I earn, it wouldn't have been possible. We bought it with the money we made from selling a piece of land my late father-in-law left us, God bless him." His sweaty face shone with gratification. "Of course, my wife's idiotic brothers helped."

He had such a pleasant expression on his face that I couldn't help but ask, "Why do you call them idiots? It sounds like they did you a favour."

"Yes," he said, his mood back intact. "They did us a favour all right, even if inadvertently. The story is this, Miss Greenwood. My wife is from Mersin. She's savvy, enterprising, and easy-going. Between us, she was the one who pushed me to get into this business rather than become an imam. And I went along with it, God forgive me... Now, where was I? Huh, yes.

When my father-in-law passed away, my two brothers-in-law insisted on taking the orange groves in their village, while my wife was to get what amounts to a barren marshland near the sea. We accepted in order to keep the peace. I don't really have my eye on female possessions anyway. Okay, death is natural, and inheritance is a legitimate right, but a man should still earn his own bread. My father was the one who taught me that. So, to make a long story short, we relinquished our rights. And that must have pleased the Almighty because he gave us a miracle."

Here we go, I thought, expecting Mennan to launch into more mysticism. But he took me by surprise when he instead said, "He sent Russians to help us. That's right. A Russian tourist company called me, offering to buy up that worthless piece of land. The real issue, that these Russians wanted to build a huge holiday village in the area, only surfaced later. So suddenly its value appreciated. Of course my brothers-in-law were both eaten up with regret. But they turned out to be good men and didn't kick up a fuss. With the money we got from the land, half went to a new house, and with what was left over we bought the Mercedes. Just so that our daughter would be happy, so she wouldn't have her eye on dogs like Serhad."

Having wrapped up his diatribe, Mennan wiped his forehead again. Suddenly, he was a completely different person in my eyes, like a relative, or a trusty friend. He must have felt me watching him because he looked up. Our eyes met. I smiled warmly at him and he turned crimson again, before quickly looking away. Then he pointed at a single storey house with a garden on the corner of the street opposite us.

"Well, we're here Miss Greenwood. This here is our Kadir's house."

"I saw a man dressed as an alien."

※

In contrast to the heat out on the street, Kadir's house was quite cool. It was small and humble but immaculately clean, and they welcomed us into a long, narrow room with windows running up both sides that made it look like a railway car. Under the windows were a faded sofa and armchairs, and situated right in the middle of the room was a widescreen TV with a lace doily draped over it, though I couldn't immediately discern whether it was there to display the doily itself or draw attention to the television. Then I noticed the same doilies laid out on the armchairs and understood that Mrs. Gemelek was exhibiting her handicraft skills. She was a lovely woman herself, Nimet. Her hennaed hair spilled onto the broad, straight shoulders under her flannel dress. Her hazel eyes shone in her round face, and her full lips seemed forever ready to break into a smile. I must admit, when we first came into the house I found Nimet's cheerful disposition odd. What with her husband having barely escaped a serious fire and the poor man still suffering trauma, her gaiety seemed out of place. But when I saw her husband, I realised I'd got it all wrong. He looked so healthy, in fact, that at first I thought he must be someone else. I was only really sure the stout, curly-haired man was our witness when Mennan spread his arms and bellowed, "Well, well, Kadir, my Golossol Gonyan!" And in one split second Kadir's thick arms had wrapped around Mennan.

"Welcome, Golossol Gonyan!" he also said, as they separated. 'Colossol Konyan' - said with hard Gs - must have been some amusing local form of address.

I kept my eyes on Kadir as I sat down in one of the armchairs they offered, but the man showed no sign of aberrant behavior. He just joked with Mennan a bit before turning to ask, "How are you, Miss Greenwood? Have you been enjoying Konya?"

"Yes, I have. It's a beautiful place."

"You should have Mennan show you round. Have you taken her to the mausoleum?" he asked, turning back to his friend.

"He has to clear it with his wife first," Nimet remarked, before Mennan could answer. "Our Mennan is a bit henpecked, Miss Greenwood. He can't even flinch without permission from home." She'd launched into the explanation with no reserve, as though we'd been best friends for years.

"Now why would you say that, Nimet," he grumbled, though he didn't really look offended. "What's so wrong with us minding the little lady now and then?"

"Nothing, usually. But in your case it seems the wife is always the one wearing the trousers, Mennan," she kept up, taunting him. "You can't even visit us anymore."

My colleague was grinning like a Cheshire cat.

"We're here now, aren't we?"

"Yes... thanks to Miss Greenwood. But if it hadn't been for her you wouldn't have come."

Mennan pretended to get an attitude.

"Now be fair, Nimet. I came to the hospital, didn't I?"

"And if you hadn't?" she griped, her hazel eyes open wide. "Your childhood friend is on death's door and you don't even bother to visit? I swear, Mr. Fidan, I would never have set foot on your doorstep again. And okay, you put in one small appearance, but then we didn't see your face again."

Kadir shot his wife a harsh look.

"All right, Nimet," he scolded. "Let the man breathe."

But she didn't back off.

"For goodness sake Kadir, what have I said now?" Her glistening eyes shifted to me. "They are always like this. Say something to one of them and the other immediately gets defensive."

If it had been anyone else I would have stayed out of it, but the woman was being so open and friendly I couldn't help myself.

"I guess that means they're great friends."

"Sure, they're great friends all right. But Mennan's wife is a bit of a socialite. She doesn't consider us her equals. She's never once been to our house."

Without knowing it, I must have hit a sore spot.

"Why would you say that, Nimet?" Mennan asked defensively. "Semra loves you and Kadir."

"Of course she does. So much so that she didn't even make it to our son's engagement ceremony." Although she was being sarcastic, the hurt expression on her round face looked genuine.

"We told you what happened. My brother-in-law was in an accident. Semra went to Mersin and took Hulya with her, remember?"

Nimet didn't look like she'd be easily appeased, but Kadir sternly warned her, "It's not nice, Nimet... in front of Miss Greenwood. You really think this is the time?"

I wasn't at all pleased to be in the middle of this argument.

"Don't worry about me," I said. As soon as the words left my mouth I regretted them, as Nimet, gaining courage from them, was now going to slaughter poor Mennan. Luckily, I was mistaken.

"Sorry if I've talked your head off, Miss Greenwood," she said, trying to swallow her chagrin. "Never mind me. Mennan is closer to us than my blood brothers. I also love Semra, and Hulya is like a daughter. Occasionally I just fly off the handle like this, intending to make conversation." She got up from her armchair. "You've got things to discuss. I'll be in the kitchen."

Kadir frowned after his wife as she walked away, her flannel skirt swishing around her knees, then turned to his friend. "I hope you didn't let her get to you. You know our Nimet is a bit touched."

Mennan wasn't really offended, just uncomfortable that I'd had to hear it all.

"Don't be silly. Nimet is a lovely woman at heart. A real gem." He turned his green eyes on me. "A little hot-headed maybe... but she hasn't got a bad bone in her."

I smiled her direction as she left the room.

"Yes, I've already taken to her," I added. "She seems very genuine."

Kadir's embarrassment was gone in a flash. He gently slapped his friend's knee.

"So. What 's your daughter up to?"

"Hulya? She's good. Preparing for her university exams. She's finally going to get this show on the road, God willing." He glanced my direction and, noticing I wasn't smiling, decided it was time to get to the subject. "Um, Kadir," he said leaning back in his chair. "I guess you know why we're here. Miss Greenwood has some things to ask you about the fire."

A look of uncertainty passed through Kadir's calm expression. His thick eyebrows approached each other on his narrow forehead as he frowned.

"If it's not too much trouble," I said, in a soft, lilting voice. "I wanted to hear your side of the story, Mr. Gemelek."

He looked away, then after chewing his bottom lip a few seconds, turned back to me with his courage intact.

"It's no trouble," he said, though he still looked anxious. "Why would it be? Only I can't sum it all up from beginning to end. You'd better ask me questions and I'll answer them as best I can."

"Certainly. Whatever's easy," I said, though sensing the change in Kadir's mood, I didn't take out my recorder. There was no sense in me pushing my luck any further. Whatever I found out, I'd have to make do with writing down from memory later. Focusing, I asked, "On the day of the incident, I mean the Tuesday of the fire, why were you at the hotel?"

"For work." His hands began to shake. He clasped them in his lap, perhaps to prevent the shaking. "We used to do the cleaning on the lower floors."

"Who do you mean by 'we'?"

"Well, Mecit and Huseyin, may they rest in peace, and Nezihe."

"Were you there every day?"

"Six days a week when it was open. We only had Sundays off. But during remodeling we only worked three days - Monday, Wednesday, and Friday."

"But this time you were there on Tuesday," I reminded him, wondering if I'd heard wrong.

"Monday was Zaim's... I mean my son's engagement." he said, looking down. "That day all the staff came to the party. Mecit and Huseyin, Nezihe... All with their spouses and kids. He gestured towards the TV. They took a video. Everyone is laughing at the ceremony, dancing and having a great time. It eats me up to see it. I wish to God we hadn't planned the engagement party for that day."

"Why, Kadir?" Mennan asked, seeing his friend squirm with grief. "Why are you so upset? I don't understand?"

"What is there to understand, Mennan? If we'd gone to work on Monday, none of this would have happened. Mecit and Huseyin would still be here."

Mennan rested a hand on his friend's shoulder to console him.

It seemed Turks, especially men, couldn't keep their hands off each other as they spoke.

"Don't blame yourself. It was God's will. Nobody can prevent what's meant to be."

"That's what I'm saying," Kadir mumbled with regret. "We lied, and this fire was divine retribution."

"What lie, huh? You're not one to lie, Kadir."

"If only I'd kept my mouth shut and not said anything, Mennan. But I didn't. You know our nephew Veyis, right? Well he works in the wedding ceremony hall downtown. Nobody ever has weddings on Mondays, so he told us if we had the engagement party then, the boss would only charge half price. So that's when we had it."

"Good for you. What's wrong with that?"

Like me, Mennan hadn't seen any fault in it.

"But I didn't tell Serhad. He was the one in charge of the re-modeling. Monday or Tuesday, I thought, what does it matter when we go in, nobody will be the wiser. And anyhow, we weren't going to clean, because the painters were coming on Wednesday. We were just going to cover everything up.

In fact, Serhad even called me to ask if we were going in the next day. And I lied and said we were. Even Serhad calling me was a sign from God. He was telling me to change my mind while I had time. But I didn't. I got greedy and lied, so then the Almighty inflicted me with this punishment."

Mennan was getting annoyed by his friend's unnecessarily eating himself up.

"You're not thinking straight, Kadir," he said. "Okay, it was wrong to lie. But it wasn't you who set that fire. Not only that, you risked your own life trying to save Mecit and Huseyin. And you got Nezihe out. You are beating yourself up over nothing. You weren't to blame. It was an accident, what else could you do?"

While Mennan tried to bring his friend round, my mind was stuck on something else.

"Mr. Gemelek," I said, looking into his puzzled face. "How long have you been working in this hotel?"

"Next month would have been three years." he answered amenably. "But you know, after the fire I was made redundant. The company is in such bad shape that they didn't even pay my compensation."

So Iknonion Tourism wasn't doing well, that was significant. I made a mental note of it and went on to the next question.

"Was Serhad in charge every time there were repairs?"

He didn't answer right away, but after giving it some thought, he shook his large head, saying, "No. The manager, Irfan, was. Either him or his assistant Orhan."

"Where were they this time?"

"Mr. Kuyumcuzade sent them on holiday and put Serhad in charge."

I looked at Mennan, clouds of suspicion were gathering in his eyes as well, accompanied by embarrassment at not having heard about any of this or specifying it in his report. But this wasn't the time to go blaming him, as we may have stumbled upon an important piece of the puzzle.

"Were there any other people in the hotel during repairs?" I asked. "I mean, if your crew had gone in on Monday, would there still have been anyone there on Tuesday?"

"No, no one," he fretted, grief-stricken. "Maybe Serhad, his sidekick Cavit and their men. You know, they're security, so they're there all the time. But they would have been in the lobby. I mean, nobody would have died." His eyes grew moist. "It was my fault what happened to Mecit and Huseyin."

"No, you had nothing to do with it," I said, trying to calm him. "In fact, if the fire started the way we think it did, you'll see the blame rests entirely on someone else."

The grief in his face was suddenly replaced by suspicion.

"What? Do you think someone set that fire intentionally?"

Mennan's eyes, like Kadir's, came to rest on me. He was still sweating buckets, despite the coolness of the room.

"We're looking into it," I said calmly. "And with your help, we hope to get to the bottom of this a lot faster. But there is a hitch. Mr. Kuyumcuzade claims you said that aliens started the fire. Did you say anything like that?"

He looked over at Mennan for assistance. Then realising he wasn't getting any, he shyly explained, "I saw a man dressed as an alien. His clothes were shiny, like tin foil."

"Did you get a look at his face? What did he look like?"

As soon as he'd ascertained that I wasn't making fun of him, he got a sudden burst of energy and confidently stated, "He had a hood on his head. I couldn't make out his face because of the costume."

"When was it that you saw him?"

"After carrying Nezihe out, on my second trip down..."

"After you left Nezihe with Serhad?" I interrupted, afraid of missing something.

"Yes, after I left her..."

"Okay, was Serhad surprised to see you?"

He wrinkled up his brow again, trying to remember.

"I suppose so. He said something like, 'What the hell are you doing here?' But I was in no state to pay him any attention. Mecit and Huseyin were still down below."

There you are. It was all slowly falling into place.

"And then you went back downstairs?"

"That's right. I had to get to Mecit and Huseyin. It was so hot down there, and the smoke was burning my eyes. I was under the stairs when I ran into that man dressed like an alien. He stepped out of the smoke. When he saw me he was startled and he started backing up. Frankly, I was pretty scared of him too, and I also began to back away. That's when someone hit me on the head from behind."

The picture in my mind was beginning to crystallise.

"There was someone else there?"

"Yes. Dressed the same as the other. I saw them both again as I was coming out. They grabbed my hands and feet and were trying to take me away."

"Kadir, these men wouldn't happen to be from the fire brigade?" asked Mennan, voicing his thoughts. "The space costumes you speak of sound like the ones the firemen wear."

"What possible reason would the firemen have to hit me on the head?" Kadir asked back, sounding extremely sure of himself.

"Well, you did swallow a lot of smoke. And you yourself said you were afraid. So maybe you just thought they did."

"No..." said Kadir, starting to get upset. "I'm not making this up. That guy was really there. There were no firemen anywhere in the vicinity. And if they hadn't hit me over the head, I could have saved Mecit and Huseyin." He must have been really miffed with his friend, because it was me he looked at as he asserted, "I know what I'm saying, Miss Greenwood. There were two men there, and one of them hit me on the head."

"I believe you," I said, my voice steady and even. "Mennan does too. The reason we are asking all this is to make sure no detail is erroneous or overlooked."

"There is not so much as one inaccurate detail in anything I've said. And, God as my witness, not one little lie. Anyhow, after this fire I'll never tell another lie as long as I live."

Mennan was looking gloomily at his friend, thinking he still hadn't recovered.

"We never thought you were lying, Kadir. We know you aren't, but in the hospital you said that aliens set that fire."

"So what if he did?" Nimet chimed in. She was standing in the doorway, two plates piled high with cakes and biscuits in her hands. When had she come in? I supposed none of us had noticed due to the heat of the discussion. "Didn't you tell the doctors that, Kadir? Didn't you say a man with antennas on his head came into the laundry room and pulled out all the plugs?"

After shooting her a look of frustration, he admitted, "Yes, that's what I said. If it were you they'd hit on the head like that, forget about aliens, God forgive me for saying it but you would have sworn up and down that you'd seen Allah himself. Godforsaken woman. Didn't the doctor say that I was lucky, coming back from the dead like that? My head took a real thrashing, so that much babble is to be expected already."

I couldn't help but burst out laughing. It was contagious; before long everyone, including Kadir, had joined in.

Mennan was the first to regain his composure.

"Now Kadir, think this over again. Don't you remember saying a rafter fell on your head?"

"Rafter schmafter, nothing fell on my head," Kadir protested loudly. "Mennan, why can't you understand? I'm telling you, somebody hit me. Everything that happened is crystal clear up until then. Okay?"

"Hey, what ya shoutin' for?" Nimet scolded her husband. She set the plates on the coffee table and, wagging a finger at her husband, continued, "Shame on you, shouting at your guests."

But Kadir was at least as incensed as Nimet.

"I'm not shouting!" he barked back. "And what are you doing here anyway, can't you see we're still talking? Go check on the tea, why don't you."

Nimet didn't immediately leave though. She stood there looking at her husband and steaming for a moment, then finally, perhaps because we were there, shrugged and left it at that.

"I'll check the tea," she said, moving towards the kitchen. "But you need to learn some manners."

Kadir was embarrassed by his behavior, but rather than looking at Mennan, whom he'd shouted at, he looked at me again.

"I'm sorry, Miss Greenwood," he said, his voice gruff. "But I know what I'm saying. I still had my wits about me when

I saw that man in the strange costume. And then he hit me, see?"

It was the perfect time for me to share what I was thinking with him.

"So, let's say you really did see a man in a strange costume. Then somebody snuck up on you and hit you over the head. You blacked out, and when you opened your eyes, two people, dressed in similar costumes, were carrying you outside."

"Yes! That's exactly what happened," he said, nodding his approval.

"Fantastic, so then we can say this. The first man you saw wearing fireproof clothes was the one who started the fire."

I could see him trying to figure out where I was going with this.

"He wasn't expecting to see you there, because the cleaning was supposed to have been done the previous day, on Monday. That's why he was frightened and backed away. Meanwhile his friend had noticed you, too. He came from behind and hit you on the head. You passed out, but when you came to for a moment, two men in strange costumes were trying to carry you out. You naturally assumed they were the same ones you'd seen before, whereas this time it was the firemen who had come to rescue you. They took you out and brought you to the hospital."

He gently threw his head back and mulled it over.

"But the first man I saw was real," he mumbled. "And the one who hit me, too."

"What about the ones after that? Weren't they real too," goaded Mennan, still unprepared to admit the fire may have been sabotage.

Kadir paused, he was confused.

"I definitely saw them as well, but that was after I'd been hit over the head. That's why I'm not insisting. I have a clearer memory of the first ones."

I'd got what I needed from him. All the pieces had seemed to fall neatly into place. There were just a few missing, and I wanted to fill them in before I left.

"Did anybody see you? I mean did anybody see the cleaning crew go into the hotel? Did you run into Serhad or Cavit?"

"No, we didn't. We went in through the service door in the back, and I didn't let anyone near the lobby so that Serhad wouldn't notice one of us. Because we'd lied to the man."

Mennan also looked confused, but he didn't say anything, perhaps because he wasn't ready to face the truth. Nimet broke the silence of the room as she entered with the teapot.

"Are you going to try and tell me you still aren't finished?" She was looking straight into her husband's eyes as she spoke. "Enough of your yapping, you are going to starve our guests, Golossol Gadir."

"Whoever enters here in half, finds himself whole."

⚅

Having waited in the sun for us for hours, the interior of the car was burning. The heavy odour of heated metal and plastic had permeated the air. Until Mennan turned on the air conditioning, I was also bathed in sweat, but as soon as the cool air began to circulate there was nothing left of the suffocating heat, nor of the smell that had turned my stomach.

"Shall I drop you at the hotel, Miss Greenwood? It's only one o'clock. We still have two hours till we meet with İzzet Efendi so you may want to get some rest."

It wasn't a bad idea. But although I'd hardly slept a wink the night before, I didn't feel the least bit tired. I didn't really feel like going to Mennan's office either. I guessed the best thing to do, seeing as I had time, would be to follow Kadir's advice and visit the mausoleum of my father's ancient sheikh, and Shams's soulmate, Rumi. But because I didn't want to reopen the topic of Shams, and I was worried he would offer to come with me, I kept my plan to visit Rumi's Mausoleum from him and pretended to be taking his advice.

"I suppose you're right."

"You'll feel better for it," he agreed, as though he were looking out for my interests. "Actually, I would love to close my eyes for a half hour too. But how? I have so much work to do. Clients to see, policies to be signed, banks to go to... And all this in two hours."

"Don't feel like you have to come with me to Ikonion Tourism. I'm just going to have a chat with İzzet Efendi. The meeting isn't work related." I felt sorry for him. All this pressure was so unnecessary and I didn't really want to discuss my father with İzzet Efendi in front of Mennan in the first place.

The exhaustion in his green eyes, which had been scrutinising me in the rearview mirror, all at once disappeared.

"If it's all the same to you, I really want to go," he said with enthusiasm. "İzzet Efendi is a wise man. It isn't every day I have the privilege of speaking to him."

It looked like it would be impossible to get away from him.

"Sure, no problem."

"Shall I pick you up in front of the hotel about three?"

"You'd better ring me first. I wouldn't want to keep you waiting." I was actually just taking measures to keep my trip to the mausoleum from him. I had the same problem at the hotel entrance, though, as I was forced to go inside when our ever polite Mennan insisted on accompanying me straight into the lobby. Fortunately, the prying night receptionist wasn't around.

"Any messages for me?" I asked the girl who'd replaced him, for show. Of course there were none. I turned to look back at the door. Mennan's car was gone. Relieved, I started back that direction, but was suddenly overcome with nausea. The child I carried was assertively warning me not to forget about it. I put my hand over my mouth, and had barely made it to the restroom before my body was wracked with waves of retching. After throwing up, I felt better. I rinsed my mouth out and patted some water onto my temples and the back of my neck. I wondered how long the morning sickness would last. I knew it wouldn't be the whole nine months, but I wasn't sure at which point it ended either. Then again, if I terminated the pregnancy, the morning sickness would go with it. I had to stop thinking about it, I had bigger fish to fry right now. I caught my face in the mirror. It was ashen, and my eyes looked tired, but it was nothing a little make-up wouldn't remedy. I opened my bag and was about to take out my lipstick when I noticed the envelope Inspector Zeynep had given me. I'd completely forgotten about it till now. I dug for the strange ring, which I found still nestled among the bills. I took it out and held it up to the light, admiring the beauty of it once more. The extremely fine detail on the silver band exhibited great craftsmanship, and the depth in the reddish-brown stone was mesmerising. No, this was no cheap ring. I held it under the tap and rubbed it firmly between my fingers, hoping to wash any last trace of dye off it. Not so much as one tiny drop spotted the beige sink. I considered putting it back on, but then what if it bled again? In the end, I couldn't help myself, and slipped it onto my finger. It suited my hand perfectly and I would give it one last try. I hastily applied a light coat of lipstick, then zipped up my bag and walked out.

Passing between Sultan Selim Mosque and a small park, I came to the vaulted outer door of the mausoleum. A group of elderly tourists, about a dozen of them, had formed a short queue at the ticket counter. As I got closer, I heard them speaking English with British accents. Their guide was a woman with silver hair cut in a short, neat bob, lively blue eyes, and skin bronzed from the sun. I didn't think she looked Turkish.

"Hey Angelina," an animated, bald man called out to her, confirming it. In his hand he held all different colours of Turkish bills, spread into a fan which he waved in the air. "Which one of these lovely papers are we giving to the ticket agent?"

Angelina laughed as she gently plucked the relevant banknote from the man's hand and held it up for the group to see. "This is the one, this red one."

This time, it was a stout woman with gray hair cut close to her head, her cheeks flushed from the heat, that pointed to a poster on the wall, asking, "Angelina, what does it say there? Yes, there. That poster with Rumi's picture on it."

Without looking the least bit imposed upon, Angelina turned to squint at the poster, and I turned to look at it with her. The man on the poster was quite different from the Rumi I'd seen with Shams. It was that classic picture of him as an old man, where he sat cross-legged, hands clasped in his lap and all curled in on himself, with languid, half-closed eyes. This cherubic dervish didn't look at all like someone who would run off to the Jewish quarter to fetch wine on his sheikh's whim. Next to his picture were lines stacked one on top of the next like a poem, though the words themselves sounded more like aphorisms. Without a pause, Angelina began to translate.

Either appear as you are
Or be as you appear
Be like the sun in compassion and mercy
Be like the night in covering others' shame
Be like a stream in generosity and beneficence
Be like earth in modesty and humility
Be like the sea in tolerance
Be like death in irritability and anger
Either appear as you are
Or be as you appear

She was obviously familiar with the poem, otherwise she wouldn't have been able to translate so quickly and precisely. When she finished, she smiled.

"Do you remember? We've read these words of Rumi's before."

The group members nodded their heads in agreement. One of them, an elegantly dressed man sporting a goatee and holding an inlaid cane, pointed a bony finger at the poem and asked, "Is it in Turkish or Farsi?"

"Turkish." Angelina explained, with the patience of a sympathetic teacher. "The Persian alphabet looks markedly different from the Latin one you're used to. However, the original text would have been penned in Farsi. It was the language Rumi always wrote poetry in."

I was impressed the woman knew Turkish well enough to translate. I wondered if she'd studied Farsi as well. And I also couldn't help but be impressed by these Westerners' interest in Rumi. I wouldn't have expected his field of influence to extend beyond Muslim mystics, and maybe hippies or marginal types like my mother once was. This, however, was a group of settled, middle-class Brits.

Angelina made sure that the stocky, red-haired man who'd been last in line had bought his ticket. Then she looked around, mentally counting them, like a mother hen afraid one of its chicks might stray.

"Are we good? Has everyone got their ticket?"

The elderly English group raised their tickets into the air like school children, and Angelina, content with circumstances, pointed towards the turnstiles.

"Now we'll go through this gate to the garden. But first, let me give you some information. This gate is called the Dervishan Gate," she said, gesturing towards it. "As you can see, it is the main entrance, and it was given the name because once upon a time it was where the dervishes entered. There are three other doors like it: The *Çelebiyan Kapısı*, the *Küstahan Kapısı*, and the *Hamüşan Kapısı*. *Çelebiyan Kapısı* means 'the Gate of the Gentleman' and is named for Rumi's lineage. Rumi's male descendants are called *Çelebi*, the females *Ünas Çelebi*. After Rumi was laid to rest here, his family bought up all the residences in this area, and the *Çelebiyan Kapısı* is that which looks onto where the houses were situated. The *Küstahan Kapısı*, or 'Gate of the Insolents', was for those dervishes who kept going astray and didn't make an effort to change for the better. When they were banished from the convent, they were taken out through this door under cover of darkness after the nighttime prayers so that nobody would see them. As for *Hamüşan Kapısı*, or 'the Gate of the Silent Ones', it faces the thousand-year-old *Üçler Mezarlığı*, the Three Saints Cemetery we visited this morning. In the Mevlevi faith, graveyards are called *Hamüşan*, meaning 'place of the mutes', which explains the name."

It appeared that Angelina was not only incredibly well-informed, but also oblivious to the heat of the scorching Anatolian sun. As I was buying my ticket, an opportunistic thought occurred to me. I should tag along, take advantage of her wealth of knowledge.

By the time the young agent with his pencil-thin moustache handed me my ticket, they had already taken their places in front of the historic ablutions fountain in the garden. The garden, with its white marble foundation, its tombstones randomly dispersed in clusters of two or three, was packed with people. As far as I could tell, apart from our English tourists, who stood waiting patiently for a commentary from the imperturbable Angelina, there were two other tourist groups, one German, the other Japanese, and a handful of Turkish visitors meandering about in small groups of three or four. That the garden was so crowded would only work to my advantage. I took cover behind the stocky red-head and tuned in to what Angelina was saying.

"Now. Imagine that instead of this huge burial chamber, there is a rose garden here."

All heads turned to look that direction.

"All around are roses in dazzling reds, pinks, yellows, and white. Breathe in the fragrance which wafts in on the breeze."

A buzz of awe arose from the crowd as though they could truly smell it, truly see the colours. Angelina was content with the group's sentiment.

"Yes, some seven hundred years ago, this was the rose garden of the Seljuk Palace. When Rumi's father, Sultanu'l-Ulema Bahaeddin Veled, closed his eyes for the last time, it was here that he was buried. Shortly after his death, those who loved him sought an audience with Rumi. 'We wish to build a shrine over the burial place of the holy Sultanu'l-Ulema,' they said, requesting his permission. But after thanking them, Rumi said this: 'O friends, tell me, could there be any greater shrine than that of the open sky, the dome of heaven?' On hearing these words, his friends retracted their proposal. But years later, when Muhammed Jelaleddin Rumi died in 1273, his son Sultan Veled consented to a shrine to be built for his father. And that is how the *Kubbe-i Hadra*, this beautiful green mausoleum with its columns thick as elephants' feet, came to be built by the architect Mimar Bedretten of Tabriz. Following that, all Rumi's relatives, his sheikhs and disciples, were also laid to rest inside this chamber."

As we approached the outer door of the *Kubbe-i Hadra*, the crowd of people became denser. Visitors were asked to slip the thin plastic booties they provided over their shoes, which was taking some time and leading to congestion at the door. I hung back from the commotion for a bit. When I finally made it inside, I was met with the smell of old cloth, earth, and wood, together with the sound of a ney coming from somewhere in the depths. The walls, which were lit with a soft yellow light that gave them the appearance of gold, displayed the most exquisite examples of Arabic and Farsi calligraphy, like the kind my father had worked on. Angelina had gathered the group a bit further on, in front of a silver door. I silently made my way over.

This site is the Ka'aba of the besotted
Whoever enters here in half, finds himself whole

Angelina was translating the handwritten piece over the door so that they could understand it.

"These words belong to the Molla Mosque," she said, in a voice just loud enough that those around her could hear. "This writing of incomparable beauty, earning its rightful place in the hearts of the people just as much for its form as for its deep significance, was written by the pen of the renowned calligrapher Yesarizade Mustafa İzzet Efendi."

"What does 'Whoever enters here in half, finds himself whole' mean?" asked the man with the goatee and cane. "I mean, is the place enchanted? Will this magical place rid us of our shortcomings?"

Angelina laughed, though without any air of condescension. I knew this look very well; I'd seen the same expression on the faces of my father, Shah Nesim, Rumi and Shams, and read the same meaning into it. They all had that same calm, patient attitude, where no matter how ridiculous a question may seem, they felt it their duty to provide a serious answer.

"To begin with, let me just clarify," Angelina said, trying to clear up the man's confusion. "When the Iranian theologian of the Molla Mosque said 'whoever enters' he wasn't talking about the visitors to this chamber. He was talking about those who come from the convent, the 'besotted' who were seeking the truth. That is not to say that the first time you enter, the holy dead that rest in this chamber will perform miracles, whisper great secrets in your ear, or turn each of you into enlightened beings one by one. Reaching this phase of enlightenment is not so easy. You must first undergo a period of suffering, bear the burden of your deserved tribulations, and become an unshakable pilgrim of divine love."

Great secrets, truth, divine love... Angelina was using language that my father, Shah Nesim, and the Shams and Rumi of my dreams had all used before her. But just like the old man with the goatee, I still couldn't quite wrap my head around it.

When there were no more questions, Angelina stepped into the inner chamber through the silver door. I followed along behind her inquisitive friends. Inside, the golden light barely filtered through. It was deeper, more honey-coloured, here. When my eyes finally adjusted, and I could see the rows of sarcophagi draped in satin cloth on either side, I remembered that my father had in fact brought me here. As a small girl, I'd been terrified of most graveyards. But here, in this dimly-lit room that itself resembled a small graveyard, I hadn't felt the least bit afraid, not even of the nearly one hundred turbaned sarcophagi that filled it. And not only was I not afraid, I felt like I was in a make-believe world, in the most splendid hall of one of the Orient palaces where my father's stories had taken place. The chandeliers that hung from the ceiling, the candelabra next to the sarcophagi, the red, brown, and yellow patterns on the four elephant-foot columns supporting the shrine, the flowers embroidered in gold tinsel thread on the satin cloths that covered the sarcophagi, the fascinating calligraphy that completed this magical atmosphere - verses of the Qur'an, the meanings of which were lost on me, poems I couldn't comprehend... The mystical, awe-inspiring atmosphere hadn't changed in decades, not since I'd first come here with my father, and it felt as though it would prevail throughout all time. The lines Angelina read now only reinforced what I was feeling.

Come, come, whoever you are
Believer, infidel, fire-worshipper, or idolator
It doesn't matter, again come
Even if you have sworn a thousand vows
Or broken your vow a thousand times

Ours is not a caravan of despair

Come, whoever you are, come

The verse was unforgettable, like the words of a very old, very well-known prayer. How many times I had heard it from my father. How many times I had set out to memorise it... Even hearing it now, I was affected. The chubby, short-haired lady, who still carried on her cheeks evidence of the heat outside despite the coolness of the room, must not have shared my sentiment though, because she brazenly blabbed, "I'm not happy with the word 'infidel'. Who is the infidel? A Christian, a Jew, a non-believer? There's something in that poem that's demeaning towards pagans and idolators. It's not nice at all. Where is this place he says to come to? To Rumi's own beliefs? What if I come with my atheism? I mean, if I try to come without changing my beliefs, would there still be room for me in this holy place of tolerance?"

Angelina kept her composure and, head held high, impassively answered, "I didn't get hung up where you did. It's true, by infidel he may have meant people not of his faith, but he was inviting those people to his table, not being condescending towards them. You may notice there is no imposition in these words, no insistence that anyone accept his beliefs. 'Mine is the religion of love,' Rumi said. And that love is the common denominator that unites all people, regardless of what religion they are."

The black clouds of doubt in the chubby woman's eyes didn't dissipate, but Angelina felt no need to explain any further, and headed towards the back of the room as we all trailed along. Arriving at the back right-hand corner, she stopped and turned to face us. She pointed out two of the turbaned sarcophagi covered with tinsel embroidered satin.

"These two sarcophagi are those of Mevlana Jelaleddin Rumi and his son Sultan Veled."

Sultan Veled. That was the older, obsequious son. The one who had trembled with the bashfulness of a young girl in front of Shams. I wondered where the other one's grave was. Alaeddin... that reckless youth who was never without Kimya by his side.

"The sarcophagi are made of marble, and were commissioned by Suleyman the Magnificent in 1565."

Angelina then pointed to one of several exquisite wooden sarcophagi behind them.

"And in that sarcophagus lies Mevlana's father, Sultanu'l-Ulema Bahaeddin Veled." The golden light reflected in her blue eyes had added a peculiar mystique to her face. "The wooden sarcophagus was originally that of Jelaleddin Rumi himself. It is said that when Rumi died, they brought him to be entombed with his father, and Sultanu'l-Ulema Bahaeddin Veled, sensing his son had come, sat up in his grave and greeted him respectfully."

I thought the group would object to this myth, but I was wrong. However, the chubby woman, still not satisfied with the response to her previous question, asked another one.

"Why isn't Shams-i Tabriz's grave next to Rumi's? Rumi's most beautiful poems were written to him specifically, so how is it the most important person in his life is lying in another mausoleum?"

The old woman was so contrary, she was actually beginning to grow on me. I was pleased to have her putting into words, questions that had been plaguing me for some time now. With intense interest, I prepared to listen to what Angelina would have to say on the subject. But then the group leader suddenly waved a hand off to the other side to the room where the books were displayed as if she hadn't heard the question, saying, "I'm sure some of us would like to see the Semahane. Let's continue on to this area over here where we can speak more freely."

I considered myself part of the group now, so I had no reservations about joining them to look into the display cases of the Semahane, which I assumed was where personal articles belonging to Mevlana and his loved ones were kept. Angelina, gathering us together in a secluded corner in front of a display case with a hand-written copy of Rumi's *Mesnevi* in it, launched into a response to this adorable old lady's question.

"It is a fact that Shams-i Tabriz was not well-loved by the people of Konya in those days." As she said this, our eyes met.

I could see her wondering who I was, this stranger hanging on her every word. I cursed myself, thinking she was going to send me away, but instead she just turned her eyes back to the chubby woman and kept talking. "How could he be? Some crazy man from Tabriz just pops up one day and steals away their great theologian, their sheikh and veritable saint, their Mevlana. You know, before meeting Shams, Jelaleddin Rumi had been a sufi of some calibre. He performed the prayer rituals, he fasted, he preached at the mosque and taught at the madrasah... But when he met Shams, he gave all that up. He took up reading poetry, talking of love, and reflecting on matters which the people of the city weren't ready to hear. And as if that weren't enough, he put Shams-i Tabriz on a pedestal, extolling his virtues to anyone who would listen and at every opportunity. There is an anecdote related to this that explains it perfectly. Does everyone remember the Karatay Madrasah? The one we passed in front of when we left the hotel? Well one night, the man who commissioned it, the Seljuk Vezir Jelaleddin Karatay, held a great feast in his residence, inviting scholars, artists, and government notables, among others. Rumi accepted the invitation, but he also brought Shams along with him. Inside, much ado was made about Rumi, and he was separated from his soulmate and given a seat near the head of the table. As for Shams, he just sat himself down with great humility at the door where the shoes were kept. At some point the subject came round to where exactly the seat of honour at the table is. Everybody had something to say about it, but when it was Rumi's turn he said this: 'For scholars, the seat of honour is at the middle of the table. For the enlightened, it is any old corner of the house, and for sufis it is off to the side. But as for the cult of lovers, the seat of honour is in their true friend's embrace.' And with that he got up and went to sit at the door next to Shams.'

As I listened to Angelina, I couldn't help but think the anecdote was based on a true story. The Rumi from my dreams was so passionate about Shams that he definitely possessed the courage to have done such a thing.

"So what did the other people in attendance say to that?"

240

The question came from the red-headed man, who looked equally wrapped up in the story.

"They didn't say anything to his face, but from that day on they harboured an ill-will against Shams and began nursing their enmity towards him. The wandering dervish was accused of all kinds of things. Some said he was immoral, others maintained he was a Mongolian spy... there were even those who claimed he was a sorcerer. There were those who asserted the madman in black should be expelled from the city, those who tried to scare him, and those who spoke openly about murdering him. Not even a year and a half had gone by since he first came here to be with Rumi when the threats reached such a head that Shams, grasping the gravity of the situation, was forced to quietly leave Konya one night without a word to anyone."

"You mean he ran away?"

It was again the red-headed man who asked. He was having difficulty accepting that such a legendary man, such a powerful dervish as Shams, would run away. To be honest I felt the same. The Shams I knew would never be frightened off by idle threats.

"Perhaps he was trying to protect Rumi," said Angelina noncommittally. "It's impossible to know, of course. But if there is one thing we do know with certainty, it's that when Rumi heard his soulmate had gone, he went crazy. He went off food and drink, sleep eluded him, and like a love-crazed madman he began scouring the land for him. But he couldn't find him. When Rumi's followers, originally glad to be rid of Shams, saw that their sheikh no longer paid them any attention, they regretted what they'd done a hundred times over. They came to Rumi again, saying, 'We did not know Shams as you do, we did not make him feel at home, and we were wrong. Please forgive us, master.' Rumi was convinced of their sincerity and forgave them. But after more than a year had passed, Shams was still nowhere to be found. Then finally Rumi got some good news; he learned that Shams was in Damascus. A caravan was made ready and his eldest son Sultan Veled set off at once. After a long and difficult journey, Sultan Veled arrived in Damascus, where he found Shams and sweet-talked him until his wounded heart was mended. The wandering dervish, who had never stayed anywhere long, was finally coaxed into coming back to Konya.

"With Shams's return, Rumi again found the happiness he'd lost. He began ardently turning out poetry, every day, like the young nightingales that blasted out songs drunk on their love of spring roses. But at the same time he kept his head together, and knew he had to take measures to prevent the town gossip. Believing that Shams's coming and going from his house wouldn't be considered so odd if the two of them were relatives, he offered his adopted daughter Kimya's hand in marriage to his soulmate."

"If I'm not wrong," the chubby lady cut in once more, "you said before that Shams was in his sixties. So how old was this girl Kimya?"

"I'm not sure," said Angelina. She looked uncomfortable. "She couldn't have been that old."

"She was under eighteen," I butted in, as if it were any of my business. "Not older."

Everyone's eyes turned on me. They were all staring at me uneasily, without saying a word. I couldn't understand why, when all I'd done was to pass along some information.

Angelina pointed towards my stomach. "Your blouse," she said nervously. "I think you're bleeding."

I looked down at my shirt in a panic, it was covered in blood just as it had been in Ziya's office. My eyes then slid to my hand, to the finger with the ring. Sure enough, Shams's ring was bleeding once again.

"...those who mess with you die, Miss Greenwood."

✳

I rushed headlong from the mausoleum and made for the hotel. Once there, I removed my blouse and slipped off the ring, wanting to get into the shower and rid myself of any trace of it. I'd just barely dried my hair when Mennan rang to say he'd left the office and would be in front of the hotel in ten minutes. Easy, I thought. I would be dressed by then, and even if we were a bit late it wouldn't be the end of the world. In the end we were right on time; it was three o'clock on the dot when we pulled up in front of Ikonion Tourism.

As we rang Ziya's bell, I felt a bit nervous about meeting my father's old friend. However, once inside, we were disappointed to find Ziya alone in his post modern room without İzzet Efendi. He asked if we'd like to sit, then fretfully explained, "My father's not feeling well. His blood pressure is up." He didn't appear to be upset about it, however, just exasperated.

"Oh, I hope it's nothing serious," I mumbled, though I couldn't help thinking there was more to it than that.

"No. Just old age. Every day it's a different story."

"Goodness, what's happened to İzzet Efendi?" Mennan uttered dismally. "He used to be able to run rings around young people even, I swear. What's wrong with him?"

"Nothing to blow out of proportion," Ziya said, trying to change the subject. "He still wants to see you. He said you should go to the dervish lodge."

I actually preferred that, as I really didn't feel like speaking about my father in front of Ziya. If I could just find a way to get rid of Mennan, too. But that would prove a bit more difficult.

"Of course," my colleague burst out enthusiastically. "I can take Miss Greenwood there."

"Is your father at the lodge now?" If the poor man was waiting, we had to get going right away.

"No, he's at home resting. He said he'll go down to the lodge after it cools off. He should be there by five, I guess." He looked relieved that I was taking this hitch in our plans in stride. "So sorry about this, Miss Greenwood, but it's out of my hands."

"It's all right. In fact, it may even be better this way. It'll give me a chance to have a chat with Serhad and Cavit in the meantime."

The nervousness in his face intensified.

"Why? What about?"

He'd put the question to me, though his eyes were on Mennan, as if asking for his help. I kept quiet, wondering what Mennan would say, but he didn't so much as twitch. It looked like he'd finally begun to grasp the situation and I'd been right to trust him. I relaxed a bit.

"Nothing terribly important," I said casually. "My report needs to be very specific, and there are still some unanswered questions concerning the fire which I need Serhad and Cavit to help me answer."

"What questions?" he asked, with renewed concern. "Maybe I can help."

I gave him a grateful smile.

"Thank you. But this time it's not your help I need, but your men's. I'll need independent statements from then before I complete my report."

"I understand," he said. "Just trying to help."

"I know. And you are, thank you."

Though Ziya was still noticeably perturbed, he pretended to be convinced by my argument and rang his secretary.

"Hi Gülşen. Can you send me Serhad and Cavit? What?... No, don't let them go anywhere, have them come here immediately. Oh, hold on a second." He looked apologetic. "I forgot to ask, what would you like to drink?"

We'd had so much to eat and drink at Kadir's there was no way I could get anything else past my lips.

"Nothing thanks. I'm fine."

"Me too," said Mennan, who was worse off than I was. His swollen belly was evident beneath his jacket. Ziya must have understood our predicament because he didn't insist. "Maybe later," he told the secretary, hanging up. Indecision was playing in his eyes.

"Um, if my presence is a problem, Miss Greenwood, I can leave you my room."

On the contrary, I wanted Ziya to be there while I interrogated the men. Being able to see all three faces and measure their responses during the questioning would only work to my advantage. Sometimes the hidden reality behind words was easily betrayed by a small gesture or a momentary glance.

"Thanks so much for the offer, but you don't have to go. As I was saying, this is just a formality."

He was scrutinising me, trying to understand whether I was being straight with him or had ulterior motives.

"This is the unsavoury part of our job," I continued. "Always finding our clients' explanations insufficient... being paranoid about everyone, even those with honesty and integrity. We end up being obtrusive and insulting whether we mean to or not."

Ziya objected straight away.

"Don't be silly, Miss Greenwood. Every job has its obligations, and you are just doing your job. Believe me, as a customer, your attention to detail only increases my faith in your company."

I supposed he was starting to relax. He leaned back in his designer chair and looked over at his fellow townsman.

"The cat got your tongue today, Mennan?" There was a sardonic, belittling gleam in his eye. "Looks like you didn't get your forty winks last night. What's up, was the wife keeping you busy?"

Mennan was in no mood to handle the joke.

"No," he answered flatly. "We were dealing with the police till the wee hours."

I was expecting Ziya to be surprised, but he wasn't.

"The police?" he casually asked. "What gives? Hope it's nothing bad."

"Miss Greenwood's bag was stolen."

His face showed no reaction. He just blinked and asked, "What? When? Why didn't we hear about this?"

He'd shot off the series of questions without waiting for a response.

"Last night," explained Mennan. "In the place where Shams-i Tabriz first met His Holiness Mevlana."

Now his look was one of genuine bewilderment.

"What's that got to do with it?"

Mennan's bulky frame spun his chair round to face Ziya.

"I don't know, Ziya." His voice was nuanced with that same mix of mystification and significance that it had had that morning while talking about Shams. "Ever since Miss Greenwood got here, situations keep arising that have somehow been connected to Shams."

Here we go, he was back on the preternatural hypothesising.

"That's a bit of a stretch," I had to intervene. "I happened to be at Merej el-Bahrain when my bag was stolen, that's all."

Ziya wore a mask of empathy on his face.

"What a shame."

"Never mind. Luckily, the police found it. And nothing was missing except my passport. They even caught the man who took it."

"Yeah, after he was murdered," Mennan blurted out. "And they cut off the hand he used to steal it, as it says to in the Qur'an, then shoved it down his throat."

Though the incident had horrified everyone else, it hardly had an effect on Ziya.

"You don't say..." he droned on calmly. "So who was this thief? And who killed him?"

"Didn't you hear about it?" Mennan replied with his own question. "The news is all over Konya."

"No, I didn't," he said, shrugging with the helplessness of someone who has missed out. "I've been in Çatalhöyük, driving a group of Japanese tourists around."

"His name was Kamil. Kamil Tenekci. Otherwise known as Lefty Kamil," Mennan divulged, looking straight into Ziya's eyes.

Ziya betrayed no sign of recognition, not a twitch, as though he were hearing the name for the first time.

"Uh... so what, should I know this Lefty Kamil?"

"You remember those horrific murders committed a few years back? Some man slaughtered his mother and two brothers?"

"No, I don't," said Ziya, shrugging helplessly again. "I may not even have been here. It probably happened while I was studying in America."

"Well then, let me educate you. Lefty Kamil is the guy who committed those murders. And coincidentally the one who made off with Miss Greenwood's bag yesterday."

"And then he himself was murdered?" asked Ziya, looking spooked. For one split second I thought it was genuine, but then he started to laugh. "Now you've really got me scared. Why don't you just come out and say it, those who mess with you die, Miss Greenwood." He turned to his friend with contrived joy. "Or wait... are you saying it was Shams punishing this bag-snatching murderer?"

Neither Mennan nor I laughed.

"Lefty Kamil was a tour bus driver," I said, trying to put a damper on his mood. "He had a minibus and was doing business with the tourism companies."

Ziya's smile instantly faded.

"I hope you're not accusing me, Miss Greenwood," he said, as though insulted. "We don't get involved in any illicit business."

I'd made him angry, which was not how I wanted him.

"Why would you think that?" I said, trying to reconcile the situation. "I just thought the man may have worked for you at some point."

Just then, there was a knock at the door, and Serhad and Cavit barged in.

"Come on in, boys," Ziya said, though they were already inside. "Miss Greenwood wants to have a word with you. Come over and take a seat."

They frowned in unison as they noticed us. Then, as though on cue, they both lumbered forward again, dragging their feet.

"Good afternoon," said Serhad, his voice bitter. As for Cavit, he nodded once and left it at that. He was wearing brown suede gloves again.

"Hello, Serhad." I stood up and extended a hand. "How have you been since yesterday?"

He couldn't understand why I was being so friendly, but he didn't hesitate to shake my hand.

"Fine thanks, Miss Greenwood."

"We left our conversation half-finished yesterday. I was thinking we should finish it up so we can put it behind us."

His lashless eyes radiated contempt.

"Certainly. And let me apologise for yesterday. I suppose the heat was getting to me."

"That's all right," I said, turning to Cavit. We were never properly introduced. "I'm Karen..."

He stared at the hand I'd put out, seeming to panic and wonder why, on top of everything else, he should have to shake it. I was about to retract it, but then he grasped it half-heartedly without removing his glove. I didn't immediately let go, but gripped his with all my might. I was expecting to read pain in his face, betraying a wound or a burn from the fire, but unfortunately there was none.

"I'm Cavit. Nice to meet you," he said, pulling his hand away anxiously. Afraid he may have to shake another hand, he went straight over and plunked himself down in the furthest, shiny yellow chair from us. Serhad had already taken his place in the metallic grey one next to mine.

"Hey Serhad," Ziya started in, obviously still hung up on the murdered bag snatcher of the night before. "Was there a Kamil..." He got stuck and looked over at Mennan. "What did you say his surname was?"

"Tenekci, Kamil Tenekci."

"That's right. Was there anyone by that name among our shuttle bus drivers?"

Serhad blinked his grey-blue eyes nervously.

"I don't know, Mr. Kuyumcuzade. We'll have to ask the accountants. They do the pay slips, so they'll be able to find his name pretty fast if it's there." He glanced at me, then turned back to his boss. "Why, what happened?"

"Apparently, the man was murdered. Konya is buzzing with the news. We didn't hear about it because, you know, we were in Çatalhöyük."

"Was it an honour killing or something?"

"It's not clear." Ziya said, not wanting to drag it out any more. "It will be soon enough, I guess. Let's just continue about our business." He nodded towards the two men. "Here they are, Miss Greenwood. Ask away."

I responded to the challenge in his voice with a polite smile.

"Thanks, Mr. Kuyumcuzade." I looked at Serhad, then at Cavit opposite me. "You already know the subject - the Yakut Hotel fire."

"But," Cavit interrupted. "I wasn't at the hotel during the fire. I don't know anything about it."

"What's that?" Feigning surprise, I turned to Mennan. I gave him a hard look that said he'd better not dare mess this up, before continuing. "Didn't Kadir Gemelek say he saw Cavit at the scene of the fire?"

"Kadir is off his rocker," Serhad cut in. "The poor guy went mad during that fire. Are you going to take the word of a crazy man?"

"He's all better now," Mennan blurted out. You could see in his eyes the pleasure he was getting from the duress his despised Serhad was under. "He seemed extremely level-headed to me."

There was the same flash of panic in all three of their faces, but it was the boss who spoke first.

"Are you sure about that, Mennan?" The nervousness in his voice was not lost on me. "Don't get me wrong, we all want Kadir to get better. But the doctors did say he's completely lost his mind."

Mennan, aware that we had them in a tight spot and feeling no need to conceal his joy, stated, "Well, I guess he's found it again, Ziya, I kid you not. He's even sharper than he used to be, you'll see. Before the fire, his wife Nimet was always shutting him up. Now he's really found his tongue. The poor woman can hardly get a word in edgeways before he predicts what she's going to say and rattles off some wisecrack."

"So what if he does?" Cavit countered. "That doesn't change the fact that I wasn't at that fire. If he's claiming he saw me, then I'm telling you the guy is still nuts."

"He gave details," I began to bluff. "He told me that you were in the lobby." I nodded towards Serhad. "Both of you. Serhad was wearing his day clothes, but you were wearing some strange silver outfit."

Cavit began to shrink in his chair like a culprit caught off guard, but Serhad didn't allow him to sink too far before cutting in, "That's impossible. Kadir and his group were never in the lobby. I didn't see any of them until after the fire."

"That's right," said Ziya, corroborating their story. "Kadir's team was supposed to work on Monday, but because of his son's engagement they came in on Tuesday instead, without letting us know. They snuck in so no one would notice them. I mean, there's no way Kadir would have come up to the lobby. He'd have been too worried about Cavit catching him."

"This whole fiasco is actually Kadir's fault," said Serhad, going into counter-attack. "If he'd done his job when he was supposed to, nobody would have got hurt."

Just when I least expected it, my colleague once again displayed his acumen.

"It sounds to me like you knew the fire was going to be on Tuesday," he said, with the resolution of a police officer interrogating a murder suspect he was convinced was guilty.

Serhad got confused and, worried he'd given something away, began to stammer, "Wha... What are you saying? I... How could I know what day the fire was going to break out?"

He was on the verge of losing it when Ziya tried to take control of the situation. "Don't be ridiculous. That's not what Mennan is saying. But there was no wrongdoing on Kadir's part either. Why would he purposely put his friends at risk? It was an accident, that's all."

I sat studying them in silence. The words they chose, the expressions on their faces, their body language and reactions, which were a mix of excitement and fear - absolutely everything confirmed the scenario in my head. But none of it, not even Kadir Gemelek's testimony, would be enough. I needed to come up with something more solid, or a reliable witness, one that didn't have doctors claiming his mental faculties weren't intact. Otherwise, none of it would be of any use. That is why I had to back off, to return to my role as an unskilled insurance agent who, despite all the pompousness, was nothing more than just a foolish little lady from abroad.

"Mr. Kuyumcuzade is right," I said, backing up their boss. "It was an accident, you shouldn't hold Kadir responsible. And I must admit, what he said didn't make much sense to me either." Out of the corner of my eye, I could see Mennan watching me in amazement. "It's true that his wife couldn't keep up with his clever remarks, but I also noticed he kept repeating himself. And he was having a hard time pronouncing his 's's and 'r's - a sure sign of head trauma."

"Wow, you are very observant, Miss Greenwood, let me tell you," he said, finally catching on. "I didn't even think about it till now. You're right, his speech was kind of slurred."

Wrapping up the investigation all at once would have aroused their suspicions again, so I turned to Cavit, saying, "Please don't take this the wrong way, but I have one last question for you."

"Ask away, but let me say again in advance, I was not at the scene of that fire."

He'd regained his courage and was acting put out at having to answer another question. I wasn't intending to argue, but the birdbrain was asking for it.

"I believe you," I said, gently cocking my head to the side. "But because Kadir's deposition will be in my report, yours must be too. That's why I'm asking."

"So long as your report says I wasn't there," he repeated, like a broken record.

Ziya couldn't take much more of his acrimony.

"What are you hemming and hawing for, Cavit? Just answer the question," he scolded.

Cavit turned red all the way up his bald head. And not just out of embarrassment, he was obviously terrified of his boss.

"Sorry, Mr. Kuyumcuzade. I mean I..."

"Fine Cavit, let's not prolong this. Just answer Miss Greenwood's question."

A deep silence fell over the room, which Ziya was presiding over with absolute authority from in front of the mosaic of Perseus. The respectful young businessman of the previous day was gone, and in his place was a tyrant who caused even the security guards to quake with fear. So this was Ziya's other face. The real one which he'd tried to hide from us. It was I who finally broke the silence.

"I should apologise to you all," I said, my manner equally bashful and sheepish. "I didn't mean for things to come to this point. I'm just trying to finish my report."

Ziya didn't let me finish.

"Please, Miss Greenwood. You don't have to explain yourself." He glared at his employee. "Our Cavit is a bit thick. It can take a while to get through to him. Please ask whatever you'd like. It's our duty to answer, and we'll do it willingly. You shouldn't have the slightest doubt in your mind about us."

"We haven't," I said, turning back to Cavit, whose face was still completely red. "All I want to know is, where were you during the fire? Just tell me that, and we'll get this over with."

Cavit fidgeted nervously in his seat. I was expecting him to start blubbering again, angering Ziya even more, but instead he answered my question, pronouncing each word distinctly.

"I was with Mr. Kuyumcuzade. We were in Sille. In the Church of Santa Eleni. Mr. Kuyumcuzade was taking photos, and I was carrying that three-legged tri... thing."

"Whoa, you are a piece of work," boomed Ziya, only half-joking. "Tripod, kid, it's a tripod. Man, Cavit, you can name every single detergent, and recognise all the soaps by smell - olive oil, daphne, lavender... and yet you can't manage to learn the word tripod?"

At that, we all broke out laughing. Even Ziya was laughing at his own words.

"It's true. He was with me in Sille," he continued. "The photos we were taking were for the new brochure. Such a magnificent setting, Sille. A settlement continuously inhabited for the last six thousand years. During Christian times it was a religious hub. Then the Turkmen came and lived there alongside the Greeks. There's still a church there, the Church of Saint Eleni, which was commissioned by the Byzantine Emperor Constantine's mother, Helen. If you have time, I'd love to show you around there, too."

"Of course. Why not?" It was the perfect opportunity to change the subject. "So you take photos then, do you?" I said, pretending to take an interest.

Ziya looked embarrassed. Interesting. This tourist agent who was trying to rip off the insurance company was also aspiring to be an artist.

"It's just a hobby is all..."

"Just a hobby?" Cavit exclaimed, kissing up to his boss. "Mr. Kuyumcuzade is a very talented photographer. Once, some guy from Istanbul came here, some jerk with a ponytail, a so-called famous photographer. He was disgusting. He stunk, must have been one of those hippy types that only wash once a month. Anyhow, he worked here for two weeks, charged a small fortune, and then took off. When we finally got a look at the photos he'd taken, they were nothing next to Ziya's. So in the end, it was Ziya's photos we used in the brochures and posters instead."

I looked admiringly at Ziya.

"I wouldn't mind taking a look at your photos, too, if we have time."

"Of course, Miss Greenwood. It would be my pleasure," he said, once again becoming the polite, accommodating young businessman.

I'd had my fill of conversing with the four men. Looking each of them over in turn, I said, "Thank you. That will be all. Forgive me for taking up your time."

Ziya and Cavit were satisfied. Smiling, they mumbled something along the lines of, "No, we thank you." But although Serhad had only listened, keeping quiet from the outset, his lashless blue eyes continued to flicker with suspicion.

"The greatest of all wars is the one against your own desires."

✖

By the time we reached the double doors of the Mevlevi convent, the suffocating heat of the day had subsided and a fragrant coolness had descended all around. The moment I entered the vast garden, I understood it was the house my father had taken me to my first time in Konya. The turbaned tombstones with their Arabic calligraphy, the tall cypresses flanking the stone path, the large garden with its pool, the two-storey clay brick house - they were all here. So I'd finally found that house. The smell of the red May roses in front of it pervaded the entire garden.

"Hello," said a soft, elderly voice from within the roses. "I'm over here."

Turning towards where the voice had come from, I got my first glimpse of İzzet Efendi, sitting alone at one of four small chairs around a wooden table at the base of the wall. He looked so thin and frail in his collarless shirt and simple, dark suit. His wide, cinnamon-coloured eyes, the most distinctive feature on his slim face, looked out with subdued enthusiasm and a childish glimmer of unadulterated innocence. "Oh, İzzet Efendi, is that you there?" Mennan called out, as though he'd stumbled onto a pleasant surprise. "Sorry. We didn't see you."

Mennan went straight over and, bending down, respectfully kissed İzzet Efendi's hand. Before Mennan could even straighten up, the old man had also put his lips to the hand of his fellow Konyan. Having witnessed this ritual years ago, I wasn't surprised, though I couldn't help but be curious as to why it was done.

"Hello," I said, approaching the old man. "How do you do?"

He looked me up and down with familiarity, as though he knew me well.

"Poyraz," he said. "It's Poyraz who has given you the meaning in your face."

"Yes, they say my eyes are like my father's."

He shook his head gently, indicating that I'd misinterpreted.

"Not your eyes, my girl, the melancholy. That pale light in your face."

Nobody had ever accused me of being melancholic, but I must have looked that way from lack of sleep.

"Most people say I look more like my mother than my father..." I was saying when he politely interrupted.

"Your mother had a beautiful face, like yours. The reddish-blonde hair, sea-green eyes, wide forehead, lips that weren't afraid to say whatever came to her mind..." Unbelievable, he remembered her so well. I was going to like this old man, I thought as he carried on. "But I'm not talking about visible beauty. It's the hidden soul that I'm referring to. A soul that can only be perceived with one's senses." He went silent. A peculiar look passed through those eyes, which age hadn't yet got its hold on. "Perhaps you think I'm talking nonsense, but believe me, you've inherited the soul that shines in your face from our Poyraz."

With that, he suddenly stuck out his right hand and interjected, "Welcome!"

I was so startled that I didn't know how to proceed, whether to kiss the extended hand or just shake it. I really wasn't comfortable with the idea of kissing hands, so I settled for a handshake. He didn't seem offended.

"Here you are, my girl. Sit here, that's right, opposite me. Let your light shine on me so that I may overcome the longing I feel for Poyraz, if only for a short time."

I wasn't so sure my father deserved his words of praise, but I didn't have it in me to say so to this exceedingly eloquent man, who searched for my father in the shadows of my face. What would I say? Sorry, but that friend of yours who you keep up on a pedestal, is actually so selfish and irresponsible that he abandoned his own child? Biting my tongue, I took my place at the table. The old man turned to Mennan, who had unceremoniously sat down before me in the chair to his left.

I would have liked to treat you to something, but the cook hasn't arrived yet. If you say you'll make coffee..."

"Of course I will," Mennan said, springing to action. "What do you think, Miss Greenwood?"

"No thanks. None for me."

"None for me, either. It makes my pulse race," said İzzet Efendi. "And the taste of conversation is far better than that of coffee." He turned to me with his expression of yearning again. "Your father was like that - ate little, drank little, spoke little... but he could listen. And he spent plenty of time reading and thinking. He was more interested in feeding his soul than his body. 'One's body consumes, while one's soul proliferates,' he used to say."

Mennan's tired eyes were coming to life again.

"Ziya told us your health took a turn," he mumbled anxiously. "I hope it's nothing serious."

At the mention of Ziya's name, İzzet Efendi's face grew dark for one moment, before he offhandedly responded, "Don't believe all you hear, my boy. Look at who said the words, rather than the words themselves."

Apparently, İzzet Efendi wasn't so crazy about his son either.

"Speaking of fathers and their children, I guess Ziya doesn't really take after you so much, does he?" I observed, trying to get a feel for the relationship between them. "I mean, not in personality anyway."

He took a deep breath.

"You can give a child its body, but you cannot impose your ideals upon its heart or soul. Everybody lives their own life, and we all choose our own paths. However, the bridge that leads a person to oneself is very delicate, very narrow, only allowing for that person to pass. The journey is not a privilege of blood ties. Unfortunately for some people, the obstacles they come across prove too formidable for them to ever overcome. Like the links of a heavy chain, they bind a person such that they can never break free."

"That reminds me of the story of that dervish at the Ka'aba," said Mennan, jumping in. "You know, the one you told us, İzzet Efendi. About the man who wanted his son to die."

İzzet's childish eyes flickered cleverly.

"Your memory leaves something to be desired, my friend," he cautioned. "That's not how the story goes."

"I guess I've forgotten," he said good-humouredly. "Tell it again, İzzet Efendi. I'm sure Miss Greenwood would also enjoy it."

If it had been up to me, I would have chosen to continue speaking about my father, but my colleague seemed so eager that in the end I had to say, "Yes, you've got me curious now."

"All right then. How could I say no?" he said, laying in. "Once upon a time in Baghdad, there lived a man who kept to himself. He was in good health, wealthy, and happily married. His only desire was to have a child, but somehow that child never came. He consulted doctors, went so far as to visit shamans even, and made many, many vows. Alas, the poor man's wife was somehow never with child. Just when he'd given up hope, he ran across a wandering dervish in one of Baghdad's covered bazaars."

At the mention of a wandering dervish, I interrupted İzzet Efendi to ask, "Like Shams-i Tabriz?"

He didn't seem at all bothered by the interruption. On the contrary, he laughed.

"So, I see you know about Shams. Yes, he was a wandering dervish just like the Tabrizi, God bless him. Now, back to our story. 'O you who have received God's generosity, would you fill the belly of this poor dervish?' asked the wandering dervish in tattered clothes.

"The man accepted his request without hesitation, saying, 'Of course. Tell me, what is it you would like to eat?'

"The dervish gave the man a grateful look. 'Plain trotter's soup with a piece of dry bread. That is a real feast for me.'

"They sat down together in the soup shop. After only two sips of soup and one bite of dry bread, the dervish pushed his bowl away and began to study this generous man who had treated him to the food. Seeing the lines of unhappiness in his face and the sorrow in his eyes he asked, 'Why do you want so badly to have a child?'

"The man was shocked that the dervish knew of his trouble, but he cordially explained. 'Praise God, my health is good. I have property and possessions and a wife I love. But I am not happy. My life is empty like a starless sky, like spring passing without the sun, as lamentable as a flowerless garden. Perhaps what is lacking is a child, I say, because I have everything I want except that.'

"The wandering dervish looked deeply into the man's eyes as he elucidated, '"It is not a child you are after, but meaning. What makes you so certain that you will be happy if you have a child?'

"But how should the poor man know the difference between the two. 'I am certain. If I have a child, the void will be filled and I will be happy,' he said.

"'All right then,' whispered the dervish. 'I will tell you the cure for your ailment.' The poor man's eyes shone, he listened with his full attention for the words that would come from the dervish's mouth. 'Tomorrow when you wake up, scrub yourself clean and go outside. Do not tell a single lie, nor use a harsh word against anyone. Do not employ cunning. Do not eat or drink anything which is forbidden. Keep evil far from your heart, and offer relief to the poor but do not boast about it. When you go home in the evening, lie prostrate with all your purity, all your heart, all your faith intact, and begin praying to God. Tell him: *O creator of heaven and earth. O merciful and gracious one. O sultan whose generosities I am incapable of counting. Clear the path to the gate of truth for me. As you know, the path to truth is different for each of your subjects. To find you I must be rid of my longing for a child. Grant me a child. Do not deny me this blessing.* Continue your invocation until the time of the morning prayers. Then after performing the morning prayer rituals, go to your wife and take her into your bed. Nine months and ten days later you will have a son.'

"The poor man fell at the dervish's feet. 'If what you say comes to be, you may ask anything you wish from me.'

"The dervish took the man's hands and pulled him up. 'Our good deeds - and our evil deeds - cannot be reciprocated,' he said, with disdain. 'We bestow on ourselves our own rewards and punishments for all our deeds.

"The poor man didn't understand a word of what the dervish said, but because he chased after every prospect of having a child, the next day he followed the dervish's instructions to the letter. He washed and was purified, and went out onto the street spotlessly clean. He neither broke any hearts, nor was unjust to any creature, nor lied, nor caused anyone pain. On returning home, he lay prostrate, repenting and praying forgiveness until morning. He appealed to the Creator. And after performing the morning prayer rituals, he came to his wife's side. Not long after, he learned that the dervish's prophesy had come true - his wife was with child. The man was ecstatic. He searched far and wide for the dervish in order to reward him, but he was nowhere to be found. Then nine months and ten days later, his wife bore him a cherubic little son. The man took the boy into his lap, kissed him, smelled him, and gave his wife gifts of jewels and gold. He came home early every day, just to see his son, to give him love, to play with that tiny life that as of yet had no concept of the world. He was happy all right but, at the same time, a nagging curiosity over how the dervish had performed this miracle would not leave him in peace. He wondered how, when the doctors and shamans and hags with all their wisdom hadn't been able to, the dervish with his shabby clothes and tangled hair and beard had. This was a question that grew in his mind as the days passed. When he couldn't work it out, he consulted wise men, went so far as to visit the theologians even, and read many, many handwritten leather-bound journals. Alas, he could find no answer. As the questions went unanswered, they grew and grew until they took on the complex form of a great secret. And that secret became the meaning of his life. He no longer got any work done, no longer spent any time with his beautiful wife, nor the son he adored. Instead, he wandered about crazed on the streets of the city.

"Then one night he heard the dervish's voice in his sleep. 'What you search for is not my secret, but God's love. To attain God's love, you must give up your love of this world.' He climbed out of bed to see if there was someone in the room, but saw no one. All night long, he turned the dervish's words over in his mind, and with the light of day he made his decision. He woke his wife and explained one by one the things that had happened to him. 'I must find that dervish,' he said resolutely. 'Only he can explain to me what has come to pass.'

"Ignoring the poor woman's begging and lamenting, her wailing and her tearing at her hair, he said, 'This is my destiny, I must live it'. Then he left all his property and possessions to her, telling her, 'If I don't return, there is enough money here for you and for our son. You may spend that.' And that was the last they saw of him.

"The woman went on to raise the child by herself. Then the day arrived when he came before his mother, no longer as a little boy, but as the strapping, able-bodied lad with a strong grasp of the world he'd become. He asked her, 'What ever became of my father? If he is dead, let me know his grave. If he lives, let me go and fetch him.'

"His mother didn't want to explain, but her son was so insistent that in the end the poor woman was forced to. The young lad tried to find meaning in what his mother had told him. 'No,' he said. 'There must be more to this than what you've said. I have to go and find him.'

"The woman begged him, just as she had her husband before. 'I have nobody in this life but you. What will I do if you leave?' she cried.

"But the child was as stubborn as a mule. Before the week was up, he was on his way. He wandered the cities, the caravanserai, theology schools and dervish lodges, asking after his father all the way. In the end, the information he gathered brought him to Mecca. He descended onto a small mosque there, where his first order of business was to ask after his father. The preacher knew straight off who he was talking about.

"'You will find him at the Ka'aba," he said courteously. 'Just as the earth circles the sun, your father walks in circles around the Ka'aba both day and night.'

"The young lad rushed to the Ka'aba and said his father's name to the Muslims there, who pointed out the old man at once. He looked and saw a man in tattered clothes, his hair and beard in tangles. He was moving around the Ka'aba with tiny steps, his hands open to the sky and the murmur of a prayer on his lips. The lad nervously approached the man but, afraid to touch him, said in a timid voice, 'Father?'

"The old man didn't hear him, so the young lad raised his voice. 'Father...'

"But the old man was in another world and couldn't hear his son's voice, so the young lad shouted quite loudly this time, 'Father!'

"The man stopped and squinted up at the lad, whose silhouette was blocking the sun. Upon recognising his son, he trembled in the summer heat, as though a wind from the dead of winter had blown through. Tears streamed from his eyes, as he looked up to the heavens and implored, 'O my Lord, I cannot share your love with anyone. Either take my life, or his.'

"While the boy stood gaping, not able to understand what had happened, he suddenly felt his breath taken away. Darkness fell across his eyes and he collapsed to the ground dead."

My hair stood on end as I listened to İzzet Efendi. This was abhorrent, I thought, but he must not have shared my feelings because for Mennan's sake he smiled and expounded, "You see, the man is not asking God to take his son's life as you suppose. On the contrary, he first requests that he take his own. But God, at his discretion, takes the life of his son instead."

I couldn't take any more of this.

"And the man is happy about that?" I snapped. "How could a father wish for the death of a son whose only sin was to try and find him?"

İzzet Efendi kept his cool.

"You're on the wrong side of the curtain, my girl. When you look from there, the story seems to illustrate a lack of conscience, but if you come to this side of the curtain, you'll see a profound story of arcane wisdom."

"Wisdom?" I asked, raising my voice. "I'm sorry, but there is no 'arcane wisdom' here. It was murder, plain and simple."

Mennan, listening apprehensively to the increasing tempo of our discussion, was about to intercede, saying, "But, Miss Greenwood..." when İzzet Efendi gently raised his right hand and cut him off.

"Wait a moment, my child, let Kimya have her say. How else can we come to understand each other?"

Yes, there you have it. I'd become Kimya.

"I can't understand how it is that the son's existence was an obstacle for the man's love." I was too angry to control my voice. "Not only that, but the God I know is not supposed to get jealous. He doesn't pick on the innocent, he watches out for them."

İzzet Efendi was studying me with a smug smile.

"Stay calm, my girl," he said in a sweet voice. "Liberate your mind from anger. Anger will only serve to blind your mind's eye and turn your heart into a stony field where snakes lie coiled." He went quiet, and after staring at me silently for a while, as though trying to figure me out, asked, "What is it that makes you so angry?"

Did this man know my father had abandoned us? Was that what he was alluding to, that my anger was just due to my father leaving? Was he trying to back me into a corner? But no, that wasn't it. You could read in his face that he was well-intended.

"I'm not angry," I said, as it was the first thing that came to mind. "I just want to know if you two really do find it acceptable to wish death on your own child?"

"It's not." His face clouded over with shame as though he himself had committed the atrocity. "It is wrong to wish death on any living creature, not just your own flesh and blood. Everyone must be allowed to complete their lives in the natural way. But this is not a story about how life ends, it's about how you live it."

When he noticed the proliferating question marks in my eyes, he carried on his explanation with even more enthusiasm.

"'Die before you die' commands the prophet Muhammed in one of the hadith."

He understood from my change of expression that I'd heard it before.

"Poyraz often quoted those sacred words; you would have heard them before of course. It is what all God's true beloveds strive to do throughout their lives. The meaning is this - you are to give up everything of your personal identity, everything that binds you to this world, to attain a spiritual death. But it is not only your property, possessions, loved ones, love and happiness you must let go of. Equally important is your hunger, anguish, bereavement, and sorrow. Here is another story that puts that message into words quite well.

"One day, a man of God was chatting with a guest in his tent when a servant came in. Slapping his hands on his knees, he bellowed, 'It's a disaster, Sayyid. Forty of your camels were lost to a flood.'

"Not a hair on Sayyid's head twitched. He just lowered his chin to look towards his heart and, placing his hand on his chest, mumbled, 'Praise be to God.' With that, he turned back to his guest and carried on the conversation as though nothing had happened. The sun rose a bit, then another servant entered.

"'Good news, Sayyid,' he exclaimed happily. 'Forty of your goats and forty of your ewes have given birth.'

"Again, not one hair moved. Again, he looked down towards his heart and put a hand on his chest. 'Praise be to God,' he said.

"The guest was taken aback. 'Sayyid,' he began in awe. 'A little while ago, you received word of a disaster. You were not rattled by the news, but simply praised God and carried on. Shortly after that, you received some good news, but did not rejoice. Once again, you just calmly praised God. Would you explain this to me?'

"Sayyid's face lit up like a summer morning. 'When the bad news arrived, I looked with apprehension towards my heart to see if there was sorrow or darkness there. There was none - I was thankful and praised God. When the good news came I was also apprehensive, and again immediately looked at my heart to see if it was swelling or gushing. It was not - I was thankful and again praised God. Camels, goats, property and possessions come and go, my dear guest. But if your heart grows dark, or swells even just the slightest bit, returning it to its original state is near impossible.'

"These words of Sayyid's shed light on the meaning of the hadith 'die before you die' splendidly. Because this world is temporary. The real world is on the other side of the curtain. And when I say curtain, I am not speaking of some heavy, cumbersome drape. It's more of a translucent wall, thinner than an onion skin, lighter than a butterfly wing, more delicate than a spider web. Those who are blinded by the world's temporary colours can see neither that mysterious curtain, nor the absolute truth behind it."

Though his words were affecting and the story compelling, none of it justified a father's wishing his son dead.

"Those who can see beyond that elusive curtain," I shot back, "would have done well to show some mercy for poor souls like the young lad who couldn't. There is more than enough evil causing people misery on this side of the curtain as it is."

"You have a conscience," he chirped. "Your natural tendency to feel sorry for others is a good thing. Mercy is one of God's many attributes. But at the same time, you are also very stubborn, just like your father. Poyraz, however, was not so quick to anger as you are. He knew how to control his temper better than any of us."

I remembered my father's loving gaze, his forehead which never frowned. I felt a knot rise in my throat and my eyes begin to water.

"I don't really remember my father so well," I said, trying to smother the anguish that had taken hold of my soul. "I was quite young when he left us."

I wasn't sure why I'd admitted that. Perhaps it was to stress the similarities between myself and the young lad, or because I wanted him to be more sensitive about discussing my father in front of me. Unfortunately, what I said had no effect on him. Mennan, whose hands had been spread out on the table in front of him, suddenly clasped them in his lap, studying them quietly to avoid looking into my eyes. Even he had picked up on my heartache. But the old man kept grinning with the naivety of a child.

"I was also pretty young when I met him," he continued, his smile displaying his smooth dentures. "He was the first one to ever greet me at the steps of this dervish convent."

I was confused. İzzet Efendi looked well into his seventies, whereas my father couldn't be much more than sixty. As though reading my thoughts, he clarified.

"Poyraz was younger in years than me, though my intellect was the less developed. His horizons were wider, his heart bigger." He pointed at the lodge behind us. "Your father was like a piece of this place. Just like these cypresses, the red roses, this ochre balcony, and this stone pool. You know how your father got here, don't you?"

"He was left here in a basket," I curtly repeated what my mother had told me the night before.

"He was left here in a basket," he confirmed. "Just like the prophet Moses on the River Nile."

"They don't know who left him here though, do they?"

A mysterious light spread in his eyes.

"The wind," he whispered. "It was the wind that left your father here. Just as the River Nile carried Moses to the pharaoh's palace, the north wind carried Poyraz here to this convent."

He was speaking of my father with such reverence, I half expected him to claim my father himself was a prophet.

"Now quit that, İzzet Efendi," I said, politely protesting. "My father had parents once too, of course."

All at once he grew serious. He pointed towards the building behind us again. "This convent raised your father, my girl. And I am your father's brother. He was born in this place, grew up in this place, lived in this place."

"And abandoned this place," I added.

The light in his eyes dulled. I carried on, pleased to finally be having an effect on him.

"And for an English girl, for a love that belonged to the physical world, no less."

He hung his head. "Yes, a love that belonged to the physical world," he repeated. He set his eyes on the roses and got lost in thought. He was thinking so intensely that neither Mennan nor I had the nerve to break the silence. Finally, he looked up and, staring at something off to the right, began to speak.

"We were standing under that tree there. It was a spring night just like this one. That day, Poyraz had spoken with Hikmet Efendi and asked the sheikh for his blessing in marrying your mother. It was your mother's second time in Konya, exactly three months after her first. While Poyraz flew around in his white robes, chasing after the truth in the *sema*, the ensuing wind picked up your mother's heart and carried it along behind him. It was on that second trip here that she decided she couldn't leave without Poyraz again. She was right; she loved Poyraz. And he also loved her. On the other hand, Poyraz's path was one thing, your mother's another. Poyraz's breeding, his code of conduct, his temperament... were all very different from your mother's. But the transitory reality was this - the two of them were in love."

The old man's referring to my mother and father's love as transitory really annoyed me. Despite my interest in what he had to say, I interrupted him, asking, "How do you know it was transitory? I don't know about my father, but my mother is still in love with him."

"Hers is only longing. Love felt for people dies just as their bodies do. For undying love, one must love an undying entity. An entity that you will never possess, never fully comprehend, never get your fill of, never be together with, and can therefore never abandon."

He had a very fresh take on religion, at least for me. I could have debated with him regardless, but Mennan, intoxicated by the old man's words, ecstatically pronounced, "You mean our love of God, don't you?"

"Mmm. Love of God," the old man affirmed without emotion. "Your father confused his love of God with love for one of his subjects. Perhaps that is why he came to Hikmet Efendi asking for his sheikh's blessing. He was trying to say,

'My heart and soul are confused; I believe my heart's desire to be my soul's desire. Please fix it, master.' But Hikmet Efendi believed Poyraz had to plot his own course for a while. He allowed Poyraz to go to London.

It sounded like İzzet Efendi disapproved of his sheikh's decision.

"Do you think it was wrong of him to condone the trip?"

"How so?" he said, coming out of his reverie. "Was it wrong? No. God forbid, it's not my place to say. No one can come between guru and disciple. Mevlana said, 'A guru is his disciple's door to Truth.' Of course Hikmet Efendi had his reasons. It seemed your father was even less certain than Hikmet Efendi was."

"How do you know that?" I threw in. "Would he follow some foreign woman to a country he knows nothing about if he weren't sure?"

"He would, my girl, he would," he said, blinking slowly. "Because the love felt for a person is but a semblance of one's love for God. And even that semblance of love is so powerful, it makes a person do crazy things. That's just what happened to your father. But don't think that's my interpretation. Poyraz himself said that, right under that plane tree. 'I'm confused,' he said regretfully. 'My heart is mixed up, as is my soul. What am I doing, İzzet? Abandoning my convent and my sheikh for my desires? Forgoing my divine love for the love of a person?'

"He was so torn, in fact, that I said something I didn't believe. 'Don't think like that,' I said, though that is exactly what I wanted him to think. 'You are taking your first steps. To attain God's love, you are first learning to love a person. To reach infinite love, you are living out one that is finite. How can you know love if you have never experienced it?'"

İzzet Efendi looked at me affectionately.

"'Do you think I haven't considered that?' your father answered. 'That I didn't ask myself these questions? But now, with only two days left before I fly to London, I still find myself wracked with doubt. But I really love Susan. Sometimes I think just like you said, God is preparing me for infinite love. Though Mevlana says *destroy the drop of water in you so that there may be a sea* I think to myself, isn't the sea also made up of drops? I ask myself, can't we reach that which is divine through a person? Then I realise all this reasoning of mine is some kind of helplessness. The helplessness of a dervish who is overcome by small passions in his heart, while burning with a desire for love of Truth.'

"His words touched me deep inside," İzzet continued. "'Do not allow your soul to grow dark,' I told him, catching him by the shoulders. 'The journey continues. Hope hasn't run out because your search is not yet over. The path itself is a means to an end. As long as your path flows, there will be hope.'

"'You are a true friend,' your father said, with a bittersweet smile. "But your words don't reflect reality. Not every path is a solution, only the path that leads us to Truth is. It's doubtful the one to London will lead me there, yet I know very well that I can't stop myself from setting off on it. The greatest of all wars is the one against our own desires, as the prophet Muhammed decreed. I hate to say it, but I've lost the first round in that struggle.'

"'But the battle continues,' I said trying to bolster Poyraz's moral. 'The battle never ends.'

"It must have worked, because for the first time his face shone with hope. 'Well, you are right there,' he said. 'Even if I lose the first round, the battle continues.' Two days later he was off to London with your mother. And I never saw your father again."

İzzet Efendi's voice had become hoarse and his eyes were moist. When he ran out of words, I took over. "My father carried on that battle during those times you didn't see him. He never gave the battle a break. Then twenty-two years ago, he got his revenge for the battle he'd lost in Konya. By abandoning his wife and twelve-year-old daughter with no explanation and setting off on the path to Truth with a Pakistani sheikh."

İzzet Efendi's cinnamon-coloured eyes looked defeated.

"It must have been terrible for you," he said. "That is why it is said a dervish must live in solitude. A dervish's strength lies within his own tribulation. But he should bear that tribulation alone. Otherwise, those close to him will have to share the burden. And it isn't a strength for them, it's a malady."

I couldn't understand whether he was accusing my father of not correctly choosing solitude, or being condescending to us, those close to him. Either way, he had infuriated me. I was just about to respond, when my telephone rang. I looked; it was a number I didn't know. I picked up.

"Yes?"

"Hi, Miss Greenwood," said a woman's voice. "This is Inspector Zeynep."

My anger immediately turned into excitement. Something else must have happened.

"Oh hi, sorry," I stuttered into the phone. It wouldn't be right to talk in front of İzzet Efendi and Mennan. "Can you hang on a minute?"

I looked over at İzzet Efendi.

"Sorry, I have to take this call."

"Of course, my girl," he said politely.

Getting up from my chair and passing beyond the rose bushes, I impatiently prompted, "Go ahead, Inspector Zeynep. I'm listening."

"We need to talk. Could I bother you to come down to the station?"

"Right now?"

She paused.

"Unfortunately, yes. Right now. There has been a change in circumstances and we need you to answer a few more questions."

Hoping to glean something from her, I asked, "What about?"

"Serhad Gökgöz..."

"You don't say. What, did you find something?"

She wasn't as happy with the question as I was; she sounded perturbed. "If you could just come down, we'll be able to speak more freely."

"Sure, I'll be right down," I gushed.

"I'm sorry, it's an emergency. I'm afraid I have to go," I explained, after hanging up and returning to the table. I turned to Mennan, whose puzzled eyes were planted on me.

"You can stay if you'd like, let's not leave İzzet Efendi by himself."

What could Mennan say now? On the one hand, he was dying to know about the phone call. On the other, he really didn't want to miss out on this rare opportunity to chat with İzzet Efendi. In the end, his curiosity got the better of him.

"No," he said, with the thinly veiled passion of a child who doesn't want to be left out of a game. "I'd better come with you. İzzet Efendi is no stranger, he'll forgive me." He held his breath as if there were something on the tip of his tongue he wanted to say, then looked brazenly into my eyes. "But we should've asked him about the ring before leaving."

I was every bit as curious as Mennan about why the ring bled, but I knew it was neither the time nor place to ask. Before I could say so, the old man cut in, "What ring?"

Mennan, noticing my displeasure, didn't want to leave it to chance.

"A ring with a stone that bleeds," he blurted out. "An old man gave it to Miss Greenwood in front of the Shams-i Tabriz Mausoleum."

"I think he was schizophrenic," I said evasively, knowing it would be rude to keep biting my tongue. "Or a beggar. And we don't know that it was bleeding. It was probably just cheap and..."

My words were having no effect on him.

"Have you got the ring with you?" he asked.

It was in my purse; I had put it in a plastic bag after it bled in the tomb. I removed it now and held it out to İzzet Efendi, who took it and held it up to his eyes.

"It's beautiful," he mumbled. "But I can't see it like this. Wait, let me put on my glasses." He took his modest, wire-framed glasses out of his jacket pocket and positioned them on the tip of his nose. He looked at the ring again. "That's some very delicate workmanship," he said, as he studied it. "Is that a topaz? No, it must be a garnet. No no, it's agate. Carnelian agate, this."

He lifted his chin and looked up at me.

"What was this old man like, the one who gave you the ring?"

"He was quite distinguishable actually. He was tall, with messy black hair and a long black beard, black clothes..."

"And mysterious. He came out of nowhere, then a moment later he vanished," Mennan enthusiastically added, believing I'd left out something crucial.

İzzet Efendi nodded as though coming to a conclusion.

"There's a book of Shams-i Tabriz's by the name of *Makalat*. In that book, he speaks of a ring with a bleeding stone."

Mennan and İzzet Efendi's enthusiasm had rubbed off on me now. "What does he say about it?" I asked.

"I don't remember exactly, my girl. That's age for you."

"We'll find the book, Miss Greenwood," Mennan burst in with his usual optimism. "I've got some second-hand bookseller friends in the bazaar. They can help us."

"And I'll look in my library tonight," said İzzet Efendi. "I should have a copy of it lying around. You've got me curious, too. Let me read it again and see what this story of the ring is all about."

"Thank you," I said, extending a hand to the old man. "For everything. I really enjoyed the conversation."

İzzet Efendi stood up and took my hand between his palms. "I should be thanking you, my girl. I was so happy to meet you. You've given me a breath of Poyraz, God bless you." He still hadn't let go of my hand. "But you can't go away with your hands empty," he said with a mock frown. "Elders should always present a gift when their young guests leave."

I thought he'd meant something concrete. Instead he presented us with a poem, which he read in a sonorous voice.

I will tell you words without tongue or lips
I will tell of secrets hidden from all ears
These words for you,
I will say amidst everyone
Though none but you will hear them
And none will understand

When he'd finished, his eyes took on a playful look.

"Rumi," he explained. "Let's see if you will hear the words of this exalted person."

"... a hunch is sufficient reason to open an investigation."

※

As we approached Inspector Zeynep's room, we came face to face with Detective Ragip. Next to him stood two plainclothes policemen, stocky like him.

"Oh, you're here, Miss Greenwood. Go on in. Zeynep is waiting for you." His voice sounded like he'd sloughed off his morning lethargy, but his already beady eyes, still swollen from sleep, had now shrunk to nothing. He leaned in and whispered conspiratorially, "Tell her everything you know. I think we're getting to the bottom of this business."

Before I got the chance to ask what he meant, he'd marched off, the two plainclothes officers in tow. Hoping Inspector Zeynep would be able to shed some light on the matter, we went in and found her behind her desk again. She'd taken off her jacket and her empty holster could be seen under the left sleeve of her lilac shirt. As she gathered her sandy-brown hair from her shoulders and pulled it into a pony-tail behind her head, she smiled warmly in greeting, though the effects of exhaustion were creeping onto her face. We politely shook hands.

"Sorry to call you down here in such a rush," she said. Then, without beating around the bush, she asked, "What do you know about Serhad Gökgöz? You said he worked for Ikonion Tourism?"

"Yes, that's right. He was the chief of security for the Yakut Hotel before it burned down."

Mennan got all excited when he heard Serhad's name.

"Actually, he's a bit of a gofer for the company," he jumped in. "He chauffeurs, oversees construction... does whatever job comes up, I mean. Mr. Kuyumcuzade, the company owner, puts a lot of trust in him."

Perking up, Zeynep turned to look at my colleague.

"I believe you called Serhad a... what was it? A shady character? Why did you say that? Enlighten me."

My co-worker shifted his feet irritably under his chair and scrunched his face up as though he found the mere thought of him repulsive.

"Because he is," he pronounced ambitiously, but then he struggled. "Because, well, that Serhad is the epitome of... He lies with ladies of the evening, eats their money... I mean, he's immoral."

What he was saying about Serhad wasn't really incriminating though, so Zeynep simplified her questions to make it easier for him.

"How long has he been at Ikonion Tourism?"

"Five years. Anyhow, he's not from Konya. It's not even clear where that crook is from. He says he's from Antalya but that's a lie. I have no idea what rock Ziya dragged him out from under, but I do know he's been nothing but trouble for us from the start."

Mennan was digressing again, as Zeynep couldn't help but notice.

"Sounds like you've got a personal beef with him."

Thank god he was clever enough to look at me before responding. As soon as he saw the look of irritation on my face, he knew better than to bring up his daughter.

"In a manner of speaking," he said, tying it up. "What real harm could the guy possibly do me?"

"How long have you known him?"

"Me? Two years maybe? Since Ikonion Tourism became our client. I saw him whenever I went there. Our relationship is based on business and nothing else."

"Okay. Has he ever been involved in any illegal activity that you know of? I mean, like gang violence, extortion, robbery?"

Mennan frowned.

"No," he said hesitantly. "God as my witness, I've heard nothing."

When Zeynep realised Mennan had nothing to give her, she started to get bored.

Trying to liven her up, I continued, "What about that friend of his, Cavit... I don't rember his surname. He's an odd one. Extremely fussy, obsessive-compulsive about germs... If you saw him, you too would have your doubts. Both Serhad and Cavit fit the typical criminal profile."

"And what exactly is the typical criminal profile?" she asked, with a twinge of sarcasm.

"You know, sociopathic behavior, exaggerated and menacing gestures, swaggering walk, foul language..."

She laughed. "I don't know what it's like where you're from, but here, if we were to throw every man fitting that description into the clink, half the country would be behind bars."

"Men are the same the world over. But," I said, to keep the subject on track, "Cavit and Serhad really are the type to arouse suspicion. And they are also close to Mr. Kuyumcuzade."

"Isn't that normal? They work together."

Was she trying to get the particulars or did she just not care about our opinions? I found her attitude demoralising, but I kept at it, stubbornly shaking my head.

"No, not like that. It's like they are all up to something together."

She seemed to revive a bit.

"Like what?"

"In my estimation, Mr. Kuyumcuzade is having them do his dirty work for him. We were just with them two hours ago. If you could have seen how they were interacting... It was like, Ziya was behaving more like a mafia kingpin than a company boss."

"Yes, yes," said Mennan, in support. "Exactly like a mafia kingpin."

"You seem quite sure of yourselves," she said, still sounding unconvinced. "Are you certain there's nothing you're not telling me?"

"No. It's just a hunch," I admitted, feeling defeated. "But you know as well as I do, a hunch is sufficient reason to open an investigation. If we keep on this trail, it will eventually turn up some evidence or testimony."

"If 'we' keep on it? What do you mean 'we'?"

"Why not?" I asked casually. "All these crimes we're talking about appear to be intertwined, including the Yakut Hotel fire I'm investigating. The fire and the bizarre murder of Lefty Kamil, aren't they both felonies?" I tried to clarify. "One of them took the lives of two workers, the other a thief. That's three victims."

"Not all victims, Miss Greenwood. Homicide," she stated emphatically, as though citing a law of some weight, "is only concerned with people who were murdered. Those who were shot, knifed, poisoned, beaten to death, strangled, thrown off some high place, or killed by other various means you couldn't possibly conceive..."

I listened, disenchanted, as Zeynep made it clear she wasn't going to collaborate with me. Had I been wrong about her? Was she nothing more than an overly-ambitious, arrogant police officer?

"Lefty Kamil's death was murder," she said, carrying on with her lecture. "But we don't know about the Yakut Hotel fire. The fire brigade's report says it was accidental and the attorney general ruled it inconclusive. Could the fire have been arson despite that? I suppose so. Something may have been overlooked by someone... the police, the fire brigade, the attorney general... Every investigation involves some intuition; you are right about that. You also may be right in thinking Serhad started that fire. But for the time being, there is nothing to back up those allegations. As I said this morning, without evidence, or a witness, there is nothing we can do."

"But there is a witness," my colleague put in. "Kadir Gemelek."

Zeynep looked at him skeptically.

"Who is Kadir Gemelek?"

"He's the head of the four-man cleaning crew," Mennan continued. "He was there when the fire broke out. They were meant to be there on Monday, but Kadir was throwing his son's engagement party that day so they went in on Tuesday instead."

She couldn't make sense of what he was saying.

"What difference does it make what day they went in?"

Mennan was having difficulty explaining himself, so I took over. "Kadir hadn't informed Serhad about his son's engagement party or their change in plans. If the cleaning crew had gone in on Monday when they were scheduled to, no one would have got hurt. Ziya and his men had specifically chosen Tuesday to start the fire, thinking no one would be there."

"That's speculation," Zeynep said, pursing her lips. "What's to say it wasn't coincidence the fire broke out on Tuesday?"

"Well, Kadir's getting hit on the head was no coincidence."

I was once again impressed with Mennan's perfect timing.

"That's right, Inspector," he carried on. "Kadir saw someone while he was trying to rescue his friends. And at that exact moment, someone else came up behind him and knocked him over the head."

Though she kept her composure, I could see our rendition of events was finally making an impact on Zeynep.

"So, who did he see?"

"He couldn't recognise him. The man was completely wrapped in one of those silver fireproof outfits the firefighters wear."

"So the man was never actually identified?" Her look was again one of smug indulgence.

"How could he be?" I answered, losing my patience. "The man was completely covered up. There was a huge explosion in the basement. The thinners and paint cannisters had caught fire. Kadir found one of his co-workers unconscious and carried her upstairs to the lobby on his back. Serhad was there in the lobby, and was shocked to see the two of them because he thought the hotel was empty. Cavit must have still been downstairs after starting the fire."

"How do you know it was Cavit who started the fire?"

"Cavit is so fanatical about cleanliness that the prospect of getting any soot on his face or hands would have made him crazy. No one else would have bothered to wear that all-encompassing fireproof suit."

"Hmm. Go on."

Serhad panicked when Kadir brought Nezihe up to the lobby. He was afraid Kadir would figure out they had set the fire themselves, so he followed him down. Kadir then saw Cavit, whom he couldn't recognise because of the fireproof suit. And Cavit saw him too, of course. At which point, Serhad snuck up behind him and hit him over the head with a blunt object, knocking him unconscious. Cavit then took off the fireproof suit and ran from the hotel."

"Then what? Did he just leave Kadir down there?"

She was finally beginning to understand.

"That's right. Instead of bringing him up, he just notified the fire station and waited for them to do it. Maybe he was even hoping Kadir would die in the fire, because he had no way of knowing for sure that he hadn't recognised Cavit. But luck was on Kadir's side. Before the flames could reach him, the firemen arrived and pulled him out."

"So isn't that what this Kadir's statement says?"

"Of course it is. But the prosecutor didn't accept his statement on the grounds of mental incompetence."

"What, Kadir Gemelek isn't mentally competent?"

"He was suffering from trauma the day he gave his statement. But now he remembers everything more clearly."

"So no one but the two of you are taking him seriously."

"Unfortunately not."

She placed her thumb on her lip and thought a moment.

"And Ziya and his men, worried this would get back to you, let loose on Lefty Kamil because..."

"Because," I said, helping her sum things up, "they wanted to scare me into completing my report as quickly as possible. The sooner I leave Konya, the less I know of the details that will expose the truth."

She clasped her hands on her desk in front of her. "Well, that certainly is some clever conjecture, but it's still conjecture nonetheless. And unless you can come up with something more concrete, I'm afraid it will remain just conjecture."

The hope I'd felt creeping up in me just as suddenly vanished.

"Perhaps if you searched Serhad and Cavit's house, you would come across that concrete something. A fireproof suit, for instance."

With thinly veiled irritation, her pretty eyes skimmed my face.

"Don't worry. We'll do that too, if it comes to it."

I hoped that meant she was really considering it.

"Really, why did you call us here?" I challenged her.

"To ask about Serhad."

"Why? Is there some connection between Serhad and Lefty Kamil?"

Laughing, she leaned forward onto her elbows, taking her head between her hands as though it had become too heavy for her neck.

"I see we've swapped roles, Miss Greenwood. You've become the interrogator and I the interrogatee."

"I'm just trying to be helpful."

She took a deep breath and leaned back again.

"Yes. We've come across certain evidence linking Serhad to Lefty Kamil."

"That dirty liar!" Mennan snarled. "Not two hours ago he was telling us how he didn't even know who Lefty was."

Suddenly Zeynep was all ears.

"He said he didn't know him?"

Mennan, overcome with doubt, turned his green eyes on me as though to ask if that weren't the case.

"He said he didn't know him," I confirmed. "That he'd never heard the name."

"That's great. Maybe we can corner him that way," she mumbled under her breath.

"So, were they friends?" I asked, unable to contain my curiosity.

All at once she grew distant, as though we'd only just come into her office.

"Who?" she said absently.

This was too much.

"Serhad and Kamil," I droned.

"We're not sure yet. We're looking into it."

"Shouldn't we be working together? I was hoping for a compromise, not this impasse. We've told you everything we know. Couldn't you return the favour? Maybe then we could help you."

"You would only get in the way, Miss Greenwood," she said, putting an end to the subject. Then noticing the hostility in my eyes she added, "Please don't look at me that way. You just do your job and let me do mine."

"But we have mutual interests..."

"No," she said, shaking her head. "We do not have mutual interests. You are interested in saving your company three million pounds. We are interested in justice."

"What? That's not..."

"Please don't interrupt me," she warned. "Maybe you think that just because you are motivated by money and stand to make a direct profit from this business, that you are working more ardently than I am. That I am merely a civil servant, and not as determined to stay on top of the situation. But you are mistaken. I haven't had a wink of sleep in exactly twenty-four hours and I am still dealing with this racket. We are in this till the end, regardless of whether your insurance company has its own investigation. And not only for Lefty Kamil's murder, but also for the husband and wife those pseudo religious freaks butchered. If your assumptions turn out to be valid, we will also find whoever it is who killed those two poor workers in the fire. But it is not my job to rescue your three million pounds, Miss Greenwood. So don't tell me our interests are mutual. They are not."

I was stunned. I felt completely wronged, yet I didn't know how to put it into words. Mennan was in a worse state than I was. His hands were sunk between his knees and he sat frozen in place, his face red as a beet.

"I am shocked," I finally managed to say. "I didn't deserve that. You are treating me like I'm a criminal."

"Wrong again, Miss Greenwood," she calmly continued. "I would never treat an innocent person like a criminal. And you are no criminal. But what you must understand is this. You are not the one heading this investigation. You are in no way conducting any of it. If you want to help, you will share with us what you know, like you did now. That is the biggest favour you can do us."

"Does it really make any difference?" I asked flippantly.

"Of course it does." She was smiling amicably now, as though she hadn't just given me a tongue-lashing. "Your input has been vital. We now have even more material with which to interrogate Serhad and Cavit."

"What? You mean you're taking Serhad and Cavit into custody?"

"What do you suppose Detective Ragip is doing right at this moment?"

Mennan and I sat stunned for one second before it sank in and our moods were restored.

"So you'll do a search of their houses as well?"

"We will," she said with a vague smile. "And of course, while we're searching, we'll keep an eye out for a used fireman's suit."

"Because we've lost our sun."

※

The darkness of night was falling silently over the city. Mennan's black Mercedes was slowly making its way through the streets of Konya's lighted boulevards. I was no longer sitting in the back, but in the seat next to his, like a friend. On either side, in the light that streamed out from the shops, crowds rushed past us; people with small packages in hand filling the pavements, the exhaustion of the day on their shoulders, the comfort of being on their way home in their faces.

Like them, I felt exhausted. I was deprived of sleep. Along with the falling darkness, it was becoming impossible for me to fight back the heaviness that spread in my eyelids. I knew Mennan wasn't much better off. After we'd left the police station, we spent some time discussing Inspector Zeynep's startling behavior. Poor Mennan had even apologised on her behalf with his usual abject demeanor, although it was unnecessary. No matter how difficult it had been for me to accept it during our argument, Zeynep was right. It was no secret that police didn't like anyone from outside meddling in their investigations, least of all someone who had a stake in the business like me. Zeynep was being patient, for a cop. The London police hadn't shown even a fraction of the understanding she had during a recent investigation I'd headed for the Tate Modern after some Picasso sketches were stolen. Still, I couldn't deny that her behavior had got to me a bit because, for whatever reason, I felt an affinity towards her.

Before returning to the hotel, we stopped off to visit a friend of Mennan's who sold used books to try and find a copy of the *Makalat*. Although he didn't have one in his shop, he rang another bookseller and within ten minutes it was in our hands. Back in the car, I opened the cover straight away and looked at the contents. Unfortunately, there was no mention of a ring in any of the chapter headings, which meant I would have to comb through the whole book. It was hard to contain my impatience, but I put the book in my bag, resigned to waiting till back at the hotel. Until eventually, like the soft darkness that descended on the city, a sweet sleepiness gently took hold of my mind, leaving me in no state to think either of the ring or of the book that held its secret. And though I knew it wouldn't be ideal to fall asleep in Mennan's car, I couldn't prevent my eyelids from slowly closing.

I had almost nodded off when the melody on my phone signaling an incoming text brought me to with a start. I knew chances were it was just one of those annoying ads, but at least it would help me wake up. But I was wrong, it was from Nigel. So now he'd resorted to sending texts, I thought, as I realised we hadn't spoken that day and he'd done all the calling since I'd come to Konya. I flashed a smile at Mennan, who was watching me from the corner of his eye, then opened the message. The first words I read gave me goosebumps.

My Shams (my sun), my moon, has come.

Hearing Shams's name mentioned by a Konyan would've been no big surprise, but it had caught me completely off guard coming from a Londoner who, as far as I knew, had never heard the name of the wandering dervish before. Mennan must have noticed the change in my expression because he asked nervously, "Something wrong?"

"No," I said, regaining my composure. "Just a friend from London saying hello."

I looked back down at the phone.

My Shams - my sun - my moon, has come
My eye, my ear, has come

My body of silver has come
My gold mine has come
My head's intoxication has come
The follower of my path has come
The breaker of my vows has come
The light in my eyes has come
Whatever else I wished for
What I wished for has come

The poem ended here, but Nigel's message continued.

That is how Rumi calls his lover Shams to him. So, my Karen, when are you coming back?

I was wide awake now. Nothing remained of the sleepiness that had weighed down my eyelids, or the daze I had been in from the day's events. Who would have thought my surgeon boyfriend would turn out to be a romantic? Maybe it was the distance between us that brought it out in him.

I scrolled back to the beginning of the message, stuck on that first line: *My Shams - my sun.* I couldn't decide if it meant the word shams meant 'sun', or if it was just one of the great poet's metaphors. My Konyan colleague would no doubt have the answer, but he was the last person I wanted to discuss Shams with now. I was considering this when our car turned a corner onto a wider, though calmer, street, with a wall stretching along the left side. A bit further on, a wrought iron gate with turbaned headstones beyond it drew my attention. It was a graveyard, and it was enormous.

"The Three Saints Cemetery. It's really old." Mennan explained, when he noticed my interest.

"Do you know the story behind the name?"

"Of course. It's also an old one. It's said that seven hundred years ago, three young men came all the way from Khorasan to see Rumi. The men were totally enamoured with their Mevlana, but sadly, they arrived to find he had recently passed away. When they realised they weren't going to be united with him, they loved him with an even greater passion. They also wished death on themselves, and begged to be buried in the earth alongside him. And they got their wish - the three youths immediately perished on the spot and were subsequently buried here in this graveyard. From then on out it was called the Three Saints Cemetery."

When I turned back round, we were coming upon some large, lighted buildings.

"Where are we?"

"You don't recognise it, do you." he said laughing. "It's Mevlana's Mausoleum. I brought you back by a different route. Your hotel is just there."

We'd arrived. I knew he wouldn't be able to drag the subject out, so I took the opportunity to ask, "Mennan, what does the name 'Shams' mean? From what I understand, it isn't Turkish."

"That's right," he said, keeping his eyes on the road. "It's Arabic. It means sun."

Sun. My childhood miracle friend, Sunny, suddenly sprang to mind. I imagined his shiny blonde hair, his eyes a blue as deep as the sky... the imaginary friend of a girl who longed for sunlight during the unfailingly grey, misty London days. Sunny, whose name so suitably evoked the brightest of stars.

"There's a nice little anecdote of Rumi's relating to the name Shams," he carried on, with no knowledge of Sunny and unaware of the strange feeling beginning to swell inside me. "One day Rumi was called to the heavens. His Holiness complied, and began ascending the tiers of heaven one by one. When he came to the fourth tier, there was darkness all around.

"'What happened? Why is it dark like this?' Rumi immediately asked.

"'It's because we've lost our sun,' the angels explained sorrowfully.

"Mevlana was puzzled. 'How did that happen? How could you lose the sun?' he asked.

"The bereaved angels answered him, 'Our sun was Shams of Tabriz. This level of heaven used to be illuminated by his light. But there were cold hearts down on earth, so he went down to warm them. And that is why we are left in this impenetrable darkness.'

"Mevlana cheered up. 'Do not worry, innocent creatures of God,' he called out to them. 'The light in Shams is so strong, so bright, so hot - it is more than enough to heat the hearts on earth, as well as those in the heavens...'"

Mennan was crazy about stories like these, whether he himself was telling them, or listening to someone else explain them. Whenever one of these mystical tales came up, he forgot all about this world and was in virtual ecstasy. Unfortunately for him, we were back in front of my hotel again.

"That should tell you what a great man Shams was, Miss Greenwood," he said, stepping on the brakes. "Those who attain his good graces are God's lucky subjects."

Meaning, the way he saw it, I was one of them whether I knew it or not. I didn't have the time or energy to argue back.

"I guess so," I said, wrapping it up. "Let's get plenty of rest tonight. Then tomorrow we'll see what Inspector Zeynep's investigation turns up. Shall we meet in front of the hotel at ten?"

"Sounds good. And if I hear anything in the meantime, I'll let you know."

"Thanks. Good night then."

"Good night..."

I paused before getting out of the car.

"I know we haven't met, but send your wife and daughter my regards."

A warm smile spread across his face.

"Thanks, I will. You'll have to come for dinner one day soon. Semra cooks exquisitely."

"We'll see. Let's get this business sorted out first and maybe then."

A cool evening wind hit my face as I got out of the car. The heat of the day was giving way to the crisp, dry chill of night. That, together with my fatigue, made me feel cold. I stepped quickly into the hotel, where the meddling receptionist was on duty again. "Good evening, Miss Greenwood. How was your day?" he asked his usual question as I was marching past.

"Fantastic." Without giving him the chance to open his mouth again, I added, "It will be even better if you could send a salad, yoghurt, and wheat bread up to my room. And if you've got any fresh-squeezed orange juice, I'll have a big glass of that as well, thanks."

I listed it all so fast, he couldn't manage to put in that it wasn't his job.

"As you wish, Miss Greenwood. I'll ring the restaurant straight away and let them know."

I knew the receptionist was dying to know what I'd been up to since the previous night's incidents, but I thanked him and headed past, leaving him unappeased.

In front of the lift was a young couple with a baby. I stood back as the doors opened, leaving the lift to them.

"Come on," the young mother said casually. "There's room for us all."

"I don't want to impose..."

"You aren't..." insisted the husband, who held the baby. "Come on in."

"Thank you," I said, stepping in.

"Which floor?" the woman asked.

"First."

"Same as us," she imparted, as she pushed the button.

From where I was standing, I could see the baby's face. It was as round as the moon, and it already had well-shaped eyebrows and long black lashes. "Is it a girl?" I asked. "She's beautiful."

The young father laughed.

"No," he stated proudly. "A boy."

"What's his name?"

"Jelaleddin."

"After Rumi," the young woman explained. "Jelaleddin Rumi."

They seemed delighted by the attention. The man twisted well round so that I could see the child's face better and, looking down at his son admiringly, murmured, "He has a middle name, too."

Was it Shams, I wondered?

"Ali," said the young father. "Like the prophet Muhammed's son-in-law, Ali."

"How old is he?"

"He'll be eight months in two days."

"Well, I wish him a wonderful life."

"Thank you," said the young mother. "Have you got one?"

I didn't know what to say. She assumed I hadn't understood her.

"A child, I mean..."

"Not yet."

I must have sounded bitter, because she tried to make me feel better, saying, "Don't worry, you will. You're still young."

Under any other circumstances, I would have been annoyed by a comment like that, especially coming from a stranger. But the young woman's intentions were so pure that I took it in stride. Or maybe I was just becoming more Turkish myself, after three days in this country.

"Thanks," I said.

While the young couple doted over their son, I tried to envision what our child would look like at eight months - its eyes and eyebrows, hands and feet... But I couldn't come up with anything. How strange, I thought. Here was this baby, growing bigger inside me by the minute, yet I still couldn't conjure up any image of the creature it would be. We came to our floor and all got off the lift together. My room was just before theirs.

"Good night," I said, moving towards my door. As I put the key into the lock, a wave of resentment passed over me. It was similar to the one I'd felt my first day here in Konya; the same profound loneliness and sense of abandonment. As soon as I was in my room, I dialled Nigel. He answered on the second ring.

"Karen!" he said affectionately. "What a nice surprise."

"Hi, Nigel. How was your day?"

"Busy, if you must know. But much better now that you've called. What about you?"

His voice was like a tonic.

"Also better now, thanks."

"You sound a bit tired."

What do you expect? I felt like saying. *The Shams from your poem has taken over my nightmares and won't leave me in peace, as even more horrific things are taking place in real life. I was jumped by a thief, who was later murdered. The police raided the hotel and questioned me, of all people. After which my colleague, fixated on a seven-hundred-year-old book, came and badgered*

*me with his mystical conspiracy theories. I finally managed
to get rid of him and got into the bath to regain some peace of
mind, only to fall asleep and nearly drown during yet another
nightmare. But it doesn't end there. There were more visits to
the police station, nerve-racking interviews... At some point I
squeezed in a visit to Rumi's Mausoleum, which would have been
the high point of my day if it hadn't come to an abrupt end when
the ring Shams gave me started to bleed again. I met my father's
childhood friend, who told me things about my father that I've
never heard before - things that shocked, saddened, and angered
me - though the old man didn't seem to care one wit. There was an
infuriating conversation with a female police investigator... Then
a short while ago, unaware of the baby I already carry inside me,
a young mother wished a child for me, unwittingly sending my
emotions all helter-skelter. And there you have it, my sweet Nigel,
that's my reason for my being so tired.*

But I didn't say any of that. I just made a weak attempt to
sound more animated and explained, "I had a busy day, too."

Nigel wasn't convinced.

"Karen, you're okay, aren't you? I mean, you aren't having
any problems with your pregnancy? Nausea, dizziness...?"

Any interest at all in my pregnancy was a plus; I would
take what I could get.

"I had a bit of morning sickness today. And I felt dizzy at
one point, like I was going to fall over."

"Promise me you'll take it easy. We'll get it taken care
of just as soon as you get back and you'll get over all these
symptoms."

I didn't know what to say, and when the silence grew too
long, he asked, "Are you there?"

"Yes, I'm here."

"Why don't you answer?

I was tongue-tied.

"Karen. Are you all right?"

"I'm fine. Just thinking about the text you sent me."

"It's a beautiful poem, isn't it? They really loved each
other... it's incredible. But," he said hesitantly, "there's
something I couldn't understand. Shams was a man, wasn't
he? Did Rumi write all those love poems to a man?"

"The ones you read were written to him."

"So were they..."

"Not in the way you're thinking," I said. "It was more of a spiritual bond. Kind of like the love Christian saints had for each other..."

"I've never heard of Christian saints writing love poems like that to each other."

Neither had I; I'd only said it by way of an explanation. I tried again. "Think of it like a love of God. Like seeing God in one of his creations... A kind of secret..."

"What secret?" he asked, puzzled.

"A secret regarding the meaning of life. The mystery between God and people..."

I could see that I wasn't explaining myself, perhaps because I didn't really understand the bond between Shams and Mevlana either. Shams was always talking about reaching the truth, what my father would call a love of God and İzzet Efendi had referred to as a secret, though both explanations were lost on me.

"So," I said, changing the subject, "are you taking my mum out for dinner?"

"I am. We spoke on the phone this morning and she didn't sound so bad. She was heading off to join the peace protests in Trafalgar Square. She said I could pick her up this evening if the police didn't arrest her."

"She's crazy," I said, worried. "I really hope she doesn't get herself into trouble."

"She'll be fine, sweetheart. She's been to heaps of protests. Have you ever once seen her hauled in by the police?"

He was right, of course. I didn't know of any other woman who was so on the ball. Gay rights, tolerance towards Muslims, protection of rain forests, animal rights... you name it. Despite having taken part in nearly any protest you could dream up, she'd only ever once been taken into custody that I knew of. And that was thirty years ago - for smoking marijuana in a bar after the protest had finished. But you could never be sure, she wasn't so young anymore.

"Please, keep an eye on her Nigel," I begged him. "She's been so sensitive since Mathew died. I'm afraid she'll do something stupid, or get herself hurt."

"Don't worry, love." he said in a deep, reassuring voice. "When you return to London, I will deliver Susan to you in the same cheerful state that you left her in. Just when are you coming back, by the way?"

"Soon I hope," I said, trying to avoid the subject. It didn't work. Nigel persisted.

"Soon? How many days?"

I appreciated his insistence, but how could I head back to London when I didn't even have a passport?

"I don't know. Three I guess. Give or take."

He wasn't appeased.

"Give or take?"

"Okay then, three days. And if I finish my job here any earlier, I'll try to come back even sooner."

"And if you can't finish?"

"Then you will come here," I said, laughing it off. "And we'll research this big secret between Shams and Rumi together."

Luckily, he went for that, and also began to laugh.

"Well, we should definitely go to Konya together one day. I really am interested in this Rumi. And their big secret... where they lived, and..." He paused. "And seeing as how you are half Konyan yourself, your father being from there and all, it would be interesting to explore his city together."

I didn't know how I would feel if Nigel really showed up here, but I jumped in without considering how it would end.

"Great, come on over. Then we can go back together."

"I'm afraid that's out of the question," he said, serious again. "I'm so busy this week. I only have tomorrow off and after that I'll be going from one surgery to the next. But whatever happens, you don't be late, okay? Look, you said three days..."

"All right, my love, I promise. I'll be back in London in three days time."

"The beauty of their bodies has made them delirious."

※

As soon as I'd hung up with with Nigel, I opened Shams's book and began searching for the story of the ring. It wasn't easy finding a single anecdote in a five-hundred-page book, but luck was on my side; as I flipped through it, I came across the story of the ring on the forty-fourth page. Shams had explained it like this:

> One day the sheikh told the dervish, "Halife has forbidden you to perform the *sema*." This restriction became a knot in the dervish's heart. The dervish fell ill and was bed-ridden. The doctor took the dervish's pulse and tried to find the reason for his illness, but it wasn't like any other illness he'd seen. He tried various cures, but none of them helped the dervish. Then one day the dervish died, but the doctor didn't give up trying to find the reason behind the illness he hadn't been able to cure. He opened the dervish's grave, exhumed the body, and moved it to the infirmary. There he cut into the chest and removed the heart. He saw that the dervish's heart had a knot in it. The knot had hardened into a stone, just like agate. The doctor kept this stone for years, but one day he fell on hard times and sold it. After passing from hand to hand, the stone was acquired by Halife, who had it made into a ring. One day, while at a *sema*, she looked down and noticed her dress was covered in blood. She examined herself, but there was no sign of any cuts or bruises. She removed the ring, and the stone turned to blood and flowed away.

That was all there was to the story, but it was enough to wreak havoc on my mind.

"What?" I breathed, horrified. "The stone was taken from a human heart?"

I got up from the book and went for my bag. It took me a moment to muster the courage, but in the end, I opened my bag and took it out. I examined the stone carefully. If it hadn't bled twice before my own eyes, I might not have believed there was any connection to the ring in the book. So whose heart had this stone come from - Shams's? Why would his heart form a knot? He was a holy man, one of the mystics that carried God's great secret. What could have possibly prevented him from performing the *sema*? There was a knock at the door as though the answer had arrived. I jumped.

"Room service," called out whoever had knocked. "Your order."

Where was my mind? Was I so daft as to have forgotten I'd ordered food? I pulled myself together and opened the door. Without allowing the waiter inside, I signed the slip and took the tray from him. Everything I'd asked for was there - the salad, the yoghurt, even the orange juice. It was only my appetite that was missing now, as I was too busy obsessing on Shams. How had things got so blown out of proportion? It was just a ring. Why was I even discussing it with Mennan and İzzet Efendi? Then, as if discussing it weren't enough, I was now reading the books they'd recommended? I had to get my head in order. I put the ring back in my bag and, taking the book from the table, tucked it into a drawer. And that was that. I sat down to my meal and, although I still had no appetite, stubbornly ate up every last bit of it.

After eating, I was overcome with drowsiness. I didn't have the energy to write a mail to Simon, so I chose the easier course and rang him. Strangely, his phone was off. That never happened, Simon was a total workaholic. But there was nothing to be done about it now, I'd have to catch him in the morning.

I got up and went into the bathroom. I threw some water on my face and hastily brushed my teeth, impatient to get into bed. I turned out the lights, but the room didn't go as dark as I expected. When I looked around, I noticed a light blinking in the mirror. Not so bright, but a persistent, yellow light. It couldn't be coming from outside, I thought, looking around. Had I left a lamp on?

When I turned back, I found myself in front of a wooden window. Inside it a candle burned, its flickering light spilling outside. I was back in the garden again, in front of the double-storey clay house with the tiled pool, the tall slim poplars and incandescent moon... Near me, very near me, I felt someone sucking in their breath. I turned and looked. There was no mistake, I could sense a heart pounding with exhilaration and fear. It was as though I were reliving a dream I'd had.

But no, this was different. My whole body was trembling with the evil that had taken hold of my mind. I was furiously searching for someone. They had to be around here somewhere. I could feel their intermingled breaths, hear their whispers in my ears. I looked towards the huge walnut tree behind me. Its branches were so thick and spiny, its leaves so broad and dense, its shade so heavy and deep, that it was shutting out the moonlight and I couldn't see what was under it. But though I couldn't see them, I knew those I searched for were there in the darkness. My spirit was so broken, my soul so wounded, like a disheartened child I'd forgotten everything I knew and held sacred and had turned into a fiery ball of hatred.

I squinted, trying in vain to make out the shapes of those I searched for. That dark, viscous shade wasn't allowing it. I had no control, my feet dragged me of their own accord into the shade of the walnut tree. As the moist chill of its leaves struck my face, I saw them. They were intertwined, two young people who had become one mind, one heart, one body. I stopped. My embarrassment hindered my steps. For a moment, I stood watching the scene play out in shadows, silhouettes in the darkness. They were so tangled up in each other that they were in no position to see me, nor this moonlit night, nor the walnut tree that shielded them. But for all the clandestine quality of this tryst, this illicit affair, this forbidden love, it was not without an oddly alluring beauty for this observer. When I'd shed all my feelings of jealousy, wretchedness, and deception and looked, the two youths appeared to be one perfectly natural entity. *Get out of here!* said a voice inside me. *Pretend you haven't seen them. Pretend this never happened. They are still so young, the beauty of their bodies has made them delirious, the fire in their hearts has made them drunk. Leave them alone. Leave them, let their own sins allocate their punishments. Leave them, let their own regret be retribution for your blackened heart. Leave them, let their own consciences tear their cursed love to shreds.*

My surging anger at once began to wane, my hatred to die down. And though my resentment hadn't completely passed, compassion outweighed it. I was about to leave, but that moon! That accursed sky! They wouldn't allow me to do what was befitting. Until all at once, a cold, hard light, like the glare of a one-eyed demon, cut a path through the trees and lit up the two entwined bodies at the foot of the thick-trunked tree. And as the full moon touched them, the two bodies, gently stirring with the fire of passion, turned into a single silver snake before my eyes. For a moment I froze. For a moment I watched their symbiotic movements as they slithered lustfully on the ground. My newly quelled temper suddenly exploded like a volcano, my abated jealousy swelled like a stormy sea, and as my compassion fell away, my anger warped into a wrath without mercy. I watched as the exposed torso of the female heaved, shining under the light of the moon, then went still as she held her breath. She stayed motionless like that for a bit, listening to the night like a startled animal. Despite my silence, she sensed I was there. She could feel the breath of my rage. She threw the body of the male off her, and the silver snake came apart, separating into two human bodies once more.

"There's someone there," said the girl, trying to button her shirt. "There's someone there in the darkness."

The boy stood up audaciously, shamelessly, pulling the girl up with him. In the light of the moon, he looked like a wild animal challenging the world. It crossed my mind to jump him, right then and there, in the very place this sin was committed. But what if someone from the houses heard? I changed my mind and backed further away. The young man squinted, looking into the darkness, but he was standing in the light and therefore couldn't see me.

"No," he said, trying to hold the girl. "Don't worry, there's no one there."

"There is... Over there, I'm sure of it."

As she said this she continued to fumble with the buttons on her shirt.

"Are you going?" asked the young man. "Are you going and leaving me like this?"

The girl was scared.

"I have to," she said excitedly. "If he comes back and doesn't see me, there will be the devil to pay."

The male was convinced now that his lover was taking her leave, but he couldn't help ask, "When will we see each other again?"

The female quickly pulled herself together.

"I don't know," she said, out of breath. "I have to go home right away."

When she said this, I turned round and, in order to reach home before her, started with long strides towards the room with the window I'd been looking through only a short while before.

The room was dimly lit with a red glow now, the light from the last smoldering candle. An ill-boding light that, with its quivering flame, scrawled the inevitable on the room's clay wall. As I stepped inside, my black shadow, like my fury, grew until it had pervaded the whole room. I snuggled into the darkness of my rage and waited. It wasn't long before the girl, who had fastened her buttons as she rose from my side this morning and opened them at the side of another this evening, came sweeping in. She didn't see me at first, she was trying to catch her breath and calm her heaving chest. She walked over and stood opposite the mirror in the middle of the room; tried to tuck her disheveled, hennaed hair, like a flag of mutiny for her forbidden love, inside her embroidered headscarf.

"Where were you?"

My voice boomed throughout the deep, high-ceilinged room and echoed like a repeated warning, "*Where were you?*"

She spun round and peered into the darkness. She still couldn't see me, but she immediately understood my intentions. She made a move towards the door but I blocked her. She darted towards the window, but I stopped her again. She shook like a willowy tree branch in my arms.

"Didn't I tell you, you were not to see him anymore?"

Her lips, rosy from kissing, parted slightly.

"I didn't see anyone. I went to the outhouse."

"Swear it," I said, trying to drag the Qur'an on the bookstand in front of the window towards her. "You will swear, with God as your witness."

Terrified, she fought back. "Let go," she cried out, turning round. "Let me go."

Her voice came out as a screech. If it went on like this, we would wake the whole house. I tried to cover her mouth with my hand. She leaned her head back and cried out, "Help me! Somebody help me, he's going to kill me!"

Unable to cover her mouth, I wrapped my hands around her throat.

"Quiet," I whispered. "Quiet, stop shouting."

She wouldn't listen to me, she wanted to bring everyone here so that she could get away. I couldn't let her do that. I dragged her into the centre of the room and we collapsed onto a cushion together. My hands tightened around her neck.

"Quiet. For god's sake, be quiet."

She wasn't listening; she kept struggling to push me off her. In a rage, I shook her neck. There was a snap, like the sound heard when a rose is prematurely plucked from the vine. Her muffled scream echoed throughout the room, in the same way the resonance of a drop, breaking free from its cloud, is amplified when it hits the ground. Then silence. Then stillness. Then in her glazed doe eyes, the reflection of myself crying - a black clad, black bearded, black eyed, black hearted dervish in the darkness. Then a door opening. The silhouette of a young man frozen in front of it. Then his delirious face, burning in the dying light of the candle flickering inside. His delirious words.

"You've killed her... You've killed her! You've killed her and the baby in her womb!"

Then I directed my gaze down to the wafer-thin body of the young girl, lying lifeless in my lap as though she'd fallen asleep. Then the sound of a baby crying in the room. The baby's insistent wail, resounding off the high ceiling and bouncing to the stone floor, and from there to the clay walls, and from there to the wooden door, and then oozing quietly into my soul's own hell. The voice of a baby that is inconsolable, knows nothing of silence, yearns for the mother forever lost to it; a voice brave like life, ancient like hope, sacred like hunger.

"Life treats women cruelly, Karen..."

✵

I woke to the sound of a baby crying. When I opened my eyes, I was in bed in my hotel room. The last thing I remembered was the light in the mirror. I couldn't remember falling asleep, or lying down even. I could, however, vividly recall every detail of my dream. The slim neck of the young girl that snapped like the stem of a rose between those powerful hands... between my hands? No, they belonged to Shams, I reasoned. But had he really killed Kimya? Maybe Shams was forbidden to perform the *sema* because he'd killed this innocent girl. If the *sema* represented ascension to heaven, then perhaps, due to this great sin, Shams was stuck in purgatory. That would explain his needing help, though not why it had to be me. He'd chosen me for my name, or because my father was a dervish like him, or for some other reason that I couldn't fathom. But how could I help him? I knew so little about Sufism, even my mother knew more than I did. The baby began to cry again. My hair stood on end. I jumped up and switched on the lights, afraid I may be stuck in the dream. I turned to look in the mirror and was comforted when it was my own image I saw there. But the baby kept crying. I stood in the middle of the room and listened, trying to figure out where it was coming from. It suddenly dawned on me that it was Jelaleddin, the baby of the couple who were staying in the neighbouring room. How could it not have woken them? They must have been sleeping even more soundly than I had. As I considered whether or not I should try to wake them, the phone began to ring. Oddly enough, that stopped the baby crying. My peace of mind restored, I picked up. But then my mother's furious voice filled my ear.

"Karen, you are going to have that baby."

Here we go, she'd heard I was pregnant.

"What baby?" I asked innocently. "What are you talking about, Mum?"

"And you have the audacity to lie about it? If Nigel hadn't let it slip out, I never would have known. You were planning to get rid of it without even telling me, weren't you?"

She was trying to shout but couldn't manage; her voice sounded raspy. Not just to change the subject, but also out of genuine curiosity, I asked, "What happened to your voice? Why are you so hoarse? You didn't catch cold, did you?"

"Don't try to change the subject," she scolded. "I haven't caught cold. There was a peace protest today and I shouted too much. Now, forget about my voice and tell me, were you going to do this without my knowledge?"

Of course. She'd been at a protest. Well, at least she'd kept out of trouble and got off with just losing her voice. My weaseling my way out of this was going to prove more difficult.

"Would I go through all that without telling you?" I evasively asked, trying to placate her. "We just found out. A few days before I came here."

"Stop prevaricating. You know as well as I do it wouldn't have made any difference when you found out. Why should you need your mother's opinion on an important subject like this? What would your mother know about it?"

"Mum, please don't. I didn't want to upset you."

"Didn't want to upset me? What could be more upsetting than hearing about your daughter's pregnancy from the bloke who got her that way?"

She must have been seriously angry; otherwise, she'd never have called Nigel a 'bloke'.

"I was going to tell you, really. Just as soon as I got back from Konya. I really do need your advice on this."

She showed no sign of calming down.

"Why should you need my advice? You've long since opted to terminate."

"Actually, if you look at it, I haven't opted for anything yet."

"You haven't?"

"No. I haven't. That's what Nigel wants, but I'm not so sure."

"Don't be, in any case." Her voice was softening. "You're almost thirty-five years old, sweetheart. This could be your last chance."

"I know, Mum. Do you think I haven't considered that?"

"You may be considering it, but you know you've got a weak spot for Nigel. This one is so different from your other boyfriends. I'm afraid you'll let him influence you. Look, I am telling you point blank, don't you dare get rid of it, Karen. You have this baby. This child will be your happiness, daughter."

"Well, I'll certainly give you points for conviction. But how can you know this unborn child will be my happiness?"

"I know, Karen. I am sure of it," she repeated. "At sixty years of age I've been there and done that already. I've known a lot of people, from all different walks of life. Men and women of every manner of sexual persuasion. I've lived a lot of lives, sweetheart. Been in and out of many of them, too. And forgive me for saying this, but I've had my share of men. Two of which I loved with all my heart, Matt and your father. Especially your father. Matt has died, and who knows where your father is now. My point is, when the time comes, each of our lovers moves on."

Her voice was getting worse.

"What, are you worried that Nigel will leave you too?" I asked jokingly, trying to lighten up the conversation a bit.

"I hope he never leaves either of us, but it's best to prepare for the worst."

She was being so pessimistic that her doubts were starting to rub off on me.

"What do you mean 'prepare for the worst', Mum? Do you know something I don't?"

300

"Don't be silly. There's nothing to know. I'm just trying to remind you of what you may one day come up against. Yes, Nigel is a good man. And yes, he loves you. I understood that again tonight. But he's avoiding responsibility. For him, life is all about having fun. He says he just wants to eat and drink and live it up. And who can blame him? Isn't that what everyone wants? On the other hand, coming into this world has a price. There are obligations. Every breath we take, every sip of water, every bite of bread, is the right of everyone else, too. We have to give back what we consume."

She was being unfair, and I immediately called her on it.

"Don't, Mum. Nigel saves lives every day. His donation to humanity is greater than yours and mine combined."

She didn't know what to say.

"You're right," she finally continued. "He does save lives daily, but that is his job. Don't get me wrong. I don't see him as some moralless person whose life revolves around money, but why would a man who saves the lives of others not give his own baby a chance? Because it's inconvenient? He won't be able to go on holidays? He'll have to get married? Nigel is used to living without any attachments. For three years you've been a couple, so to speak, but you still live in the same places. You haven't moved in with him, nor has he chosen to come live with you. What about when he is fifty? What will you do if he falls in love with a thirty-year-old co-worker and leaves you?"

"What could I? I would just keep living my life."

"That's not what I'm saying. You'll be forty-five then, I mean, far beyond your childbearing years. But if that dark, handsome gentleman of yours changes his mind, there'll still be plenty of time to have a child with his new thirty-year-old lover, or whoever it is he chooses. Life treats women cruelly, Karen, you have to understand that. Not just life, men are also cruel. Not to change the subject but, there's a place called Çatalhöyük sixty kilometres from Konya where we went with your father the second time I was there. It's a settlement that dates back ten thousand years, and possibly the first place on earth that people lead sedentary lives. Ten thousand years ago in Çatalhöyük, the gods were female.

The earth was ruled by a mother goddess. But then what happened? It was taken over by men. And with it the gods' sex changed as well. From the Babylonions to the Marduks, the Greek Zeus to the god of Abraham, the father of Christ, the prophet Muhammed's Allah... all of them, men. Before that, there was the Sumerians' *Inanna*, the Babils' *Ishtar*, the Egyptians' *Isis*, and the Hittites' *Hepat*. It was these goddesses who determined people's fate; they were the embodiment of fortune, abundance, joy, fertility, and mystique - that is, all life. Men may have divested us of all these things over the last ten thousand years, but we are still endowed with one ability they can never take from us, and that is childbirth. The privilege of bringing another human into the world. On the condition that the biological clock hasn't stopped ticking, of course. If we are late, then nature takes over. And even if you want to, you won't be able to have a child. Look, Karen, I really hope you and Nigel live happily ever after, but what if you don't? What if my odious prophecy comes true? Nigel and you break up, and it's too late for you to have a child anymore?"

I didn't know what to say, and my silence only encouraged her.

"If I had any say in it, it would be your heart you listen to, not Nigel. Please don't do anything rash, Karen. Just look at me. I'm getting old and everyone I love is dropping out my life, but it's not a problem because I have you."

"And I've got you too, Mum."

"True, but it's not the same thing, sweetheart." Her voice had got all emotional. "My time will be up before yours. I won't always be here, that's the reality, and then you will be alone. Nigel or some other man may be sharing your loneliness, but if you have a child... Just don't do it Karen, keep this baby."

I took a deep breath.

"Okay, Mum, I'll give it some thought."

"You do that, and don't stab yourself in the back for Nigel's sake."

I tried to laugh but couldn't manage.

"Don't worry, Mum. I won't."

A silence settled between us.

"Thank you, Mum," I said, breaking the silence. "I really do value your guidance."

"So tough love works then," she said, also trying to laugh. Her voice was shedding its sentimentality. "I hope it worked on Nigel."

"Please don't tell me you chewed him out, too?"

"And she immediately defends her lover... What could I possibly say to Nigel? The man was being polite and taking me out to dinner. When I could get my tongue around it, I just tried to explain the virtues of having a child. He was content with hearing me out and didn't interrupt. There was not even one little altercation between us."

"Because he didn't argue back," I offered, certain of what had happened even though I hadn't been there. "You gave him hell the whole night long."

"He was asking for it," she grumbled, without the least hint of regret in her voice. "I hope it paid off and he'll change his mind on the subject."

"You are relentless, mother."

"Not relentless, my dear. Experienced. And courageous enough to defend the life of my soon-to-be grandchild."

Courageous was a word I would use for my father. The dervish Poyraz Efendi, who'd followed the woman he loved to a country he didn't know.

"Mother, today I met this man," I suddenly started to explain. "He used to be father's friend. İzzet Efendi. He says he knows you, too."

"İzzet? Ah yes, the jeweler, I remember him. The slender, soft-spoken man with the beautiful hazel eyes..." She paused. "...that looked straight through you. Your father and he were quite close, like brothers practically. " There was another brief silence. "Did he mention your father? When did he last see him?"

She sounded vaguely hopeful.

"He talked about father but he hasn't seen him in years."

"I'm surprised. They were so close." The optimism in her voice died as quickly as it was born. "I would have thought your father had visited him. He was a good man, İzzet. But...

do you know... in those days he was against your father's coming with me."

"Yes, I sensed that too."

She let out a small laugh.

"He still feels that way?"

"I guess so. He still doesn't understand how his friend could forsake God's love for the love of a woman."

"Forsake God's love for the love of a woman," she repeated, sarcasm in her voice. "That's not really what happened. Your father never forsook God's love. The love he felt for me was nothing more than a piece of the love he always had for God."

İzzet Efendi's words rang in my ears: *To reach infinite love, you must live out one that is finite.* But I didn't repeat them to my mother. On the contrary, I protested, "You can't be sure of that."

"Actually, I can, sweetheart. Because it was your father himself who said that to me."

"He said your love isn't important? That he's just preparing for his big love with God?"

She chuckled sweetly.

"Not in those exact words, but something along those lines. After Rumi, there was another folk poet that your father really loved. The Anatolian mystic and poet, Yunus Emre. He would always recite this one line of his: *That we love the creature is due to the Creator.* After your father repeated that quote, he would add, 'And I love you, due to my infinite love of Allah.' What you need to understand is, your dervish father never gave up his beliefs for my love."

"But he left his sheikh and his convent, and came back with you."

"He came back with me because in those days he wasn't strong enough to overcome his desires. That's your father's explanation of course. When it comes right down to it, yes, he was in love with me, and I with him. But later that love wasn't enough, or maybe it just lost its old intensity. Either way, he no longer had any interest in love. Or family, or his life in London, for that matter. He started searching for something more. And he lucked out - he found his soulmate, Shah Nesim. We all made do together for a while, as you know. But when I could no longer tolerate that life, your father was once again forced to make a choice. A choice that was considerably different from the one he'd made in Konya. In the end, he gave up his 'small love' and returned to his 'big love'."

"He went with Shah Nesim," I said meaningfully. "I mean, he came full circle, ending up back in the life he'd abandoned in Konya."

"In the beginning, anyhow. Shah Nesim represented the doorway that would take him to God. But your father would soon mature a lot, and probably didn't need Shah Nesim for much longer."

I was confused. Though what really puzzled me was my mother's extensive knowledge of these subjects.

"How do you know all this, Mum?"

"What do you mean, how do I know? I lived with a sufi for no less than thirteen years. In fact, you should know all about these things too. These subjects were always being discussed in front of you."

"I don't know, I guess I've forgotten. But certain things are coming back to me here. I've had dreams about some of it."

"You've had dreams?" She sounded concerned. "What kind of dreams?"

It crossed my mind to tell her everything I'd been through since coming to Konya. The ring I was given, the nightmares, Shams, Rumi, Kimya, Alaeddin... Perhaps if I explained it all I would relax. But I was afraid if I told her I was having nightmares again, or walking in my sleep, she would drop dead from worry, the poor woman. No, I had to remain tight-lipped on the matter around both my mother and Nigel until it was sorted out.

"It's not important. Just dervishes, *semazen*, dervish convents and the like."

"Sounds like culture shock." Her voice was calmer. "Don't let it worry you, dear. And keep your distance from İzzet Efendi. Sure, he's a good man, but what he says will only confuse you. So, you'll be back here in three days, eh?"

"Did Nigel say that?"

"Yes, he did. When our own daughter doesn't tell us, we have to hear it from her boyfriend... Okay, I'm joking. I'm happy you are coming back. I've really been missing you since you left, with all that's happened. Look, the second you're back you have to come over. I won't tolerate any 'I've got to see my boyfriend' excuses. He can come too, if he wants. We'll all have a nice meal together. I'll make you one of those Japanese dishes you love so much."

"And miso soup?"

"Of course. It wouldn't be a meal without it. Then onigiri, or maybe donburi..."

"Which one was that? You mean that one that I tried to make and failed? The rice bowl?"

She laughed. "The very one. And we'll get some sake to have with it. For you and Nigel, that is."

"All right. As long as you promise not to bring up the subject of babies with him again. Let me handle that matter by myself."

I could tell she wasn't happy about it, but she knew she had no choice. "As you wish, Karen," she said flatly. "You know I've always trusted you."

"Death is not annihilation."

※

My mother's voice still rang in my ears as I hung up the phone. "Life treats women cruelly, Karen." She was dead on. Oddly enough, I'd already reached almost all the same conclusions long before. The future was as clearly cut as the sun in a cloudless sky for me. But what about that weakness for Nigel I had, for reasons I myself couldn't understand? She was right about that, too. I got so much pleasure just from being with him. Walking leisurely through the park, lying around listening to music, going out for dinner or cooking together, making love... I didn't want to lose any of that.

Occasionally, I would run into one of the female doctors he worked with, some prettier than me, some younger and cleverer. When I did, I couldn't deny I was overcome with jealousy. Nigel spent all day, every day with them. It would be delusional to think none of them were attracted to him. And falling for one of them back would be as easy as falling off a log. Then again, maybe it would be me who left Nigel one day. It wouldn't be unheard of. People's feelings changed. We were all capable of falling in love with someone when we least expected it. The important thing was to be able to stand on your own two feet; and as women got older, the whole issue of having children probably played an important role in this. That must have been my mother's point. Though she hadn't said it in so many words, it would have been that much more difficult for her to get through my father's abandonment if I hadn't been there. No lover can be our sole source of happiness over long periods of time. Unless, of course, we were talking about a dervish's love, like my father's. The fire of passion would never burn out in them, because they would never get their fill of it. They would never reach the object of their love in any real sense of the word. They would be forever chasing after it in fits and starts; and as they got closer, it would move further away. But then maybe it wasn't like that at all. Maybe it was just two totally different perspectives on love. When it came to love, their satiation point was completely spiritual, but that didn't necessarily make it any more abstract. Seeing as how my father left with Shah Nesim without even feeling the need to look back over his shoulder, he must have been influenced by some very powerful, very real emotions. Whatever their relationship was, however, I was convinced that it involved abstinence. Abstinence from eating, drinking, making love, and even sleep. What they loved was a divine being. And to reach that being, to become one with it, they had to break free of their carnal needs, relinquish their bodies. Becoming a divine being is impossible for one with a physical body. Either the corporeal body becomes a divine being, or the divine being must become flesh. You couldn't have it both ways. It is the corporeal body that falls in love, therefore self-sacrifice also lies within its responsibility. I remember my father celebrating the anniversary of Rumi's death. I was so confused, not understanding what there was in death to celebrate. "For us, death is not annihilation, my girl. Death is the moment of unification with our beloved," he'd pronounced.

It was difficult to grasp. I wondered if I even wanted to. But the time had come, I supposed. It was like I'd been wrapped in an unfamiliar sensation since coming to Konya. Not a negative one exactly - I was no longer afraid, despite the numerous nightmares. There was only that mix of excitement and curiosity, without which I hardly expect I would've stayed on in Konya after all I'd been through. I still didn't have a passport of course...

I got up and my eyes involuntarily settled on my bed. Even if only for a short while, the sleep had done me good. I felt refreshed. All at once, that pleasant smell wafted in again, followed by the exhilaratingly sweet breeze. I wanted to get a breath of fresh air so I went onto the balcony and filled my lungs. My eyes slid down to the ablutions fountain where Shams had been standing. There was no one there; the small lot in front of the mosque was completely abandoned. The wind picked up speed and the cold air hit my face. I shivered. I looked up at the sky wondering if it was going to rain, but there was not a cloud in sight. On the contrary, hundreds of stars, both big and small, twinkled softly in the deep blue sky like blinking eyes. Looking back at the mosque, I saw what I at first took to be a street dog - a poor, derelict animal taking refuge in the shadows of the fountain. On more careful inspection, I realised it was a child. A little boy. What on earth was he doing on the street at this time of night? He must have noticed me watching him because he pulled away from the shadows, stepping into the light that illuminated the walls of the mosque. That's when I recognised the wide forehead and the curly blonde hair, and felt a pang of sadness. It was Sunny. My Sunny. But Sunny didn't know the first thing about Konya. What was he doing here? My mind was obviously playing tricks on me, though it all seemed so real that I couldn't help waving at my imaginary childhood friend.

He beckoned to me, but I was torn. Just the day before I'd been attacked, and Inspector Zeynep had spoken of a gang of religious zealots on the street who weren't opposed to killing people to implement shari'a law. Leaving the hotel would be madness, but on the other hand Sunny was down there, waiting. I remembered what he'd said to me in my dream. "You told me not to dare move a muscle, that you'd be right back. And I have been waiting for you since that day." Whatever happened, I couldn't leave my childhood friend there alone. I signaled for him to wait, then went back inside my room. Luckily, I still had enough of my wits about me to not go out half dressed. I slipped into my blouse and jeans, pulled on my shoes, and sprang from the room. Rather than wait for the lift, I went for the stairwell, taking the steps in twos.

Once in the lobby, I was pleased to see that the nosey receptionist had his head down on the desk, asleep. I tried not to make a sound as I slipped out the entrance door. And there he stood, alone in front of the fountain where Shams had been before him, the dim, yellow light giving him the dramatic appearance of a dejected, abandoned child. I wanted to go straight over and give him a big hug. But just as I stepped into the street, a rubbish truck came out of nowhere. I stepped back in alarm as the truck went roaring past. I was about to head across again when I noticed Sunny was no longer there. I looked around but he was nowhere to be seen. Hoping to find him behind the fountain, I headed over to the opposite pavement, but he wasn't there either. I looked around in the garden of the Sultan Selim Mosque, but it was deserted. The entire area was desolate, there was not a soul in sight. I wondered if I'd been seeing things. I was suddenly struck by the absurdity of it, and found the idea hilarious - that I'd imagined seeing my imaginary friend. It really suited a crackpot like me. I was glad the receptionist hadn't seen me walk out, he would have thought I was crazy. He still may, I reminded myself, there was more of a chance that he'd notice me on my way back in. For a moment I considered not going back in at all. But what was I going to do, curl up on a bench in front of the mosque for the night? If he sees me, he sees me, I thought. I would just say I couldn't sleep and had gone for a walk, it's not like I really gave a damn. As I headed back across, the nursery rhyme from my childhood could again be heard coming out of the night. First the melody, then the distinct words.

Hu hu hu dervish
The dervish opened a dervish lodge
His skirts they scattered secrets
Although no one knew about it

Hu hu hu dervish
His head it reached the sky above
His beard it brushed upon the ground
His lips they scattered secrets
Although no one could hear them...

The voice echoed off the stone walls of the historical mosque. I looked in the direction it had come from. He was there, standing in a shadowy spot of pavement next to a grave about fifty metres beyond me to the left. How is it I'd never noticed that grave before? Never mind, what was important was that I'd found him. "Sunny, stay there. Wait for me," I called out. But he ignored me and ran across the street as though forgetting he'd signalled for me to come meet him. There was no stopping now, I thought, running after him. Once across the street, he slowed to a walk and followed along a short wall towards a door. On closer inspection, I saw that it was the very same ice blue door that had appeared in the wall of my hotel room. There was no clue as to what it opened onto, but the ambiguity of it didn't put Sunny off. He just paused briefly to look back at me, then dived inside without warning. I knew it wasn't wise to go back through that door, especially after what had happened last time. Then again, it hadn't been wise to go chasing after my childhood friend at this time of night in the first place. I had to remind myself that, apart from the last time we'd met, he'd never let me down. And although I'd left him at the head of the pool, not searching for him all those years, now that I'd finally found him it didn't make sense to lose him again.

I slipped through the door after him. On my first step I was struck by the cold, with that same dizzying howl, like wind slicing through a forest. I quickly took a second step and found myself inside a graveyard, the one the Mevlevis called *Hamüşan*, the place of the silent ones.

Everything in this realm of the dead was wrapped in the same icy blue - the trees, the tombstones, the flowers on the graves... It made me shudder inside. What business did Sunny have in this graveyard? A long narrow road with graves on either side stretched into the distance. I set off up the road and was quietly looking back and forth in hopes of seeing Sunny when I instead noticed three people to my left. At first I thought they were tree trunks, three tree roots that had come up together and twisted around each other forming one big mass. But then I noticed the faces, the serenity in their eyes, mouths that didn't speak... They must have been the three brothers Mennan had spoken of, the ones who had come to see Rumi, who on hearing of his death had wanted to shut their eyes for good on this spot. So this was the Three Saints Cemetery. That historical graveyard named after the three brothers from Khorasan. As I turned to look at the other graves, I recoiled in fear. The black forms I had thought were gravestones were actually the proprietors of the graves; wrinkled old men, women settled into middle-age, young lads, their pent-up energy still palpable, girls with coquettishness frozen on their faces, babies who had passed away before even learning to smile... For a moment I was overcome with horror, and in that moment wanted to forget all about Sunny and run away. But sensing the profound peacefulness in the faces of the dead, I stood my ground. An overwhelming sensation swept over me, as if by looking at them I had shaken off the oppressiveness of death. Death wasn't to be perceived as an end, or a catastrophe, but rather a part of life. Like the cycle the rose bush went through each year, budding, blossoming, wilting, shedding its petals, but then sprouting again the following year. In this house of the silent, I felt but a branch on humanity's family tree. If this wasn't how eternity felt, then what was? Then there came the whisper of indistinctly murmured words. The whole graveyard heard the voice along with me. All at once a gale whipped through the graveyard as the icy blue night was plunged into a deep azure darkness. The trees moaned as though gripped by storm, the earth jolted with a crash, and the graves opened one by one as the mutes gently retired to their places. The whispering had frightened them. I turned to look towards where the voice had come from and there saw Sunny, just beyond me with his back turned; he had stopped at the foot of a huge plane tree and was fixated on a tombstone, its inscription no longer decipherable after who knows how many hundreds of years. He continued to whisper. Was it directed at the tombstone? With deliberate steps, I drew closer. As I did, the tombstone began to shrink, and Sunny's body to grow. "Sunny, what are you doing?" I asked in a timid, hushed voice.

This time he didn't move away, but calmly turned round. It wasn't Sunny, it was Shams.

"Come here, Kimya. I've been waiting for you."

And he still had the audacity to address me as Kimya.

"You are disturbing the dead," I rebuked. "You shouldn't speak in this place of the silent."

"Good for you, Kimya," he said, with an appreciative grin. "You've learned our customs. Your perception, however, leaves much to be desired. It was not my voice that caused them to withdraw, but rather the fear in your heart." He drew a hand across the grave. "They were ashamed of the fear their presence gave you. That is why they returned to the earth, the same earth Adam came from."

Whatever I said, he would have an answer. Rather than dragging it out, I asked, "Where is Sunny?"

He gave me a long, dismal look.

"You still don't understand?" he asked, disappointment in his voice. "I am Sunny. I have been with you since your birth. Your father, you, and me..."

A chill passed through me.

"That's a lie!" I shouted. "You are not Sunny. You could never be my friend. Sunny would never kill anybody."

He gave me an injured look.

"How do you know I have killed?"

"I saw it with my own eyes," I said, giving him a dose of reality. "You snapped that poor girl's neck like a twig."

He placed his left hand on the black tombstone and pronounced, "You suppose your nightmares are real, but it's reality that is a nightmare. I didn't kill Kimya, what killed her was her own sin."

And he could look me in the eye and deny it.

"Funny, I've never heard of sin killing a person," I said dryly. "How exactly does that work?"

"She went where I told her not to go," he began explaining patiently. "She did what I told her not to do and saw who I told her not to see. All I did was look into her eyes with scorn. Just stared into her face with my sad, desperate eyes. But the poor girl took her neck into her own hands and fell to the ground. I never wanted her to die, never wanted to lose her. I didn't want her light to go out, but it was predestined by God."

That was too much.

"Don't you dare say it was predestined by God. You killed that girl with your bare hands. You were an instrument of your rage. And now you are asking for my help."

"I'm not asking for your help," he said decisively. "Why would I?"

"To clear your conscience."

He looked at me vainly.

"If there is such a thing as a conscience, I am that conscience from head to toe. A man born of a conscience has no need to clear it."

"If that's the case, then why have you given me the ring?"

"You are not even trying to understand," he said, shaking his head with its grizzled hair.

"Then educate me. What is it I need to know?"

"The truth," he stated with finality.

"The truth, you keep saying," I snapped. "Tell me and let me learn it already, what is this truth?"

I expected him to launch into his spiel about how it's not so easy again, but he surprised me.

"Do you know of Judas Iscariot? The disciple who betrayed Jesus into the hands of the Romans? The Jew who sold his messiah for thirty pieces of silver?"

"Of course I do. What has Judas got to do with this?"

"A lot. Everyone assumes Judas was a traitor."

"Wasn't he?"

"If Judas hadn't informed on the prophet Jesus, would Jesus have been crucified? If Jesus hadn't been crucified, if he hadn't paid for people's sins with his own body, how would he have been resurrected, and therefore become immortal? Of the twelve disciples, Judas was the one to carry the heaviest burden by far. The other disciples reached sainthood by putting their lives at risk for their beliefs. This was also virtuous. However, the real accomplishment lies not only in doing good for your beliefs, but even more importantly in doing evil for them. In risking eternal damnation in the same way the fallen angel, Lucifer, did. In being the sole person to carry the burden of what only you know to be the truth. In being totally alone with your archaic secret, while the whole world thinks you a traitor. That is exactly what Judas did. So

314

that a sacred destiny could be fulfilled, he offered himself at the foot of Jesus, sacrificing not only his body, but his soul."

"So you are saying you did this for Mevlana?"

"How can I explain," he said, sounding hopeless, "when in understanding, you employ nothing but reason. Logic has enthroned itself on your intellect like a tyrannical king. Whatever I tell you, you will fail to understand. Whatever I say, you will look under it for hidden meaning. And you will always blame me."

"But I saw what happened with my own eyes."

"What you see with your eyes is not always real. Let me tell you a story to help you better understand:

"One day a male swallow made a declaration of love to a female swallow from atop the prophet Solomon's temple. As luck would have it, at that moment Solomon himself was inside. On hearing the swallow's voice, he pricked up his ears, and this is what he heard the male swallow say to the female. 'I am so thoroughly wrapped in your love that if you commanded me to bring this dome down on Solomon's head, I would do so without hesitation.' Solomon was enraged upon hearing these words, and called the swallow over to him on the spot. He told him, 'Explain yourself, why don't you? What was it I heard you say just now?' The swallow replied bravely, 'O Solomon! Don't be so quick to punish me. Those in love speak in such a tongue, only the mad can understand it. It's true that I uttered those words. It's true, I said I would bring the temple down on the prophet Solomon's head. But I am in love with that bird. On the lovers' path, there is no law, no morality. They have but one route: love. They have but one law: love. They have but one moral: love. They speak only the language of love. Beside this colourful language, the language of knowledge and reason remains lifeless like a smothered flame.' And that is what the swallow said to Solomon. Whereupon the prophet Solomon forgave him. Because when it comes to love, evil is not evil anymore. And as for goodness, it is also no longer goodness. There is but one single truth - absolute love. A love which fulfills miracles."

"So then which miracle have you fulfilled, doing evil that isn't evil?"

He ignored me and raised his head to look towards Rumi's Mausoleum, which stretched into the sky like a giant jade stone beyond the low walls of the cemetery.

"This place was once a rose garden. If Khüdavendigar had not become our Mevlana, not even the rose garden would be here now. These greedy people would have long since erected their multi-level buildings in its place. Khüdavendigar would have been laid to rest in one of these ordinary, centuries-old graves. As it is, he continues to have an influence on the sons of Adam as though he never really died. His poems warm souls. His words chisel those who are still rough. Like a roving star, his light illuminates the path for those who, in their search for meaning, have lost their way in the dark. It is said of him, 'Though he was not a prophet, he has written sacred texts.' Next to a miracle like this, evil, cruelty, even murder, lose all meaning."

He stared at the mausoleum with the pride of an architect looking on his own masterpiece.

"No, they don't lose their meaning. Evil is evil and murder is murder, even if done for love. You cannot achieve righteous gains through doing evil. You cannot bring one new life into existence by ending the life of another."

"Who said anything about bringing new life into existence? It was enough to appreciate that which already existed."

"Evil is not a prerequisite to appreciating someone's life, no matter how important that life may seem."

"It is," he said assuredly. "Where there is no evil, one cannot recognise goodness. And we have both within us. That is what is meant when Jelaleddin says, 'There are times when angels are envious of our innocence, and times when Satan sees our evil and looks for somewhere to hide.' Life cannot be shaped, breath cannot be locked up, yearnings of the flesh cannot be totally snuffed out. Whether it is goodness that is fruitful, or evil, cannot always be determined. Sometimes a day comes when more is to be gained from one evil act than from a thousand good ones."

I took a step back and watched him with a contemptuous smile.

"So, whatever evil you did, you did for Rumi. Is that right?"

He looked back at me pityingly.

"Evil or goodness, whatever I've done, I have done for love. Not for Khüdavendigar."

"Isn't that the same thing?"

"It is not. The journey of love is set in motion by a single person. When a beloved is found, two people proceed together for a while, but the end of the road finds us alone once again. What begins with us, ends with us."

"But Rumi didn't share that view. He wrote so many love poems to you. He was enraptured. What exactly did you say to him during those days you stayed cloistered together in his room, after that first time you met in the place they call Merej el-Bahrain? What did you say that would make him give up his prayer rituals and sermons and start writing poetry?"

"I said nothing. We sat in silence. He uncovered my secret despite my silence. He saw the fire inside himself reflected in the mirror of my soul. It was not I who enraptured him, but his own fire inside him. Everyone believes he was burning with my light, but that is wrong. Rumi was burning from within himself. I just stoked the furnace."

I could feel my awe of him creeping in as he explained these things, carried away by his boundless emotions. But then I saw Kimya's face, and summoned all my rage to combat my rising fascination with the strange man.

"By murdering Kimya?" I asked, interrupting. "You stoked that furnace by stealing the fire of life from a young girl?"

His eyes looked moist and I thought I could see his beard trembling.

"Not by killing Kimya, by killing myself," he said.

I stared at him blankly.

"You killed yourself?"

He was about to answer, but then suddenly turned his gaze upward. Something had got his attention. I followed his gaze, trying to see what it was that was dazzling him. A bright light rushed towards us, like one of the stars had broken off and was falling to earth. "When the sun of the material world rises, that of the spiritual world sets," he whispered cryptically, as the deep azure sky gave way to a bright, sunlit blue.

"... the shame of a dervish defeated by his hatred..."

✖

Morning had broken. I was standing between the freshly dug grave of a recently deceased child and one a thousand years old with a worn black tombstone and no semblance of a mound left. As the soft light of the morning sun struggled out from among the purple clouds, I was still trying to make sense of what had happened. I wasn't hurt. Nobody had attacked me or stolen anything from me this time, but what was I doing here? Had I really seen Sunny and had that bizarre dialogue with Shams? And what about those corpses sleeping in the cold blue night that had come crawling out onto the surface, mud smeared on them like shrouds? I turned it over in my mind as I walked through the graveyard, through the tall, eternally green cypresses, until it finally dawned on me. I'd probably started sleepwalking again, picking up where I'd left off as a child. If that were true, I reasoned, it may be time to pay a visit to our beloved psychologist Oliver. And it weren't, if there was some other explanation for it, it was still time to pack up and go. This wasn't the first time I'd been abroad for work. I'd been offered bribes before, threatened even, but never before had I experienced such bizarre, unnerving events. That being the case, why was I insisting on waiting till my report was written? Nigel was right, I should be jumping on the first plane back to London. What else was there for me to find here? I wasn't a detective. I didn't have a team of armed police at my disposal, as did Inspector Zeynep. It shouldn't have all been up to me to shed light on the nuances of this case, or come up with evidence proving Serhad and Cavit guilty. And yet here I was - examining, researching, organising evidence, taking witness statements, writing reports... Not that I was downplaying the arrests Inspector Zeynep had planned for the night before. On the contrary, I was curious how it would all turn out, though that was hardly reason enough for me to stay. There had to be more to it - whether the subconscious belief that this city held the secret of my father's disappearance, simple curiosity about the ring, or even the prospect of reaching the absolute truth that Shams spoke of. But I was neither a devout Muslim, nor a sufi trying to wash my hands of the world like my father had been. I'd never really considered religion. Nigel called himself a Protestant, though he didn't question it much either. He had enough to do in his daily life that he didn't worry his head over religion. But me, I wasn't sure. If my mother and father hadn't spent all that time arguing over these subjects, I may not care either way. And frankly, I hadn't cared anyhow till I came here. Or was I fooling myself? Was it really possible that I hadn't been at all affected by their discussions? Maybe I just hadn't bothered to give the matter much thought till now.

In any case, I had to put all this aside now. It's the sleepwalking I should be asking my mother about. I remembered reading somewhere that somnambulists have no recollection of what occurs during an episode, whereas I could recall every last detail of what had happened over the course of the night, apart from the actual moment I'd fallen asleep and woken back up. So how much could I trust my memory of those details?

Near the cemetery gates was a sizable grave surrounded by an iron fence that I couldn't help but notice. A shiver went through me as I read the sign: *A prayer of El Fatiha for the souls of three brothers who have come from Khorasan to see the prophet Mevlana.* I'd seen those brothers as a massive single body, like three embracing trees, but did that really prove my nighttime experiences were real? Mennan had told me the story before, that was all it was.

Without warning, I found myself staring into the sleepy, surprised eyes of a guard stepping out of the booth next to the gate. I picked up my steps and, not giving him a chance to ask any questions, left the strange, thousand-year-old cemetery behind me.

Unfortunately, I wasn't so adept at evading the nosey receptionist, who stared at me incredulously as I entered the hotel. "Good morning, Miss Greenwood," he shot in, as I tried to ignore him and rush past. "You're up bright and early. I didn't even see you leave."

"Not surprising since you were sleeping away at your desk."

He frowned, confused.

"Sleeping?"

"Yes, and quite soundly at that. Better take care your boss doesn't catch you like that," I said over my shoulder as I kept walking. I didn't look back, but I knew he'd be watching me with a long face until the door of the lift closed.

Once back in my room, I showered, put on a change of clothes, and lay in bed for a while until I fell asleep. When I woke again it was coming on nine o'clock. Breakfast was already being served downstairs, but I wasn't the least bit hungry. My mother was probably awake by now; she'd been an early riser for at least ten years now. I took out my phone and dialled her. It rang a few times but she didn't answer. Wondering if maybe she wasn't awake after all, I let it keep ringing until her answering machine picked up. I hated speaking on that thing, but I was beginning to worry about her. She had no mobile phone, so if she'd already left the house I wouldn't be able to reach her all day. I decided to leave a message in the hope that, if nothing else, she'd call me when she got home.

"Hi Mum, it's Karen. Ring me when you get in. Love you," I said, brief and to the point.

Where could the woman have gone at this time of morning? Maybe she was watering the flowers in the garden. Then again, she may just as well be spearing and bagging rubbish along the banks of the Thames River, or lying down on the asphalt, blocking a road in support of a save the seals project. Who knows? She could be anywhere. So long as there's a cause, so long as there's a justified reason to protest. She would never settle down, that woman. She felt compelled to 'be involved' and her involvement would never allow me to rest easy. My nerves were shot. I got up and began to pace the room. The laptop on the table grabbed my attention, reminding me that I hadn't reached Simon the night before. It was too early to call now. My boss wasn't yet at that age where he could get by on little sleep, like my mother. I turned on the laptop and wrote the few lines about my progress that I'd felt too lazy to write the previous night. Then I asked about my passport, and sent it off. I was about to turn off the laptop, then thought to look up what Shams had had to say on Kimya's death. I couldn't recall the name of the book Mennan had mentioned, so I typed 'Rumi' into the search engine and scanned the English sites to find it. Plenty of book names popped up: Rumi's *Mesnevi*, the Divan-ı *Kebir*, *Fihi Mafih*, *Mecalis-i Seb'a* and *Mektubat*. There was *Risale* by a writer named Feridun Ahmed-i Sipehsalar, Sultan Veled's *Veled-name Rebab-name* and *Ma'arif*. Among those was also Ahmed Eflaki's *Ariflerin Menkıbeleri*, which I recognised right away as the one Mennan had mentioned. I was lucky enough to find a copy of the text in its entirety, but it must have been a thousand pages long. I opened the find tool and typed 'Shams' into the window, but his name was highlighted uncountable times, so I narrowed my search to 'Shams and Kimya'. Poor Kimya's name only came up three times in the entire text, and those, it appeared, were just to clarify something about Shams. In the first, it merely mentioned that Shams had left Konya after Kimya's death. The second was a story about how God had appeared to Shams as Kimya, an allegory on the tight bond between Shams and God using some striking illustrations, which was at least more interesting. But what interested me most was the third. This is what it said:

The bride of Shamseddin, Kimya Hatun, was a chaste and beautiful lady. One day, the other women, including Sultan Veled's grandmother, went for a stroll in the vineyards. They took Kimya along with them, although without Shams's permission. When Shamseddin came home and couldn't find her, it was relayed to him that she'd gone out for a walk in the vineyards with the women and the grandmother. Shamseddin was furious. As soon as she arrived back home, she came down with a stiff neck straight away. She remained as rigid as a dry blade of grass, crying and moaning for three days time, after which she passed on to the other side.

This seemed to confirm what Shams himself had told me. I started to wonder if what I'd dreamt was not the real story after all. In the end it didn't make much difference. Although it was Shams's bare hands that had killed Kimya in my dream, whereas in Eflaki's version it was his anger, the outcome remained the same. A man had brought on the death of his wife because she hadn't listened to him. But even more curious was why a person so full of love, a model of compassion like Mevlana, would give a young girl of not even eighteen years of age to a sixty-year-old man as a wife in the first place. How he could keep quiet in the face of the poor girl's death. My father, İzzet Efendi, and Mennan would all say the same thing: for love. I recalled the story Shams had told me. What the swallow, mad with love, had said to the prophet Solomon. "... on the lovers' path there is no law, no morality. They have but one route: love. They have but one law: love. They have but one moral: love." But the swallow in that story had been revolting against an authority many times greater than itself, putting its life at risk for its lover. The victim in this story, on the other hand, was a young girl too weak and helpless to even protect herself. I visualised Kimya's slender neck, her slim body and pale face. In the young girl's inert eyes, I again saw the shame of a dervish defeated by his hatred. I struggled to repress my surging anger, trying to make sense of it by convincing myself it had to be kept in the perspective that era, but my mother's words wouldn't allow it. "Men took over the world." And after that, nobody paid the least bit of attention to the tears of young girls when they were presented as wives to men of wealth and standing in society. Nobody asked their opinions. Nobody enquired as to whether they wanted to be with the men. For a moment I felt like my mother. Perpetually angry, rebellious, and ready for a fight. I was normally more objective, and had to remind myself to stay that way. Maybe none of this was what it seemed. What if Kimya was in love with Shams and she herself had wanted this marriage? Was that such a far-fetched notion? It did happen. Simon's sixteen-year-old daughter, Jenny, was a case in point - completely smitten with her maths teacher despite the decades between them. But it wasn't the same thing; the Kimya in my dream hadn't shown the least bit of interest in Shams. It was Rumi's middle son, Alaeddin Çelebi, who seems to pull on her heartstrings. So where exactly did Alaeddin fit into this story? And what ever became of him? The boy was not one to sit back and quietly resign himself to whatever happened. And another thing, Shams had said that he'd killed himself. Had he meant suicide, in the literal sense? It was hard to believe; he didn't seem the type. Not to mention suicide would have been against his beliefs. Only God could take a life he created. So how had Shams died? Could his death have been related to the ring? Was the bleeding brown stone a knot from the heart of the dark dervish?

My thoughts were interrupted by my phone ringing.

"Hello?"

"Good morning, Miss Greenwood?" a woman's fatigued voice asked. It wasn't my mother's. I recognised it as Inspector Zeynep's.

"Good morning. Yes, speaking."

"I've got good news for you."

Not good enough to erase the lethargy in her voice, I thought.

"What, did you find the fireproof suit?"

"No, but we found your passport," she explained with a sigh. "You can come and get it whenever you want."

I should have been thrilled by the news, but I was too hung up on the Ikonion arsonists.

"What about that suit?"

"Look, Miss Greenwood," she mumbled sluggishly. "I haven't slept in nearly two days. The last ten hours have been spent running from one inquiry to the next without a moment's rest, and it looks like it'll be a few hours more before I get one. So please refrain from asking me questions like this over the phone. Come in and get your passport. And, assuming I haven't passed out in some corner by then, I'll answer all your questions."

"My father cannot live if he learns of the death of his sheikh."

✳

As I waited for Mennan at the hotel entrance, I noticed that the bright morning sun was now covered by black clouds. A strong wind that felt left over from the cold winter days had started to blow from the direction of Rumi's mausoleum towards Konya's older neighbourhoods. I buttoned up my leather jacket, and while trying to gather my flying hair, Mennan's car pulled up in front of me. I opened the passenger door and sat next to him.

"Good morning..."

"Good morning, Miss Greenwood," he answered with a wan smile.

"I looked him over from the corner of my eye. The grey clothes he'd had on his back the last two days had been traded in for a dark blue suit, though the exhaustion on his face had stayed firmly in place.

"I guess you didn't sleep so well last night."

"I did, actually."

He combed a hand through his hair.

"But before I slept, my curiosity got the best of me and I started rereading that book I was talking about."

"*Ariflerin Menkıbeleri?*"

His eyes opened wide with admiration.

"What a great memory! I can't believe you remembered the name."

"It sounds like an interesting book, not easy to forget," I sufficed in saying, not wanting to disclose that I'd just been reading it myself that morning. "Did you learn anything new?"

"Quite a bit actually. It looks like you were right; the book does mix quite a bit of fiction in with its fact," he admitted, as he manoeuvred the car.

Though more interested in the contents of the book than what had changed my colleague's mind, I was pleased he'd finally started talking sense, and prompted, "Like what?"

"Some of the subjects struck me as a tad ridiculous."

"Ridiculous?" I repeated, enjoying myself now. "Wasn't that you who only just yesterday claimed Shams was our murderer based on what's written in the book?"

Avoiding my eyes, he went on to shyly explain, "Well, there's one part, for example, that tells how God met with Shams while in Kimya's image." He went quiet, then fidgeted. "Not met with exactly but... spoke with, philandered with even, God forgive me for saying it."

Apparently, Mennan considered reducing God to Kimya's image an act of sacrilege by the book's author. It was a pretty daring passage, I had to admit, though it really came as no surprise to me. From what little I'd seen, the chapters relating to Shams were full of these songs of praise for the wandering dervish. To people like Mennan, these kinds of allegories must have seemed repugnant. There had been a pretty strong reaction against the relationship between Shams and Rumi, too, once upon a time.

"I guess Shams doesn't really resemble your average Muslim, does he?"

"God forbid!" he spit out quickly, as though he'd burnt his tongue. "I'm not saying anything against His Holiness Shams. Just that the book's author, Eflaki Dede, exaggerated a bit. What I was explaining last night about Shams being a killer may also have been a bit of an exaggeration. If we were to believe everything Eflaki wrote, we'd see Shams as a man with a heart of stone who takes out anyone who crosses his path."

I was once again struck by how naïve Mennan was.

"Don't worry," I said, smiling. "I never form opinions on people based solely on what I read. I don't doubt that Shams was an entirely different person from that in the book."

The definitiveness of the comment threw him off. I could see him contemplating whether I knew more about the wandering dervish than I let on.

"What about you? Have you had a chance to read Shams's book? What does it say about a ring bleeding?"

"Not much," I said, so as not to confuse him more. "There is a story about a dervish who couldn't perform the *sema* so a knot forms in his heart and he dies. But I mean, there's no connection to our ring."

Disappointed, he grumbled, "So you think İzzet Efendi was wrong about it?"

"Not wrong. There was a ring in the story, just not ours."

He gave me a skeptical look and was about to speak again, but I beat him to it.

"Mr. Fidan, that book... I mean *Ariflerin Menkıbeleri*... does it also explain how Shams died?"

"Um... it does touch on the subject. Let's see what I remember. Now, the first meeting in Konya between Shams and Rumi took place in 1244."

"Merej el-Bahrain. The place where I was attacked and Lefty's body was dumped," I said, sighing heavily.

He turned to look at me and see if I was making fun of him, but seeing that I was dead serious, he just nodded gently.

"Merej el-Bahrain. From the moment the two men of God met, they were inseparable."

That wasn't news for me. Angelina had explained it all in the tour of the mausoleum.

"Rumi's conservative disciples were overcome with jealousy, and went so far as to threaten Shams," I said, taking up where he left off. "Then one night he went missing."

"You already knew that!" he exclaimed.

His astonished eyes were focused on my face when a woman suddenly ran out into the street.

"Look out!" I shouted in warning.

Mennan stepped on the brakes just in time, any later and we would have mowed the poor woman down. Leaving the woman behind as she jumped hurriedly onto the opposite pavement, he grumbled irritably, "Where did she come from? I didn't even see her."

"You might want to keep your eyes on the road."

"I am. It's just... you said you didn't know anything about Shams, and then..."

"You're right, I'm sorry. I do know a bit. When Shams disappeared into thin air, Rumi went to pieces, after which the jealous disciples realised their mistake and regretted it. Meanwhile, Rumi learned that his soulmate was in Damascus, and he sent his son Sultan Veled to bring him back to Konya. Then, to put a stop to all the rumours, he married off his adopted daughter, Kimya, to Shams."

"That's it! That's exactly what happened!" he exclaimed, still surprised by how much I knew.

"However," I said, wondering what his reaction to my words would be now, "at that point Kimya wasn't even eighteen years old yet, whereas Shams was in his sixties..."

He stirred restlessly in the driver's seat.

"So it seems. Shams was a bit old... But in those days that was the norm. And what girl wouldn't give her right arm to marry such a noble man as Shams? What family wouldn't be thrilled to have him as a son-in-law?"

"Is that right?" I asked, with no attempt at hiding my indignation. "So you would also marry off your daughter to a sixty-year-old man if times were different?"

He wasn't expecting a comeback like that and didn't know what to say.

"Of course not now," he repeated, keeping his eyes on the road. "No one would do that now."

A look of uncertainty passed through his eyes.

"I sure wouldn't do it, at least," he said, with more conviction this time.

I knew there was no point in prolonging the debate.

"Okay, let's get back to what we were saying. That's all I know about Shams. But what happened after he married Kimya? Did the people leave Rumi and him alone? And how was his marriage to Kimya?"

With no more bones about it, Mennan eagerly set out to tackle the subject.

"Unfortunately, those same jealous people started right back up again shortly after he came back to Konya and married

Kimya. They spread rumours all over Konya, slandering the two harmless dervishes in ways that defy imagination. And it's a shame, but Rumi's middle son, Alaeddin Çelebi, was also part of this gang of provocateurs. Some say Alaeddin was in love with Kimya, others say he was just jealous of how close Shams was to his father and older brother, Sultan Veled."

I remembered my dream from the night before and the expression of pain in Alaeddin's face as, seeing his beloved Kimya's lifeless body, he cried out. Having witnessed the murder of his lover, the child seemed capable of anything. Somehow I felt I had to defend the boy.

"Kimya's death could have pushed Alaeddin off the deep end. Maybe if Kimya hadn't died..."

"You're right. If it hadn't been for Kimya's unexpected death, perhaps Alaeddin Çelebi wouldn't have joined that group of traitors. But he was a troubled child from the start. While Shams had Mevlana's and Sultan Veled's utmost respect, Alaeddin Çelebi stayed cold and remote, marching to the beat of his own drummer like always. At any rate, that pack of seven killers, of which Alaeddin was one, knocked on Shams's door late one night and called him outside. And when Shams stepped out, unaware of the trap laid for him, the seven men each stabbed a knife into the saintly man's chest. It's said that His Holiness Shams let out such a powerful wail that all seven of them fainted on the spot. When they came to again, there was nothing left of him. Nothing but a single drop of blood on the stone."

"What? You mean the body disappeared?"

"Into thin air. There was that one drop of blood, that was all."

I was puzzled again.

"Okay, but I've seen Shams's sarcophagus."

"Be patient, Miss Greenwood. I'm getting there," he continued, smiling politely. "Days had passed since Shams's death when the great dervish appeared to Sultan Veled in a dream. Shams said to him, 'O Bahaeddin Veled, I am cold. I am in water; find me. O Bahaeddin Veled, I am in a well. Get me out.' Sultan Veled woke up drenched in sweat and, paying no attention to the time of night, gathered together three friends that were closer to him than his own brothers and went to find the well Shams had been flung into. When he pulled Shams's body out, tears were streaming down his face, but the foreboding in his heart outweighed his sorrow. 'My father cannot live if he learns of the death of his sheikh,' he said. 'He will fall down and die.' So the three friends swore to keep the matter a secret. They buried Shams's body in a grave alongside a good Samaritan by the name of Bedreddin Gevhertaş. None of the friends betrayed the secret, until one night when Sultan Veled again woke up screaming, tears streaming from his eyes. He wanted to protect the secret, but his anxious wife, Fatima, refused to let the matter rest. Sultan Veled finally broke down and told her what had happened to Shams, though not until after she'd sworn on a Qur'an to protect the secret as well. And Fatima did keep that secret for years, just as the others had, right up until His Holiness Mevlana and Sultan Veled passed on to the other side. After they died, she told her son Ulu Arif Çelebi what she knew. And he passed it on to Eflaki Dede, asking him to write it down."

"And yet you're angry with Eflaki Dede." I smiled, so he'd know I was giving him a hard time. "If he hadn't written down what happened to Shams, it would have remained a mystery."

"I'm not angry but," he said, jumping to his own defence, "he exaggerated a bit is all I'm saying."

"So then whatever happened to Alaeddin?"

"He left Konya, and later died of malaria while still quite young. According to Eflaki, Rumi never even attended his son's funeral." He threw me a timid look then offered his opinion. "Why would he? Why would anyone have a smidgeon of esteem left for a delinquent son like that who murders the man you love."

Mennan sounded so callous, and so convinced. But what I'd dreamt and what Eflaki had written didn't match up. According to Eflaki, or rather Rumi's grandson, Arif Çelebi, who'd had him write the book, his uncle Alaeddin had been a malicious, jealous son to Rumi. Whereas in my dream Alaeddin was just a desperate adolescent whose mind had been conquered by love, exactly like his father.

"... as rebellious as Rumi's rebellious middle son, Alaeddin Çelebi."

⋙

A harsh wind whipped our hair and clothes about as we stepped out of the car. We quickly threw ourselves into the police headquarter gardens as Mennan looked up at the sky and mumbled, "Poyraz. The northeasterly wind. That means rain."

The garden was more sheltering; the wind's force had no effect here. A man's bulky form was just emerging from the main entrance. I squinted, trying to pick out some identifying feature. It was Detective Ragip. Still agitated, still high-strung, he was barking orders down his wireless with a frown on his face, so carried away with what he was doing that he didn't notice us. Behind him was a group of about fifteen men, most of them police, but my attention was on the brawny, athletic-looking man with greying hair and thick moustache standing straight and tall between two officers in the front row of the crowd. Though his hands were cuffed and the officers had a tight grip on his arms, he still managed to strut with his chest out as though challenging the world.

"Miss Greenwood, look!" exclaimed Mennan, grasping my arm.

I looked to where he was pointing and there saw Serhad and Cavit, each flanked by police officers like the suspects in the first group. I was wondering if they were all part of the same gang when I came eye to eye with Serhad, whose expression went quickly from surprise to suspicion, before settling into hatred. Cavit had also spotted us and, unable to immediately make sense of the situation, nearly smiled. But then he noticed his friend's hostility and got confused. As for Serhad, he was well aware of everything. With growing animosity he stared into my eyes as though trying to curse me by sheer will. If it weren't for the police presence he would have done more, maybe even jumped us. But the police didn't even allow him to slow down. Dragging him quickly along, they crammed him, along with Cavit and the other gang members, into a van.

"I guess they've been arrested after all," Mennan pronounced happily. "That Inspector Zeynep sure is a woman of her word."

"Don't get your hopes up. I spoke with her this morning and she said they didn't find any evidence in their houses."

A quizzical expression replaced the delight on his face.

"So then where are they taking these guys?"

"I don't know," I answered, starting forward again. "If we can find Inspector Zeynep, we'll find out."

It wasn't difficult. She was back behind her desk in the same lilac blouse and blue jeans, giving instructions to a uniformed police officer and looking even more exhausted than Mennan and me. When she saw us at the door, she gave a vague smile in our direction and paused just long enough to direct us to the chairs in front of her desk, saying, "Come on over and have a seat. I'll see to you right away." Then, while we plunked gracelessly into the chairs, she carried on with her efficient explanation of which documents were to be taken to the district attorney's office.

Her desk was piled quite high, but there appeared to be a kind of logic to the clutter. Her computer was to the right, the paperwork was all in neat stacks to the left, and in front of her was a small, empty desk pad wedged in between a crowded pen holder and an incessantly buzzing police scanner. Just in front of the scanner was a small photo in a simple frame that I hadn't noticed the day before. It was of Zeynep standing between two men. I leaned in to get a closer look. One of the men was middle-aged, his face weary though kind, the sort of person you could instantly warm up to. The other was younger, with a turbulent look in his eyes. He looked every bit as rebellious as Rumi's middle son, Alaeddin Çelebi.

"Curious about the photo?"

I jumped as though caught red-handed.

"I'm sorry, it just grabbed my attention for a moment."

"It's all right, Miss Greenwood." Her smile was relaxed. "It's right in front of your nose, it's only natural you would look at it."

Encouraged by her reaction, I asked openly, "Is it your family?"

"No. They're closer than family, actually."

She looked longingly at the picture.

"The grey haired one is Detective Nevzat, my superior in Istanbul. And the one with the crazy eyes is Ali, Police Commissioner Ali."

Her eyes were lost in thought as she repeated Ali's name. Apparently, the young man was more to her than just a co-worker.

"Detective Nevzat is the finest man I have yet to meet in this world."

Zeynep had begun to offer some insight into her personal life, and I couldn't let the opportunity pass. I smiled and asked, "Why finest man and not finest police?"

"Well, he's that too. But he has principles. He always puts his conscience before his profession, which is what he tells us to do, too. 'Be human first, then police.'"

"And the young one?"

For one moment the fatigue in her chestnut-coloured eyes disappeared.

"Ali?" She leaned back in her chair and her eyes shone as she looked off to one side, as though in the middle of a beautiful daydream. "Ali is crazy. A real maniac. But he also has a heart of gold. I think being a police officer is the worst possible job for him." She paused and looked back at us, realising she'd got carried away. "That's not to say he isn't good at it," she said coming back down to earth.

She took a deep breath and leaned forward. "Right. Let's get back to business." She pulled an envelope out from the stack of documents to her left. "Here you are, your passport."

"Where did you find it?" I asked, taking it from her.

"You know this Lefty Kamil who assaulted you? Well, we found it in the house of the guys who murdered him."

"So then you've caught them?" I asked, amazed.

"Yes, two of them got away, but never mind. We disbanded the gang. It's just a matter of time before we catch them too."

Mennan swallowed and asked, "What sect are they from?"

Zeynep's normally smooth forehead wrinkled up.

"Sect?"

"You said yesterday," continued Mennan impatiently, "that the men were religious fanatics. Remember, Inspector Zeynep?"

Zeynep gave him a mischievous smile.

"Well, they weren't. Actually, we've known this for quite some time, but couldn't say so until the operation was finished."

"So what was it really about? Why did they kill him?" I asked.

"They were settling a score with another gang..." she'd started to explain. The wind blew open a window behind us and she didn't finish her sentence. "I'm sorry, I'd better close that."

She got up from her chair and walked sluggishly to the window, closing it firmly. Turning back around she asked, "Has winter returned or what?" She settled back in her chair then carried on from where she'd left off as though she'd never stopped. "We've come across this kind of mafia plenty of times before. But this time the group we were facing was better organised. Or more accurately, they had a very crafty ringleader, a captain who was dishonourably discharged from the army. Yılmaz Deresoylu, known by many as Psycho Yılmaz."

"Is this Psycho Yılmaz a grey-haired guy with a thick moustache? I think we just saw him in the garden."

"That would be him. Chief Ragip was taking him to the DA's office. Now, contrary to his name, this Psycho Yılmaz is extremely clever and cunning. He worked as an intelligence officer in the gendarme for years, before getting caught up in some corruption during the time he spent in the war in the southeast. After getting kicked out of the army, he rounded up a handful of crooked cops and created a ring in Konya. When they came across an older gang, one of whose member's was Lefty Kamil, things got out of control."

"You said Lefty Kamil had got out of that business," I said, pointing out the contradiction with what she'd told us the day before.

"We thought so, too, until last night. Turns out he hadn't. He was lying low, for sure, but he still did the occasional job for the gang. It is true that he had a minibus. But he was using it for both tourism and gang activity."

"This gang you keep mentioning, what kind of things were they involved in?" I asked, wondering if Ikonion Tourism was just a front.

"All kinds of things. Collecting 'protection' money from restaurants and beer houses, selling drugs, prostitution... But Psycho Yılmaz had set his sights on higher horizons. He'd started to collect on illegal cheques and bonds, extort money from wealthy businessmen, and was attempting to acquire government property through illegal means. Konya is a small place, and one day the two gangs' paths crossed. Lefty Kamil's gang came down hard on them. Psycho Yılmaz appeared to be backing off, not wanting to risk an all out war, but secretly he was devising a plan. Using his previous experience at intelligence gathering, he began hunting down the members of the rival gang one by one. First he had the prostitute and her pimp husband stoned to death on the Afyon motorway. And as I explained yesterday, he had his men give the crime scene the appearance of a ritual stoning carried out by fanatical Muslims. Following that, he had the rival gang's tavern burned down and verses from the Qur'an written on the wall opposite. Which brings us to now. Just like the others, he orchestrated the murder of the already widely hated Lefty Kamil and made it look like shari'a law was being implemented. But Lefty was already dead by the time his hand was stuffed down his throat. It was Psycho Yılmaz himself who snapped his neck."

"You mean, Lefty's murder had nothing to do with the assault on Miss Greenwood?"

It was Mennan, every bit as stupefied as I was by the news, who had asked the question.

"Nope. Total coincidence. But it is highly possible that the killers saw Lefty assault Miss Greenwood. Because at that point they were already after him. And there were five others on the list after Lefty. If we hadn't managed to bring that ring down, they would have killed them all. Psycho Yılmaz was determined to dispose of the lot of them and make it look like the work of some radical Islamic group like Hizbullah or Al-Qaeda."

It was a compelling story, not the kind I came across every day in England. Still, I couldn't manage to keep thoughts of our company's three million pound payout from creeping in.

"So was there any connection between Lefty Kamil and Ikonion Tourism?"

Her face fell.

"Afraid not. We were only able to establish a connection with Serhad and Cavit. Lefty spent one year locked up in the Eskisehir Prison with those two. The three of them were good friends."

"So Serhad was a previous offender," Mennan spit out indignantly. "I knew he was scum all along. And that clean freak Cavit, even worse."

"They were doing time for shooting a man," Zeynep continued. "The two of them were members of a boatmen's mafia in Antalya. After three years of incarceration, like Lefty, they were released on a general pardon. After that they came to Konya, where they were employed by Mr. Kuyumcuzade."

At last we'd come to the subject that concerned me.

"And Mr. Kuyumcuzade, was he also part of this gang?"

"I don't think so," she said, shaking her head. "His name didn't show up on Psycho Yılmaz's gang's black list, nor was he among the members of the rival gang. Presumably, Mr. Kuyumcuzade has no ties to any gang."

I immediately objected.

"He may not have ties to a gang, but he certainly had no qualms about setting Lefty Kamil on me."

She looked at me wearily, though acknowledging I had a point.

"Yes, it was most probably Mr. Kuyumcuzade that set Lefty on you. Via Serhad and Cavit no doubt. Both Serhad and Cavit are denying the charge, however. Serhad admits to calling Lefty on the phone, but claims they are old friends and were just going to meet for lunch.'"

The hopelessness of the situation was starting to get to me.

"But they're lying. They said before that they didn't know Lefty. But look, it turns out they were prison mates."

"I'm aware of that, Miss Greenwood," she said, looking browbeaten. "But I already told you on the phone, in the search we conducted of their houses, we found no evidence that they started any fire, nor any indication that they had an incentive to. Regardless, I sent them both over to the DA's office, taking into account that they are repeat offenders."

She didn't sound too hopeful. She may not have been admitting it, but she believed the DA would let the two of them go. I felt totally defeated. For a while no one said anything. The nerve-wracking buzz of the scanner on the desk was the only sound in the room.

"I don't know that it will be of much help, but I'd like to tell you something regarding Ikonion Tourism," said Zeynep, taking up the conversation again. "I looked over their credit details and it turns out Ikonion Tourism was in very bad shape from a financial standpoint. Ziya was seriously overspending on that apart hotel he insisted on creating. He had outstanding bank loans of close to five million dollars. If he hadn't come up with at least part of that in the next six months, all his possessions were going to be seized. And this isn't the first time Mr. Kuyumcuzade got himself in a tight spot. Five years ago, he was a partner in a Konya-based limited company that lost ten million euros he'd collected from religious Turkish citizens living in Germany, after conning them into believing he and his company were also devout Muslims. I mean, the individual we know as Ziya Kuyumcuzade is not exactly pure as driven snow. And if you want my opinion, then yes, he is also the one responsible for the fire in the Yakut Hotel."

Now I'd lost hope, too. I repeated what Zeynep had said on our last two visits.

"We have no evidence and no witnesses. Ziya planned this down to a tee."

"What?" Mennan exploded. "Are we giving in to this blatant scam, Miss Greenwood?"

"Do we have any choice?"

"Let's speak with his father," said Mennan stubbornly. It didn't look like he was going to give up without a fight. "İzzet Efendi won't stand for this disgrace."

I pursed my lips helplessly.

"Maybe you should speak to him," Zeynep cut in. "Ziya may not have much regard for his father, and may not be too forthcoming with the old man, but you never know. He could have something for you to go on."

Apparently the idea of Ziya walking off with three million pounds also made her uncomfortable. She couldn't swallow the idea of a crook like him winning out at the end of the day.

"I'll take your suggestion into account," I said, picking myself up. "Well, we should get going. Thanks so much for all your help."

As we got up, she also stood and extended a hand.

"I wish I could have done more, but I'm afraid it was all I could manage."

Her expression was sincere, her voice regretful.

"Destruction is your prerogative,
just as creation is."

✳

As soon as we left Zeynep's office, I had Mennan call İzzet Efendi, though not for help with our investigation so much as at the prospect of finding out more about Shams and my father. Their exchange was short. İzzet Efendi welcomed the request and invited us to the Mevlana Museum director's office, where he would be meeting with the director who was an old friend. We settled on twelve o'clock. I should have then called Simon and updated him, but somehow I just didn't feel like talking to him. Despite the failure of our investigation, my mind was more occupied with Shams than work. So many questions had cropped up in my head, I didn't know what order to take them in, which ones to try and get answers for. The only thing I knew for certain was that I wanted to be alone to think. I told Mennan I was going for a walk around the city.

"Where do you want to go?" he asked enthusiastically.

The man was crazy about helping me. But this was my story, I'd already involved him enough in the matter, and I was sure he had plenty of work to do in his office.

"I don't know," I said nonchalantly. "Wherever. And please don't take this the wrong way, but I'd like to do it alone if you don't mind. Nothing to do with you, I just really enjoy sightseeing by myself."

He didn't understand, but he didn't push the subject either. "If there's somewhere in particular you'd like to be dropped off..." he was starting to say when I cut him short.

"No," I stated firmly. "Thanks, I can look after myself."

"Okay then. My phone will be on if you need me."

After Mennan drove off, I walked around the streets aimlessly for a while, thinking. It looked like I'd finished up here. I'd found my passport and there was no reason for me not to head back to England. I would speak to Simon, and set off to Istanbul the following morning, then get the first plane back to London. Yet I knew it wasn't what I really wanted to do. I couldn't pinpoint it exactly, but a feeling of having left something unaccomplished throbbed like a hidden wound in my mind. After being apart from my father for so many years, I'd now come to his city, and face to face not only with his beliefs but the ghosts of people he himself had chosen to guide him. The situation had caught me off guard and I could have done without it. But now that I was here, I couldn't see any point in leaving before tying up the loose ends. My ringing phone pulled me back down to earth. It was Nigel. For some reason I didn't feel so ecstatic.

"Hi, Karen..."

"Hi, Nigel. How are you?" I said morosely.

"What happened? You don't sound so good."

Clever man, my boyfriend, he'd immediately detected something was wrong.

"No, I'm fine. There was a snag in the investigation is all."

"Really?" he said, less cheerful this time. Who knows what he was feeling when he dialled me, maybe he'd even been planning to read another of Rumi's poems.

"Never mind that," I said, changing the subject. "First, let me thank you for taking my mum out to dinner last night. It made her very happy."

"Is that right?" He sounded doubtful. "Didn't seem that way to me. She was happy enough to begin with, but was a wee bit pissed off when she heard you were pregnant."

I didn't ask him why he'd told her in the first place, because I didn't want him to think of this pregnancy as a mistake that needed hiding. On the contrary, a woman my age should be thinking of it as a fortunate last shot, as my mother had pointed out.

"Then when I told her we weren't going to have it, she got even more upset," he continued. "I guess your mother wants a grandchild. You'd better talk to her soon so the poor woman doesn't get her hopes up."

It sounded more like he was warning me. Maybe my perception was off because of all the stress I'd been through. Though I knew it was neither the time nor place, I didn't feel like hiding my feelings any more.

"Nigel, there's something I want to say."

"And what is that?"

I could discern a challenge in Nigel's voice. My perception hadn't been off after all. I knew that tone so well, it was the same one he used whenever I wanted to talk about something he didn't. But this time he wasn't going to get his way.

"I'm not so sure about this abortion," I stated assertively.

Despite the thousands of miles between us, I could feel the full weight of his disapproval.

"We've already been over this," he said after a short silence. "I've already made an appointment for you at the hospital, for that matter."

"I'm sorry, Nigel. You're right. We have talked it over, or rather you told me what you think and I kept quiet. I admit it was wrong of me not to share my thoughts then, but from now on I promise to be more upfront. The point is, I don't think I want to go through with it."

"So. You want to have a baby?"

He'd raised his voice like he was nagging, scolding even.

"I don't know," I said, my tone neither meek nor defensive. "I have to give it some thought."

"Haven't you given it some thought already?"

He was becoming more hurtful by the minute.

"No, I haven't."

"You're letting your mother influence you."

"It's not just my mother. It's everything." I didn't want to argue with him. "Give me time, Nigel. Let me think a bit, and you think too. We'll continue this conversation when I'm back in London."

My levelheadedness must have been having an effect.

"All right," he said, managing to control his temper. "All right, we'll speak when you get back then."

"Apart from that, how are you?"

"Fine. No surgeries today." His voice was impassive and unemotional now. "I'm going to play tennis this afternoon. I have a match with this psychologist of yours."

"Oliver?"

"Mmm. He wiped the floor with me last time, you know."

"Well, maybe you'll beat him this time."

"It won't be easy, but I'll do my best."

"Good luck."

We were talking, but the chill between us was somehow not thawing, inferring that it was time to bid our farewells. He didn't say he missed me, or ask when I'd be back, but just randomly uttered a dry, "Take care," before hanging up.

My heart stung, but I held myself back.

"You too," I said, leaving it at that. "You take care too."

As I hung up, I couldn't keep the tears from welling up. Where had we gone wrong? How had we reached this stalemate? Why were we falling apart? I suddenly realised how pessimistic I was being. Our relationship wasn't failing, I told myself. We just disagreed. Maybe when I got back to London I could bring Nigel round and he would also want this child. I hadn't yet disclosed all my thoughts on the subject. He may surprise me and understand. But what if he didn't? What if he really didn't want a child? I didn't know what I would do. It felt so complicated. As I mulled all this over, I picked up my step, as though by walking faster I'd arrive at a solution sooner. I rushed around the city streets as though competing with the intensifying wind, inextricable questions in my head and a baby in my belly awaiting answers. I suddenly realised I was lost, that all the streets and boulevards were starting to look the same. For a moment I panicked and didn't know what to do. The solution appeared in the form of a taxi passing a few metres beyond me on the avenue. Without a second thought I flagged it down.

"Where to?" the driver asked as I got in.

"The Shams-i Tabriz Mosque," I answered purposefully.

The first drops of rain were falling as I climbed out of the taxi. Dark blue clouds covered the sky as though the day had given way to nightfall. Hoping to avoid the downpour, I impatiently entered the mosque. A young man with a wispy beard and luminous face met me at the door, politely requesting that I remove my shoes and cover my head.

"If you haven't got a scarf, we can provide you with one," he offered.

"That's all right. I've brought my own," I answered, thanking him.

I pulled it out of my bag and covered my head, then took off my shoes and placed them on the lower left row of the shelves that stood on both sides of the door. Compared to Rumi's Mausoleum it was an extremely modest place, a mosque and tomb combined in just one room. But maybe that was what suited Shams. Had they asked him, he may not even have wanted the tomb. Wasn't it Rumi who had rhetorically asked what more beautiful dome there could be than the sky? I was sure that Shams would have agreed. Still, after the crowds at Rumi's grave, it was disheartening to see no one but the attendant here. The solitude inside this centuries old mausoleum was more than just somber, it was downright eerie. I looked around gingerly before making my way further in. Passing under a wide archway to my left, I noted the wooden *mihrab*, the niche showing the direction of Mecca, which meant prayer rituals were actually still performed here. But I didn't waste much time on that area. A few metres beyond me, separated from the rest of the mosque by a low wooden railing, stood a large, stone sarcophagus draped in green cloth, a stone turban balanced at its head. As I neared the foot of the sarcophagus, I read the plaque to the left.

Whatever the friendship, affection, and bond between our great Prophet Muhammed and His Holiness Ali, such is the friendship between His Holiness Shams and His Holiness Mevlana.

I found it sad that people still felt the need to defend the relationship between them seven centuries on. On the other hand, it wasn't as though the bond between these two extraordinary men didn't warrant that kind of interest. They themselves called it love, though I suppose there was a huge discrepancy between the meaning they applied to that feeling and our concept of it. Perhaps if I could figure out

343

the relationship between Shams and Rumi, I could also grasp the bond between my father and Shah Nesim, as well as the reason behind my father's leaving us. Maybe what I should have been asking İzzet Efendi is not why my father went away with Shah Nesim, but why Rumi was so passionately bound to Shams. The mystery of the ring may also lie there, in that great secret Shams referred to as 'the truth'.

As I was considering this, a series of gongs reverberated through the dome of the mosque. I turned to look where the sound was coming from, and for the first time noticed the antique grandfather clock against the wall. I watched, mesmerised, as the clock's pendulum swung back and forth, continuing to gong stubbornly as if signaling the time for some important event. When it finally stopped, the door in the lower part of the clock creaked open, and there in front of me stood yet another mysterious corridor. Once again, I heard the familiar howling and felt that biting wind. Again I was wrapped in a sweet breeze that carried with it the scent of geraniums, and a shiver went through me. The spirit of the black-clad dervish was somewhere nearby. Ignoring the feeble voice inside me telling me not to dare go in, I grabbed my curiosity by the shirttail and let it lead me towards where the scent was most intense. As I entered into the passage beyond the clock, a dampness from deep within the ground struck my face and my body was overcome with trembling. But that didn't stop me. I kept going, along a narrow vaulted corridor lit with yellow candlelight. A few more steps and I came to a glass door framed in thick, gilded wood. But there was no knob, no keyhole even. As I contemplated how to get in, a shadow fell on the other side of the door. On closer inspection, I saw that it belonged to a person, and that the person it belonged to was our wandering dervish.

"Why have you stopped? Why don't you carry on walking?" he asked, as though there was nothing preventing it.

I pointed out the door blocking my way. "Can't you see this glass? How can I get through?"

"It is not glass, it is a mirror."

"Then the mirror's enamel must have chipped away, because I can see through to the other side."

"You cannot," he said, his dark, almond eyes squinting at me. "What you see is your reflection."

I looked down at my body. He was right. Once again, I was dressed in those black garments. Once again, my hands were those of an aged man and my body that of Shams. I lifted my head and looked at myself in the mirror, though this time without surprise. One pace beyond the image of the Shams I'd become was a wooden hatch with an iron ring, and I understood the path I was to follow. I turned and, grabbing the iron ring, lifted the hatch. At my feet lay a stairway twisting into the depths of the earth. Without hesitation, without finding it the least bit odd, I started smoothly down the stairs as though altogether familiar with them. With my first step, a whispering could be heard.

"This Iranian dervish has cast a spell on His Holiness Mevlana. Why else would he be so bound to him?"

With every new step, a new voice spewed out new hatred.

"They say he is a sodomite. That it is only male bodies he's fond of, this Shams-i Perende..."

As I descended further, the whispering could be heard more clearly.

"They say he declared his own prophethood the other day in the bazaar."

Following in my footsteps like wingless demons, the whisperings soon became snarls.

"They say he is a blasphemer who worships many gods. God forgive me, they heard him say of himself that he is Allah."

Their snarls became a flag for their blatant enmity.

"They say he is a Mongol. That he is going to give them a map of Konya so that they may enter the city with ease..."

Their virulence ultimately turned to threat.

"This black dervish shall be condemned to death. It's to be carried out quick as lightening."

As I was taking my last step down onto the stone floor, all at once the voices cut out. I was in my room. In the room Jelaleddin had provided me to live in, though it had been emptied of all its things. There was no longer the divan along the wall, nor the carpet spread on the floor, nor the ornamented water pitcher, nor the Qur'an bookrest which the Vizier Karatay had presented to Jelaleddin as a gift. There was only a casket. A casket made of glass, displaying its contents to the world as though for all to see and learn from. For inside the casket was a young girl, my wife, Kimya. She looked as fresh as though she'd never died. Her cheeks were as pink as roses, as though she would soon wake from her slumber with a smile. Perhaps if I touched her she would open her eyes, or rise up if I called out to her. But I was weak at the knees. Where was my fortitude now?

At that moment I heard a knock at the door.

"Shams Efendi... Oh Shams-i Tabriz, come to the door a minute, will you?"

I wasn't surprised at what I heard. Neither was I daunted, nor afraid. I knew that it was time. I shifted from one foot to the other, then walked resolutely to the door. Before bringing my hand to the lock, I turned to take one last look at the girl's chaste body lying unshrouded in its glass casket. If it weren't for my covenant with God, I would have exchanged my life for hers in a heartbeat. But the promise I was made had been fulfilled, and I must therefore fulfill mine. I opened the door. The chill from the dead of winter blasted in. A cold wind licked my face like an invisible, flameless fire.

"Here you are," I said to the seven men, whom the full moon had reduced to shadows. "See? I have come. What is it you have to say?"

No one could utter a word. The silence of the winter night fell over us like a penetrating frost. I seemed to be able to distinguish the one in front. This was Khüdavendigar's rebellious middle son, Alaeddin.

"Alaeddin," I uttered, reading the judgement passed on me in his eyes. "Alaeddin, is it you?"

The shadow I imagined to be Alaeddin took one step forward. I saw my own face in his image.

"Remember," my own lips commanded me. "Remember the promise you made."

Before my eyes, I saw a silent garden, lit by the light of the full moon. On that blessed night, I had implored God:

"O he who created the heavens and the earth, O he who makes possible that which is not possible... I beseech you to name for me one of your recondite beloveds."

He who becomes unreachable as one approaches, said this unto me:

"The life you ask about, hidden from the eyes of all, a life with favour and grace upon it, is Muhammed Jelaleddin Rumi, son of Belhli Sultanü'l-Ulema Baha Veled."

And I had said unto him:

"O hope of hopes, O sacred light of our existence. Will you reveal the image of Muhammed Jelaleddin, the blessed face of your beloved?"

He who sees and knows all, enumerating and increasing manyfold what we know, had asked me:

"How will you repay your debt of gratitude?"

And without faltering, I had stretched out my neck and responded:

"With my head!"

The Creator had seen merit in my gift and said to me:

"This is spiritualism. This is love. Love has but one price and that is one's life. Love that is not consecrated by death is not really love. And because of this Muhammed Jelaleddin Rumi, son of Baha Veled, is for you lawful and legitimate. Go now and find him. Go, find him, but do not forget the promise you have made."

I hadn't forgotten. How could I forget the sacred purpose I struggled to fulfill with every breath I took, every step I put forward? I smiled as I looked back on myself from the body I supposed was now Alaeddin's.

"Is it time?"

"It is time," said the one who appeared in my image. "Are you ready?"

"I am ready," I said without so much as blinking. "Destruction is your prerogative, just as creation is."

First I heard a sound, a knife being pulled from its sheath like the hiss of a viper spitting poison. I looked, and now it was Alaeddin who stood before me again. I tried to smile, but they didn't let me. I attempted to explain with my eyes, but they wouldn't allow it. Under the light of the full moon, seven knives reflected seven synchronous flashes of light. Seven jolts ripped through my body like muffled screams. Seven flowers of fire bloomed in my open flesh. And out through those seven fiery blossoms, my soul rose gently into the sky. Then blood dripping on stone. Then the full moon in the sky, the scent of earth in the garden. The trees swimming in an unsettling chill. The burgeoning winter roses and the narcissus in full bloom. Seven men had torn my body to shreds. Seven wrathful hearts, seven minds seized by hatred, seven finely-honed knives. Seven pitiable humans, who knew not what they'd done. And then blood on the stone. As though absorbing every creature in existence as it congealed, that one drop of blood.

"Why have you given me this ring?"

✖

When I opened my eyes, I was lying on the red and blue embroidered carpet at the foot of Shams's sarcophagus. The heavy smell of dye rising from the carpet was making my head spin and my stomach queasy. I propped myself against the wall as the attendant with the wispy beard caught up with me.

"Hey, lady... Are you okay?"

I pulled myself up with the help of the wooden rail in front of the sarcophagus.

"I'm all right..." I said, trying to smile. "I blacked out for a second."

"You shouldn't get up. You're very pale," the attendant muttered, with genuine concern.

For a moment, I thought of sharing with the concerned attendant that it was the man in the sarcophagus he was guarding who was responsible for this. That I'd been forced to live out his murder, and the violence of it had made me faint.

"Don't worry, it'll pass," I said instead, as I tried to suppress the queasiness rising in me. "Could I trouble you for a glass of water?"

"Right away, I'll be right back with it," said the young attendant, rushing off.

Alone now, I felt better. I was picking myself up when another plaque next to Shams's sarcophagus caught my eye.

Here lies Shams's-i Tabriz, martyred by seven jealous, ignorant men.

I must have seen it without realising, and it had influenced the vision I'd had when I passed out. Then again, after what I'd been through these last three days, just visiting Shams's tomb alone was sufficient to wreak havoc on my nervous system. Either way, it wasn't the first I'd heard of his death. Mennan had already told me how Shams had been killed. But while my mind sought out plausible excuses for what I'd been through, I inwardly believed more and more that these were not just random nightmares I was having, but a reflection of reality itself. In this arduous war between mind and soul, a strange silence was wrapping around my psyche, as though it were content with just helplessly watching events play themselves out.

"Here you are, lady."

The attendant held out a glass of water. I took the glass and brought it to my lips. The water was flat and tasteless. I wondered if it had come from a well. There was a smell of damp soil again and I imagined those stairs leading into the depths, the threatening whispers, Kimya's fresh corpse lying in the glass casket, blood dripping on stone... The nausea intensified. I needed fresh air. Thrusting the glass into the young attendant's hand and hastily thanking him, I rushed outside. I didn't even manage to get my shoes on till outside the mosque.

I leaned back against the low wall of the fountain a few metres beyond the mosque and took a deep breath. Feeling better now, I continued towards the pavement. This was all to do with the pregnancy - dizziness, fainting, nausea... But the nightmares? I thought pregnant women just had unusual food cravings. Watermelon in the dead of winter, chestnuts in summer... I must be the only one for whom seeing ghosts was a symptom. Did this mean I was going to be dealing with dead saints when I got back to London? It seemed ridiculous. These things I was experiencing were all related to subjects discussed in our home, and to my father's being Mevlevi, just as my mother had pointed out. And I had to admit I was completely ignorant when it came to pregnancy. I would have to see an obstetrician as soon as I got back, if for no other reason than to overcome my total cluelessness on the subject. But maybe it wasn't such a good idea to tell anyone about the nightmares. Even my mother would think I was crazy. It's true she'd always been understanding. She hadn't sent me to a doctor about my imaginary friend Sunny or my sleepwalking when I was young. But now, with this baby thrown into the equation, I was afraid she would have me checked into one of London's exclusive psychiatric clinics in a heartbeat. And there was no reason to cause her unnecessary concern. I was sure everything would go back to normal the second I left this city. Or would it? I didn't understand the first thing about these nightmares, what Shams was trying to say or why he kept showing me his own life, his relationship with Rumi. What was this secret? This absolute truth that not everyone could reach? Was it some specific occurrence in his own life? Was it his knotted heart in the ring's stone? Was he trying to explain to me how he had died? But how he'd died was no secret. Ahmed Eflaki wrote on the subject hundreds of years before. So then why wouldn't he leave me in peace? There must be a reason why he seeped into my dreams at every opportunity, stirring up nightmares and terrorising my sleep. I wished my father were here. This was his faith, his culture. If he couldn't explain it, who could? But who knew where my father was now? Even if he were here with me, I wasn't really sure how he would react. He, too, may not believe me and think I was crazy. And he may not be so off the mark, I wasn't so sure myself anymore. Maybe it had nothing to do with pregnancy or my father's beliefs, but I really was gradually losing my mind.

All at once I found myself in the place I'd come upon Shams three days before, where he'd given me the ring. I looked around, expecting him to appear to me again, but could see neither the strange dervish nor his black shadow. The park was quite calm. Two men and a covered woman with a market bag stuffed full of groceries rushed past, but there was no one else. Another raindrop fell on my face. I looked up at the sky, but there were no more drops. On the contrary, the dark blue clouds were quickly dispersing and a timid sun slowly emerged. I recalled what Shams had said.

"When the sun of the material world rises, that of the spiritual world vanishes."

His voice resounded in my head again and his words preoccupied my thoughts. I somehow couldn't get away from him. It was as if some invisible being was lodged in the convolutions of my brain. And he was right. I'd only ever seen him at night, or when the daylight disappeared. That, I reasoned, was when our minds were at their most vulnerable, when it was easiest for our sub-consciouses to take over. The explanation made me feel better. I looked at my watch. It was nearly twelve, almost time to meet with İzzet Efendi. I started towards the entrance of the park with its scattered trees. As I neared the pavement and looked round for a taxi to take me to Rumi's Mausoleum, my phone rang. It was Simon. Though I still had no desire to speak with him, I no longer felt I had the luxury of not doing so, so I picked up.

"Hi Simon."

"Hi Karen. How's it going?"

I launched into the bad news.

"Terrible, I'm sorry to say. We couldn't prove that the men purposely set fire to the hotel..."

"But your email said Ziya's men were being taken into custody. That their houses were being searched..." he complained, disappointment registering in his voice. He was so desperate he was almost blaming me. Without dressing it up any for him, I relayed all that had happened. How all my efforts had come to naught, and how Ziya was craftier than we'd supposed... He listened in silence. I couldn't help thinking he must have expected all this from the start. He'd probably just been keeping his fingers crossed that I could change the outcome. In the end, I'd been incapable of performing miracles. Our company should have taken more care when insuring the hotel, I told him. Ziya already had a reputation for getting involved in illicit business deals, and it had been a big mistake accepting someone like him as a client in the first place. When I'd said all I had to say, Simon kept silent a bit longer. Who could say what was going through his mind? He was scheming though, for sure. Maybe even contemplating jumping on a plane to Konya himself. But I was wrong. He must have realised he had no choice but to accept defeat.

"What do you recommend? What do you think we should do?"

"The smart thing would be to back off. Sit at the bargaining table. Try to reduce the three million pound payoff as much as possible."

He went quiet again.

"I guess you're right," he finally said. "We should start the bargaining. Still, let me give it some thought first. I'll meet with our lawyers, maybe they'll come up with a better plan." He took a deep breath. "In the meantime, you have another chat with Ziya. Try to figure out what's going on in his head. But whatever you do, don't let on about our intentions. We'll be in a much stronger position if you can figure out how low Ziya is prepared to go on the payment. We'll speak again this evening."

"All right, I'll see Ziya today and let you know what happens."

"Sounds good." I thought he was hanging up, but he didn't. Not before he added, "Don't be demoralised over how things turned out, Karen. I know you did your best. And good luck today."

Frankly, he'd surprised me. Although in general Simon was a decent manager, his worst habit was that of shrugging off his share of a failure. When the outcome of a case was negative, he would try and put the burden of responsibility on anybody but himself. This may be the first time since working together that he actually showed some understanding.

"Thank you," I said appreciatively. "I'll see you later."

A taxi passed in front of me just as I was saying goodbye. But rather than hailing it, I decided to dial Ziya while my phone was still conveniently in my hand. His phone started ringing, but Ziya wasn't picking up. I persisted, however, and he took it on exactly the eighth ring.

"Hello, Miss Greenwood." His tone was cold, his voice rushed. "Sorry about that. I was in a meeting with the bank and..."

"It's me who should be apologising, Mr. Kuyumcuzade. I'll make this short. We have to get together. I need to share some findings regarding the investigation with you before I write them in my report."

"What kind of 'findings' are we talking about?"

He'd intuited from my tone of voice that it was serious, and was getting nervous. That was a good sign. With two of his men already in custody, he must be wondering what I had up my sleeve. I knew stalling would make it even harder on him.

"Not over the phone. And it sounds like you're busy now. I'll explain in person when we meet."

"All right then, I'll see you soon."

There must have been some pretty high stakes involved in this business meeting he was in, because he seemed more concerned with avoiding an unsavoury conversation in front of his customers than of hearing what I had to say. Maybe he was worried he'd risk compromising a deal.

"How and where?" I asked.

"Don't worry, Konya is a small place. I'll find you," he responded confidently. "Good day now."

Before I got a chance to ask how, exactly, he intended to find me, he'd hung up.

"... the devil is the guide of he who has no guru."

※

Arriving at the Dervishan Gate, I came across a small queue like the day before. This time, however, it wasn't English that filled the ticket booth at the entrance, but a group of French in burgundy fezzes. Mennan was nowhere in sight. I checked my watch again, and it was twelve on the dot. As my eyes scanned the surrounding area, I suddenly picked his voice out from among the chatter of tourists. He was calling to me from behind the turnstiles.

"Over here, Miss Greenwood... Over here."

I made my way to the turnstiles, where the uniformed attendant let me in. The garden of the mausoleum was packed with visitors again. "You must have got here early?" I asked, as we cut through the enthusiastic crowds.

"That's right," he said sheepishly, as though it were a fault. "Right after I left you, İzzet Efendi called. He asked if I could give him a lift here since I was coming this way. He sounded really down. It was obvious something bad had happened. So I picked him up from his house and delivered him to the museum director."

"So what happened? Why was he upset?"

"He caught that low-life son of his trying to take out a mortgage on his home. Apparently, the gentleman wanted a loan, and was planning to use his father's house as collateral," he droned angrily.

It sounded desperate; Ziya must have really been in dire straits. It would make for a nice bargaining tool, I considered, before concern about his father set in.

"What does İzzet Efendi have to say about it?"

"Of course he said not on your life. And he didn't just leave it at that. He immediately set about implementing his own plan, one he'd been mulling over for ages but hadn't got round to. That's why he wanted to come here."

I didn't understand.

"Why?"

He smiled an angelic smile and his eyes glistened.

"To donate his house to the museum. That's right. He wants to leave all his worldly possessions to the Mevlana Museum. That's what he and Saim, the museum director, were discussing. There are still a few legal hurdles though, so when we leave here I'll take İzzet Efendi to see my lawyers."

I really admired İzzet Efendi. It couldn't be an easy decision, leaving everything to a museum while your son was still alive.

"What will his other relatives have to say about it?" I asked. "He has other children, doesn't he?"

"Nope," he joyfully proclaimed, before chuckling to himself. "It's just Ziya."

"Ziya will be ruined."

"Let him," said Mennan callously. "That reprobate has had it coming for a long time."

Leaving the colourful crowd of tourists in the garden, we entered a corridor, where he pointed to a wooden door on the left.

"This is it, Miss Greenwood. The director set this room aside for us."

İzzet Efendi was sitting in front of the room's only window. After what Mennan had told me I expected to find him tense and angry. But just like the day before, he met us with a tranquil smile. He stood up as we were walking over and I decorously extended a hand.

"Hello again, my girl," he said, taking it in his gentle grip. "Every time I see you, I catch the scent of Poyraz, God bless you."

"Actually, we owe you a big thanks," I answered the warmhearted man. "It's such a pleasure for us to meet with you again."

His wrinkled face beamed.

"Don't mention it. You think I wouldn't jump at the chance to talk with Poyraz's daughter if she wills it? That's out of the question."

He pointed to the chair opposite him.

"Go on, have a seat."

I looked around as I settled in. The room appeared to be a small library. On the glass shelves were rows of gilded, clothbound books, on the walls, a framed picture of Rumi, and a few others of whirling *semazen*. The faint sound of a ney could be heard, though where it came from wasn't clear.

"What a beautiful place!" I exclaimed. "Small, but so cozy."

"That's to be expected. This room belonged to the Mevlana." His cinnamon eyes grew solemn. "It needs some repairs, but unfortunately that takes money. A lot of money from what the museum director, Saim, has just told me."

"Surely, thanks to charitable people like yourself, they'll come up with it..." I was saying, when İzzet Efendi frowned and looked over at Mennan. Poor Mennan went bright red and shrank in his seat. It looked like I'd really stuck my foot in it this time.

"I'm sorry," I said, trying to remedy the situation. "I really pressured Mennan for an explanation. It wasn't his fault."

İzzet Efendi's resentment passed as quickly as a summer rain.

"Nobody is at fault," he said. "It's not a good thing for a charitable act to become common knowledge, but since it's out in the open... let's just call it a blessing in disguise and move on."

There was a brief silence. We'd got off to a bad start and it wouldn't be appropriate to ask him about his estranged son now. I was considering leaving the subject of Ziya off to one side and jumping straight into that of Shams, but then İzzet Efendi suddenly launched into an explanation of what I hadn't wanted to ask.

"In the Hud verse of the Qur'an, there is a fine example of a relationship between father and son. God informs the prophet Noah of an imminent deluge and instructs him to build a huge vessel. He tells him to invite those who believe in him onto the boat. But those who didn't believe made fun of Noah's words and refused his invitation. Unfortunately, among those who declined was one of Noah's own sons. Despite Noah's insistence, the boy would not get on board, but said, 'I will take shelter on high ground, and will there escape the floods.' There was no escaping, however, and the floods picked Noah's son up and dragged him away. After that Noah asked the Almighty, 'He was family, why did you not protect him?' To which the Almighty replied, 'O Noah, he was not your family, for he had gone astray.' Hearing these words, Noah understood the truth and stopped questioning God."

He turned his cinnamon eyes on me.

"Yes, my lovely girl. Despite Ziya's being my own flesh and blood, he is no longer a part of my family. May God protect others from his wickedness. I know you do business with him, but that is all I have to say on the matter. And if you want to do me a favour, let's not bring him up again."

He'd put me to shame.

"Don't worry," I said apologetically. "We aren't here to talk about Ziya. What I wanted to ask you about is the relationship between Rumi and Shams."

"Did you read the story about why the ring bleeds?" he immediately interjected, as though the subject had just occurred to him. "I mean, the one in Shams's book. I couldn't find it, so..."

"We found it," I said, though I didn't want to get into that now. "And I read the story. It was interesting, but it had nothing to do with the ring I was given."

"Oh, all right," he said, not pushing the subject. "Now then, let's get to your question. Tell me, why is it you are so interested in the love between these two sages?"

I knew I'd best be honest.

"Actually, it's the relationship between my father and this Pakistani Shah Nesim I spoke of yesterday that I'm interested in. I believe my father may have been trying to emulate the relationship between Shams and Mevlana."

358

My sincerity pleased him.

"You're right. We all try to follow their example. So what exactly is it you want to know?"

"How can two people be this close? What kind of friendship was this, that two grown adults could become so inseparable?"

He closed his eyes as though the question itself had had a profound affect on him. Then he nodded his head slowly and gently explained.

"Their love bound them to each other. His Holiness Mevlana had this to say about it. 'This love, that leaves nothing to remind me of myself, is truly liberating.' But those who are content with only what they see cannot understand this." His eyelids parted, he turned his languid eyes on me. "Most people, like you, wonder what exactly Rumi and Shams got up to in those days of withdrawal to their room after their first meeting. What could have happened in that period of seclusion that would make Rumi give up lecturing and preaching to chase after this greatest of secrets? Even his wife, Kira, fell prey to her curiosity. Though fully aware of how wrong it was, she couldn't help herself. She peeked through the keyhole of the chamber where the two men of God were cloistered. What she saw was the two of them sitting opposite each other without so much as a word between them. There was a deep tranquility, a peacefulness and profound joy on their faces. Two souls within two bodies who, without tongues, lips, or gestures, spoke only with their eyes. And knowing nothing of this means of communication, Kira couldn't make sense of what they were doing."

Not just Kira, I thought. I couldn't understand it either.

"So what were they doing?" I burst in. "What were they getting out of it, sitting there together all quiet like that?"

"They were searching," he murmured patiently. "In that silence, without flinching, without asking questions, without offering explanations, they sat just so and searched within themselves. But what they sought in themselves was none other than God himself. That's how one became the lover and the other the beloved. Because without love, they knew they would never be able to attain Truth. Mevlana expressed it like this:

The heart, and love, were stripped of a hundred curtains
Both side by side and soul to soul they sat
If at that moment Gabriel himself were to come between them
Unable to escape the fire of love, he would go up in flames

And that is how, my dear girl, they chose love to reach Truth."

İzzet Efendi's words really confused me. "This love, it's different than the love between a man and a woman, isn't it?" I asked, to confirm what I'd already come to believe.

There was no contempt in his face, but he did appear disappointed by my ignorance.

"As I said yesterday, the love between man and woman is miniscule, finite, and temporary. It is a weak flame, and it cannot ignite the human soul, it cannot burn." Raising his index finger slowly into the air, he shut his eyes once more. "Can you hear the music?" He was drawing my attention to the melancholic motifs of the ney. "Now this, this is love. Mevlana says, 'We are like the ney, our song is from you.' That great man believed there were many paths to God, but says he chose music and the *sema* as his.

"According to what Eflaki Dede wrote, one day Mevlana was sitting listening to music. A friend came in, who turned to the musician and harshly admonished him, saying, 'Keep quiet! *Ezan* is being recited from the minaret.' Mevlana immediately intervened. 'No,' he said, forbidding the musician to stop. 'This too is *ezan*. Each is a call to God. But while one is to worship from outside, the other is to intimately know him and feel his love. Do not hold music in contempt; there is a secret hidden within its rhythm which is so great that if I revealed it, the world would be turned upside down.' Yes, that's what he said. The hidden meaning Mevlana spoke of was love. And music was the *ezan* that called him to love. This is why his *Mesnevi* starts off with a folk lyric in praise of the ney: *Listen to the ney, to the story it tells, to its lament of separation.* Cutting a reed from the lake's edge, they made the ney by opening seven holes in the body of the reed, giving it a form that allows for music. But no matter how skilled the *neyzen* who plays it, with every breath, in whatever *makam*, or style, the ney gives voice to its own longing. That is, a longing for the lake's edge from where it was cut. It is a piece of the whole from what was the lake's edge, and real tranquility, real happiness, real love, can only be had when it is made whole again. By the same token, the ney carries the attributes of the lake's edge in its body and soul. Just like the Almighty created Adam from mud, opening seven holes in his head and breathing life into him. As he breathed life in through Adam's nostrils, God gave a piece of his own soul to that life. God, creator of heaven and earth and master over the four seasons, seven continents, and seven levels of heaven, is within us, so to speak. But our desires drag us down the wrong path. The hunger we feel for food and sleep, our lust and our swelling egos, push that piece of our soul into such a deep well within us that most people are not even aware of this sacred element. The person who does, however, become aware of it, and sets off on their quest, is called an *aşık* - a besotted. And what is being sought is *aşk* - or love itself. I mean, the crucial thing is the quest. It is not a quest to be undertaken alone, however. One must have a teacher, a guru if you will, what we call a *maşuk*, meaning a beloved person. Because that bridge of love, which is thinner than a hair and sharper than a sword, cannot be crossed alone. Once the person has made it across, however, he no longer needs the *maşuk*. Because the *aşık* and the *maşuk*, the one who loves and the beloved, will be just that one person now. Just like the Almighty."

"So Shams was Rumi's catalyst to God?"

He smiled and nodded.

"His guide, that's another way of putting it. Shams's illustration of the relationship between disciple and guru is quite astute:

"One day a disciple was asked, 'Who is superior: your guru or Bayezid of Bistam?'

Without giving it a thought, the disciple answered, 'My guru is superior.'

'Then who, God forbid, is superior between your guru and the prophet Mohammed?'

The answer was the same. 'My guru.'

'Is your guru superior, or God?'

'My guru,' came the answer again.

'Isn't what you say blasphemy?'

'It is not,' the disciple explained proudly, confident in himself and his words. "Because it is my guru who taught me of God's existence, his singularity and all his superior attributes. And because the devil is the guide of he who has no guru."'

When he'd finished his anecdote, İzzet Efendi looked us over and added, "The moral of the story is, the relationship between guru and disciple runs deeper than that of the greatest love."

"That is why Mevlana champions love as his religion," Mennan murmured admiringly, again overwhelmed by what he'd heard.

The old man patted his fellow townsman's hand affectionately.

"What other subject is there for Mejnun but Leyla, seeing as how he lives and breathes her?"

So Shah Nesim was my father's *maşuk*, or beloved guru. The one who would lead him to God. That must be why he had meant so much to my father. And why Rumi could not forsake Shams. But what about Shams? He would no doubt hold the same significance for Rumi. It seemed so complicated. Who was the besotted and who the beloved? Which was the disciple, and which the guru? But Shams couldn't put his feelings into words so eloquently as Rumi. He didn't speak so much of love, and wasn't overcome by such ecstasy. Whatever he may have been, he was no poet, not like Rumi. He was nothing of the sort. On the contrary, his role seemed to be that of someone on a mission. He was never without the weight of that sacred duty in his thoughts, and was determined not to give up until it was accomplished. The mission itself was clear – he was to lift the ordinary theologian known as Muhammed Jelaleddin out of the *ulema,* and mould him into the miraculous Mevlana whose words would be kept alive for hundreds of years, to pull the true soul of this holy man from Belh up from the depths where it lay hidden.

"That's why they killed him?"

The question had come out so direct that İzzet Efendi was at a loss.

"Who?" But then he pulled himself together at once. "Shams-i Tabriz?"

I nodded.

"It was their ignorance," he stated flatly. "Their inability to understand. The Qur'an was being taken too literally. Whereas every letter in that great book holds hundreds of different explanations, every word thousands of meanings. And because Shams had unraveled those hidden meanings, he had a grasp of the Qur'an that this pack of blind believers didn't. Then, because those ignorant people could understand neither Shams nor the Qur'an properly, they became his enemies, declaring him a sinner and a heretic. They didn't even try to understand what a jewel he really was. Their hearts and minds had grown black. They became zealots. And whether Muslim, Jewish, or Christian - a zealot is a zealot, my girl."

"And Alaeddin Celebi? How did he get mixed up in all this?"

He smiled bitterly.

"We started off with the Hud verse. Well, what the Almighty said to the prophet Noah also applies to Mevlana and Alaeddin."

I didn't want to contradict the old man, but I felt it unfair to put the entire burden of guilt on Alaeddin.

"But İzzet Efendi," I said, speaking in as soft a voice as possible. "Alaeddin was in love with Kimya. And I'm pretty sure Kimya had taken a liking to him as well. Mevlana was entirely aware of this, and yet he had no qualms about giving Kimya to Shams. What's more, Shams accepted willingly despite his advanced years, marrying Kimya though she hadn't yet come of age. Eflaki's book attests to Shams having been responsible for Kimya's death. Though he may not have had any solid evidence, suspicion alone could have been enough to drive Alaeddin Celebi off the deep end. Of course, I'm not condoning murder, even under those circumstances. But shouldn't we at least take into account Alaeddin's state of mind?"

İzzet Efendi's face had paled. He stayed silent chewing on his bottom lip for a moment.

"I have heard similar accounts," he said, when he finally spoke again. There was no indignation in his voice. "I, personally, believe they were all concocted to slander Shams. I don't believe those great men were defeated by their desires. That cannot have happened. It's true that Shams could be ruthless, but only when it was called for and to those who deserved it. As for Rumi, he wasn't even capable of thinking evil thoughts, let alone committing evil deeds."

It didn't seem right that he was so sure of himself, especially while admitting to not knowing what really happened.

"What if those accounts weren't hearsay, but fact?"

"I doubt that," he said, shaking his head stubbornly. "But even then, there would nonetheless be meaning in everything that happened, beyond what we can see. Meaning that lies hidden from us on the other side of the gate of secrets. We will never be able to completely fathom what happens here on this side of it."

It was the typical argument for every religion. And when it came down to a discussion on belief or the lack thereof, it was his own beliefs İzzet Efendi chose without a moment's hesitation. I realised then that this discussion was going nowhere. I gave up. Still, I was curious as to how Rumi had reacted towards his murderous son.

"So did Rumi then disown Alaeddin when he learned that he'd had a hand in Shams's death?"

He gave me an odd look as though I'd said something outrageous.

"You think Rumi would do a thing like that? Rumi is incapable of holding a grudge. He is like the water that runs pure after the snow melts in the mountains, sweeping along and collecting the twigs and soil in its path while leaving the filth in its wake. It is beyond doubt that he forgave his son. This is what Rumi wrote on Alaeddin's sarcophogus: *O Allah the Munificent! If it is only the righteous you embrace, then who shall those with sin on their conscience pray to?*

"And to those friends of his who questioned why he'd written it, he gave this explanation: 'I spoke with the rose-faced Shams in the unseen world. He told me he has forgiven Alaeddin for all his sins.' And when the great sheikh pardoned Alaeddin, Rumi also embraced his wayward son."

That may have been İzzet Efendi's explanation, but I construed Rumi's words differently. To me they seemed to express a father's deep regret after finally having recognised the grave mistake he'd made.

"What it all comes down to is being truly humble."

※

It was dark again when I got ready to take leave of Mevlana's Mausoleum. Although it was still afternoon, the sun was lost behind the layers of dark blue clouds that stretched across the sky. The rain that somehow never managed to fall was about to finally shed its drops. I was leaving İzzet Efendi and Mennan behind to discuss some details of the estate with the management, after which Mennan would take the old man to see his lawyers. But as I stood up, İzzet Efendi stopped me.

"You're leaving without your present again. I guess that means you weren't happy with yesterday's poem."

"Of course not, I loved it," I said turning red. "I just forgot. Getting used to your customs may take a while."

"Our customs?" he scoffed, feigning indignation. "They're your customs, too. Don't you ever let it slip your mind that you are Poyraz's daughter. Your father is a good man."

I had no intention of getting into another discussion. When I didn't say anything, he continued.

"I'll recite another of Rumi's quatrains for you then, with your consent of course."

"I'd love that," I exuberantly put in. "Please, go ahead."

I looked over at Mennan, who appeared more eager than I did. He'd already locked his hands together on his chest and assumed his listening position.

We are sinners for love, what are Muslims to us
We are tiny ants, what is Solomon to us
Ask from us a face gone pale, a piece of heart
What is the silk cloth of greedy merchants to us

The old man finished reading his poem and asked.

"So, what do you think?"

"It's beautiful." I said admiringly.

Though I didn't agree with most of what İzzet Efendi said, I had really begun to enjoy his company; whether it was his old-fashioned, gentlemanly ways, the tolerance with which he met everything I said, that glimmer preserved in his eyes despite his age, or his tranquil expression, the reflection of a lifetime devoted to one belief, right or wrong. If it weren't for their business with the museum director, I could have sat there with him for hours. And just as İzzet Efendi saw his old friend Poyraz when he looked at me, I saw my father in him. Maybe the saying 'out of sight, out of mind' wasn't so far from the truth. It would certainly explain why I missed my father so much now. Though I still couldn't forgive him for leaving us, the anger I harboured towards him was releasing its grip on me.

My phone rang again. I assumed it was Mr. Kuyumcuzade, the good-for-nothing son who didn't remotely resemble his father. I took out my phone. It was my mother. Though the meeting with Ziya was inevitable, for the time being I'd be happy to hear her voice instead.

"Hi, Mum."

"Hello, Karen," she said, sounding worried. "Are you all right? There's nothing wrong with the baby, is there?"

"No, Mum. I'm fine. And fairly sure the baby is too. Why are you asking?"

"The message you left... You sounded upset, like something bad had happened."

She was right, of course. But I couldn't tell her I'd spent the night in a graveyard, so with affected joviality, I said, "That's you being over-worried. Everything is fine. I just got a bit of a worry myself when I couldn't find you at that time of the morning. At which protest were you?"

"I wasn't at a protest. I was in the cemetery. In Highgate."

I remembered once going to Highgate Cemetery as a child, to commemorate the hundred year anniversary of Karl Marx's death. Though my mother was open to all leftist and progressive ideas, she by no means thought of herself as a Marxist. Her good friend Betty, on the other hand, referred to herself as a staunch Trotskyist. She'd been the one to drag my mother to the memorial and, because my father was elsewhere that day, I'd also gone with them.

"Visiting Karl Marx's grave again?" I asked, confused.

"No. Matt's grave. In his family's plot," came her deadpan response. "But you're right. Marx has no choice but to share his burial grounds with Matt, even though Matt never really cared much for radicals like Marx."

"Sorry," I muttered. Then, trying to cover up my blunder, I continued, "But I thought you said you weren't going to Matt's grave."

"You're right. I really didn't think I would, but then I had a dream about him last night."

She was my mother all right. Her daughter spoke with the dead in her dreams, why not her?

"So what did he want from you?"

"Flowers..."

"Flowers?"

"Seriously. He said he wanted flowers. He even went so far as to specify the kind and colour."

"So what kind did he want?"

"Roses. Seven yellow roses. That's why I left the house so early, to honour his request."

It suddenly dawned on me that my mother and I had probably been in the graveyards at the same time. While she'd been in the hundred-year-old Highgate Cemetery on a mission to put flowers down for her first love, I'd been in Konya's thousand-year-old Three Saints Cemetery, searching for who knows what.

"Was it nice at least, where they buried him?" I asked, not knowing what else to say. "It's a gorgeous place, from what I remember."

"What does that matter, Karen? It's not like the people buried care what it looks like."

My mother had flipped again. She'd gone to the graveyard as Susan the romantic, putting roses on her lover's grave because of a dream she'd had, and had come back as world-weary Susan with her ever so logical outlook on death. Meanwhile, I had come to the front of the Sultan Selim Mosque, and in another ten metres or so I'd be at the hotel entrance. I didn't want the conversation with my mother to be interrupted, so I put off going into the hotel and headed towards a bright, red bench under a willowy cypress tree in the small park nearby.

"Mum," I said, as I got to the tree. "At what age did I stop walking in my sleep?"

"What? Now where did this sleepwalking nonsense come from?" She sounded nervous, as she did whenever the problems of my youth were brought out into the open.

"It's not nonsense, Mum. You and I both know I used to do it. I just want to know until what age."

"Why? What happened that you suddenly started thinking of your childhood afflictions?"

She wasn't taking the bait.

"Nothing happened," I said, sitting on the empty bench. "This woman in a film on TV last night was sleepwalking, and it made me think of it. Now, are you going to tell me when?"

"You were a completely normal child, sweetheart."

My probing was just adding to her stress; she was doing her best to avoid answering.

"I know that, Mum. That wasn't my question."

"Karen, are you sure you're okay? I mean, you're not hiding anything from me, are you?"

"What could I possibly be hiding, Mum. Things are going swimmingly."

"And the baby?"

"The baby is fine. Stop worrying. You're getting worked up over nothing."

"All right then. But you should know, I've never really been comfortable with the idea of your being in that city."

My mother was a very perceptive woman and had always been able to pick up on even the smallest tremor in my voice, so I resorted to what I always did in these situations - I objected.

"Relax, Mum. There's absolutely nothing to feel uncomfortable about. You think I wouldn't tell you if there were?"

"No, you wouldn't," she said, quite sure of herself. "You would keep it to yourself, as though that were an accomplishment. You got that from your father, too. Honestly, Poyraz had plenty of redeeming qualities, but sometimes I think you purposely went for his negative ones."

I didn't want the tension to escalate, so I tried to joke my way out.

"Oh, now I get it. You're just pissed off because I take after my father."

"Not at all. Why should I be angry with you when I'm not even angry at him?"

There was a brief silence.

"You really have forgiven him, haven't you, Mum?" I asked bluntly. "You aren't angry anymore, are you?"

"No, I'm not," she finally said, after another long pause. "If you love someone - I mean really love them - in the end no matter what they do to you, you will always forgive them. And I have forgiven your father. The worst thing is Poyraz doesn't know this. I wish I'd had the opportunity to say it to his face."

"Maybe you will," I said, to console her. "Maybe one day..."

"You haven't run into him in Konya, have you?" she excitedly interrupted. "Is that why you are asking all these questions?"

Her voice suddenly sounded younger. I wanted so badly to tell her I had, but in the end I admitted, "No, Mum. I haven't seen him. I'm not even sure I would want to."

"I think you would, Karen." Her voice had softened, become more compassionate. "You may not want to admit it to yourself, but you would welcome the opportunity."

She was right, of course. I'd love the chance to see and speak with him one last time. I couldn't bring myself to say this to my mother, however.

"That may be so, but I still seriously doubt that he would want to see me. He could have found me years ago if he'd wanted to."

"I'm sure he had his reasons for staying away, darling... Reasons we wouldn't understand."

Typical. My mother, who was known to fight like a vicious tiger over the least little thing with anyone else, suddenly turned into a monument of understanding completely incompatible with her character the moment my father was mentioned. And she said I had a weakness for Nigel? My weakness for Nigel paled in comparison to the passion she had for my father. Frankly, I found her continued allegiance to him after everything he'd put us through extremely irritating. Not least of all because she'd made no effort to actually stop him at the time.

"Come on, Mum. What's not to understand? The two of you just couldn't make it work. You stayed, thank you very much, but my father took off without the least thought as to what would happen to me."

"I couldn't have lived without you, Karen. But try to show some mercy for your father. You don't know what he was up against, what he was going through."

There she went defending him again.

"So then if you loved him so much, why did you let him go?" I asked. "Why didn't you try to stop him?"

It had come out sounding like an accusation, though that wasn't my intention. Luckily, she didn't take it to heart.

"Because he couldn't live with us," she calmly explained. "The path he chose would never merge with ours."

My attention was drawn to the door of the Sultan Selim mosque opposite me, from where two men with long beards were just emerging. They simultaneously tucked their strings of prayer beads into their pockets and began putting on their shoes, all the while chatting with the peace of mind that comes from having fulfilled one's duties. I suddenly longed for the peacefulness I saw in their faces, for the contentment they radiated. Maybe that is why I stubbornly contradicted her, saying, "Why shouldn't our paths have merged? My father was no Muslim fanatic. He lived in your country,

371

conforming to your culture, for years. He never once tried to push his beliefs on you. And I seriously doubt he was any more puritanical than your average Christian."

"He wasn't."

"Then why did you let him go? Don't say because you had different beliefs. Because the way I see it, your beliefs, or even lack thereof, were closer to my father's religion than to any branch of Christianity. Tell me I'm wrong."

"No, that's true," she responded tersely again.

The more she agreed with me the angrier I got, and the shriller my voice became. "So if that's true, then why did you let him go, Mum? Why did you let Shah Nesim drag him off? Couldn't you have just been more tolerant?"

"It wouldn't have made any difference, Karen," she said helplessly. "No matter what I did, your father was going to leave."

"Why should he? I remember him as being very affectionate, and totally devoted to us both. If I'd had the capacity in those days to think or act as I do now, he might still be with us."

"I'm sorry, Karen," she said, her voice trembling. She was clearly having difficulty speaking. "Maybe you're right, I should have tried harder."

It was her shaky voice, rather than what she said, that made me snap out of it. Regret had begun to gnaw at me. What was I doing, blaming this poor woman for something that happened years before? If there was anyone to blame it was my father.

"But even if I had, he still would have gone," she continued. "He was determined to rectify the huge mistake he'd made."

"What mistake?"

"The mistake of leaving his sheikh and the dervish lodge in Konya and coming to London with me all those years ago. His passion for me eventually began to dwindle, and when it did, his old passions were rekindled. He missed the lodge, his sheikh, his life as a dervish..."

"Okay, I agree with you, Mum," I said softly, trying my best not to hurt her any more. "But maybe if you hadn't fallen out with him, if you'd accepted him for who he was, he never would have missed his lodge, his sheikh, or his life as a dervish life to begin with."

"What you can't seem to understand, Karen, is that your father was going to leave us whatever we did." She was struggling to keep a lid on her grief. "Even if you and I had lived in perfect harmony with him, he still would have stepped out that door."

I really couldn't, or didn't want to, make sense of it.

"Why? How could he leave the people he loved most?"

"Because, just like all other dervishes, your father believed in that 'great secret'. A secret that meant more to him than you, me, and all humanity combined. A secret only accessible to him via the path of love, and I'm not talking about mine."

The faces of my father, Shah Nesim, İzzet Efendi, and the Shams and Rumi from my dream, all passed before my eyes in succession. The self-assured, boundlessly charitable demeanor they all shared. The indifference towards, but fathomless tolerance of, the material world. The constant allusion to a 'great secret' that poured with sacrosanct respect from their lips.

"Are you talking about his love of God?" I asked to clarify. "Divine love?"

"More than that, sweetheart. I'm talking about becoming God. Love was not just an emotion your father felt for God, it was the very road which led him to being one with him."

Lightning flashed in the sky and the bench I was sitting on shook with the thunder. The rain was finally going to fall. But I paid no attention to the sky being ripped apart by lightning, nor to the impending downpour. I was too busy turning the words of İzzet Efendi over in my mind: *As He breathed life in through Adam's nostrils, God gave a piece of his own soul to that life. God is within us, so to speak. But our desires drag us down the wrong path. The hunger we feel for food and sleep, our lust and our swelling egos, push that piece of our soul into such a deep well within us that most people are not even aware of this sacred element.*

Yes, this was the great secret, the absolute truth that Shams spoke of, that all these men shared. Being God... And was that so wrong? The meaning behind this was vaster, more profound and complex, than either the question or the answer themselves.

My mother kept talking, unaware of what was going through my mind.

"And that God doesn't need the love of a person - not that of a wife's like mine, nor of a child's like yours..."

I thought of the dervish who, when his long lost son had finally found him, requested that either his son's or his own life be taken. It was a sad, bitter story... Disgusted, I chased away the images from İzzet Efendi's story.

"Do you believe that? I mean, that my father will become God?"

When she answered, her voice was weary but full of conviction, "Of course I don't believe it, but I respect it. I find his beliefs easier to accept than the majority of today's religions, as you said."

"Still," I interrupted, "you find it a bit over the top, don't you?"

"It's not a new thing," she said. "Hittite kings used to believe they would become God when they died. Roman emperors proclaimed themselves God even before they died. Christianity is in and of itself the story of one man becoming God. The desire to be God may be the oldest dream on Earth. But there may be something to it, already. Whether as a pillar of religion or a scientific fact, it's agreed that humans are the only living creatures that can fathom the world's existence. And they are the only living creature that can consciously change this world. Both are characteristics attributed to God, don't forget. But of course I find the idea of being God preposterous, at least in the sense your father and the other sufis meant. And even though I knew it was God at the core of their motivations, I still sympathised with their courage, their tolerance, their openness to different interpretations of the Qur'an, and their ability to find room in their hearts for people.

"But you never embraced it all."

"No, I didn't. Because I believe in simple living. My view of the world and morality are pretty basic and transparent.

Just live your life - without asking for privileges, or coveting power, or claiming your ideas are superior... I believe this Earth is the mother of all living things. And just as her soil, water, and sky belong to everyone, her wisdom also belongs to us all. In my book, hoarding what you have learned under the guise of a 'great secret' qualifies as privilege, and I can't accept that. I also cannot accept selling life short by controlling your desires in the name of discipline."

"But I never saw father look down on others," I objected. "He was always so cordial with everyone."

"Yes, but he used that cordiality to keep people at arm's length, both from himself and his ideas. Cordiality was protective armour for your father and those like him. Because they couldn't convey to everyone, or share with everyone, their true thoughts. This was their secret. And they carefully selected whom to share it with."

"Don't you think you're being a bit unfair, Mum?" I interrupted. "I don't think that reaching that 'secret' or 'absolute truth' they believe in, and becoming a spiritually wise person, or God, as you put it, is a thing that everyone is capable of understanding. There are stages to pass through, and consequences within that wisdom itself. Not everyone is capable of immediately grasping a belief like this. They run a huge risk of misconstruing what is being said."

"Well, you're right there," she said, surprising me. "And I'll give you another very good reason for them to keep their wisdom to themselves - self-preservation. Your father used to talk about a sufi called Hallac-i Mansur who was killed under horrific circumstances in Baghdad a thousand years ago. Hallac-i Mansur, reaching a pinnacle in his beliefs and intoxicated with his divine love, for one split second shouted 'Ene'l Hak!', which means I am God! The orthodox Islamists of the Abyssinian Dynasty immediately arrested the pious sufi and, after keeping him in prison for years, cut off his limbs and publicly tortured him to death."

"That's revolting," I said under my breath. "What kind of savages were they?"

"The kind that history is full of, dear. Jews, Christians, Muslims... it really makes no difference. Like the history of nations, the history of religion is also written in blood. But what I was saying was that there were plenty of good excuses for keeping heterodox beliefs like those of your father's shrouded in esotericism. But that isn't the only problem. Another thing I find wrong is their undervaluing the life we live now. They don't appreciate it in the least. All they care about is the one on the other side. They believe that, even if those of us who are slaves to our desires can't see it, there is a curtain, beyond which lies a world with real freedom, real peace, and real contentment. What's important for them is that other world, because it is there that everyone becomes one with God."

"You, on the other hand, don't believe that world exists."

"Is there any evidence for it? The smallest indication? A sign, a message, a voice, a vision? No. And there never has been. Each of those miracles is a beautiful myth, a colourful fairy-tale, and no more. But that is the very reason I love religions. Even though it's not their aim, they offer us clues to understanding the human condition. They make us face our fears, reveal the weaknesses of our souls, and test our courage. In order to understand people, you have to understand the religions they create."

I'd never heard my mother talk like this.

"Are you saying religion is indispensable? That it's something we all need to understand?"

"Whether it is or not, Karen, we all know it exists. And that people are still deeply affected by it. You can't ignore what's right under your nose, that would be no different from burying your head in the sand. But I know this, too - no religion has even the slightest evidence of the magnificent life they profess to exist beyond the curtain. They all promise us a world that just isn't there. Meanwhile, the world we live in is real, not only in its abundance, but also its scarcities. A child dying of hunger is real. Disease is real. War is real. The decline of humanity's happiness is real. While every morning people on Earth open their eyes to life like this, while there's so much cruelty, poverty, and hopelessness, I can't reconcile myself to just living my life contemplating the paradise beyond. Even if that paradise did exist, I wouldn't do that. I want to do good for the sake of doing good, not because I'll be rewarded for it. And I'll refrain from doing evil because I'm not evil, rather than out of fear of punishment. I don't need a master in order to be a good person. Goodness and evil are both within us, we were born with them and they will die with us. The important thing is which you choose while you're alive - without the reward of heaven or punishment of hell as motivation. Secure in the belief that you are going to end up dead and gone and that there is no paradise beyond any curtain. And at the same time keeping jealousy of those who will come after you at bay, struggling for their happiness too, despite knowing you will never see them. What it all comes down to is being truly humble. This is my contribution, to show my appreciation for this life, which is both beautiful and thrilling. For me, life is just that simple. "

"... an enormous sword in one hand and Ziya's severed head in the other."

※

I stayed on the red bench under the tall, slim cypress tree for a while. Ignoring the sky's furious growl, the flashes of lightning that struck one after the next, and the sky which grew darker by the minute, I sat thinking about all my mother had said. So my father wanted to be God. And no matter what we'd done, he still would have left us because he just didn't care enough about my mother and me. But these were my mother's words. I had no idea what my father's actual thoughts or motivations were. How could I when I never got an explanation from him? My mother could be mistaken. She could be making up excuses to make herself feel better. But as much as I would have loved to believe that, İzzet Efendi's explanation seemed to confirm what she'd said. My father had been prepared to sacrifice us for his ideals. It was that simple. In trying to reach that absolute truth, to gain spiritual wisdom, he'd had few or no reservations about leaving a wife on her own or a young daughter fatherless. On the contrary, he must have been proud of himself. In his war against his desires, he'd come out victorious. He'd broken free of all his worldly bonds and was indifferent to his longings, pain, and sorrow. He'd succeeded in 'dying before he died' and had put a very significant leg of his journey behind him. And Shams? What Shams, I argued, frustrated with myself. He was only a figment of my imagination, a nightmare, my mind playing tricks on me. I suddenly realised my mother had actually succeeded in pussyfooting around the subject of my sleepwalking. She must have been afraid that admitting it would cause her daughter's neuroses to resurface. I wasn't intending to just let it go, but as I considered ringing up my mother and asking her again, the rain began to fall. But what rain! It was as if the sky had opened up and was pummeling us.

I jumped up from the bench and made a beeline for the hotel. Leaving the Sultan Selim Mosque behind me, I'd passed in front of the fountain and come to the pavement's edge when a black jeep pulled up at my feet. I first noticed the emblem painted in white on the door. It was the warrior with the enormous sword in his right hand and the head of Medusa with her fiery eyes and hair of snakes in his left, the complete picture of Perseus that was the Ikonion Tourism logo. As I looked up at the window, the back door opened and Ziya's face appeared.

"Go on, get in," he said, moving over and making room for me.

I leaned forward to look inside and saw Cavit sitting in the driver's seat. He had also noticed me and gave a half-hearted smile in greeting. Despite the rain that came down in buckets, for one second I thought it best not to get in.

"What are you waiting for?" Ziya persisted. "We've been trying to reach you for a while now but your phone was engaged, so we waited in front of the hotel. Don't tell me you forgot we were supposed to meet?"

He was right. And I was the one who had requested this meeting, so why was I being so hesitant?

"Hello," I said, getting in. "You've got perfect timing. I would have been soaked by the time I made it to the entrance."

As the rainwater trickled off me wetting the seat, I turned to Cavit the clean freak, who was watching me in horror.

"Sorry, I've made a mess."

"It's not important," Ziya quickly blurted out. "I hope that's the worst of our problems." He turned to Cavit. "Let's go."

"Where are we going?" I asked, trying to hide the apprehension in my voice. "We could have spoken in the hotel."

"We're going on a little trip," Ziya answered, without looking at me.

With that he faced forward again. The welcoming expression on his face was gone now, as was the artificial smile pasted to his lips whenever he tried to be charming. His eyes appeared to be locked on the blades that struggled to wipe away the rain striking the windscreen, but I knew they weren't. His fury at having been betrayed was snowballing inside him, preparing to explode. All at once I understood just what a bad move getting into the jeep had been. As the two of us sat frozen in the back seat, Cavit, following his boss's orders, changed gears and accelerated. I started to wonder if I were being kidnapped. But no, they wouldn't dare. It couldn't have been more than a few hours since Cavit's release. If anything happened to me, he'd be the first one they'd suspect.

I turned to watch the deluge on Konya's streets through the rain streaming down the window, trying to push aside the pessimistic thoughts and stay calm. But when neither Ziya nor Cavit said a single word, I began to lose my composure. I needed to know what was happening, so I settled an expression of curiosity on my face and addressed our driver.

"Cavit, am I wrong or was that you I saw at the door of Police Headquarters this morning?"

Our fussy driver didn't know how to respond, he looked from me to his boss in the rearview mirror.

"And Serhad was with you," I said, encouraging him.

"Serhad has been arrested, Miss Greenwood."

The response, said in the monotone, mechanical voice of a judge handing down a sentence, had come from Ziya.

"Really?" I asked, trying to appear sympathetic. "Why? Why would they arrest Serhad?"

"Quit with the act," Ziya menacingly snapped at me, staring daggers. "We know what you're up to."

I felt Cavit's jeep pick up speed. The cards were finally on the table. The men were now accusing me outright of having a hand in their arrests. I kept maintaining my innocence, while inwardly cursing myself for getting into the jeep.

"I don't understand. What is it you know?"

"Don't play ignorant with us," he shot back. His right eye was twitching with rage. The polite, knowledgeable, enterprising businessman was gone, replaced by a bully who looked capable of anything. "You were the one who turned him in."

"And me," growled Cavit, smacking the steering wheel with his gloved hands. "You told the police it was me and Serhad who started that fire. They turned our houses upside down."

"You've been shamelessly pretending to be our friend," Ziya said, supporting his cohort. "And I was gullible enough to believe you."

"You're mistaken..." I began to say when Ziya spun round and caught my left arm in his hand.

"Don't play games with me." His eyes stared into mine. "I'm pretty damned irked right now, Miss Greenwood, believe me I am. All morning long I've been in a meeting with the bank, and in the end absolutely nothing came out of it. They refused my loan, and even my own father has turned his back on me. I'm going to lose everything. The insurance payment from your company is my last hope. And it looks to me like you're doing everything in your power to prevent that. You are leaving me no choice, Miss Greenwood, you understand? You're backing me into a corner..."

He gave a tug on my arm and his jacket was swept aside, exposing the black butt of the gun on his hip. I wondered if the move was intentional, to scare me. We were well beyond the point where I could fool myself with more optimistic prospects. These guys were dead serious.

"Look Mr. Kuyumcuzade, you are making a big mistake," I stuttered. "I... I was just at the police station to pick up my passport."

"Stop bullshitting," he said, shoving me hard.

"Ow," I cried out, as my arm rammed into the door handle on my right. "What are you doing? This is barbaric... Stop the car. Stop, I'm getting out."

In response, Cavit sped up even more, while making a point of smirking at me in the rearview mirror.

"You're not going anywhere," Ziya said, extending a hand towards me again. I flinched, thinking he was going to hit me, but he didn't. He reached over and grabbed my seatbelt, fastening it before I had time to realize what he was doing. Presumably it wasn't for my safety, but so I wouldn't jump out of the car.

"I'd advise you to go along with us if you want to get out of this jeep alive," he hissed.

"Killing me is not going to get you anywhere," I said, trying to control my shaky voice. "If anything happens to me, you'll be the first ones they arrest."

A virulent smile spread across Ziya's pursed lips.

"That's if they found your body."

"Oh, they would," I said, trying to sound confident. "Inspector Zeynep is an extraordinary cop, as Cavit can tell you. She's already on your trail. Neither of you would stand a chance." I caught Cavit's eye in the rearview mirror and, noting his hesitation, carried on. "Even if you don't talk," I addressed Ziya, while nodding towards the driver, "he will for sure."

"Don't drag me into this..." Cavit was saying, when at that moment the car slipped noticeably to the right.

"Shut up and keep your eyes on the road," his boss scolded. "You're gonna crash."

Cavit turned his eyes back to the road. "What the hell?" he immediately uttered, looking like he'd seen a ghost.

Ziya and I both followed Cavit's eyes. A man dressed in black stood in the middle of the barely visible road, ignoring the pelting rain. Though I couldn't see him clearly, I knew who it was. And for the first time I was happy to see him.

"Shams," I breathed with renewed hope.

Ziya didn't hear me.

"Hit the gas," he ordered, his voice crazy with rage. "Run him over."

Cavit hesitated, squinting at the silhouette in the middle of the road.

"Ziya Abi, this man's not getting out of our way. Look, he's coming towards us."

Ziya smacked Cavit's seat.

"Don't you 'Ziya Abi' me. Just do as I say."

Cavit changed gears and stepped on the gas again and the car lurched forward with a grinding sound. They had both forgotten me now and had their eyes riveted on the man. As the jeep drew closer to him, it seemed to fly. There was a sudden thunderous roar followed by a flash of light. I watched as the lightning struck just behind the man in black. But the man held his place as a huge ball of fire appeared, ready to swallow us up. Cavit hit the brakes and we were thrown forward, before the jeep began spinning out of control. All I could do was grasp the door handle helplessly as though it would protect me. Ziya's words were the last thing I heard before the jeep rolled over.

"What have you done, you idiot!"

I opened my eyes, surrounded by a deep silence. The colours and forms around me were all blurred together and I couldn't see so well. But then I heard the whisper of a gentle breeze, the kind that follows rain, as it blew over the puddles in the road. I breathed in its sweet scent. I tried to get up but couldn't manage, my seatbelt was holding me firmly in place. I reached down and pushed on the buckle and it popped open. I'd got lucky. I was sure the jeep had flipped, but strangely it was upright again. I noticed a large red blob on the windscreen, which I squinted at trying to get my vision back. When I realised what it was, I recoiled in horror. It was Cavit.

"Oh my god!" I exclaimed.

Where Cavit's face had been, there was now just a red mash of blood and bone. I turned, horrified, to look at Ziya, but his seat was empty and his door wide open, the glass shattered to bits. I moved slowly towards the open door, prepared to witness an equally gruesome scene. Leaning out a bit, I saw Ziya lying on his back about a metre from the door. There was no noticeable blood on his body so I relaxed a bit, but the rough landscape prevented me from seeing his face. His head must have been bent to one side. Then I heard the faint murmuring. I concentrated all my attention on it. It was the nursery rhyme Sunny and I used to sing.

Hu hu hu dervish
The dervish opened a dervish lodge
His skirts they scattered secrets
Although no one knew about it

Turning to look in the direction of the voice, I found Sunny rocking back and forth gently on the asphalt as he sang.

Hu hu hu dervish
His head it reached the sky above
His beard it brushed upon the ground
His lips they scattered secrets
Although no one could hear them...

I noticed a shadowy figure, which I took to be Shams, standing a few metres beyond Sunny in the middle of the road, holding something up in front of him. I tried to focus. Then I saw Ziya, or more accurately, Ziya's head. While his hair had become menacingly twisting snakes, his eyes, reduced to pools of blood, were gushing with horror. I observed the hand that held his head, then followed the arm up to the strange man in black to whom it belonged. From within the cover of fog that had seeped in on the rain's heels, he stood looking back at me with the undaunted grin of a hero from a legend, an enormous sword in one hand and Ziya's severed head in the other.

"... now you can perform the *sema*."

✳

I was surrounded by ice blue light; that unblemished, cold, familiar radiance. The ground beneath me was a lighter shade, almost white. I was free of all my clothes, though not naked, as my body was wrapped in that same icy blue. The trees and hills, the boulders and the pebbles, everything my eye could see was shining in that same colour, like crystal. It was as though I were in another world. My body had broken free of its heaviness, my steps were as light as feathers and I walked without purpose. There was a wind. When it touched my skin it formed into tiny droplets which trickled down, collecting in my palms. My whole body was tingling. There was a smell in the air, a pungent odour that burned my nasal cavity and moved down into my throat. I threw my head back, but I couldn't get away from it. I started to cough, but no sound came out. My voice was melding into the silence. I was imprisoned in the eternal hush, just as I was wrapped in this blanket of freezing blue. Then I saw a golden light coming slowly towards me, melting away the snowy white ground beneath it as it cut its path. I tensed up, terrified of falling off into the yawning abyss it left in its wake, and as I did, a whisper sliced through the silence.

"I think she's coming to..." It was a woman's voice. "She coughed."

"The IV must have done the trick." This time it was a man who spoke. "Let's get another hooked up."

385

When I opened my eyes, a woman with auburn hair was pointing a medical instrument resembling a tiny flashlight into my face. Behind her stood a thin grey-haired man in a white smock.

"Well now, how are we feeling," the woman smiled, "now that we've finally come back to life."

The man in the smock took my right hand. "Try to relax, please."

I glanced down at the man's white plastic gloves and remembered Cavit, and everything replayed itself before my eyes. The downpour, the jeep I'd been whisked away in, the dervish in black who had stood fixed to the middle of the road, the car flipping over, Sunny and his nursery rhyme, Shams holding Ziya's Medusa-like severed head...

"What happened to me?" I asked, despite remembering every last detail.

"You've been in an accident," the man mumbled, as he changed the IV bag. "But you were lucky, you got off quite easy."

My hands automatically slid towards my belly.

"The baby," I directly asked. "How is it?"

"Easy," said the woman with the auburn hair, trying to calm me. "Your baby is fine, and so are you. Someone upstairs must have been looking out for you."

Relaxing a bit I lay back down, and though I knew the answer, I asked, "And the others?"

They didn't know what to say. They must have been worried Ziya and Cavit were close friends or relatives and didn't want to give me the bad news.

"They're dead, aren't they?" I said, making it easier on them. "Go on, you can tell me."

"Yes, I'm sorry. Neither of them made it," the man said.

"How? How exactly did they die?"

They looked at me with alarm, probably wondering why I was so interested in the details.

"Cavit's head hit the windscreen. I saw that," I said, pausing so they could confirm it. "And Ziya, his head..."

The grey-haired man, giving in to my persistence, averted his eyes and admitted, "Yes, it was pretty gruesome. He was decapitated."

"How?" I kept up with renewed insistence. "How did that happen?"

The same perplexed look came over both their faces. They must have thought it was the trauma speaking, but I didn't care. I was too curious to hold back.

"Please, tell me. How exactly was his head cut off?"

"It happened when he flew out of the car. The car window acted as a guillotine slicing through his neck. You were going pretty fast. It's a miracle that you survived, actually."

"And the sword?" I knew I was trying their patience, but I had no choice. "Did they find a sword at the scene?"

The man gave me a stern look.

"A sword? What are you talking about?"

"There should have been a sword there. I saw a sword. And there was a man... dressed in black."

A knowing, apprehensive look passed between them. Without a word, the woman proceeded to take a glass vial and syringe from the small tray next to her and, breaking open the vial, pulled the liquid into the syringe. As the woman injected the contents of the syringe into the IV line, I realised they were sedating me, and made one last final attempt to explain.

"I know you don't believe me but there was a man there with a sword in his hand. A dervish, dressed in black, tall and slim with a tangled beard and kohl-lined eyes..." My speech was slurring and the lines of the woman's face blurred and then melted away. I tried to keep my mind clear. "Kohl-lined eyes..." I repeated.

On the roadside stood the man in black goat's felt, his kohl-lined eyes staring into mine. The light of the full moon left half his face in shadows, so that it melted into the endlessly vast steppe, becoming one with it.

"Why do you always see me as a killer?" he asked discontentedly. "Why am I always plotting to take someone's life in your dreams?"

He stood tall and defiant, putting the question to me as though I were responsible for all this.

"I don't know," I answered, trying to collect my thoughts. "Maybe you can tell me."

"I cannot say," he stated, shaking his head of unruly hair. "These things have nothing to do with me. It's true I'm not blessed with passivity, yet although I am filled with rage towards those who deserve it and do not refrain from letting them know, neither am I in the habit of making attempts on the lives of everyone who crosses my path. Besides, even the Archangel of Death, Azrail, cannot unduly take a life out of turn."

"So how did Ziya and Cavit die then?"

He smiled. His smooth, white teeth glistened in the moonlight.

"Speed killed them. Why would anyone drive so fast in the rain?"

His eyes displayed genuine pity. He paused, then continued emphatically, "Fortunately, nothing happened to you. Or the life growing inside you."

That he would even mention my baby angered me.

"What do you want?" I asked frowning. "Why are you stalking me?"

He stroked his beard as he looked me up and down.

"I don't want anything from you."

"But you do." I said, boldly drawing closer. "Why else would you hound me so much. Is it that you need my help? If that's the case, just come out and say it. If there's something I can do, I'll do it."

He was losing his temper. There were sparks in his black eyes as he almost imperceptibly leaned towards me.

"Who are you to help me?" he chided. "What could you possibly do for me, when you cannot even determine whether to give birth to your own child?"

"My personal life is none of your concern."

"In fact, I am an intrinsic part of your life. I always have been," he said, with the ease of someone stating a well-known fact. "I have been with you since even before Sunny. Not that you were aware of it. As a child, your days passed in a stupor. You were forever ambivalent. Were you to hold a place at your father's side or your mother's? In the meantime, so much time has passed one would think you'd have grown up. But you are still in the same predicament." He pointed towards my belly. "Will you give birth to the child or will you be coaxed to get rid of it by your surgeon lover? Will you live your own life or his? Rather than attempting to help me, do yourself a favour and settle that matter once and for all."

The man's tongue was poison. My gut instinct was to rip him to shreds, but I held myself back.

"It's true I have unresolved issues," I said, managing to keep my cool. "But thankfully, I at least have a sense of compassion and don't go around killing people. And I certainly wouldn't harm my loved ones."

His face grew dark and he looked away.

"Must you bring that up again, Kimya?"

"Yes, I am bringing her up again... that poor innocent girl. The young bride slaughtered by her husband because she loved someone else."

He had no answer. I saw my opportunity and took it, spitting out all the rage inside me. "Perhaps you are hoping I'll clean up your dirty conscience, wash the blood off your hands."

All at once, the slim neck over his slumped shoulders seemed to have difficulty carrying his head.

"There was a covenant. I had to honour my word to God, who had already kept his word in revealing Jelaleddin Rumi to me. The Creator inquired as to what I would give him if he did so and I answered 'my head'. Blood is the only price for love. And I honoured my word. I paid my penance with my own life, my own soul, my own sin."

"By killing a young girl? What part did she have in all this to deserve it?"

"You understand nothing," he grumbled despairingly. "You have misinterpreted everything I have revealed to you. Because your soul's eye is closed, you cannot see beyond the bounds of your mind. You do not know real love, therefore you do not know the meaning of sacrifice. Just look at your insignificant love, long since faded away, with all the fire gone. You can only endure each other by traveling to faraway lands, pursuing entertainment, satiating your appetites with rich foods, and love-making until your bodies are practically mauled, and yet you still dare to criticise ours."

As he said this, I couldn't help but wonder how he could compare those days he stayed cloistered away with Mevlana to my relationship. But this black-clad man carried on intently, either unaware or unconcerned with what I was thinking.

"You've never known real love that you may judge me. You've never thrust your hand into the fire, so you cannot see how the fire of love does not die out in the human heart, but instead turns into a raging flame. You've never died for your lover, and you've never killed for him, so you cannot understand me."

It was his usual ploy. When I accused him, it was I who couldn't understand, who couldn't conceive of a reality beyond appearances. But this time I wasn't backing down. Letting the chips fall where they may, I continued to defy him.

"It doesn't take being a murderer to understand murder. Murder is what it is. Whether now or seven centuries ago. And a killer is a killer, whether an ordinary man on the street or an enigmatic dervish."

"Watch your tongue, my girl," he said, looming over me. I'd managed to get him worked up again. "You cannot talk to me that way."

"I can," I stated, without flinching. "Everything I say is true."

We faced each other under the full moon like two archenemies in a standoff. He could do with me as he liked, I didn't care anymore. It was time for these nightmares to end, time for me to find my way out of this labyrinth of riddles.

He surprised me by unexpectedly breaking into laughter.

"You are a brave woman," he said, when he'd finally stopped. "I appreciate that. But you are also mistaken, I am not asking for your help. My conscience is clean, as are my hands. It is you, in fact, who seeks my help." Seeing my eyes open wide, he continued, "I know you aren't aware of this yet. People like you cannot always clearly voice their needs. Sometimes they don't even know what they are, and ask for help without knowing it."

I also tried to laugh. He was making no sense, and I asked him sarcastically. "So what kind of help is it I seek from you?"

He leaned forward and stared vacantly into my eyes, in the same way one calmly watches a river flow past. "I've told you many times, it's not something to be explained. You must see. Come watch with me." He spoke with a slight inflection of tedium, like a teacher certain his thickheaded student would fail again.

For one short moment he kept his eyes on me. Then, with no interest whatsoever in what I was about to say, he turned and walked off. As the slim form of the black dervish drew away, a boundless stretch of white appeared before me.

"The salt lake," I murmured. "The lake I saw on my first time in Konya."

Shams kept walking with determination as if he hadn't heard me, and despite having beckoned to me, didn't bother to check if I was following him. I quickened my pace, trying to bridge the distance between us. As I did, the melancholic lament of a ney split through the silence of the night. Where was this music coming from? I looked around but couldn't see a soul. Shams, sensing my dismay, pointed towards the light ahead.

"They are preparing for the *sema*," he said in a soft, sweet voice. "The ney has already begun."

I looked to where he was pointing, fifty metres beyond on the moonlit lake, to where seven men sat widely interspersed forming a broad circle. They sat on their knees wrapped in black cloaks, with the tall felt hats they called *sikke* on their heads. I felt my lips grow dry and my palms begin to sweat. My stomach cramped and my legs were shaking. I couldn't bear the weight of this mix of sentiment and suspicion gradually awakening in my mind.

"One minute," I begged. "Please, can't we stop for just one minute?"

"What's wrong? Are you tired?"

"No, not tired but..." I felt something rising in my throat. "I just need a moment. Please."

"They will not wait for us," he warned. "We must be there before they rise for the *sema*."

"Why? Why do we have to be there at all?"

His black eyes looked into mine as though offering an explanation.

"Because my words have no effect in this place. You must see it with your own eyes."

Having caught my breath, I kept pace with him as he started forward again. We passed over a rough patch of earth and neared the lake. The entire place was pervaded by that ice blue light I'd become so familiar with. It was as though the moon had fallen into the lake and begun to light up the air from under a dense pane of salt. A luminescent stage was formed as the lake seemed to shrink to where it only surrounded the broad ring of the seven *semazen*. We stopped just outside the circle's perimeter and observed the men from there. I looked into the face of the dervish seated directly opposite me and was surprised to find that it was Shams. But the one nearest him was also Shams, I suddenly realised. In fact, it seemed all seven of the *semazen* were the dervish from my nightmares. Hoping for an explanation, I turned back to the Shams who had brought me here, and was met with the earnest eyes of the dervish in black.

"Don't be surprised," he murmured, his tone consoling. "We were all put here for the same reason. We are all points of the same light. We all came into being with a breath from the same God, so what does form matter?"

He looked back at the seven *semazen* in his image. The cry of the ney faded away like an oil lamp burning itself out. As the music stopped, the seven dervishes, taking one deep collective breath, slapped their hands gently on the ground and simultaneously stood up. All but one of them, the one directly opposite me, who had lowered his head and remained sitting with his legs tucked under him. As the others shed their black cloaks, the skirts of their white *tennure* billowing under the moonlight, the music started up again. This time the resounding beat of a drum could be heard accompanying the ney. I looked back towards the dervish who hadn't risen, and gasped. The fleeting thought I'd first had on seeing the dervishes had come to pass. This dervish, who had remained seated and curled in on himself as the *sema* started, was none other than the father who had abandoned me all those long years ago. My father, who for years was never the least bit worried about us, who in all that time had not once enquired as to whether we were dead or alive. I grabbed hold of the Shams at my side so as not to collapse, but kept my eyes on my father. Time hadn't touched him, he looked just as he had the day he'd left us. Although his hair was hidden under his felt hat, I could easily recognise the big black eyes, the Roman nose, the copper-coloured beard sprinkled with silver... And more importantly, there was that same chronic melancholy, that anguish that my mother had so loved, in his long, thin face.

"You wanted to find him. Here he is," Shams said, breaking the hypnotic gaze I had on my father. His voice was full of self-conviction. I turned my moist eyes on him. "The time for denial is over, Kimya. This is what has occupied your thoughts since coming to Konya. It was always your father. Even this matter of the fire was merely an excuse. You've come here to find him, and you have found him."

I was so amazed, so overjoyed, that I couldn't even protest.

"It's true," I said, bowing my head. "I wanted to know what had become of him. And you have helped me to do that," I said gratefully.

He looked at me coolly.

"It is not you I am here to help, but rather your father, Poyraz Efendi."

Why was this man still breaking my heart? Was he playing games with me, trying to mess with my head? I needed to know for sure.

"Why should my father need help? He is a man of God, like you."

"Yes, there is no doubt about that," he stated flatly, as though it were old news. It is said that the greatest of all wars is the one against our own desires. Sometimes, just when we think we've arrived at the light, we look, and find our feet are tethered as though bound by lotus vines. A heaviness has settled into our hearts which hinders our path. It holds us back, when in fact, buoyancy is the essence of our journey. Our hearts cannot bear more than the weight of divine love. Every other tie that shackles the soul must be loosened and thrown off. This is what a dervish is – he must shed his body, cast aside this life, be rid of all emotion. Not that this is an easy task. A dervish stumbles as he walks - a day arrives when he becomes a crane and flies effortlessly in the skies; a day arrives when he loses his way between the precipitous mountains; a day arrives when he flows like a mighty, gurgling river; a day arrives when he flounders in a waterless desert, or searches for a way out of a bottomless well, or lies waiting for a breeze on a perfectly still sea. Your father is now in that waterless desert, searching for a way out of that bottomless well, waiting for a breeze on that still sea. There is a stain on his conscience, a knot in his heart. And that knot is you. Though he has shed his body and cast aside this life, his feelings for you are pulling him down, preventing him from performing the *sema*."

I thought of the story of the ring. The story of the dervish whose heart knotted and turned to stone because he couldn't take part in the *sema*.

"And that is why the ring you gave me bleeds. Isn't it?" When I didn't get a response, I ventured to ask another question that plagued me. "Can a person who is tied to their child 'die before they die'? Is a person like that capable of reaching a state of *insan-i kamil*, of spiritual perfection?"

"It is because he cannot that your father doesn't rise to join the *sema*. This is the reason you are here."

I turned round to look once more at the father I hadn't seen in years. He was so unhappy that he could no more see me than Shams; it was like his eyes had turned in on himself and were watching in utter despair as his heart hardened and turned to stone.

"Yet there is no coercion on our path," he carried on. "We have strived to make you understand the matter by showing you how events unfolded. Everything else rests on your nature. Poyraz Efendi's heart is knotted with the love he feels for his daughter. Whether you choose to loosen that knot or just carry on living your life is up to you."

As Shams spoke, his face betrayed not the slightest sign of emotion, as though he were purposely refraining from influencing me, leaving me to make my own decision. He

394

reached out and took my right hand, placing it in the palm of his left. Just as he had the first time, he opened it up and placed the silver ring with the brown stone in it. I couldn't even remember where I'd left it last.

"If you want to loosen the knot, you must return this ring to its rightful owner."

Tightening my fingers around the ring, I looked back to where the *sema* was being staged. The ritual continued. The *semazen* had begun to bow in salutation to each other. Things were moving quickly and there was no time for wavering. Keeping my nerves in check, I walked over to the *sema*. The moment my foot was inside the circle, the music stopped and the *semazen* froze in their places. Only my father and I were still able to move. My father, noticing the music and movement had stopped, looked towards the dervish nearest him to try and understand what had happened. Finding him motionless, he then turned and saw me. I didn't think he'd recognise me because I no longer even remotely resembled the little girl he'd left behind years before. However, my father's face was soon distorted with emotion. Without taking his eyes off me, his trembling hands reached out, as with difficulty he cried out, "Kimya! My little girl!"

Little girl? I looked down at myself and, sure enough, I had become a child again. In fact, I was exactly as I had been on the day my father left me, down to the navy blue plaid skirt and red boots I wore. I wanted so badly to go running over and throw myself into his arms, but something was holding me back. Instead, I walked over with heavy, deliberate steps. Tears were streaming from his eyes. His hands were open to the sky and he was murmuring to himself. I thought he must be thanking God for sending me to him, but this was not a prayer of gratitude, as I soon understood. He was pleading, just like the dervish who had asked God to take either his own life or that of his son. Could my father be making that same appeal? I was mortified, overcome with a profound sadness. How could I have been so hopeful about this man? He had turned his back on us once, after all, and now he was doing it again. I felt this, and yet I still couldn't resist listening to what he was saying.

"My God, have mercy on her," came his heartfelt plea. "If you must take a life, let that life be mine. I was incapable of loving you as I should. That is not Kimya's fault."

All at once, I was bursting with joy. My father hadn't forgotten his child, not like the other dervish had. On the contrary, it was his love for me that had kept him from reaching God, just as Shams had claimed. No matter what he did, he could never renounce his little girl. And though he'd abandoned us, he had never managed to rid himself of the pain in his heart from having done so. The pain had clipped his wings, bound his hands and feet, formed a knot in his heart and prevented him from performing the *sema*. I stood in front of him and took the hands he'd opened to God into mine. They were cold, uncertain and weak. He turned his teary eyes on me. I wanted to smile at him but couldn't, wanted to stifle the sob rising in my throat, but it was impossible. I grabbed hold of him and started to cry. He held me tightly in his arms. I inhaled the smell of geraniums that spread from his slim body. And I cried to my heart's content, sobbing for several minutes the way an abandoned child does, without reserve, without shame, in whatever manner they feel compelled to. He also cried. Though unlike me he did it silently, spilling his tears inwardly as though ashamed of them.

It felt good to cry. I felt that magical property of tears to soothe the human heart. As I cried, I unwound, relaxed, and remembered what it was I had to do. I gently extricated myself from my father's embrace and took his hands into mine again.

"Stand up, father," I said, finally managing a smile. "Stand up."

He hung his head, void of hope.

"I cannot, my girl," he said, sounding crushed. "I cannot leave this circle. I cannot come with you."

"It's not so that you can come with me," I explained, wiping the tears from his beard with the back of my hand. "Stand up. It's time for you to join the *sema*."

A light spread through him, as though all the moonlight reflected on the lake were concentrated on his face.

"Have you forgiven me?" he asked with uncertainty. "Is it over?"

He was looking towards the sky rather than at me, but I knew I was the only one who could answer.

"Yes, I forgive you," I managed to say, unable to control the shaking in my voice. I opened his hand and slipped the silver ring with its brown stone onto his finger.

"I'm returning this to you. Be free of this knot now, and of all that bound you. You are free now. You are free to join the *sema*."

He gazed into my eyes with bewilderment, then turned his eyes on the ring. As he examined it, I quietly pulled away from him, then made my way discreetly out of the ring of the *semazen*.

As I stepped out of the circle, the music started up again, and the *semazen* picked up their salutations where they'd left off. My father rose as light as a feather from where he was kneeling and joined his companions. Though he was reluctant to show it, I could sense his elation. He came to a halt opposite a dervish of his own height and gently bowed in salutation. The dervish raised his head, and I saw the image of my father in his face. I looked at the other five; all of them shared my father's countenance. Smiling, I turned towards the Shams at my side. But the black-clad dervish with the kohl-lined eyes had disappeared. In his place stood my childhood friend, Sunny, his blue eyes twinkling with glee in the moonlight.

"... the wind that brought my father here, and the wind that carried him away."

✕

Someone was touching my hand. Puzzled, I opened my eyes and found myself back in that disagreeable hospital room with its stark white lighting. The salt lake that had become a stage for the *sema* was gone, as were Sunny and the father I'd left whirling in ecstasy. So the dream was over. In the chair next to me sat Mennan, in all his reality, grappling with my IV tube, unaware that I'd woken up.

"Hi, Mr. Fidan," I said, trying to shake off the impact of the dream. "What are you doing there?"

He wriggled in his chair as though caught red-handed.

"Um... The serum bag was empty, I was taking the needle out. The doctor charged me with that duty."

"So, in the end you've become my nurse, as well," I said admiringly.

"I thought I should stay with you since there's no one else," he explained sheepishly, looking off to one side.

"Thank you," I continued, touching his arm lightly. "You're a good man, Mr. Fidan."

"No, don't mention it," he answered, his red face gone completely red again. "You are our guest. I mean, you were entrusted to us, even though we couldn't protect you very well. You've spent half your time in Konya in a hospital. And only narrowly escaped death this time." His became grave. "How did this happen, Miss Greenwood?"

Although the incident was fresh in my mind, I began to explain calmly, as though I'd had days to reflect on things.

"I suppose Ziya and Cavit were attempting to kidnap me. But I'm not sure, maybe they were just trying to scare me. Cavit was driving, going very fast at that, and the roads were wet."

"Of course he lost control, and when he hit the brakes..." he said, adding his own conjecture.

I didn't try to explain what I'd seen or heard after that, because I wasn't sure how much of it was real. I just nodded slowly and finished his sentence, "We started to roll, and you know the rest."

"Yes, I heard, I heard," he repeated, lost in thought. "God have mercy, both of them are dead and gone but... seeing as how they went so far as to kidnap you, they must have been the ones to start that fire."

"I suppose so, but we still have no proof. Looks like the company will have to pay the damages after all."

He shrugged his shoulders indifferently.

"Who is there to pay? Ziya is dead. And he hasn't got a partner or anything."

"His wife, his children..."

"He did get married once, but he divorced two years later. He hasn't got any children. I guess the money will go to pay off his bank loans."

"I suppose so. Though the amount we'll be paying out exceeds what the banks will get. And then there's the Yakut Hotel property, the old Konyan houses..."

His lips spread into a childish grin.

"Why don't you just come out and say it – all that will go to İzzet Efendi," he chirped, having just thought of it. "And he'll leave what's left over to the Mevlana Museum. The mausoleum could really use it."

Simon would never hear me say it, but this was the first time I was actually pleased that the company would have to pay out. As for the old man, would he be happy about the outcome? It wouldn't change the fact that he'd lost a son, albeit it an estranged one.

"Has anyone informed İzzet Efendi about what happened?" I asked, concerned. "Does he know that Ziya is dead?"

"Don't even go there, Miss Greenwood," Mennan fretted. "We were together when we heard. We were with my lawyers, discussing donating his house to the museum. As soon as we heard the news, the poor man collapsed. I thought he was dying. We barely got him to the doctor in time. He came to in the hospital, but he's still in pretty bad shape. I don't know how he'll ever recover from this. They may not have got on, but Ziya was still his only son."

He was going to say something else but a phone rang, interrupting him. I realised it was mine, and looked around but couldn't see it. The sound was coming from somewhere nearby. I glanced over at the wooden cupboard on my left, just beyond my bed. Mennan had figured it out before me and was already making his way over.

"It must be in my bag. If the bag's in there, just take a look inside," I instructed him.

But instead of doing that, he took the bag out and handed it to me. He must have felt uncomfortable with the idea of rummaging through it.

"Thanks," I said.

I went through the bag myself and removed the phone which was still ringing insistently.

"It's my mother," I said panicking. "Does she know about the accident?"

He looked upset, as if he himself had been the cause of it.

"I don't know, Miss Greenwood. I didn't speak to your mother. Maybe if the hospital did..."

It didn't bode well for my mother to keep ringing so stubbornly. Before answering, I took a deep breath. Mennan was watching me anxiously.

"Miss Greenwood, with your permission I'll be on my way."

"Of course. Thanks again for all you've done for me. You go home, I can take things from here."

He kept his skeptical green eyes on me.

"Don't look so worried," I insisted. "If I need anything, I promise you'll be the first one I call." He still didn't look like he was going to budge until I good-humouredly protested, "Go on. Look, I can't even answer my phone with you here."

"You'll call if anything happens though..."

"I will. Good night now."

Mennan left and I answered the phone.

"Hello," I said, assuming a casual tone. "What's up, Mum?"

"What took you so long?" she asked dismally.

Here we go, my mother had found out what had happened after all. Who could say how badly she'd panicked when she heard two people had died, poor thing.

"Karen," she said, again with difficulty. "I have something to tell you, but it's important that you brace yourself."

I was taken off guard when I realised it wasn't about the accident.

"What? What is it? Is something wrong?" I asked nervously.

"You need to stay calm, Karen," she said, though she was the one who sounded upset. "Try to be strong."

"Mum, what is it? You're scaring me."

She took a deep breath. "Okay, look. A little while ago I got a phone call. From Pakistan." Her voice was shaking. "It was Shah Nesim. He was calling about your father. He... Your father has died, sweetheart." She couldn't hold back any longer and started to cry.

I sat motionless with the phone to my ear. I pictured my father's beaming face as he whirled in the *sema*. Maybe it was what kept me from going into shock. It hurt, of course. My heart was aching. But at the same time I didn't feel torn apart with grief. My father was content, he'd lived as he wanted to and died as he'd wanted to. Even if how I felt now was reliant on a dream, I believed it. I had to believe it. By the same token, I was more inclined now to believe my dream, having heard the news of his death after seeing him liberated by the *sema*. I believed this, and so there was no need to feel wracked with grief. My father was at peace.

"How did it happen?" I asked, when my mother was calmer.

"The Americans were bombing a village in Pakistan, a village in the north of Waziristan. The dervish lodge where your father and Shah Nesim had been living was destroyed. Seven people died and many more were injured. Poyraz was among those injured, he was in hospital for a month."

"A month?" I barked. My heart was suddenly gripped by rage. "Why didn't Shah Nesim call us before?"

"Your father wouldn't let him. He didn't want us to worry. Apparently, he was in a lot of pain. He wanted it to end, but somehow he couldn't manage to die. Then finally, just today, he passed away. Shah Nesim says a wind rose up, a cold wind blowing down from the north. Poyraz heard it howling and he was delighted. He says your father murmured, 'What brought me here will also carry me away,' then closed his eyes and set about listening to the rising din. Shah Nesim said he was smiling as he took his last breath."

"Well that is some consolation, Mum," I said, to comfort her. "Not everybody dies happy."

"I just wish he hadn't suffered so much..."

"Me too. But try to remember, he did so struggling to keep us from being sad till his last breath."

"That is how it happened, isn't it? He didn't want us to hear he'd been injured because he didn't want us to feel bad?" Her voice was trembling, she was going to cry again, fall to pieces even.

"Of course that's how it happened. He wanted to complete his journey on his own. Without being a burden to anyone." The alternative, that he didn't care about us, was one I knew she didn't want to consider.

"When will the funeral take place? Where will we have the ceremony?" I asked to distract her.

"He didn't want a ceremony, sweetheart. And he made Shah Nesim promise not to tell anyone where his grave was going to be. I don't know... What do you think? Should we go to Pakistan and bring him back?"

"No, Mum, we have to honour his wishes."

"Of course. You're right. Your father always said the body is insignificant, what was important for him was the soul," she said, regaining her composure.

"His soul will always be with us, Mum."

"I don't know about his soul, but at least his memory will be."

We said our goodbyes and hung up. I leaned back and got lost in thought. Who was my father? Had he really wanted to be God? Or had he chosen that way of life because fate had dragged him down that path? Did he really not have enough love in him for my mother and me? Or had he, as I'd dreamt, simply been torn between his family and his beliefs? My mother, myself, Shah Nesim, even İzzet Efendi, may all have entirely different things to say on these matters. But there was one thing I knew we could all agree on - it was the wind that brought my father here, and the wind that carried him away.

"Because every child is hope."

※

The plane was only half an hour from starting its descent. The sky was clear. A scarlet sun was sinking on the horizon. Thousands of metres beneath us, a cluster of thinning clouds stretched over a dark brown expanse of earth. I was suddenly startled out of my reverie. Which flight was this? I glanced at the woman sitting next to me but she was no longer paying me any attention; her eyes were fixed on the screen above, perhaps trying to find out when we'd land. I turned round, perplexed. The seats behind me were empty. I faced forward again... to where a young girl and her boyfriend were sitting, her blond hair all mixed up with his black hair. I pressed my forehead to the plane's tiny window and peered with curiosity to the earth down below, hoping to pick out some identifying feature. Was this Turkey's Anatolian heartland or the European island of my birth? Was the plane going to land in the sunny city of Konya, or perpetually foggy London? I could have asked the hostess what we were flying over at that moment, but wasn't sure her answer would help much. I really didn't know if everything I'd been through was just a tangled web of nightmare and delusion, or reality itself. I could no longer perceive where fantasy ended and real life began. Had Shams appeared to me in his corporeal form, or only in spirit? Had I really seen my father and made my peace with him? Was he free to perform the *sema*? Was he dead? I wasn't sure of anything anymore, but strangely, I